Joan O'Neill's Novels

'A dramatic plot, very believable human characters. Their emotions and reactions are so true, irrepressible and natural.' *Katie Donovan* on *Turn of the Tide*

'This is her best yet. The story of these three brave Irish women will get Joan O'Neill a whole new readership - and her fans will love it.' *Betty Burton* on *Leaving Home*

'One is soon captivated by O'Neill's gift for storytelling. Human interest plots abound, peopled with characters various and engaging . . . all ages and psychologies are sketched with a wise hand.' *Irish Times*

'Joan O'Neill takes the most ordinary, everyday, trivial details of life and by ordering them in a certain way elevates them to the level of art. This is life as we know it.' *Robert Dunbar, The Gay Byrne Show*

'A compelling sense of storytelling.' *Woman's Way*

'O'Neill has a strong sense of place and wonderful descriptive powers – so lively that one can almost smell the rashers sizzling or feel the heat of the lush Wicklow meadows.' *Maureen Cairnduff* in the *Irish Independent* on *Turn of the Tide*

Also by Joan O'Neill

TURN OF THE TIDE

LEAVING HOME

PROMISED

for young adults

DAISY CHAIN WAR

BREAD AND SUGAR

DAISY CHAIN WEDDING

About the author

Joan O'Neill began her writing career in 1987 with short stories and serials. Her first novel, *Daisy Chain War*, published in 1990, won the Reading Association of Ireland Special Merit Award and was short-listed for the Bisto Award. Acclaimed by the *Irish Times* as Ireland's first teenage novel, it was a bestseller. Two sequels followed, *Bread and Sugar* and *Daisy Chain Wedding*, and *Promised*, a love story. In 1997 her bestselling novel *Leaving Home* was published, followed by its bestselling sequel *Turn of the Tide* in 1998. She lives in County Wicklow with her family.

A House Full of Women

Joan O'Neill

CORONET BOOKS
Hodder & Stoughton

First published in Great Britain in 1999 by Hodder and Stoughton
First published in paperback in 2000 by Hodder and Stoughton
A division of Hodder Headline

A Coronet Paperback

10 9 8 7 6 5 4 3 2 1

A CIP Catalogue record for this title is available
from the British Library

ISBN 0 340 75171 1

Typeset by Palimpsest Book Production Limited,
Polmont, Stirlingshire
Printed and bound in Great Britain by
Mackays of Chatham plc, Chatham, Kent

Hodder and Stoughton
A division of Hodder Headline
338 Euston Road
London NW1 3BH

To *my* House Full Of Women
(Past and Present)

ACKNOWLEDGEMENTS

My thanks to Helen Litton for her help in the early stages of the writing of the book and to Phil Farrelly of Lace Boutique, Bray, who was so generous with her time and expertise.

Thanks to Sheila Barrett, Renata Aherns-Kramer, Alison Dye, Catherine Phil McCarthy, Cecilia McGovern, and Julie Parsons for their encouragement, and to Anne Cooper, Jackie Dempsey, Maureen Keenan, Mary Kirby, and Rita Stafford for their support.

My heartfelt thanks to all my family and friends, especially Elizabeth and Laura O'Neill for their inspiration, time and invaluable comments, and to John and Robert O'Neill and Edeana Greene for their helpful advice.

With particular thanks to Carolyn Caughey for her continued faith, and especially, as ever, to Jonathan Lloyd of Curtis Brown for his expert help.

Chapter One

We were in the back room of my grandmother's shop, a hot, stuffy room in Abbeyville, with the windows shut tight. Trish Traynor and Doreen O'Donoghue, my neighbours and best friends, were trying on identical bridesmaids' dresses in blue *peau-de-soie*. My grandmother, Queenie Boyle, was removing my wedding dress from its layers of tissue paper, helping me slip it over my head, smoothing it down with her palms. The half-completed flower-girls' dresses hung around the walls.

'You look beautiful, Olivia,' Doreen said, in a small voice.

'It doesn't fit,' Mum said, a note of triumph in her voice. 'I knew you'd lost more weight.'

I couldn't deny that the dress hung loosely on me, and I appeared, even to myself, gratifyingly thin.

'Don't panic,' a weary Queenie said. 'It's only tacked together.'

'And only twenty-two years,' Trish added.

'Hard to imagine that soon you'll be married.' Doreen's watery eyes were on the drifts of duchesse satin that fell in a white arc around me.

'Still a baby,' Queenie said. 'Now hold still,' she added, reaching for her pins. Leaning forward, she repinned the dress.

'Leave her room to breathe,' Trish said.

'Hmm.' Queenie sighed abstractedly. The fact that she was making my wedding dress was statement enough of her devotion to me. Taking orders from Trish was not part of her remit. 'I'm going to get more pins to turn up the hem,' she said.

She left. Mum went with her to take care of the shop.

I gazed into the mirror at the sweetheart neckline, the tiny waist. Recent dieting had transformed me. I could see myself, a ravishing bride, walking up the aisle, Barry next to his best man, the guests falling back in a blur of pastel shades.

'How'll you manage without us on the honeymoon?' Trish was reminding me that, apart from the occasional weekend, we'd never been separated.

'You'll think of something to occupy yourself.' Doreen sniggered. 'I envy you.'

Wrinkling her nose, Trish said, 'I don't. Men are bastards.' She looked round to hear the rebuke from one or other of us.

All Doreen said was, 'I'm keen on Kevin Regan.'

Trish was in her 'off men' mood. Her womanly curves and long, shapely legs were 'wasted on the desert air', as Mum said, in her imitation of a Scottish lilt. Mum had spent happy summers in Scotland, in her youth, when she was with the circus. 'She'll soon change her mind when she meets Mr Right,' Queenie said.

Mum had shaken her head. 'I'm not so sure. Tommy doesn't want anyone sniffing around her.'

Tommy was Trish's father. 'A nasty piece of work', according to Dad, who was jealous of his money. 'A sad git,' Trish said.

Tommy Traynor was the proprietor of the betting shop and a friend of Queenie's, mostly because she liked to bet on the horses, and he gave her good tips. Mrs Traynor, Trish's mum, was a quiet little woman with gold-rimmed glasses and a quivery voice. She always referred to Tommy as 'my husband', the way the Queen of England referred to Prince Philip. We called him 'Snozer' because of his broken nose, a testament to his prowess in the boxing ring.

Trish took a vow of celibacy when her boyfriend, Willie Westward, went off with Samantha Lynch from Cedar Crescent, and swore on her grandmother's grave to have nothing more to do with men for the rest of her life. 'There's a lot to be said for being a single woman in the nineties,' she offered, leafing through a magazine. 'You can do what you like, when you like, how you like.'

'No fear of pregnancy,' Doreen added.

'No in-laws,' Trish continued.

'That has to be an advantage.' I was thinking of my obnoxious mother-in-law to be.

'Sole custody of the remote control,' Doreen rejoined.

'Not having to watch rugby or football. Not having

to pretend he's fantastic in bed.' Trish was getting carried away.

'Mmm,' I said, feeling a familiar heaviness in my heart as I thought of Barry, far away in France. His mother, Mrs Bernie Breslin, had phoned to invite me to lunch, to discuss the 'wedding arrangements', her voice thinning with impatience to impress upon me the necessity of us 'getting together' or 'toogether' as she pronounced it in her Cork accent. The question of how our marriage would be presented to Mrs Breslin in the first place had been our primary concern for a long time. She had lived uneasily in our neighbourhood for the past thirty years, cutting herself off from the community, her dislike of people from any county that wasn't her own County Cork evident in the suspicion that showed in her face.

'Men want it all the time.' Doreen sighed, looking at me pityingly.

We guffawed.

'Cathy Coyle told me that her fella and herself have an unspoken agreement not to have full sex until they're married,' Trish informed us.

'The poor bugger must be on fire all the time,' Doreen said. 'Mind you, if I had to kiss him I'd vomit.'

'I couldn't imagine doing it with him either,' I agreed.

'We'll want to know how you get on,' Trish said to me, winking at Doreen.

'A blow by blow . . .' Doreen took a sudden fit of the giggles, bending forward, holding her sides. We all burst out laughing together, breathing deeply to calm ourselves, as Queenie's footsteps approached.

She bent one stiff knee and tweaked the hem as she began her final adjustments: tucking, pinning, signalling to me to turn round slowly, her mouthful of pins rendering her silent for once. Rising to her feet, her face flushed, she stood back and said, 'I think that's it.'

Trish sat back on her heels and pronounced the hem straight.

Queenie took down the veil from the hatstand and began to manipulate it this way and that. I stood like a statue, cold and powerless, until the desired effect was reached.

'It's amazing how you survive on the little you eat,' Mum lamented, drizzling gravy over Queenie's dinner, placing the dish carefully in front of her.

'A dainty eater,' Queenie said, picking up her knife and fork, throwing me a daft, tender glance.

Queenie, a nimble woman, not a pick on her, could eat as much as she liked and did, often finishing what was left of a bread pudding or an apple pie, encouraged by Mum saying, 'A hardworking woman needs sustenance.' Not that she needed any encouragement. Queenie never stopped. Mealtime for her was 'a break', an experience that gave her as much pleasure as she would ever get in this life, I suspected.

'You're skin and bone,' Mum said to me, 'isn't she?' she added, with a quick enquiring glance in Queenie's direction.

'So is Audrey,' I said defensively.

'She eats like a savage,' Queenie said.

I avoided their eyes. Queenie, aware of the dangers of

allowing this conversation to go any further, said, 'Soon we won't be able to get into the house with all the presents.'

'Soon it'll all be over,' I said defensively.

'A lamb to the slaughter.' Mum sniffed.

'Go on with you, Lorraine,' Queenie said. 'You'd love to be getting married all over again.'

'Not if the experience was going to turn me into a skeleton.'

'Fat chance,' I said, under my breath.

The truth was that I could take food or leave it, preferably leave it. A mealtime, as far as I was concerned, was an ordeal, a price to be paid in order to be able to stand up and walk around. For Mum and Queenie it was a different story. They loved food.

'A slice of heaven,' Queenie said approvingly, helping herself to a huge chunk of sultana cake.

'Thank you.' Mum smiled.

Mum loved cooking. Her unspent passion had gone into the baking of the wedding cake. She had stood in the hot kitchen, her busy hands covered in flour, an expression of pure concentration on her face as she stirred, the mixture. A clutter of utensils lay on the kitchen table, a spoon at the ready to add lemon juice, a dash of brandy. Now, she raised her eyes and stared fixedly ahead.

Because of my inclination to put on weight my natural greed had to be controlled at this crucial time.

'Why don't you have a taste, Ollie?' Queenie enquired.

'Later,' I said, glanced at the clock and gasped theatrically.

'Is that the time?' I left Mum to come to her usual conclusions about me with Queenie.

I undressed quickly, folded my clothes neatly over the pink velvet boudoir chair, and stared at my reflection in the full-length wardrobe mirror. Only ten weeks to go to the wedding and I could see my face was pinched and white, already settling into the likeness of Mum's, without the fat, of course.

I was sixteen, working in McDonald's, overweight from too many burgers and fries, and miserable, when I had my first date with Barry Breslin. I was enclosed by an overpowering mother, and a grandmother who instilled female self-sufficiency in me and felt threatened by any young man who called, for fear that he might challenge it.

It was a time of obsession. My obsessions were boys, fast cars and premarital sex. It didn't go much beyond sitting together, or a bit of rough-and-tumble on the green when one of the gang would trip me up so that Barry could come to the rescue. Six foot tall, introverted because of his home life – a domineering mother and drunken father – Barry was shy. He did as his mother told him, studied hard, worked in the family bakery at weekends and had never asked a girl out on a date.

He was my first real boyfriend, handsome in a rough sort of way, and older than me. Our first encounters were interludes of tactile pleasure, sticking out a foot to tackle or be tackled when we passed each other, then holding hands in the cinema, our palms sweaty. Our first kiss was a disaster:

me puckering my lips, his open mouth coating half my face in saliva.

I hadn't had much practice at kissing. Sister Justine, our religion teacher, had informed us, her face screwed up, that 'French kissing is to be avoided until it's time to give oneself to marriage.' Trish said it was an art to be learned, like a language. We discussed the subject endlessly. I came to the conclusion that kissing Barry was OK once the initial terror of it subsided. Things improved when I began to relax in his arms. When he became too ardent I would suggest a walk to divert a full surrender, wanting the evening to end on a note of promise.

Trish, known affectionately by the class as 'the man-eater', was the most experienced girl in our class. Beautiful, witty, smart, energetic and bitchy, she was too much for the boys. She would sit with her blonde hair pulled back into a perfect pony-tail, legs crossed, gymslip riding high, showing off her incredible legs, a smirk on her face. The leering boys would giggle and fidget.

Trish and I had got off to a bad start. She was barefaced and different, which scared me enough to ignore her for the more ordinary girls. Her wisecracks provided the humour during break. But when Rachel Parry taunted me one day in the schoolyard with 'Your mother ran off with the circus. Bet she turned a trick or two in her time,' Trish saw red.

'Shut your gob,' she hissed at Rachel, who hissed back, 'Make me,' screwing up her face and pointing her index finger in the direction of her chest.

'Don't interrupt the class,' Sister Justine warned.

Outside I called Rachel over. She wouldn't come.

'Come 'ere I want you for a minute. I want to ask you something.' I crooked my index finger at her.

'What?' She sidled up to me. I made a fist and whammed it into the side of her jaw. She grabbed my leg, pulled me to the ground with her and bit my thigh.

'Ouch!' My cry brought Trish and the rest of the class to the scene. 'Give it to her, Ollie!' Trish shouted, as I grabbed Rachel by the hair.

'Hey. Stop that.' Jim, the caretaker, came running up to us, lifting me in the air amid cheers and roars from the boys and disapproving clucks from Miss Murray, our games mistress.

We were marched down the corridor to the headmistress's office, and made to stand there, waiting for our punishment with our dishevelled hair and torn blouses.

'You were great,' Trish said, walking home with me.

'Yeah,' Doreen, her friend, agreed. 'Did your mother really run off with the circus?'

'Yes.' I sighed.

'I think that's great,' Trish said. 'Fair fucks to her.'

'You keep away from that vicious little tramp,' Mum said, shocked at my appearance when I returned from school. She wanted to know the precise details of the row.

'I forget,' I lied.

'She's setting herself up for trouble, that one,' Mum said. 'If it happens again I'm going over to see her mother. A decent poor, hard-working oul divil if ever there was one.'

'Calm down, Lorraine.' Queenie's countenance was grim.

'Let it be a lesson to Olivia not to grapple with the lower elements.' Leaning towards me she said, 'Rachel comes from an unhappy home, and you, Olivia, should have known better than to get into a fight with her. You're too quick-tempered. You should act like a lady and a Christian at all times. Remember that we're a respected family around here.'

After that Trish invited me to join her group. I was often 'the outcast' because I didn't like her schemes. The head of our little trio, she would sometimes attach herself to one of us, excluding the other. Keeping secret the latest gossip, or the newest hideout, was another trick of hers to isolate the third party. Fresh information was given to the new Best Friend, who was then prevailed upon not to communicate with 'the outcast'. 'The outcast' would straggle behind while Trish and Best Friend walked ahead, chanting little rhymes under their breath, loud enough for the outcast to hear.

As time went on I learned the rhythms of her moods, how to keep everything light. Becoming her friend was an advantage because of our close proximity in the neighbourhood, and if anybody else attacked me she would let rip.

As we grew up Trish's success at parties became guaranteed. Her conquests came to her with ease, and good nature replaced the unkindness of childhood.

Daily we dawdled home from school, Trish, Doreen and I, stopping to gaze longingly at the models wearing flimsy bras and briefs in Sylvia's boutique, imagining the wisps of lace on our burgeoning breasts. Trish's boobs were the biggest. 'The lads like them,' she explained, sticking them out.

'Yes.' Doreen laughed, trying to imitate her, but too skinny to succeed.

Doreen always went along with what everyone else said. As a child she was nicknamed Dumbo because she wasn't very bright, which did not detract from her prettiness. She was a follower, without initiative, without ambition, acceptable because she understood the main rule of our little group (Trish the chief, us the Indians). She hung on, oblivious to all obstacles.

We had lived on the same tree-lined street since I was born. The houses were set well back in narrow gardens, solid, no-nonsense houses with jutting chimneys, all looking the same. Ours was the end house, attached by a party wall to my grandmother's drapery shop, the last of the old shops crouched beneath the dominant new shopping centre. Trish's house was at the other end of the road, Doreen's in the middle.

I was the only girl in our family, 'spoilt' according to Dad. Billy had left home a long time ago and, much travelled, he now lived in New York with his wife, Faith.

Through the shop we heard lots of gossip, rumblings about the financial irregularities of neighbours, or about the woman 'friend' Mary Nugent's dad had in England. We remained unfazed, hungering for details of the local boys, most of which were denied us by our elders, who felt we had no right to know. But we wanted to know.

We wanted to know why Roger Rogan had this heroic urge that kept getting him into trouble. Doreen had a fixation about him, going so far as to visit him in hospital to see the bullet wound in his shoulder. She wanted to hear from his own lips how much blood he'd lost when he'd intercepted the raiders in Breslin's bakery, and see the hole the bullet left in his shoulder.

Elton Reilly's suicide transfixed us. We sat in the summer sunshine on our front step, unashamedly dissecting the incident with unhealthy curiosity, listening to the gory details with dread. What type of rope had he used? Had he acquired it specifically for that purpose? Where had he located the chair? Had the last fatal pull taken place in his shadowy back bedroom, a room we played cards in once when his strict mother was out? Who had found him? What excuse had he given so that no one would look for him? What was going through his mind? The episode horrified us. One day he was there, hurling abuse after us, joining us in Murphy's pub on Saturday nights, before the disco, reeling off jokes. The next he was gone.

For a while we became caring, tolerant members of our families. We stopped jeering at Joey Long, our slightly retarded neighbour, and we didn't call out maliciously after Frank Grimes, the street's drunk, stumbling up the street, his head thickening under the brim of his felt hat. It didn't last.

With no discernible talent for anything except a love for acting, I went to drama college. I liked acting. I got on well with the teachers, especially Frank Holmes who explained everything in a way that made it easy to understand. I enjoyed the challenge of mime. Frank would watch me closely and say, 'You're good,' in his soft, Galway accent.

In my spare time I liked sketching. Sometimes I would

take my paper and pastels to the park and draw flowers: primroses, fuchsia, dullish yellow, purple, filling in one colour after another, the blues of petunias and greens of foliage smudged with my fingers to blend them.

Barry Breslin went from school to his inheritance, the bakery. Big, broad-shouldered, awkward, there was something about him as he drove his delivery van in the early mornings, and took his father home at night. He was the neighbourhood good guy, and the dream of a mother who lived in a world of her own. After leaving school he studied economics at night at University College, Dublin, and worked every available hour in the bakery.

When he realised that he was missing out on the joy of life he decided to go to France to learn how to make French breads and pastries, to bring new, innovative ideas into the business and extend his range. And to get away from his mother. He proposed to me the night before he left. 'As soon as I come home we're getting married.' This was said matter-of-factly; he did not invite my opinion. Now I had letters and cards from him pinned up over my bed, stirring my imagination, filling me with a sense of primitive longing for nights and days of languorous lovemaking, in which I would abandon myself completely to the worshipping of him.

Chapter Two

Regina Coeli Murphy, or Queenie as everybody knew her, was born in Ringsend in 1920 to a fruit and vegetable merchant named Mick Murphy, and his wife Barbara. She was the elder of two daughters, her sister Statia being ten years younger than she was. From the age of fourteen she had served in Maybella Modes, a large drapery shop in Suffolk Street. Queenie had always had an eye for fashion and liked having a wage to take home on Fridays to her mother. Each day and each customer was a new challenge. Concentrating fiercely, she learned the business, daydreaming of having a shop of her own one day.

Maybella Modes was managed by Miss Ashton, a tall, pigeon-chested Englishwoman of forty-five who sounded like a man when she said, 'Yes, Modom?' Her black hair was swept up in a bun and her heavy makeup gave her face the severity of a mask.

On Tuesdays and Thursdays Mr Harrington, the owner

of the shop, would arrive, and take Miss Ashton into the back room to brood over the books. He was a short man with horn-rimmed spectacles and big fleshy hands, which he would clap at eleven o'clock in the morning and four o'clock sharp in the afternoon, a signal for Queenie to brew the tea.

One morning, while Mr Harrington and Miss Ashton were in the back room, Sean Boyle, the wiry delivery boy who had taken Queenie to the pictures a few times, burst through the door, stopped, then lifted in a huge parcel. He plonked it down before Queenie, with the air of a man on a secret mission. 'Delivery for Miss Ashton,' he said, his big eyes shining blue and slightly bloodshot. 'It's marked urgent.'

'She's busy,' Queenie said importantly, brushing him off, glancing at the parcel. 'It's the hats she ordered from Bond Street. I'll sign for it.'

'That'll be her last lot. There's going to be a war.'

'What? Where?'

'In England,' Sean said, hearing the rattle of cups in the background, sidling up close. 'What about a cup of scald?'

'Certainly,' Queenie said. 'But there's no sugar.'

'Doesn't matter.' He smiled. 'I'm sweet enough.'

As he sipped his tea he said, 'You look different,' his eyes on her lips, coloured with a touch of lipstick, and the new high heels she'd substituted for her summer sandals.

'Do I?' she asked, surprised that he'd noticed her attempt to look grown-up.

'Mmm.' He ran his fingers up her arm, moving away with the slow, sullen, weight-shifting of the sexually aroused when Miss Ashton appeared.

She glared at Queenie, who shrugged and went out the back.

Raising his cup, Sean said to Miss Ashton, 'Here's to Britain,' more to take her mind off Queenie than for any other reason.

'What about it?' she said testily.

'You're going to war with Germany. According to the wireless.'

'I know.' Miss Ashton was blushing and smiling all at once, suddenly proud of her nationality. 'At least our country's not afraid to go to war,' she said.

'You should go back and give them a hand,' Sean persisted. 'They'll need all the help they can get.'

'Maybe I will.' Miss Ashton gave him a withering smile.

'I'm thinking of joinin' up meself,' Sean confided.

Queenie had just come back into the shop and a quiver ran through her. It was her first scent of danger.

'Will that be all, Sean?' Mr Harrington said, coming into the shop.

'Yes, sir,' Sean said, and scampered out of the door, calling, 'See ye,' to Queenie.

Miss Ashton said to Mr Harrington, 'Sean was talking about the war.'

'Rumours,' Mr Harrington said dismissively.

'If there is a war Ireland will be dragged into it.' There was a smile on her face and a faraway look in her eyes.

'Not a chance. De Valera'll keep us neutral,' Mr Harrington barked, dashing her hopes of excitement.

'You weren't serious about joining up?' Queenie asked

Sean, the next evening on their way home from the cinema.

'Never more serious about anything in me life.' Sean looked at her.

Queenie couldn't believe her ears. 'Why would you do a stupid thing like that? You'll be killed.'

'Thousands are joinin' up. Mickey McGuire and Liam Redmond from our street are going to Belfast to find out about it. I'm going with them.'

'Fight for bloody Britain!' said Mick Murphy, Queenie's father, a weasel of a man with a goatee beard and blazing blue eyes. A great patriot, he was motivated by the same ideals as Patrick Pearse and Robert Emmet, and had a cache of arms hidden up the Dublin mountains. At the moment he was paralysed by fear of a surprise attack on his camp.

'It's a regular job with good pay, and I want to get married,' Sean spat defiantly at the old man and left the house.

'I think he's very brave,' Queenie said defensively, and got a slap across the face for her trouble.

Sean's decision to go to war and his marriage proposal outside the Metropole Cinema made Queenie realise that she was in love with him. Not in the frenzied way she'd seen in the films but in a slow, unfolding, magical way. She was suddenly unable to meet his gaze for fear it showed in her face. She thought of telling him but was too shy.

He must have noticed because all at once the two of them merged together, kissing, hugging, in the dark street. High-spirited with their plans they hurried through the crowds, oblivious to the dangers and reprimands.

Sean got his call-up papers. They sat on the steps of the pavement outside Queenie's house, heads bowed.

'We'll get married before I leave,' Sean said.

'What?' Queenie's eyes widened. 'It's too soon. We don't know each other well enough.'

'It's a good idea,' he insisted. Seeing her still doubtful he said, 'Let's toss for it.' He wanted her for his wife at that minute, knowing that the war would change things, that human needs never lasted. 'Heads we get married. Tails we don't,' he said.

There was the musical jingle of coins. Queenie waited. The penny went dead as it hit the ground.

'Heads it is,' Sean said, punching his fist in the air. A disquieting loneliness crept over Queenie while she waited for him to pick it up.

On her wedding day, 10 May 1939, Queenie wore a blue silk sheath dress copied from a sketch in a women's magazine, pinched in at her small waist with a navy patent belt that matched the tulle hat she'd made the day before, and her high heels. Her bouquet was a single red rose given her by Sean. Proudly she stood beside him and vowed to love him in sickness and in health. All decked out in his British Army uniform, the only suit of decent clothes he possessed, he looked silly.

'You'll know him the next time you see him,' her sister Statia said, caught by Queenie's peculiar calm, as she came out of the church.

'What do you mean?' Queenie said.

'You're holding on to him as if you owned him.'

'Well, I do,' Queenie protested, knowing as she said it that she would never own Sean. He was an independent free spirit, one who would go away and return, always acting as if he'd never been away. He had never wanted anything in his life until he met Queenie. Without her he was lost, though he would never admit it. She knew this instinctively. She also understood that his essence was a balm to something vulnerable in her that, until she had met him, had been raw and exposed.

The reception was drinks and sandwiches in Mooney's, Statia flirting furiously with Jockser Ward and the best man. On the first and only night of their honeymoon Sean took Queenie in his arms in the back bedroom she usually shared with Statia. Clumsily he opened the tiny covered buttons that ran down her back. Her heart beat like a bird in a cage to the rhythm of his thrusts that stopped almost as soon as he found the soft place he sought. Pressing her against the oak headboard he said with desperation, 'I'll be back. We'll do it properly.'

Queenie, amazed that the whole process was over so rapidly, and lonely for the new husband wrenched so suddenly from her, before she'd got a chance to get to know him, cried to Statia, 'It was over before it began.'

'A lot of stuff and nonsense it is anyway,' Statia agreed, bitter-faced. She'd let Jockser Ward go too far on the same night and suspected that he might be gone altogether.

14311157. Pte Sean Boyle,

97 Coy, Pioneer Corps,

No 5 Sec.
B.L.A.

Dear Queenie,
Just a few lines and a Christmas card. I am also enclosing a letter and card for Mother that I hope you will give her. I know you will not part with them, as it is a card that you will not get again for I shall never think of coming here for a holiday. Tell her I'm sorry that I could not send her one of her own as I could not get another green envelope, we only get one of them a week and I'm saving my next one for a letter to you. I have not received your card yet but I have received your letter dated 1–12–39 so I expect the other one will follow as it has happened like that before.

I have changed my address as they've called all our trucks in so I am now back with the new company as I am now Bx7. I am working in camp on maintenance that is repairs to the company's transport and as spare driver so I am very happy here but would be much happier at home. It will not last forever. I went into a town on Friday night but could not get you anything as there was nothing to buy. Look out for New Year's card and letter. Sorry the cards do not have any verses. I don't think there is any more at present. I will close.

God bless you and keep you safe. I should be home on leave next year some time as leave starts for men soon so I should be somewhere in that.
Xxxxxxx
P.S. Remember me to all, especially Statia.

For a long time after that Queenie kept looking up and down the street, afraid to go anywhere, half expecting to see Sean appear. Nothing happened. A strange peace settled on her when she discovered she was pregnant. As she waited for her baby's arrival, contentment made her oblivious to the dangers of the war.

'Call her Lorraine,' Sean wrote, the only clue he ever gave as to his whereabouts. Queenie saw his return in the waiting chair by the fire, beside her own, in his scent that wafted on the air as clearly as the scent of the bluebells on the May altar. He wouldn't fail her. Her certainty carried her through.

She continued working while her mother minded baby Lorraine. There were no imported goods, so a dressmaker friend of Mr Harrington supplied frocks, costumes and coats. When Miss Ashton returned to England to 'do my bit for the war effort', Queenie was put in charge of the shop and Ellen, a sad-eyed, quiet girl, became the new assistant. A girl who took pride in her appearance, Ellen made all her own clothes. She taught Queenie how to make frocks out of remnants, and liven up an old coat with a bit of fur around the collar and a fur hat to match.

'War's broke out,' Queenie's father said, excited with the news that the mail boat *Cambria* had been bombed and machine-gunned by a German plane, forty minutes out of Dun Laoghaire harbour, with fifty passengers on board. 'I knew de Valera wouldn't be able to keep the Huns out.'

'De Valera's a good man,' Queenie's mother said. 'I won't hear a word against him.'

German bombers, thinking they were over Belfast, dropped a couple of land-mines on the North Strand, killing twenty-eight people and leaving 2,500 homeless on 31 May 1941. Queenie was in bed asleep when a sound ripped through the sky, followed by a thud and a bang that shook the house to its foundations. Dazed, she went to the shattered window to see a ribbon of smoke trailing up from the city centre.

Mick Murphy found his shop on the edge of the North Strand intact, except for broken windows and doors blown out. Grey cabbages were strewn among the glass and rubble, the rest of the fruit and vegetables buried beneath it. Shanks, the dray horse, lay under his cart, in what had been the back yard of the shop, in a pool of purple blood, his grey body twisted and legless. The 'Fresh Fruit and Vegetables' sign was suspended on the jutting window-frame. The roofs and walls of the houses further up the road had collapsed. Further along whole houses were wrecked, and dazed homeowners were crawling over craters to retrieve their possessions.

'There'll be hell to pay over this,' Mick said, sobered by the shock, his head and shoulders covered in grey dust.

Mrs Coyle, whose small shop had been demolished, sucked on her cigarette. 'To think that it's not even our bloody war, and not an air-raid shelter between us.'

'That oul bulldog Churchill has finally managed to drag us into it,' Mick agreed.

'Compo,' she said, meaning 'compensation', stirring tea laden with sugar, snug in a rug the ambulance man had wrapped around her.

'Sad bloody state of affairs,' Mick Murphy mused to his pals over his pint of Guinness in Kenny's pub.

Queenie was sadder because she hadn't heard from Sean and she was pregnant.

'He's dead,' Statia said.

'I don't feel he's dead. I feel he's alive.'

'Never heard such rubbish in all me life,' Statia scoffed dismissively.

VE Day, 8 May 1945, was marked in Dublin by a series of small celebrations, some of which turned into riots. Queenie received a telegram from Sean stating that he was on his way home. She waited at the docks the day he was due, her body tightening in the effort she was making to keep still as the boat came into view. He wasn't on it. Elbowing her way through the crowds, she searched for him. On the way home she gazed into every shop and up every alley, blindly looking into lamplit windows in case she'd missed him. She refused to believe that he wasn't coming back. As the months went on she became frantic, avoiding the streets that she had known with him. Often outside her parish church, the priest would ask her how she was bearing up.

To everyone's amazement Sean eventually returned to Queenie with an artificial leg. Horrified, she couldn't get used to the sight of it. Nor could she get used to his nervous ways, his sunken cheeks, his large bones jutting out of his skeletal body. He said, in a slow, noncommittal way, 'Got out of the tussle before the tide washed me up.'

'He's washed up, all right,' Statia said, watching him limp

off to Kenny's bar in Amien Street, under the illusion that the exercise of raising his glass to his lips would cure him.

They got a house of their own on Ivy Terrace, two streets from Queenie's home. Life was quiet. Sometimes Sean would say, 'It's that bloody war that's done me in. It's responsible for my condition.' Which particular condition he was referring to Queenie had no idea. As he recovered they took up where they'd left off in the back bedroom. Shaking and shivering Queenie climbed the stairs each night, her eyes swinging away from the stump where his leg should have been, the sight of the crude stitching at close range repelling her. She would stare at the cabbage-rose wallpaper, her back ironing-board straight as 'the wonders of her body' were rediscovered.

'My last remaining pleasure,' Sean would say, by way of foreplay, forgetting about the nights he spent in Kenny's bar drinking health to the King and the Commonwealth.

'Mind yourself,' Queenie would say every time he left the house, standing at her front door looking out over the sea, hoping a great ship would appear over the horizon and pick on him up and she wouldn't have to smell the sharp sourness of his breath.

'There's something not right about him,' she said to Statia.

'It's the mad glare in his eye,' Statia said.

'Things done are never undone,' Father Farrelly stated when Queenie consulted him. 'It's a mistake to try and rectify them.'

Queenie walked the streets in the evenings to get out from under her own disturbing thoughts. Sean became more morose, reaffirming Father Farrelly's belief that it had been a monumental mistake for Queenie to twist the arm of Jesus, with her novenas and rosaries, and will him back.

With Lorraine, now five years old, in school until half past two in the afternoon Queenie continued to work because Sean was unemployed and money was scarce. Trade was bad with hardly a soul coming into the shop. Sean wasn't the only one who'd changed. Queenie was changing too. She was beginning to hate him, and she didn't much care for the world around her either. The war had dragged on so long, with Ireland experiencing none of the excitement she'd heard about from Miss Ashton's letters to Mr Harrington: American troops, free nylons, cigarettes, chocolate, chewing-gum, air-raid shelters.

A dig in the ribs from Statia was guaranteed to bring Queenie out of her long silences. Queenie would put up a pretence for a while but mostly she felt terribly alone. Only with Ellen in the shop was she released from the necessity of pretending that she was coping, and managing on the few shillings a week she earned. Her eyes were dazed from sleepless nights and days looking at Sean sitting in the corner, staring at nothing.

'Leave me alone,' she screamed, one Christmas Eve, when he came home drunk and grabbed her on the stairs, hitting her across the face because she refused his advances there and then, with Lorraine not yet asleep. Lashing out at his red, distorted face, she ran away from him into the city to lose herself in Moore Street with her cousin May, among hawkers, mounds of cabbages and cauliflowers decorated with holly and tinsel. She crossed the Liffey in the early hours of the morning, sorrow, shame and bitterness directed at her husband.

Looking at her sheepishly he said, 'You won't tell your oul fella, will you?'

'No, I won't,' she said, aware that if she hadn't run away she might be hiding a different story. Sean knew too, from the flick of her eyes, that if he ever touched her again, even accidentally, she would carry out her threat and do for him.

After that on her day off she started taking Lorraine on little outings to get away from him. She headed south, past the delicately painted houses, the shops, until she came to a junk shop near the church with a for-sale sign over it. 'I want it,' she told Sean, knowing he had savings in the post office from his war wounds.

Together they went to see the premises with the auctioneer. When Queenie said, 'We'll buy it,' he gave her the down payment of fifty pounds, afraid she'd tell her father that he'd hit her.

When Lorraine got the whooping-cough Sean got a part-time job in the coal yard, checking the orders. In the evenings, before going home, he would scavenge through the heaps of slack for big lumps, then drag them home. Occasionally he brought rashers, fresh loaves and the odd cake. Spilling chocolate drops from a bag he would say to Lorraine, 'It's raining chocolate on Lorraine.' He would lie down beside her, his stories of Little Red Riding Hood, Cinderella, the Babes in the Wood sending them both to sleep, her doll in his arms.

'He's stark staring mad,' Queenie said to Statia, after a night of listening to Sean ranting and raving in his sleep. But she knew he was not well. A fever found its way through the drawn flesh of his skull, into his eyes and the pucker of his mouth. She sent for Dr Long, who said, 'Pneumonia.'

Before Sean died he looked at her from red slits in his face. She slipped next door and knocked up the neighbours to run for the doctor, the priest, and to hurry up. Urging him to take deep breaths she held him while he gasped and panted his last.

Afterwards, at the wake, her rosary beads twined around her fingers, her eyes dry, she remembered him as he had been when she first met him: a tall, lanky lad, with a broad back and bright eyes under the ridge of brows. His smile stretched to his high cheekbones.

Chapter Three

The Breslins' house was tall and square, grey-faced and unyielding. Its staring windows, blinded by the afternoon sun, gave nothing away.

Bid, the daily help, led the way into the sitting room. 'Cold weather,' she said, bending down to blow on the fire and replenish it with a huge log. 'How have you been keeping? And you having to manage everything on your own,' she asked, with charming sympathy.

'Oh, I'm fine,' I said. 'Everything's organised.'

'And your mum?'

'Fussing as usual.'

'Ah, well. It'll be grand,' Bid said. 'I'll tell Mrs Breslin that you're here.'

The whole countenance of the sitting room was cold, the deep leather chairs like stiff-backed ladies. Looking around I wondered how soon I could extricate myself from this plush prison, with its heavy velvet drapes, the slippery satin cushions, the heavy brass and gleaming silver.

Mrs Breslin came into the room, a tall, broad woman, followed by her yappy little dog, Poppy, who growled at me.

'Olivia, come and sit down,' she said, drawing me to a side-table in the bay window, overlooking the flower-beds. 'I hope there's enough here. If not, I'll get Bid to bring us more.'

'There's tons,' I said, surveying the egg-and-cress finger sandwiches, scones, and coffee cake.

She settled herself at the table tucking her linen napkin into the belt of her blue silk dress, the hostility in her eyes leaving me in no doubt of her dislike. I was the obstacle between her son and the millionaire's daughter she had hoped he'd marry. 'How's everything coming along?'

My natural instinct for trouble warned me to smile. 'Mum's made the cake. The hotel's booked. We saw the florist yesterday.'

'Quite,' she said, dabbing her lips with the corner of her napkin. 'I'll need a copy of the seating plan.'

It should have been a time when all barriers were set aside. Instead, Mrs Breslin was determined to keep the wedding ritual rigidly conventional, each member of the cast playing his or her part.

'The wedding invitations. Nothing gaudy, I hope?' Her eyes bored into mine.

'Plain white with silver writing.'

She nodded approvingly. 'Where were you thinking of for the honeymoon?'

'Italy,' I said.

'Perfect,' she said, joining her fat, ringed fingers. 'Barry's been there plenty of times. He'll make sure you come to no harm.'

Silence ensued, broken only by an insistent beating of pigeons' wings in the trees outside, and a lawnmower in the distance.

'Well?' She looked at me. 'More tea?'

'Yes, please.'

'Of course, once the wedding is over things will be easy for you. You're very fortunate to have a home to walk into.'

'I know.'

'Mind you, it won't be all plain sailing being married to Barry. His place in the family business, particularly in view of his father's impending retirement, will keep him very busy. You, as his wife, will be expected to entertain. I hope that you will make a conscientious effort to learn the practical concerns of being a businessman's wife.'

'I'll do my best,' I said, gazing at the bright, reflecting surfaces that surrounded us, longing for a smoke. Lifting my bag I rooted for the packet, then hesitated. 'Do you mind?'

Mrs Breslin said stiffly, 'You realise that Barry will be judged by business associates on how he conducts himself in his own home.'

It was horrible to be forced to sit with a woman who was hoping that her new daughter-in-law would not disgrace her. With trembling hands I lit up.

'I'd be happy to instruct you on the various courses

suitable at dinner parties, and on table etiquette. I worked in catering myself, you know.'

'I know,' I said, keeping my gaze on the roses.

'I hope you won't think me interfering for asking, but tell me, what provision have you made for a family?'

'A what?'

'I was wondering if you intend to start a family straight away, now that you have your own home. A sense of family is very important. There's a strong tradition in the Breslin clan to start within three months and I'm old-fashioned enough still to believe in that tradition, despite modern notions of young wives keeping their jobs, and the availability of contraceptives. Still, I'm sure that you'll be happy to give up working in the shop. It isn't as if you're hankering after a career.'

With clarity I saw the price to be paid for marrying into the comfortable façade of respectability. It occurred to me that this was how life would be from now on: an eternity of her sitting in her chair, knees pressed together, her hands uneasily on her lap, gazing at me, quizzical and disapproving. If her intention had been to shock me, she had succeeded. She didn't care. Her age and seniority seemed to give her permission to say what she liked.

I said, 'I don't think that's any of your business.'

She gazed at me, her mouth open. Conscience-stricken, I said, 'I'm sorry. I was overreacting. It's pre-wedding nerves. Barry and I haven't discussed it. Sure we've hardly seen each other in the last year.'

She brushed imaginary crumbs from her lap and said, thoughtfully, 'Perhaps I spoke out of turn but, you see, I'm a woman of means and that imposes a terrible responsibility. Barry is our only child and stands to inherit quite a lot. In protecting the interests of the bakery I want to ensure that the Breslin name continues.'

'I've never thought about Barry's wealth,' I said, and it was true.

'No?' she said, her mouth bitter. 'I think you have.'

She gestured round the room. 'There's far more at stake than the bakery, you know.'

'I'm not interested in your property.' My voice rose high and defensive.

'Oh! Come now, you hardly expect me to believe that. The question is, would you be willing to marry my son if he hadn't a penny?'

'Of course I would,' I said, indignantly.

'I don't think so,' she said, her mouth tightening.

I don't have to put up with this, I thought. I stood up, quelled an urge to rush for the door and said, 'I don't know what's going to happen in the future. We haven't discussed it.'

'Well, I have no intention of being left out in the cold. I want to know your plans,' she said, her diamond brooch gleaming in the sunlight. 'For the life of me, I can't think why you and Barry are rushing into marriage. He's young, his whole life ahead of him.'

I couldn't stop myself. 'He's probably marrying me to get away from you.'

'How dare you?' For a moment I thought she was going to reach out and hit me but the door opened suddenly and Bid came into the room. 'Did you call me?' she asked.

'No.' Mrs Breslin rose to her full height.

'Right you are.' Puzzled, Bid left.

I glanced after her retreating back, longing to get out of there. I glanced uneasily at my watch, said, 'Is that the time?' and walked towards the door.

Mrs Breslin came up behind me as I opened it. 'Wait,' she said. I stood poised. 'It serves no purpose us being at loggerheads like this,' she said, her eyes moist. I could feel her terrible loneliness, was aware of it in the depths of her eyes. I knew that her fear of losing her son outweighed her dislike of me. She extended her hand. I shook it and said, 'I suppose we'd better make the best of things. We're stuck with each other now.'

She gave me a wet-eyed look, her shoulders raised.

I felt guilty. This woman had brought out the worst in me.

'We'll meet again,' she said.

'See you,' I said, and ran down the steps.

'She's gone too far this time,' I said to Trish and Doreen, still seething, two days later, white and close to tears, 'and all because we haven't any money. Half the time I couldn't think of anything to say. It was a nightmare.'

'The repulsive old slag,' Doreen said. 'You're going to be married anyway, whether she likes it or not, and there's nothing she can do to stop it.'

The morning of our last girls' night out I sat in the beauty parlour.

'Facial first.' The beautician, a young girl with several earrings pierced into each lobe, leaned closer and sighed, her eyes critical.

She shook out her hennaed hair, took down a bottle from an array on a shelf, squeezed an expensive blob on to the back of her hand. 'Then leg and bikini wax, manicure, eyelash tint, tanning, and finally hair,' she said, splaying her fingers across my face, 'You won't know yourself when I'm finished with you. Your skin needs nourishment. Drink plenty of water, you're dehydrated.' She squinted at me, dabbing my face with cotton wool. Eventually, several hot flannels and lavender water later, my skin was raw.

Tweezers poised, she attacked my eyebrows.

'Ouch,' I whimpered, but she took no notice. 'You want to look beautiful, don't you?'

The strip of wax across my top lip made it impossible for me to reply.

'Legs,' she said, with the alacrity of a Gestapo officer, pointing to the massage table covered in a thick towel. Facing the wall mirror, I could see myself for the ugly, revolting slob I was.

'Do you shave your legs?' she asked, pulling a face.

'Yes,' I said. 'Regularly.'

'Leaves a disgusting rash.' She smeared my legs with wax, and yanked so hard my eyes bulged.

By the time Slinky Sue, the hairdresser, took the scissors to me I was ready to dissolve. As she worked she talked about the poor condition of my hair, its need of a treatment, and wedding etiquette, a subject on which she seemed to be a connoisseur, her cantilevered bosom tilting over my eyes.

Trish and Doreen called for me early and lolled on my bed while I finished my makeup. Beautiful in coloured tops and short skirts, cheeks glowing with anticipation, they drank vodka and lime while they waited.

'Come on, you'll do,' Trish said impatiently, downing her drink, making a *moue* with her mouth. 'I don't know why you're bothering so much. You're spoken for.'

'You never know. I'm not married yet,' I said.

'That's what we're afraid of.' Doreen giggled.

Laughing at our own silliness we left the house.

As we got nearer to the city the Friday-night traffic swelled. We stopped in Leeson Street at the Pink Elephant.

'Nothing over eighteen.' Doreen looked at the arrogant young men milling around, girls squashed together dancing.

'Tough-looking, too,' Trish said.

'Who cares?' Doreen's voice was high with the combined stress of trying to make a good impression and remembering to breathe in.

'What did you say your name was?' Trish asked the bold, earringed stud standing next to her.

'I didn't. Here's the number of my mobile.' He handed her a business card. 'Call me,' he said, 'but only on Thursdays.'

'Married creep,' she hissed, and moved away.

'I want to dance.' Doreen dug me in the ribs every time she saw a delectable male, wondering with schoolgirl optimism if tonight was the night her efforts would be rewarded and she would meet her Prince Charming. The dimmed lighting did wonders for our appearance but made it difficult to check out the talent.

We plonked ourselves on bar stools, and smiled surreptitiously at everyone. Trish leaned forward to order, insinuating her cleavage on to the bar, flicking her eyes suggestively at the barman. His face creased into an ingratiating smile.

'What can I get you?' he asked.

She shrugged dramatically, her over-madeup face glowing. 'What have you got?' she asked, with a smirk, her resolution on men forgotten.

'What would you like?' He grinned.

'Surprise me.'

I focused on the girl seated next to me, who was extracting a silver snuffbox from her handbag, her hair a frizzy halo around her head, her talons the same colour as her drink.

'There's a party in Killiney. We're invited,' Doreen said, returning with a new recruit from the dance-floor.

'I'll drive you there,' the recruit said, his face in mine, his shaved head shining in the fluorescent light.

'Has to be better than this,' Trish said, sipping her cocktail, the barman forgotten.

The venue in Killiney turned out to be a large, rambling house and grounds owned by a film star at the end of a tiny cul-de-sac that overlooked the sea. Girls in thigh-high skirts circled with trays of champagne and caviar. The place was full of well-known people, enjoying themselves. I felt depressed, watching the beautiful glistening women as they sipped cocktails, their faces vacant. The men leered at them, seeing them as beautiful but useless objects. It was a stage upon which to be seen, to barter personalities and tell great adventure stories. A drink would transform me into a silly, acceptable, girlish version of myself. I grabbed a passing glass of champagne. Doreen and Trish were dancing while a few men standing in groups looked on.

'Come and meet Simon. He's really sweet,' said a blonde woman with a tan, whom I took to be the hostess.

Simon, small, fat and bald, was languishing on a couch, surrounded by several cats.

'Did you hurt yourself when you fell from heaven?' a soft foreign voice behind me said, as I backed away.

I turned. Standing before me was a tall, olive-skinned man with long, shiny black hair curling behind his ears. I blinked to make sure I wasn't dreaming. 'Hello,' he murmured, his wide sensual mouth smiling to expose teeth as white as his starched shirt. I returned his stare because it seemed the natural thing to do.

He had brown eyes, a narrow nose, and looked as if he'd just stepped off a film set. I said, wanting to touch his cleanshaven cheek, 'Hello. I'm Olivia.'

'Ol-iv-ia.' He drew it out in a long breath.

'After Olivia de Havilland, my mother's favourite film star. Haven't we met before?'

'I don't think so,' he said, dropping his eyes over my body. 'I would have remembered,' he added, with emphasis.

'I thought perhaps we might have met at Lillie's,' I said, not sure why I was pursuing this line of conversation. I hadn't ever been to Lillie's Bordello, Dublin's famous nightclub.

'Oh, no,' he said, in a tone that implied that he would never set foot in the place unless he absolutely had to.

'It's just that you look familiar.' I gazed at him with innocent eyes. 'Do you live locally?'

'I'm the manager of the new Italian restaurant, Shrimps, in Abbeyville. My name is Lorenzo O'Brien.'

'Lorenzo O'Brien! I knew I'd seen you before. With a name like that you couldn't be Irish.'

'I'm half Irish, half Italian.'

'Oh! I like Italian men.'

'Have you known many?' he asked.

'A few.' I shrugged. 'Great lovers,' I added teasingly.

'So I hear,' he said.

I repressed the urge to shift sideways and align my body with his. The place became stuffy, and his arm rested along my back. I leaned towards him and touched his hand.

Doreen came up to us. 'Lorenzo!' she crinkled her eyes when I'd introduced them.

'He's half Irish, half Italian,' I explained. 'Tell me,' I asked, 'which half of you is Italian and which is Irish?'

'You'll have to find out for yourself,' Lorenzo teased.

'Don't worry, I will.' I gave him a dig in the ribs. We roared.

'Can I get you a drink?' Lorenzo asked.

'Yes, please,' I said.

'Nothing for me, thanks,' Doreen said. 'I'm off to seek my fortune.' She was gone, weaving through the crowd.

'Wait there. I'll be back in a minute,' Lorenzo told me.

He returned almost immediately. 'I'd like to get to know you better. You're beautiful.'

'Oh! Thanks.' I sipped my drink, trying to look sophisticated. This gorgeous man was giving me his undivided attention and I wasn't sure how to react. 'You're beautiful too,' I said, appraising him, something rising in me with the warmth of the champagne.

'Let's go somewhere.' His voice vibrated in my ear, his breath was feathery on my face. Dizzily I moved back, watching his mouth, wanting to kiss it slowly, for a long time. I think he was thinking the same thing because suddenly he leaned dangerously close. 'Come on,' he said.

Trish glanced sardonically at me, making it clear that she saw what was going on and didn't approve. Undeterred, I continued my exploration of his body with my eyes. There was something dark and dangerous about him.

'A walk on the beach,' he said, his voice husky with restrained desire.

'Lovely,' I said, mumbled something to Trish and swayed to the door, Lorenzo's arm around me.

The path was thick with brambles, the beach strewn with seaweed, the moon reflected on the dark water breaking on the shore. Taking off my shoes I felt the soft sand beneath my feet as I walked along the strand.

'Nice breeze,' he said casually, gazing up at the stars, his head tilted so that his hair fell back.

'It's beautiful,' I said, breathing in the salty air. The champagne had mellowed my mood, and diminished my sense of responsibility, making him hard to resist. We sat down and gazed silently at the moonlight, my head resting on his shoulder, Barry forgotten. He shifted, settling himself more comfortably. For all his restraint I sensed the lust in him.

'A girl like you must have a steady boyfriend?'

I stared into space. 'There's plenty of time.' When I turned he was smiling radiantly.

The breeze blew my hair into my face, to catch in my mouth. I was sitting so close to him that I could feel the heat of his skin and told myself to get up and walk away, all the time knowing I wouldn't. I looked at the stars, and the moon encircled in its white halo.

'Why did you come to live in Ireland?' I asked.

'It's where my father originated. I spent a lot of my childhood here. You see, my parents were separated.'

'Oh!' I waited, but he didn't say any more.

I stretched out my legs in front of me. Beneath the moon my skin took on a sheen, a magic glow. There was an alertness about Lorenzo, as he took me in his arms and kissed me. I put my arms around his neck, liking the warmth of his body.

'Um,' I murmured, feeling his hands on my waist, laying me down gently on the sand. He touched me as if he knew my body, had already possessed it. I turned to him, my hands on his hips. My body was ripe beneath his hands, my breasts arching up to meet his mouth. I opened my eyes. He was staring at me, his gaze tense.

'Ollie!' Trish's voice ripped out like a bullet.

'Stop,' I said, breathless, scrambling to my feet, brushing sand from my dress. 'I have to go.'

I stumbled blindly towards the house, thinking I might

never see him again. Then, turning back, I called, 'I'll see you again.'

Lorenzo ran, caught up with me. His arms reached out, pulled me to him. He pressed his mouth to mine, his breathing rapid. I broke free, running before Trish saw too much.

'Olivia.' Lorenzo's voice was dying on the wind.

'You were gone a long time,' Trish said, on the way home. 'I was getting worried.'

'We went for a walk.'

'Is that all?'

'Of course.'

'You seemed to be getting very cosy.'

'Oh! Not really.' I shrugged nonchalantly.

'He fancied you.' She giggled. 'And I got the impression that you were enjoying yourself.'

'I just hope I don't wake up with a hangover in the morning. There's so much to be done.'

Next morning I could hear Mum vacuuming, her voice high-pitched and girlish as she sang, 'I want to be loved by you, la, la, and you alone,' her loose polyester dressing-gown swirling around her as her hips swayed.

'There you are, Olivia,' she said, following me into the kitchen, a duster in her hand. 'I've been up since five. Everything's done. Kitchen, sitting room, dining room. I've even swept the yard.' She gestured widely towards the back of the house. 'I've got to phone the hairdresser, get my hair sorted. Auntie Tess is bringing Polly over for a fitting. Oh! Mr Hall, the hotel manager, phoned. He wants us to organise the seating arrangements. If you'd chosen to get married in September Billy and Faith would have been able to make it, you know.'

'Blame Barry,' I said. 'It was his idea to get married in June. As a matter of fact it was his idea to get married.'

'On the other hand,' Mum said, ignoring me, 'the flowers are more reliable this time of year.'

I went to the fridge to get out the orange juice, thinking of the previous night and Lorenzo.

'I've got the guest list somewhere.' She went to rummage in the drawer.

I sighed deeply and turned away.

'I wish you'd take an interest in your own wedding, and for goodness sake go and get dressed and put on some makeup. You're as pale as a lily. I'll see you in the shop,' she said, yanking off her apron.

'Right,' I said, thinking how his strong hands had brushed over my body, driving me mad with desire, before Trish had broken the spell.

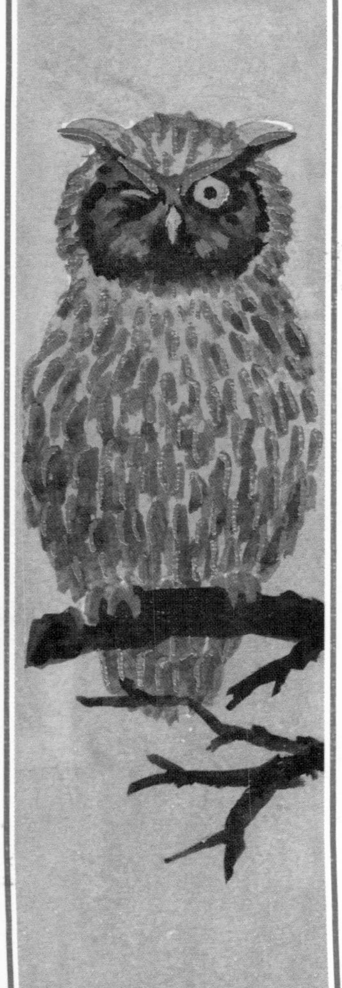

Chapter Four

Widowhood changed Queenie. She ruled her shop, Regina Modes, with determined efficiency, but in the privacy of her home she was frantic, her eye on the next disaster. She smothered Lorraine with her fussing: buttoning up her cardigan to the neck every morning before she left the house, bringing her lunch to school if she forgot it, doctoring her with medicines and potions, nourishing her with the best she could afford to buy. All her efforts went into the care of her daughter. That and her contact with her customers brought a little satisfaction to her joyless life.

Lorraine was a girl with ideas of her own. From the age of ten she elected to serve customers, her nose barely visible above the counter. At the age of fifteen, devilment in her huge, dark eyes, she ran off with Ginger, a young animal trainer she met when the travelling circus came to town. Wild with the release from Queenie's rules, she shared in his fun, moving from place to place with the circus. To him she was a pet, someone to share his jokes, and his main interest, apart from his horses, was in keeping her happy. She wrote home saying that she regretted any worry she had caused, but that she couldn't stick school and taking orders from everyone a minute longer. 'No Fixed Abode', where the address should have been.

'Worry!' Queenie had roared. 'The irresponsible little scamp. She hasn't finished school.'

'Tramp, you mean,' Statia said, a gleam of envy in her eyes.

In the parish Lorraine's disappearance remained a mystery. Queenie told the customers that she'd sent her to boarding-school to give her a final polish, but her story backfired when, the following summer, neighbours encountered Lorraine at Butlin's in Skegness, or 'a girl who looked the spitting image of her', bulging with life and 'eating fire'.

'The devil's got hold of her,' Queenie said to Father Farrelly.

Statia said, 'She'll have to get married,' wishing it was her own story. Jockser was the only man who'd 'stolen her heart', she said, and 'Anything else he could get his hands on,' Queenie added.

Lorraine returned with a suitcase in one hand and baby Billy in the other. She was all in black, a wedding ring on her finger, her raven hair falling forlornly into her eyes. 'A widow,' Queenie said tragically, wrapping her arms around her, knowing what it was like to bring up a child alone.

'No,' Lorraine, said, looking her straight in the eye, 'but I can do a good impersonation of one.'

Within days the news of Lorraine's return was out. The neighbours came to sympathise and console. Queenie had a memorial service to authenticate the story. The whole parish turned out: 'God help you,' and 'What a cross to bear.' Lorraine was flanked on either side by Queenie and Statia, sentinels in long black coats and tall fur hats, faces inscrutable.

'Tragic,' Father Farrelly said, to the congregation.

'Mauled by a lion,' Lorraine told Mona Corcoran, her best friend from schooldays, in her new English accent. They were sitting in the back kitchen, Mona with her feet tucked under the table, her chair drawn up close to Lorraine's.

'What was he like?' Mona asked.

'Huge, powerful, golden eyes, striped fur.'

'Your husband, stupid!'

'Oh! Gorgeous.' Lorraine sighed. 'Dark, glossy hair, beautiful white teeth.'

Mona sighed regretfully. 'Shame he had to go and die.'

Later, in the pub, Mona confided to Curley Mathews, 'I can't put a finger on it but that story of Lorraine's doesn't ring true.'

'There was someone killed by a lion in a circus.' Curley Mathews sipped his beer.

'That was in recently, all right, but I doubt it was her husband.' Mona sniffed. 'I smell a great big rat.'

Sunshine, the scent of strawberries and raspberries from the shop next door, and the return of Lorraine brought new life to the street. Shoppers strolled by, their greetings interspersed with laughter. Some dropped in to see Lorraine and Billy. Lorraine regaled them with the fantastic tales of her days in the circus. Business picked up.

From the age of twenty-five Queenie had relinquished all contact with men, and hoped her daughter would be sensible enough to do the same, but after a year's mourning Lorraine dropped her widow's weeds and shortened her skirts. Often she could be seen pushing little Billy in his go-kart, her skirts hitched up, her long legs bare and bronzed, shopkeepers gazing up the road after her. Queenie was appalled. Billy, a big, round eighteen-month-old, with golden curls and a smile to melt ice, was too lazy to walk but he could unclip his straps and unscrew the bolts that held his pram together. According to Queenie he had been robbed of his true identity and belonged to the circus. Billy Smart, she called him, in the privacy of her own home. His only reply was da-da.

Full-skirted suits and dresses, latest *haute-couture* designs from famous designer Sybil Connelly, were all the rage. Queenie overstocked her shop with Irish linen and fine wool fabrics, convinced of a sell-out to her thrifty, collar-turning customers. The women, headscarves tied severely under chins, gazed longingly at it all, and shook their heads sadly. Material for new clothes for themselves, they explained to Queenie, was out of the question. There were too many mouths to feed, and a lot of the husbands were out of work.

'We're broke,' Queenie said, panic-stricken, one hot summer's day.

'What'll we do?' asked Lorraine, who longed to escape

again, but seemed doomed to a lifetime of shop routine because of Billy.

'Take in lodgers.'

'Lodgers!' Lorraine broke into a peal of high-pitched laughter that exposed her white teeth and made her eyes dance. 'You've got to be joking.'

'It wasn't meant as a joke.' Queenie was hurt.

'Of course it wasn't,' Mary, the general factotum, said. 'It's not even a bad idea.'

'You think so?' Lorraine scoffed.

'Someone's sensible,' Queenie said.

Lorraine raised her eyes towards the ceiling. 'There's only the spare room, which is damp. The box room, with that hideous wallpaper, is no bigger than a cupboard. You won't get much for that.'

'Swap,' Queenie said. 'I'll have the box room, you and Billy take the other one. I'll have them done up.'

'Who'll look after lodgers?' Lorraine wasn't convinced that it was a good idea.

'You will. Mary'll help.'

That's how, at a time of massive unemployment and emigration, Queenie had enough to live a tight-comfortable life, and to keep on Mary. Her strict economies – scrimping with soap, using rough Bronco toilet paper, saving string and paper – grew after the war years rather than diminishing. Each morning she rose at six o'clock, went for a walk and bought the newspaper, which she scoured over breakfast to formulate her opinions on current affairs.

Breakfast was for early risers, newspaper readers, and Mr

Appleby, the first lodger, made early-morning discussions lively. He and Queenie debated, rather than discussed, global affairs. Mr Appleby's Adam's apple hopped up and down, his *pince-nez* balanced precariously on his nose. They thrashed out their views on de Gaulle taking over in France, Castro becoming premier of Cuba, Krushchev succeeding Bulganin, the riots in Notting Hill and the increased activity at the border.

On the morning Mr Healy, the second lodger, was due, Lorraine was alone in the shop. She was several inches taller than her mother, loose-limbed and fleshy, with long black hair to her shoulders. She wore a long blue dress and smart, comfortable shoes and a touch of lipstick.

'This is Regina Modes?' A round-faced fair-haired man in his early forties put a foot inside the door then walked forward with a suitcase in each hand.

Lorraine said, 'Yes,' and waited, smiling, her bright earrings setting off a sparkle in her watchful, blue eyes.

'Healy is the name,' the man said, shaking the rain off himself like a dog, lifting a hand to his shirt-collar, loosening his striped tie. 'I've been walking in the rain, looking for the place, and it's most unpleasant.'

'I'm so sorry.' Lorraine stepped forward and shook his hand. 'Come in. I'll show you to your room and get you a drop of something. Bring your cases.'

'How charming,' Mr Healy said humorously, following her. 'I saw from the sign outside that it was the shop, but couldn't locate the living quarters.'

'To the side,' Lorraine explained. 'We take up the whole corner.' She gestured expansively to the hall and stairs.

'Fascinating.'

Lorraine hoped she had adopted the right manner, for it was essential, Queenie had said, that she should be friendly and welcoming.

'I'm afraid it's a bit old-fashioned,' she said, following his eyes around the dingy bedroom. 'I'm sure it's not the sort of place you're used to.'

'My dear, I love it.' Mr Healy took in the maroon flowers on the wallpaper and the green-painted window and door. 'I can't stand hotels with cocktail bars and fussy staff. I've had my fill of those. This is . . .' he paused, gazing around '. . . wonderful. I'm glad I found it.' He really meant he was glad he'd found her.

'There's only my mother and myself, and my little boy.' Lorraine was apologetic. 'I do the cooking.'

'I love the way you talk.' Mr Healy stared at her. 'I'm willing to pay good money for this room.' He leaned over the bed to test the springs. 'And a nice meal in the evenings.' He was smiling at her, as though her presence made up for the sad, empty spaces in his life.

'Wonderful!' She smiled back. 'I'll make us a pot of tea. Or would you prefer something stronger? A glass of whiskey? Only I'm afraid we'll have to take it in the shop. I'm the only one here at the moment. My mother's gone to town.' She took a breath and laughed. Lorraine laughed a lot. The sound echoed through the place but was not always a good barometer of her moods. It was a camouflage.

'I'm happy to have a cup of tea with you. I like listening to you,' Mr Healy said.

'Oh! I'm not here all the time,' Lorraine didn't know why she said that. 'I do a bit of acting in my spare time.'

'How marvellous.'

'Only with an amateur company. But I'm learning so much.'

His eyes were full of light and interest as she spoke.

While they drank their tea she watched him. An attractive man, nothing out of the ordinary. Her heart lurched a little when he said, 'You're extraordinary.'

'Not really,' she said, finishing her tea.

'Well, I'd better be off too,' he said. 'I need a wash and a change of clothes,' his hand shook a little as he raised his cup to his lips, 'before my next appointment. By the way, please call me Phil.'

Lorraine watched him leave the room, opening the doors so that the sunlight blazed in from the hall. He was not a Dublin man. He had no accent. Perhaps he was English. There were quite a few English people in the area. Looking back she felt that she had known something was happening to her, that her brain was piecing together facts about him even while he was smiling at her, and thanking her for her hospitality.

She was a member of the amateur drama society, and had played Jessica in *The Merchant of Venice* and the White Rabbit in *Alice in Wonderland*. She wished she were Audrey Hepburn, the film star she'd seen in *My Fair Lady*, or Olivia de Havilland, the Hollywood actress she'd seen in *Gone with the Wind*, and admired so much. Often she pretended that she was Olivia de Havilland strolling through the Hollywood boulevards, her hair piled high, her high-heeled shoes enticing men who stopped to engage her attention, smiling, saying, 'Aren't you Olivia de Havilland? Let me buy you a drink.'

Her own name – Lorraine – was interesting, the name her father had given her. She remembered him taking her hand, walking her through the streets of the city. She remembered his tobacco, and the hardness of his hands. He was always smiling at her too.

There had been terrible rows between her parents. Sometimes her father banged around, in the middle of the night after the pubs closed, shouting for her mother. Lorraine would listen, confused. At other times he was gentle, giving tea-parties for her doll, Nell, and Teddy, with tiny tomato sandwiches that he would make and they would eat, then recounting stories about animals in the jungle, lying beside her, cradling her doll. He'd brought Nell home under his coat, a big, walkie-talkie doll that looked like a real baby. 'Life's for living,' he would say to her. 'Enjoy it. When you grow up be sure to do something that you love. Something you want to do more than anything.'

When he got sick she was sent to Dollymount to stay with Statia, and she didn't see him after that. When she asked her mother if her father had died Queenie replied, 'It's all for the best,' and gave her the silver locket with her baby picture on one side and Queenie's smiling face on the other, the scratched surface proof that he'd worn it all during the war. She had loved her daddy, and had cried bitterly.

She had seen herself on the stage, in the opulent costumes

of Shakespearean ladies, and had said so to her mother. Queenie's reply, 'All that glitters is not gold', and that as an actress she might not make enough to keep body and soul together, was disheartening. On her fifteenth birthday she had visited the circus for the first time, smart in her new blue backless sundress. That was when she caught the eye of Ginger. He invited her for tea and cream buns in his caravan afterwards. Every night while the circus was in town she went, and her desire for the roar of the crowd and the smell of the greasepaint flared. Ginger told her that the circus had fallen on hard times, that he and his horses were off to seek their fortune in Britain, the land of opportunity, and that she was welcome to join him if she wanted to.

Lorraine was tired of studying, of the nuns and of her acerbic mother, so she agreed. 'It won't be a bed of roses,' he had warned, his eyes on her abundant cleavage. They sealed their plans with a kiss and a walk down the pier, when he said, 'I love you.' Thinking that they would be together for the rest of their lives, she let him take unrestrained liberties with her body. After that he never told her he loved her again. But he kept his promise and took her away with him.

During her time in England with Ginger she worked hard. She learned to bang nails into walls and to attach bolts and screws to metal or wood. Any task in the erection and maintenance of tents, the sewing of sequins on costumes, and the care of animals was hers. Ginger lost interest in her as she slowed down, and didn't look out for her as he had in the past. He was happier performing in his new act, showing off his tap-dancing skills taught him by his new partner, Griff.

Lorraine would watch them, their hair slicked back, their soft leather cowboy boots pressing together, their heels clicking under the flares of their trousers, their jewelled studs glittering in their cuffs when their hands touched. 'Ah, Ginger, you look great,' she would say enticingly, hoping he'd come to bed with her but knowing he was happier dancing in his new act. When Griff and he left for the States she was heartbroken. Courted by Dimitri, the lion-tamer from Cyprus, who preferred large docile women to wily little chicks, she coped. He had money and security as the best lion-tamer in the business. He took her to the theatre in Leeds to see *The Taming of the Shrew*, coached her in the art of stage presence, even went with her to the cinema to see Olivia de Havilland. He bought her chocolates, which she ate while his roughened hands struggled with her clothes, her pregnancy making it difficult for him to locate his target.

She would cook supper for him, which he ate, assuring her that some day she would make someone a great wife. Often she wondered what life would be like with this nomad. She tried to imagine the two of them sharing a house, and couldn't, because he would leave without saying where he was going, for days, returning unruly and intoxicated. She would remove his boots, and wait silently in their tiny caravan, while he slept, not making a sound until she heard him moving about, calling her to bed.

'I'm leaving the circus,' she said to him, when Billy was a year old and Ginger had not returned to claim her. She had had enough of Dimitri and had saved the money to go home. He beat her first, then said, 'Don't go. I'll buy you a ring.

We'll live as husband and wife.' Lorraine was amazed at his sadness.

She'd watched him remove his clothes, putting them carefully across a chair, then walking towards her, his powerful body slightly thickened at the waist. Suddenly she could see her future clearly: Dimitri and herself, and eight beautiful children, wandering from place to place, homeless, regular beatings.

Seized by bitterness she said, 'Thanks for the offer, but no. I'm leaving.'

For years afterwards she remembered his tears as he said, 'Let's go to the pub. It'll cheer us up. Forget all this nonsense.' Lorraine imagined her mother at home, working hard in her shop, and decided to take her baby home to meet his family.

Having to take orders from Queenie again, and always being reminded of her 'unfortunate' circumstances, made Lorraine resentful. She was back where she'd started, full of doubts and unfulfilled curiosity about life, her youthful *joie de vivre* gradually dampened by tedium. She knew she'd have to find a husband. All her friends were married. Billy was getting bigger, and more and more dependent on Queenie. Lorraine, overcome by the terror of ending up like her mother and anxious to have some status, married Phil Healy, the lodger.

At a time when poverty was rampant and good jobs were scarce, Phil Healy, a salesman with the printers Cherry and Smalldridge, was considered a good catch. He wore pinstriped suits and carried an attaché case of samples. Sometimes he took Lorraine to afternoon tea at the Russell Hotel.

Occasionally, he treated Queenie and his wife to a night at the Theatre Royal.

He settled in well to a tradition of female self-sufficiency, although there was no relationship between him and Queenie. However, she intruded upon the intimacy he shared with Lorraine to such an extent that they had to resort to going away together for weekends for privacy and to ward off the shame of being discovered 'at it' by Queenie. How they managed to produce a daughter remained a mystery to everyone, Queenie not least.

Chapter Five

I was weary of the wedding preparations. Mum's references to 'bridal nerves' and 'your groom' and the mention of catering, church, priest, new hats, made me feel trapped. Mention of the honeymoon sent me into a panic.

'I can't stand all the fuss and tension,' I said to Queenie. 'It's like living in a play with me as the central character.'

She gave me a sidelong glance. 'Too much booze last night. I know the feeling,' she said, her eyes unfathomable.

Queenie, a vital woman with a handsome face, had a ready smile, but a sometimes turbulent expression in her eyes. She was tall, but she carried off her height well in elegant clothes. Her Harris tweed coat was always teamed with matching gloves and neat hats, made by herself. A fashionable woman, though not exaggeratedly so, she was comfortable with herself.

Sitting down at the table, in the back room, on which were sliced cold ham, tomatoes, lettuce, bread, cheese and hard-boiled eggs, she said, 'Forget about it. Have something to eat.'

'I'm not hungry,' I said, helping myself to a tomato and a lettuce leaf. 'I'm meeting Trish and Doreen later this evening at the new wine bar in South Anne Street. I'll have something to eat then.' There was always the chance of unexpected company when Trish and Doreen were around, and a change of surroundings wouldn't go amiss.

'The portions they serve in those places wouldn't fill a bird,' Queenie said. 'And the prices they charge!'

'You won't see middle age if you go on like this,' Mum said, coming into the room, her eyes on me. 'You know that there are various psychological disturbances attached to eating disorders,' she continued, helping herself to the ham.

'You don't want to get into all that,' Queenie snapped, 'but you *are* like a whippet, Olivia. Turn sideways and you'll disappear.'

I tossed my head carelessly, determined not to be rattled. 'You exaggerate.'

'Have one of those savoury slices to keep you going,' Mum urged, carrying a cheese and broccoli pie, topped with puff pastry, following me to the door.

'No, thanks,' I said.

'It's all this fussing,' Mum said, glancing into the shop to ascertain that the 'Closed' sign was in place.

'I blame Barry's mother,' Queenie said sourly. 'Trying to keep up with her expectations is impossible. And you'll never get her approval, even if you stand on your head.'

'Christ! I can't stand it,' I said, thinking of the city, how

I would rather be in that terrific hum of people and traffic than listening to Mum and Queenie going on and on.

'I'm only warning you for your own sake.' Queenie continued munching.

'There's no call for swearing,' Mum threw me a look. She hated my sudden outbursts of what she called vulgarity even when there was no one there but ourselves.

'Cheer up,' Queenie coaxed. 'Only one final fitting. That should do the trick.'

That evening my aunt Tess, Statia's daughter, arrived with her two girls, Polly and Audrey. Polly was ten, Audrey a year younger. They were to be my bridesmaids. Queenie closed the shop early so that there'd be no distractions. 'We'd better get everything right this time,' she warned.

'I want to go to the park.' Audrey sulked.

'Olivia'll take you if you behave yourself for a half an hour and stop moithering,' Mum said, handing her a packet of chocolate biscuits and a bottle of Kia-Ora. 'There. You'll need a bit of refreshment after the swings and slides.'

'I won't be staying that long,' I said peevishly.

Queenie gave Audrey a sharp, sideways glance. 'Don't you dare open those biscuits in here. They're for later, and I didn't hear you say thank you.'

'Thank you,' Audrey said sulkily.

Eventually I tried on my dress one last time to please Queenie.

'It doesn't fit,' Mum observed, with triumph in her eyes.

Queenie had to concede that it hung loosely on me and, irritated, said she'd have to take it in more at the seams.

'I don't want you skipping any more meals between now and the wedding or the dress'll fall off you,' Mum warned, as Audrey, Polly and I left for the park. I was glad to get away: only I could feel the extra inches creeping up on me, the slack muscles, the thickening waistline.

We walked quickly past the petrol station, Brady's Lounge, the launderette, spreading suburbia, with its bare-stripped gardens, close-clipped hedges. A capricious wind scattered flower petals with wild abandon. My forthcoming wedding was affecting everybody. Queenie, a woman who despised men, had always said, 'Be independent,' and 'Go your own way.' When Barry came on the scene she seemed to accept him. She did not admit to anyone that she found his jokes and his ready-to-please good nature irritating, but it was evident to me in the way that she gritted her teeth when he was around. Unlike Mum, she was not impressed by his family's social position, or their bakery. Realising that I was neither exceptionally beautiful or clever she tolerated him for my sake, knowing that I would be well set up in an alliance with him.

A red BMW coupé stopped in front of us. Lorenzo got out, calling, 'Hello!'

'Hi,' I replied, surprised and not a little disturbed.

'Want a lift?' He grinned.

'We're on our way to the park.' I was desperate to seem nonchalant.

Audrey jumped into the back before I could stop her. Polly scrambled after her.

'Thanks.' I got into the front passenger seat.

'Did you enjoy yourself the other night?' he asked, as

the car shot off down the road and the girls squealed in excitement, their hair streaming in the wind.

'Very much.'

We came to a halt at the park.

'Your car's smashing,' Polly said, alighting.

Pleased by this Lorenzo marched them to the swings.

'Give us a push, will you?' Polly asked.

They charmed him with their playfulness, and their energy and high spirits forced us into a false liveliness, which we kept up while their squeals of delight rent the air.

'Ice-cream,' they chorused, and tore after the Mr Whippy van. While they ate their cones, quiet for once, we strolled along in front The sudden calm and harmony gave me time to take this man in. He was older than me, at least twenty-seven perhaps even thirty, and so handsome. Impressed by the attention he was paying me I laughed at his silly jokes.

The following day I was dressing the shop window when I caught sight of him walking down the street with a purposeful air and an armful of roses, the curious stares of passers-by eliciting a smile from him. A man who loved his own body and lived comfortably in it. I seized my jacket and threw it on as the shop bell rang. Before I could stop her, Mum had leaped at the door and pushed past me, interest and anticipation in her eyes. Queenie stared from behind the counter. 'Well, hello,' she said. 'You must be . . . ?' She gazed at him, leaning to open the door further.

'Hello,' I said to him, and to Queenie, 'See you later.'

'Why didn't you let me in?' he asked. 'Are you frightened of me meeting your family?'

'It's not a good time,' I said as we drove off, staring at the road ahead, which was deserted but for a few afternoon shoppers.

'What are you nervous of?' he persisted.

'Nothing. I'm not afraid of anything.'

'Are you frightened of your mother?'

'Maybe a little,' I said.

He shook his head, laughing. 'We've only just met. I hardly know you. Do you want me to rescue you from her?'

'No!'

He took my hand. 'What could she do anyway?' he asked, brought my fingers to his lips and kissed the tips passionately. 'The only woman I want, and she has to worry about what her family might think.'

'Lorenzo!' A shiver ran through my body.

He took me to an Italian restaurant in South Anne Street where the home-made pasta was superb and the atmosphere was lively yet relaxed. On the way home he stopped the car and kissed me, his lips soft as he pulled me hard against him.

'I want you,' he said, sure of himself, his fingertips sliding up under my top.

Electric pleasure shot through me. I wanted to say, 'Stop' but the word wouldn't come. I had to tell him about Barry. 'There is something you ought to know,' I began, not in control of my voice.

'Not now,' he said, fumbling with the buttons of my blouse.

Catching his hand in a firm grip I said, 'Lorenzo, listen.'

'What?'

'We shouldn't do this.'

'Why not?'

'We don't know anything about one another. There are things we should discuss.'

'What things?'

'You're not the first.'

'I should hope not.' He sucked in his breath.

Glancing back towards the shop I said, 'I have to go,' and removed his hand.

He murmured into my hair, 'I'm going away for a few days but I'll phone you when I get back.'

'Soon,' I whispered, and the word drove a nail through my relationship with Barry.

Next morning Queenie came into the kitchen asking, 'Who was that handsome man who brought the roses?' She eyed me suspiciously.

'Interflora,' I said, my aptitude for lying in full flight. 'Barry sent them.'

'Ah! He's missing you.'

I walked out of the kitchen and shut the door, pleased with myself for managing to keep my secret – what secret? I had done nothing of any consequence. For the rest of the morning I worked, suspended inside my imagination, resentful of any unnecessary interruption, taking deep breaths to keep myself steady, my thoughts focused on Lorenzo O'Brien.

'We're not making any money,' Queenie said, looking around the shop disheartened.

'There's plenty we could do to brighten up the place.'

I followed her gaze to the deep mahogany counter with its tarnished brass fittings, the rows of dark drawers, the old-fashioned fitting room.

'Oh?' she said, waiting.

'Widen the display window for a start,' I said, nervous of pointing out the need for change. 'Expand in different directions.'

The idea came to me when we were checking the order list: patterns, dress shields, safety-pins, tape measures, crochet hooks, bodkins, needles, cards of pins, spools of thread, drawers of assorted buttons. Bravely, I said, 'I think we should change the whole place. Get rid of this lot.'

Queenie eyed me suspiciously, then lowered her head over the button drawer. 'What exactly did you have in mind?' She dropped a pin. 'See a pin, pick it up,' she said. 'You see, I'm careful. I've a saving nature.' As if she needed to tell me. 'I can't understand what happened to the business.'

'You need to bring it into the twenty-first century. Modernise. This shop needs something,' I said, my eyes on dull dresses and coats, drab hats, the drawers of gloves for every occasion: leather, cotton, crochet, net, string. 'Something new, exciting, something to draw the customers.'

'My customers know exactly what they want and it's what I sell them.'

'We need an event in this shop. Something to entice them in,' I persisted.

'I dare say.' Queenie's corseted body restricted the movement of her hips as she moved around behind the counter, counting, checking.

'Sexy underwear like they had in Sylvia's would do it.'

'What, in God's name, are you thinking of?'

'Black wispy lace, oyster satin, red silk, white Lycra frilly pants, cami-knickers.'

'Have you lost your mind?' she said, slamming a drawer shut.

'That wispy, cobwebby underwear Sylvia's used to have before it became a garden centre.'

'I don't like to sound old-fashioned but it's not respectable. Look at the way poor Sylvia ended up – in a home for the bewildered.'

'She sold out for a lot of money,' I protested.

'This is a traditional shop. Our customers wouldn't welcome a change like that,' Queenie said flatly.

'There's a new, younger generation in the town, and visitors that we haven't managed to—'

'I pride myself on the fact that my customers can rely on me to supply their requirements. Where else can they replace their corsets?' she asked. 'Trivialities like you're suggesting are a passing fad.' She was counting bundles of knitting needles, the contents of the bottom drawer. 'I like to think we provide a reliable service. Which reminds me, I want you to post the order list this afternoon.' She banged the drawer shut and the conversation was at an end.

Chapter Six

That afternoon, I walked the long way home from the post office, past the park. Lorenzo stood on the steps to the entrance.

'Hello,' I said.

He made as if to touch me but drew back, looked about him and grinned. 'I saw you coming out of the post office. Come and have a drink with me – or is someone waiting for you?'

I glanced up and down the street, at the windows opposite. 'I'd love to,' I said, 'but I'd better not. You know what this place is like, eyes everywhere, and I'm supposed to be working.' I began to walk away.

He followed me. 'I'm parked over there,' he said, pointing to the car. 'We can drive out of town.'

'I suppose one drink wouldn't do any harm,' I said.

'Where'll we go?'

'Anywhere away from here,' I said, and climbed into the passenger seat.

We glided away and turned left at the traffic lights, past the rows of houses that led to the main road. He took a cigarette from the packet on the dashboard, his hand grazing my thigh, filling me with desire and a sense of foreboding. 'Where will you say you've been?' he asked.

'I could have met Doreen or Trish, got delayed.'

It was as if we were acting a play, the audience the inquisitive neighbours behind the chinks in their curtains.

He picked up speed and drove through the traffic, his restrained passion obvious in the hunch of his shoulders, and his grip on the steering-wheel. 'Where to?' he asked, his voice husky.

'Seapoint.'

He came to a halt in the car park. Stretching his arm along my back, he drew me to him. With his hands firm on my shoulders, he kissed me. My entire body responded to his caresses, and blossomed with desire.

'Were you hoping to see me?' he asked, his breathing shallow.

'No,' I lied, a bit too quickly, quivering with excitement. I pulled away from him. 'We can't do this.'

He jerked back, took a deep breath and switched on the car stereo. Sinead O'Connor's haunting voice, singing 'Nothing Compares', flooded the car.

'I'll have to go back,' I said.

'I want you so badly.' His voice was taut. 'Come to my place.'

'Not tonight.'

'When?'

'I'll think of something,' I said softly.

'If you don't I will,' he said.

'I know.'

'I'll ring you,' he said.

'Sunday's not a good time,' I said. 'Monday night?'

Our arrangement made, we drove home, the sense of danger drawing us together.

'You'll be in Monday night?' he said, as we drew up outside the shop, anxiety creeping into his voice again.

'Of course,' I said, trying not to think of the deception I was embarking on. 'I'll be waiting for your call.'

'Okay. I'll see you.' It was raining as I got out of the car and walked quickly back to the shop.

'Hey!' He caught up with me as I was about to break into a run. The rain was soaking me. He caught me, kissed me full on the lips. 'I love you,' he said.

I couldn't believe it. Joy surged through me as I ran round the corner, out of sight, the rain beating a steady rhythm in the gutters, the ground hard beneath my feet.

I dripped all the way up the stairs to the bathroom, removed my clothes, took a shower, and emerged just as the phone was ringing.

'Hello, Ollie. It's me.'

'Barry!' I stood still. No words came.

'I know it's late but I tried earlier and you weren't there.'

'I was out . . . at the wholesaler's,' I lied.

'Oh!' Silence. Shivering I wrapped the towel closer around me.

'How are you?'

'Fine, thanks.'

'Getting excited?' His tone was serious.

'Yes. I can't wait.' I covered the mouthpiece with one hand so he wouldn't hear my chattering teeth.

'How's everything coming along?' he asked.

'Fine.'

'Olivia. I can't leave here yet.'

'Great – I mean, why?'

'We haven't finished the course.'

'Oh!'

'I really miss you.'

'Me too.' He seemed an eternity away, as if he'd been gone for ever.

'I'll make it up to you, I promise.'

'There's no need.' I could still feel Lorenzo's lips on mine as I searched for the right words to say, something that was true.

Tears sprang to my eyes as he said, 'I wish I was with you now.'

'Me too,' I mouthed, wishing it were sincere but, at that moment, I couldn't even imagine him.

'I'll see you soon.'

'Yeah.' I held my breath in the long pause that followed. The line crackled.

'You there, Ollie?'

'Yes.'

'I wanted to make sure everything was going all right. With the wedding and all. If there's anything you need, let me know.'

'Yes.'

'I love you.'

Unable to say it back I hung up, my skin taut with the ease of the lies that had sprung from me.

That night I went to bed so full of secrets that I thought I would burst. Staring at the dark, I thought of Lorenzo, of Barry's brittle voice smashing my peace, forcing me back to the present, and our imminent wedding. Cringing inwardly, I wished the evening had never happened. I felt trapped by the chaos of the wedding preparations. 'Bridal nerves,' Queenie had diagnosed when she saw how pale I was.

'The honeymoon will do wonders for you,' Mum said, and meant it.

She had lived my life for me to a great extent and now I was being handed over to my bridegroom who was eager to claim me.

I snuggled down with images of Lorenzo floating through my mind. When I finally fell asleep I dreamed I was sliding down a deep tunnel, and woke up so dizzy that my head felt separated from my body. Next morning I made up my mind that I would not see Lorenzo again.

A few days later the phone rang. 'Hello. Listen.' Lorenzo's voice was urgent. 'I have to see you this evening.'

'But . . .'

'No buts. Trinity College, eight o'clock.' The phone went dead.

All the way there I went through the list of film stars I admired most, not the sophisticated, distant types but the sexy, glamorous ones, like Sharon Stone and Meg Ryan. My heart was pounding. I had examined myself carefully in the mirror before I left: my face, my arms in the sleeveless top, my legs. Barry was forgotten. Lorenzo was all I could think of. It was an exciting act of defiance to go out alone with him leaving no message behind and my engagement ring in its velvet box. I wanted to be glamorous and beautiful, mysterious and sexy, worthy of him.

'Let's go,' he said, opening the door of his car.

We drank cocktails in the rooftop bar of a new hotel, and then he insisted on taking me back to his apartment. 'So tell me,' he said, pouring me a vodka and tonic, 'what is it about me that scares you?'

'Scares me? What do you mean?'

'All of a sudden you're shy, backing away. What's the matter?'

My heart thumped in my ribcage. I stared at him, wishing I could disappear. He removed his jacket and stood before me invitingly. I looked at his broad shoulders, and narrow hips. I wanted him to whisk me away to a desert island and make love to me for ever.

He kissed me, his lips hard and demanding. A shock of pleasure coursed through me. Releasing me, tilting back my head, he said, 'You want me as much as I want you. I see it in your eyes.'

I slipped out of his grasp. 'Lorenzo! Please.'

'I won't wait much longer,' he warned.

Next day I met in him in Grafton Street. He insisted on buying me a dress in Brown Thomas, a divine black dress with a *décolletage* that was positively embarrassing. 'Go on, show them off,' he encouraged. He bought me chocolates, a teddy bear, a gold necklace and bracelet to match. I was fascinated by the way he wanted to buy everything, see everything, like a prisoner let loose from a life of deprivation. This worried me. Could he afford to indulge me so extravagantly? Was it necessary? 'A beautiful woman like you,' he said, 'why not?'

We talked, him of his life in Italy, the restaurant his mother owned in Venice. His trip to Ireland was work experience: he was learning about the food of different nations. 'I want to get to know my Irish family too,' he confided. 'I haven't had much to do with them because my father abandoned my mother before I was born.'

'I'm sorry,' I said, not knowing what else to say. I told him little about myself and it didn't seem to matter: for the present he was amused at my lack of sophistication and my desire to please him.

On Saturday I sat, drinking coffee, with Trish in the back room of the shop, the rain pouring down outside, careful not to mention Lorenzo.

'What'll we do if it rains like this for the wedding?' she said.

'I don't know.'

'You don't seem bothered.'

'Too tired. I didn't sleep much last night.'

Puzzled, she said, 'But you look terrific. Your skin's glowing, your eyes are shining.'

I wanted to tell her that I had met someone who had set me on fire but I kept silent, going to the window every so often, hoping to catch a glimpse of him.

'You expecting someone?' she asked.

'No.'

'Then come away from that damned window and tell me what Barry said when he phoned.'

The quiet evening was pierced with the shrieks of raucous children outside playing tip and tig, in and out of open doorways, and hiding in the gloom. The town itself was lonesome with no sign of life as I drove through it on my way to Shrimps. Coloured lights shone in the windows at tables with snowy white cloths and paper napkins. Inside, men in shirtsleeves sat opposite tidy-limbed girls, their just-washed hair drenched in light. A girl in crimson silk sat at a corner table, her shining head bent over a menu, a man beside her.

I slipped down the path to Lorenzo's rented apartment, clutching the collar of my jacket against the light wind blowing in from the sea. A chink of light behind the window grew more incisive as I drew nearer. The door opened. He stood there, tall and mysterious in his silence.

'Hello,' I said.

'Come in.'

I went into the dark hall. He shut the door and his arms were tight around me, his lips seeking mine.

'You're cold,' he said, running his hands down my back, his voice tense with excitement, his tongue flicking over my lips. 'Come on,' he said, leading me through an enormous sitting room to a patio, where a table was set for two, the city lights twinkling across the expanse of dark water. 'I've made something special. I hope you're hungry. Let me take your jacket.'

I watched his movements as he served a Caesar salad, his hands, the way he stood, the way he walked, absorbing each gesture. Barry had never cooked me a meal. It was a beautiful balmy night. Stars studded the black sky. The sea was calm. Lorenzo brought me chicken carbonara with asparagus. 'You went to a lot of trouble,' I said.

'For you, anything.'

I was scared out of my wits, knowing what was coming next. He would want to take me to bed and I wasn't sure if I could resist him. After home-made ice cream he poured coffee and liqueurs at a low table beside the sofa. 'Come over here,' he said, putting his arm round me and leading me to the sofa. 'Relax,' he said, when he saw how tense I was.

At first his kisses were gentle. Then his tongue parted my lips and invaded my mouth.

'Lorenzo,' I said, pushing him from me, afraid I wouldn't be able to resist him.

'You're beautiful. I want you. You want me. I know you do. Let's go to bed.' He leaped off the sofa, grabbed my hand and almost danced across the room.

He pulled me to him and kissed me until I almost fainted. 'Now tell me you don't want me.' He was breathing fire into my ear as he nuzzled it.

'I want you.'

'Come on.' We ran upstairs to his bedroom. He pushed me on to the bed and slid down beside me. 'What is it?' he asked, when he saw how hesitant I was.

I was wishing I was more experienced so that I'd know what to do. 'I've never been in a strange man's bedroom before.'

He laughed. 'Relax, I'm no stranger.' He took my face in his hands and gazed into my eyes. Smiling, he kissed me.

I shivered, relishing the taste of his lips sensing the dangerous side of his romantic sensuality. Then I drew back. 'We shouldn't be doing this.'

'Why not?' he said, raising his shoulders in a shrug of confusion.

I longed to tell him about Barry. I also longed for him.

'You'll be all right. Trust me.'

My caution slipped as I gazed at his handsome face. I felt a yearning in the marrow of my bones that pulled me towards him. Rigid with passion he kissed me again. I no longer wanted to think of anything except the pleasure we were both about to give to one another.

Slowly, he began to undress me, the light from the opening in the curtain falling across our bodies. I felt his lips on my breast and lay back, arching my body, closing my eyes, breathing deeply. But I knew it was all wrong.

'You're beautiful,' he muttered, kissing my neck, opening my blouse, playing with my hard nipples.

Murmuring endearments in Italian he began to remove the rest of my clothes. Before I knew it he was on top of me, his hips grinding into mine.

I was so filled with desire that I cried, 'Lorenzo.'

I opened my eyes.

He was staring down at me, as if he were asking me if

this was what I really wanted. I pulled his head down, took his tongue between my teeth, all doubt abandoned.

Frantic, he tore off the rest of my clothes. He entered me, slowly, until I started moving on him, sliding up and down. Then we rode together, climbing higher and higher up a great tidal wave until it burst over me in a wave of pleasure.

Then I lay back and looked up at him. He was grinning wickedly down at me. 'For an amateur you're not bad.'

I felt myself flush.

'I love you,' he whispered.

'It's late, I'll be in trouble if I don't go,' I said, as he started to make love to me again.

Disappointed, he stopped. 'I'll take you home,' he said.

I got home at five o'clock in the morning. Carrying my shoes I sneaked past Mum and Dad's bedroom, then Queenie's. I closed my door, and began to undress. The doorknob turned. Cautiously Queenie entered, concern in every wrinkle of her face. 'You're back,' she said, walking carefully towards me, squinting a little. 'Everything all right?'

I nodded, backing away from her, scared she'd smell him on me.

Puzzled she said, 'Sleep tight,' and left, closing the door gently after her.

I slid between the sheets, my mind full of Lorenzo O'Brien.

Chapter Seven

I was all strung up waiting for him to phone, but at the same time scared that Mum or Queenie would find out. One evening, when I couldn't stand the waiting any longer, I drove to his apartment. There was no sign of life but his car was outside. I rang the bell. From inside I heard a sound. I saw his shape in the glass. The door opened and there he was. The blood rushed to my head as I tried to think of something to say.

'Oh! It's you. What a pleasant surprise.' He was smiling.

'Thought I'd call and see how you were.'

'Come on in.' I followed him inside.

'Glass of wine?' He pointed to the opened bottle on the table, his profile sharp in the evening shadows.

'Yes, please.'

He poured the wine, handed me a glass.

'Thank you.' Perfectly chilled, it cooled the burning heat inside me. 'Delicious.' I sighed. 'I'm glad I came.'

Lorenzo ran his hand over my thigh, pressed it down, then said, 'That's not what you came for.'

'Lorenzo!' I shook off his hand. 'You think you know everything about me.'

'I know what you look like naked.'

'Lorenzo!' Instinctively, I put my arms protectively across my chest.

'That'll do for a start.' His eyes were teasing, and sly, his breath hot on my neck. He grabbed my hair, and pulled me towards him. I put down my wine glass and kissed him hard on the lips. Fondling my breasts, stroking me, he said, 'Let's go upstairs.'

In the bedroom he undressed me. Cautiously he moved inside me, his eyes glittering. When I began to move too he quickened his pace. Together we exploded and Lorenzo cried, 'Olivia!' as if he couldn't believe the miracle of it.

Exhausted, he slept. My mind drifted. This was different. I was different. I was not Olivia Mary Healy, daughter of Lorraine Healy, granddaughter of Queenie Boyle. I was a woman who had tasted the sweet nectar of liberation and liked it. I was free to do as I pleased. Free to take what I wanted. What I wanted was this man, body and soul, night and day.

Then, with unwelcome clarity, Barry's face floated before me, clouding my happiness.

Lorenzo woke. 'Come here and kiss me.'

'Lorenzo. We've got to stop this,' I said.

Startled, he sat up. 'What is the matter?'

'I'm engaged to be married,' I cried out in desperation.

'What?' Lorenzo's arms around me loosened.

'I've been with him since I was sixteen. He's the only boyfriend I ever had. We grew up together.' I was talking too fast, like a defensive child.

'I'll kill him,' he said. 'Kill him,' he repeated, his voice rising dangerously. 'I'll kill anybody who touches you.'

'Lorenzo, you don't mean that.' All of a sudden I was frightened.

'I do mean it,' he shouted.

'I'm sorry. I should have told you sooner.'

'Why didn't you?'

'There wasn't an opportunity.'

'Rubbish!'

'I didn't want to lose you.'

'Wonderful!' he said sarcastically. 'When's the wedding?'

'In a couple of weeks. Lorenzo, I didn't mean this to happen. You've got to believe me.'

My heart was pounding. This couldn't be happening to me. It was a nightmare, like something you'd see in a movie. Time stood still.

'And now what?' Lorenzo picked up a packet of cigarettes and offered me one.

'I don't know. I'm sorry.' I collected up my clothes and disappeared into the bathroom to get dressed.

When I returned, he was gazing out of the window his back to me. 'I'll take you home,' he said curtly.

'I'll get a taxi, if you prefer.'

'No.'

All the way home he didn't say a word but kept his eyes on

the road. When he pulled up outside the shop I said, 'Thanks for the lift,' and jumped out, slamming the door behind me. He roared off.

I'd done it. I'd told him. I wasn't sure how I'd feel in the morning but at least I wouldn't have a guilty conscience any more.

Queenie was waiting up for me. 'I couldn't sleep so I came down to make myself some hot milk. Would you like some?'

'Yes, please.'

'God knows what I'll do when you're married. I won't be able to sleep at all.'

'You'll sleep sound, knowing I'm safe.'

'I will.'

I picked up the steaming mug of milk. I had made my decision. My fate was sealed.

Chapter Eight

Barry returned home a few days earlier than expected. When he walked into the shop I didn't recognise him. He was tanned and handsome, but it was the joy in his face that surprised me. 'You look terrific,' he said, pulling me to him.

'Good to see you, Barry,' Mum said, from the other end of the counter. She took his arm and led him through into our kitchen. 'How's your mother?'

'She had a touch of flu, but she's over it.'

'Dangerous time of year,' Mum said. 'Hot one minute, cold the next.'

'Aye,' Queenie said. 'Let's hope it picks up for the wedding. Otherwise Olivia'll be freezing in that flimsy frock.'

'Indeed,' Mum agreed, her arms folded across her plump chest.

'How's Mr Healy?' Barry asked.

'Very well, thanks. He'll be home later on. Sit down

and have a cup of tea. I've just taken an apple tart out of the oven.'

'Thanks.' Barry patted his flat stomach, a glint in his eyes. 'I know I shouldn't but . . .' He took a huge slice of apple tart.

'Olivia?' Mum looked at me.

I swallowed. 'No, thanks.'

'She's eating nothing,' Mum whined to Barry.

'Mum . . .' I was mortified.

'Here have this, Ollie.' The hairs on his wrist glistened as he passed me a plateful. 'Don't worry, Mrs Healy, I'll straighten her out.'

'Good.' Mum nodded with approval.

Barry sat straight, head erect, Mum and Queenie's presence commanding his respect. It was as if they were all drawing up some unspoken contract to do with me. He talked about how the new skills he was learning were important, that the bakery would have to be modified to accommodate them. Mum listened, nodded and cut him more apple tart. 'This is delicious, Mrs Healy. The French couldn't hold a candle to you.'

'Oh! Go on with you.' Mum was delighted.

'No, I'm serious, Mrs Healy. I haven't tasted anything as nice as this since I was here last.'

'Time to go,' Queenie said to Mum. She was restless, her eyes on the clock.

She and Barry stood up.

'Sit down, sit down,' Mum protested. 'You don't mind us rushing off like this.' She went to get her hat and coat.

'Only it's bingo night,' Queenie called over her shoulder.

'You'll be here when we get back?' Mum asked.

'No,' Barry said. 'We're off to the house. I'm dying to see what the new wallpaper looks like.'

'It's nice,' I said.

'Very tasteful,' Mum agreed, bouncing out of the room, with Queenie following.

I began to clear the table.

Barry was looking at me slyly. As the front door closed, he said, 'Come here.' He straightened his powerful shoulders, his eyes gliding over my body. 'Give us a kiss.' His voice was hoarse as he pulled me to him.

I had kissed him so many times in the past but now it felt strange.

'I'll give you three guesses as to what I'm going to do with you when I get you to myself.' His voice cracked. 'Let's go to see this house of ours.'

As The Gables loomed up before us, Barry switched off the engine. 'The end of the road,' he said quietly. 'I'm tired of travelling. I'll be glad to settle down.'

I could hear the happiness in his voice.

There wasn't a soul in sight, just acres of green fields on one side, the sea on the other. 'It's so isolated,' I said.

Barry's eyes were on the fields. 'You'll get used to it,' he said. 'You won't miss the town, not with this view. It's nature at its best.'

It was a big, plain house, reached from a narrow, curving lane. The red brick was mellow with age, the tiles on the roof grey, but the recently replaced windows jarred. Barry walked round to the back, past the kitchen garden and the rows of vegetables planted by the previous owners, and in at the door.

He lit a fire in the sitting-room. The whole place smelt of fresh paint and damp. Ladders and tins cluttered one corner. I looked around at the sparse furniture. 'Mum and Dad are giving us money towards the carpets,' I said.

'Great. I bought a bureau and a few other bits and pieces at a market in Brittany on my way home. They're being shipped over.'

I could see the cosy home we would have eventually: pine floors, yellow curtains, thick rugs, built-in wardrobes to match the solid pine bed in our room, and the big chest of drawers Barry had bought. It would all take time, but it would be worth it.

Barry sat back on his heels. 'There you go,' he said proudly, as the fire spurted up and the wood shavings crackled and hissed.

'Lovely,' I said, as he came and sat beside me on the sofa, Queenie's wedding present.

'How have you been?' His eyes were on me.

'Okay,' I said.

'Did you miss me?'

'I got used to it,' I said, wanting to say, 'I met some-one else.'

'Let's go and see the new wallpaper,' he said. A stab of guilt shot through me.

After inspecting the wallpaper in all the rooms Barry led

me back into our bedroom. 'It was hell without you,' he said, leading me to the bed.

'We said we'd wait until . . .' I was panic-stricken.

'I've waited long enough.' His voice was rough.

In the bedroom my stomach fluttered. Barry began to kiss me. 'Mmm,' he said, nuzzling my perfumed neck, then undressed quickly and took a condom out of his wallet. 'I've missed you so much,' he said. He undressed me awkwardly. His love-making was hasty, almost brutal in its lack of tenderness. I kept my eyes closed, imagining I was with Lorenzo, seeing in my mind the planes of his face, his almond-shaped eyes, his high cheekbones.

'Ouch!' I cried out, digging my nails into his wrist.

I could feel his instant withdrawal. I glanced at him. He looked tense, wounded. 'What's up?'

'It hurt.' Ashamed, I wanted to press my lips to his, reassure him that everything was all right. That once all the hullabaloo of the wedding was over, and we belonged to one another, things would be different. We would get to know one another on our long voyage of discovery, where I would be revealed not just to him but to myself.

But all I could think of was Lorenzo, the feel of his hands, rubbing my back, pressing me to him. I pushed these perverse thoughts from my mind. I would have to forget Lorenzo.

'Sorry, Barry, it's all so sudden. This house is so strange.'

My excuses sounded lame, but he accepted them. 'It'll get better,' he said, with conviction.

We spent surprisingly little time together after that. He

was busy renewing old business acquaintances, and playing golf, determined to get the most out of what remained of his bachelorhood. When he came to tea, his behaviour towards Mum embarrassed me: he treated her word as law, deferring to her, seeking her advice and support.

'And how's the bridegroom?' Trish asked, when she called into the shop.

'He's fine,' Mum answered. 'Very considerate to Olivia, giving her plenty of time to organise everything.'

'It's so long since I've seen him I've almost forgotten what he looks like,' Trish remarked. 'Has he changed?'

I thought for a moment. 'Yeah, he has. He's more . . . mature, I suppose.' I wrinkled my nose.

'Barry was born with a waistcoat, he's so mature,' Trish joked.

'He's sensible,' Mum retaliated, 'and what harm is that?'

She was angry because she could see that I had meant Barry to sound boring.

'You look miserable.' Trish eyed me curiously.

'When she's married she'll brighten up.' Mum spoke as if I wasn't there. 'Marriage doesn't tolerate sulking or selfishness.'

'Maybe I should break it off, then,' I said unpleasantly.

'Don't talk daft.' Mum laughed dismissively, and went on to Trish, 'He's a good boy, only wants the best for Olivia.'

I stopped listening. I wished I could have discussed marriage seriously with someone: whether I loved Barry sufficiently, and if my feelings for him were strong enough to see me through my crush on Lorenzo.

Just before she left Trish asked, 'Will Billy be coming home for the wedding?'

'No,' Mum answered, peeved.

She had been outraged when Billy wrote to say he couldn't spare the time, but the cheque he sent made her forgive him quickly. She realised, too, that life would be less complicated without him. Billy had always been a trouble-maker, and I suspected Mum was relieved that he lived far away.

'I was looking forward to meeting his wife,' Trish said.

'So was I,' Mum said sarcastically.

'What's she like?' Trish asked, her eyebrows raised innocently. Trish had fancied Billy for years and was bitterly disappointed when she heard he'd married an American.

'She's a nice-looking girl, judging by the photographs,' said Mum half-heartedly.

'You don't seem too enthusiastic,' she said.

'How can I be? I've never even met her.' Mum was indignant. 'Still, he seems happy. And he's settled down, that's the main thing.'

I wondered if Mum had ever loved Dad with the consuming passion I felt for Lorenzo.

'What are you thinking about Ollie?' Trish said. 'You seem miles away.'

'I was thinking about what you were saying,' I lied, memories of Lorenzo flooding back.

'I want to be madly, passionately in love when I get married,' Trish said.

'Choosing a partner for life has more to do with qualities of character than anything else,' Mum advised. 'Now, take Barry, for instance.'

'No, thanks, I'd rather not.' Trish's cigarette smoke went down the wrong way and she spluttered.

Suddenly I realised that I was marrying a man Trish didn't like and the thought filled me with fear. She was my best friend: I didn't want to be alienated from her by my marriage.

'Well, we can't stay here settling the world,' Mum said. 'Olivia has clothes to sort out for the honeymoon.'

'Let me help,' Trish said, excited at the prospect.

Upstairs she examined the contents of my new wardrobe. It was filled with the results of many trousseau-buying trips to Dublin with Mum, and Queenie had made nightdresses in soft silk.

'Take that red dress. It's lovely on you.'

'It's not new,' I objected.

'As long as it flatters you and arouses his interest who cares if it's not part of your trousseau? If you were rich you could throw out all your old clothes, but you're not, so you have to make the most of what's there.'

I laughed. 'You sound like a parent.'

'You're about to be married to a successful man, Ollie. You'll have to look your best most of the time.'

'I'm dreading that part.'

Trish tittered. 'Think of all the money he'll make. That'll ease the burden.'

She continued examining my clothes. 'God knows what

you'll discover about yourself when you've some real spending power. You don't think you'll change but, believe me, you will.' She spoke with authority.

'If you mean I'll take him to the cleaners every time I go shopping you're probably right.'

'I told you, marriage has its compensations.'

We looked at each other and roared laughing. In that moment it was just as if we were children again.

I said, 'I'm scared.'

'You'll be fine,' Trish said. 'Look at the time! I must be off – I've got to get to the supermarket before it shuts.' She gave me a hug and was gone, off down the stairs in that swift way of hers, her mind already on something else. Suddenly I felt bereft.

Lorraine sat in the hairdresser's perspiring quietly in the warmth of the hairdryer. As Tony, the proprietor of Turning Heads, snipped, she blinked and brushed a hand over her eyes. At fifty, her round plump face still held the beauty that had captured Ginger's heart, all those years ago, and kept Phil Healy still in thrall. It was in her smile, and in the depths of the sea-green eyes. She looked like a girl in a Renoir painting, Queenie had said, on her wedding day. Now the fine lines around her eyes were the only sign of ageing.

'All set for tonight?' Tony asked, referring to the handful of people who were coming over that evening.

Lorraine nodded. Queenie had referred to the dinner as a 'pre-wedding warm-up', an introduction to the Breslin family. Father Nobel, the parish priest, and Father McMahon, his curate, would be present. They usually attended family occasions, because Queenie, an ardent churchgoer, assumed that they were not fed properly by their dotty housekeeper, Miss Muldowney. This time they were urged to come and help break the ice.

Tony leant forward and asked, 'How's the mother-in-law?'

'Don't talk to me.' The presence of that woman in her house for a whole evening was something she anticipated with dread. Glancing round to make sure nobody was within earshot she said, 'That oul wan all but asked Olivia if she was pregnant. I ask you?'

Tony's eyebrows shot up to his hair. 'Cheeky cow.' He pursed his lips. 'Will I take a bit more off the back?'

Lorraine looked at her halo of bouncing curls. 'Just a teeny bit. Heaven forbid she implies anything like that tonight. I'll clock her one.'

Since it had become known that Olivia was to marry Barry Breslin, the wedding had been the main topic in Abbeyville. 'A lucky girl,' people had said. Breslin's bakery had established itself as a cornerstone of the town and its environs. In the realms of wealth and social position Olivia couldn't have done better, according to the neighbourhood.

'Nosy parker. It's a wonder she didn't scare Olivia off,' Tony said, snipping away.

'It's too late for anything like that,' Lorraine exclaimed. 'Everything's ready. All we need now is a fine day.' She kept her eyes on the passing shoppers, sipping the tea Jenny, the junior, had brought her, visualising Mrs Breslin like an explosion of fireworks. She shivered, foreseeing nothing but argument and dissent, wishing that she had the charm to ease the tension.

'It'll be all right,' Tony said comfortingly, seeing the worry flit across her face. He brushed the trimmings from her neck and shoulders. 'There's a lovely shine off your hair,' he said.

'It's starting to fall out.'

'Stress,' he declared. 'I've a great wax treatment for that.'

'How much?'

'Ten pounds for the tub.'

Lorraine gaped at him.

'Four applications, though. It should do the trick.'

'I'll take it.'

'Right. Just a spray to hold it and you're done.' He held up a mirror to show Lorraine the back of her head.

'Great, thanks, Tony.' Lorraine removed her wrap.

'Wish the happy couple well from me.'

'I will.' She beamed, cheered by the glamour of it all.

Abbeyville was a quiet town, with one main road, Church Street, its shops sloping to the church on the hill, and the Franciscan abbey, with three priests. Residential streets branched off, blending into suburbia. The modern grey building on the corner housed the bank, the building society, Fitzgerald's auctioneers next to Everyday Cleaners, the post office, and Blunt's the butcher's. The double-sided fronts of Breslin's bakery took up the whole corner. Opposite, the new supermarket stretched to Regina Modes, incorporating Turning Heads, Jaunty Blooms, the florist, and the video centre.

Sunshine sparked off the blade of the huge knife Mr Blunt

was expertly wielding in and out of a free-range turkey, boning and rolling it, cursing the fly that hovered nearby. 'Ready now, Mrs Healy,' he bellowed, scurrying from the far end of his shop in his blood-spattered white coat, to hand her the parcel. 'You're looking splendid.' He smiled obsequiously. 'All set for the big day?'

'Just about,' Lorraine replied, avoiding his eyes to keep him at bay.

'All very exciting. Honeymoon in Italy, I hear?'

'That's right.'

'I wouldn't mind a bit of that meself.' His voice was full of innuendo, and not missed by the other customers.

'Yes, well . . .' Lorraine, unnerved by the butcher's leer was at a loss.

'A lovely girl. Just like her mother.'

'Thanks,' was all she managed.

'You have every right to be proud of her,' Mr Blunt called after her. 'Isn't that right, Mrs Dodd?'

She was out of the door and walking down the street by the time Mrs Dodd gave her answer. In the supermarket she selected a dry white wine and a selection of cheeses. Soon Olivia would be married and living in her new house. The plan for her to return to drama college to complete her studies in the autumn had been a generous gesture on Barry's part, Lorraine thought, as she hurried to the church. There she knelt to say a prayer while she waited for Father McMahon. She had believed from childhood in an all-seeing, all-powerful, all-merciful God looking down from the sky, bestowing benefits to the pious people of Abbeyville. Now she implored Him for a fine day for the wedding, and remembered her own marriage to Phil, her quest for security through it. It hadn't been so bad, she reflected, a bit uneventful but they'd managed. After the blow of his redundancy Lorraine had developed an interest in the city markets too, often getting up at dawn to scavenge for bargains with him, setting up stalls here and there, determined not to be haunted by their plight.

Queenie, considered Lorraine's concern for her husband misplaced. 'You don't need to go that far,' she'd said. 'He's well able to take care of himself.' She was tougher than her daughter, her views were sharper, and she was not especially well disposed towards Phil. As a contender for her daughter's hand she had hailed him with surprise and scepticism. Their relationship, though polite, was tainted with jealousy and doubt.

'Lorraine.' Father McMahon was behind her.

'Father! You gave me quite a start.'

'You got your hair done. It's lovely.'

'Thank you.' A pleasant feeling of recklessness invaded her senses, making her feel like a schoolgirl again.

Chapter Nine

I woke up groggy, then remembered that the family get-together was that evening and I felt sick with nerves. I flung off the duvet and hopped out of bed. When I got downstairs Barry was in the kitchen eating breakfast, chatting to Mum, protesting as she put two more sausages on his plate. 'You've got a good one here,' she enthused. 'I was just about to bring you breakfast in bed,' she added.

'I won't be spoiling her like that.' Barry laughed. 'She'll be bringing *me* breakfast in bed.'

'Hello.' I yawned, pretending to be half-asleep.

'Barry brought us over some cakes for tonight,' Mum said. 'And some wine. Isn't he great?'

'Not at all,' Barry said. 'My mother sent the wine.'

'How is she?' Mum asked dutifully.

'Grand, thanks, looking forward to the evening.' Barry smiled at me. 'I'm looking forward to it too.' As soon as Mum left the kitchen he said, 'Ollie, I couldn't wait to see you. About last night.' He took my hand, held it firmly. 'Talk to me, Ollie.'

I hesitated. 'It's the new house. I wasn't expecting anything to happen before the wedding. We said we'd . . .'

'I know.'

I leaned against him, my betrayal making me want to cry. Barry smoothed my hair, his hand steady, soothing. 'It's my fault. I shouldn't have tried it on.'

I felt a cad, letting him take the blame, but I didn't know what to say.

That evening my family gathered, warm with the affection of years, eager for each other's company, nothing about them changed, though changes had occurred. Since they'd last met they'd quarrelled, made up, laughed, cried. Now, all that showed in their faces was the pleasure of seeing one another again.

The Breslins filled up the place, self-conscious in their prim greetings. It was obvious from their wide-eyed curiosity, as they inspected one another, that they hadn't met since the last family wedding or funeral. We remained divided into two camps, the Healys eyeing the Breslins with suspicion, the Breslins regarding the Healys with disdain.

Mary Morgan, the help, had discarded her black dress for the first time since the death of her husband. Her hair was freshly hennaed and she wore a touch of eye-shadow, a slash of lipstick. In her new floral frock she stood to one side of the long snowy-covered table and the mahogany sideboard. From their gilt frames the family ancestors kept vigil over the proceedings.

Mrs Breslin, cool and calm, marshalled her own clan, her status as their head evident in her demeanour and her place at the top of the table opposite Queenie.

'How do you do?' Queenie shook hands with everyone around her and sat down, covering her knees with her skirt.

'How's the bride?' Trish asked. 'Feeling more cheerful?'

'Much better thanks,' I lied.

'It's only your hormones playing up. They'll settle down as soon as you're hitched. Where's Barry?'

'He's around somewhere.'

Mum, coming hot and bothered from the kitchen, apologised for the delay in serving the meal. 'It's almost ready to serve,' she said. 'Just a little contretemps with the gravy.'

Father McMahon smiled encouragingly. 'I've got too much on my mind,' she said to him, letting him know that she was bearing the full burden of the forthcoming wedding.

'You're a marvel, Lorraine,' he said, then turned to look at me as if to say, 'Why don't you pull your weight?'

Barry came into the room with Trish. No sooner had Father Nobel said grace than Mrs Breslin settled into her seat, and began to eat, oblivious to everyone, as if an invisible blind had been pulled down. Her surreptitious intake of alcohol sustained my interest. It was nice to see Barry attentive to his mother, nice too that she was enthusiastic about our honeymoon in Italy. Queenie had been to Rome to see the Pope, in Holy Year, but she'd no desire to return. She didn't like foreign food or the peculiar customs of the Italians.

Father Nobel, impeccable in his clerical attire, was deep

in conversation with Dad about their favourite greyhounds. Voices low, heads close together, their shared interest was a private affair. Next to Dad sat Father McMahon. Younger than Father Nobel, and handsome, his dark hair fell forward over his eyes as he inclined his head towards Lorraine. I felt a flutter of unease and wasn't sure why.

'I said, would you like more wine?' Mr Breslin touched my arm.

Pulling myself together, I said, 'I beg your pardon. I was miles away.'

'Let me fill your glass.'

'Thank you.' The conversation continued around me. I turned my attention to Barry's cousin and best man, Tom, and Tom's brother Jim, grateful for their presence, a buffer between myself and Mrs Breslin. They were eating and drinking with gusto, cracking jokes.

Father Nobel was talking to Queenie about local affairs and the corruption of politicians. Barry refused to be drawn into their argument: he remained indifferent and aloof. Even on this occasion he seemed out of place. It was as if he didn't properly belong to the nineties, and was from an earlier period altogether. There was some mystery about him, something unconsciously withheld. It had captivated me without me realising it. By now Father McMahon was exercising his charm on Mrs Breslin with compliments about her beautiful home. Smiling sideways, she spoke of her paintings and antiques.

After the meal the men sprawled in the lounge watching TV while the women drank coffee. Queenie was talking to Father Nobel about the merits of family life. Father McMahon and Mum stood at the window, still deep in conversation, heads silhouetted against the evening light. However much he tried to mask it, I had known for some time that he was in love with Mum.

Mrs Breslin sat apart, a look of grim amusement on her face. Queenie addressed her every so often with snippets of information about various members of our family, but Mrs Breslin made it obvious that she wasn't interested.

Audrey and Polly arrived with Auntie Tess.

'Come and help move back the chairs.' Dad clapped his hands. 'We're going to have a bit of dancing from the girls.'

Uncle Tommy brought out a couple of dozen bottles of Carlsberg.

'We'll drink the place dry,' Mr Breslin said, with glee.

'There's plenty more where that came from.' Dad laughed.

'Laughter today, tears tomorrow,' Mrs Breslin put in. Then to Queenie, 'Well, my relatives have a long journey ahead of them. They'll need something before they go.'

Queenie said, with cold sarcasm, 'It'll take a lot to sober them.'

'I think you'll have to keep them overnight,' Father Nobel said. 'It would be dangerous to let them loose on the roads.'

'It went well,' Queenie said, folding her arms across her chest, surprised that she'd enjoyed herself.

'It did,' Mum said, with satisfaction. 'I was dreading it.'

'You were great, Lorraine,' Dad said, relaxing into his chair, a look of pride in his mild eyes.

'I suppose,' Mum said, stretching out her arms in pained

exhaustion. 'Only for me heart playing tricks on me legs I would have danced more.'

'It's the weight that's killing you,' Mrs Breslin said, returning from the bathroom.

'Is that so?' Mum turned on her with the speed of a tornado.

A pang of panic seized me as Dad stood up. 'Come on, Lorraine,' he said, helping her up. 'Let's get you off to bed.'

On her way out Mrs Breslin stopped walking suddenly, causing Mum and Dad almost to collide with her. She stood, poised to make a speech, but all she said was 'Marriage can be a disillusionment,' and left, Mr Breslin trailing after her.

'I'll keep an eye on things here,' Queenie said.

Mum and Dad went upstairs, knowing that everything would be all right in Queenie's capable hands.

She surveyed the dirty plates, cups and glasses littered across the room, gift wrapping beside them. In a corner deflating balloons bobbed from the ends of coloured ribbons, in a tired attempt at gaiety.

As Queenie helped clear up, she voiced her wretched thought to Mary that they were celebrating a totally unsuitable alliance. 'I can hardly say this to Lorraine, any more than I can protest that this marriage shouldn't take place.'

'Maybe you should, if you're that worried,' Mary advised.

'Who'd listen to me at my age?' Forcing herself to smile, and keep smiling, Queenie waited to see off the last of the guests.

Chapter Ten

'This is very nice,' Queenie declared, gazing at the river and the fields stretching as far as the eye could see.

'Nicer than Abbeyville on a Friday afternoon,' Lorraine said, lifting her glass of white wine to her lips.

'A treat.' The meeting of the waters was one of Queenie's favourite beauty spots. Especially now, sitting at the wooden table beside her granddaughter, in the stillness of the evening.

Olivia was just twenty-two years old and here she was getting married, a child, Queenie thought, as she gazed at her granddaughter's fine features, and long blonde hair. A beautiful, gangling girl.

Olivia poured her another glass of wine and they talked about the wedding. Queenie had thought that Barry's return would end their Friday evening drives to somewhere pleasant, like Avoca, or Glendalough. It hadn't.

'Of course this wedding is a big event in the town.'

Olivia nodded. 'The town where nothing exciting ever happens.'

'You'd be surprised,' Queenie said.

Although the preparations were almost complete and the wedding cake was at Breslin's bakery waiting to be iced, Queenie felt that this was as good a time as any to mention the apprehension she'd felt on the night of the dinner party. The worry had persisted ever since. It refused to go away.

Olivia said, 'Mrs Breslin's in her element bossing everyone in her family about.'

'Poor Mr Breslin will be glad when it's all over.'

'There's something I wanted to—' Queenie began to say,

'Oh! I was talking to the organist about the hymns,' Olivia rushed on. 'I told him it's Schubert's "Ave Maria" we want.'

Queenie nodded.

'I mustn't forget to ring Father McMahon and let him know. I hate having dealings with priests but he's so nice.' Olivia emphasised the 'nice'. 'And he's really looking forward to it.'

'Mmm.' He was nice, Queenie thought, but had Olivia discovered his true feelings for her mother she might have thought differently. Yes, he was charming, Queenie thought, but there was something about him that put her off. Not that she saw much of him. Lorraine was the one he sought out every time he called.

They talked of all the things that still had to be done. Queenie's attention drifted. There would be no need for her to continue with the shop when Olivia was settled. She could sell it if she liked. She'd taken to reading the property section in the papers in case there should be anything of interest, but there never was – and she didn't really want to part with her shop anyway. What kind of a life would it be with nothing to do? But that wasn't what was worrying her. This alliance between Olivia and Barry was all wrong. Why, exactly, she couldn't explain to herself, never mind to Olivia, who'd known Barry for the best part of seven years and wouldn't welcome her grandmother's opinion at this late stage. In fact, she'd probably think her 'gone in the head' like all the other old dears of her acquaintance.

'I wanted to say . . .' she began again.

'Here comes the rain.' Olivia grabbed the rug from Queenie's lap. 'Come on, or we'll be drowned.'

It rained all week. Queenie sat at her sewing-machine among tape measures and threads, patterns strewn about, working feverishly to get the dresses finished.

'I think poor Olivia doesn't know what she's letting herself in for,' she said to Lorraine.

'What makes you say that?'

'I don't know exactly. She's naïve still. Sees the good in everyone. I don't think she knows what's involved in marriage.'

'She'll soon find out.'

'By then it'll be too late. He'll be her next of kin, family.' Queenie made a face.

Lorraine, surprised at her mother's sudden apprehension, said, 'It's too late already. I don't know what your objection is. Barry's a successful, presentable young man who can look after Olivia and provide her with the lifestyle she wants.'

'Does she want a life with him?'

'Of course. She can't wait to be married.'

'I've a peculiar feeling about him and I can't put a finger on it. Call it intuition.'

'He couldn't be more suitable, more responsible. He loves her. That's plain to be seen.' Lorraine was getting angry.

'Something's stuck in my mind that I heard Olivia say and I can't for the life of me think what it is.' Queenie was at pains to explain further. 'She might feel she's been drawn into something and can't see her way out of it.'

'Ridiculous. Olivia's happy. She knows Barry's a good catch.' Lorraine wanted to say, 'The trouble with you is that you're seventy years old and prone to obsession,' but she didn't. All she said was, 'It's natural enough for you to worry, Mother, but there's no need. Your nerves have probably got the better of you with all the commotion and fuss.' Her face suggested that Queenie was in her dotage.

A burst of sunshine brought a hazy summer feel to the early-morning market. Men leaned in a line against the gaunt stone wall, warming themselves, watching stalls being erected, waiting for the bustle of trade to begin. Dresses and jackets were being hung from stands, brass and china, used bits of cutlery, lampshades, but no real bargains.

'Mother's worried about Olivia,' she said to Phil, who was unpacking books for his bric-à-brac stall. He reflected for a minute and said, 'Why?'

'She's not sure.'

Phil threw his eyes to heaven. 'Typical of her to become anxious at the last minute, making everyone panicky. All you can do is humour her.'

'I suppose you're right.' Lorraine hurried off to buy herself a comfortable pair of shoes so that her feet wouldn't kill her on the wedding day.

A week before the wedding Billy arrived home. Queenie was overwhelmed when she saw him.

'My baby.' Tears poured down her face. 'I can't believe it. I'm so happy to see you.'

He held her. 'You've gone soft, Queenie,' he said.

'Baloney.' She pushed him away from her, laughing through her tears. 'Let me have a good look at you.'

His blond hair was brushed back, boyish as ever, but his mature face was bronzed by the Kentucky sun.

'You look wonderful, Queenie.'

Overwhelmed, she was conscious of the dowager image she portrayed to her grandson as he moved her under the light. 'I'm glad you think so. You look pretty wonderful yourself,' she said.

Then Billy said impatiently, 'Come here, darling.'

A brash blonde woman came forward, her hand held out. 'Hello, I'm Faith.'

'Billy's wife!' Queenie's surprise was matched only by her curiosity as she took the proffered hand. Finally she said, 'Holy Lord.' That this was Billy's wife was difficult to take in.

'Isn't she just darling?' Billy enquired.

'She's a fine woman.' Queenie spoke as if Faith wasn't there.

'She's my heart's desire, Queenie,' Billy said, with passion. 'Aren't you, my love?' He turned to Faith, worship in his eyes.

'Gee,' Faith drawled, 'Ah've heard so much about you.'

Queenie said, 'I'm glad he didn't forget me.'

'No chance of that.' Billy laughed, his big face full of happiness.

'We had to make it home for the wedding, Mrs Boyle,' Faith said formally.

'Call her Queenie,' Billy instructed her.

'May I call you Queenie?' Faith asked.

Billy laughed. 'No need to stand on ceremony, for Chrissakes.'

Queenie lambasted him with a look, then said to Faith, 'You may, certainly.'

'I wanted to keep our visit a surprise.' Billy said.

'You managed to do that, all right, but it's lovely to have you here.' She longed to hold him, stroke his hair as she used to when he was little. Instead she stood stock still, examining him. 'You're the same Billy. Just the same as the day you left,' she said, knowing that he wasn't.

'Faith's going to love it here too. I can tell,' Billy said. 'Maybe we could develop something good between here and my contacts back in the States.'

'Oh!' Queenie was taken aback with this assertive streak in Billy.

'First of all,' he continued, 'I must see everything.'

'First of all,' Queenie said, 'we'll have a lovely time getting reacquainted. We'll start with a cup of tea in the kitchen. Your homecoming has my nerves in an awful state of excitement.'

'Perfect.' Billy led the way to the back stairs. 'Mind your step,' he cautioned, holding Queenie's arm, careful not to let her trip.

'I do these stairs several times a day,' Queenie reminded him.

'You can't blame me for being careful of you.'

How thoughtful he was. Behind the rough exterior he had a heart of gold. With each step Queenie's apprehension dissipated.

They drank their tea, her mind flitting to his childhood, and the delight of having him to live with her. Her eyes were on him as she recalled the school events she never missed, his tenth birthday when he won the cross-country event with the Bray Pony Club. That was when he decided he wanted to be a jockey. From then on his schoolwork had been eclipsed by Pony Club events.

Queenie thought of his going away to Kentucky to learn about horses. The pain she'd felt at his departure had gone now, as had her anxiety for his safety and well-being, but the fears she had had for him then were not forgotten. Now, watching him sitting there, happy to be home, she knew that she was the embodiment of all things secure in his past.

'I still can't believe he's actually here, even though he's sitting opposite me,' Queenie said to Lorraine, who came into the kitchen searching for her son.

'Neither can I.' Lorraine looked adoringly at him.

'You'll get used to it.' Billy smiled. 'We'll be here for a while.'

'Good. Where's Faith?' Queenie asked.

'Freshening up for dinner. She'll be down in a minute,' Billy said.

Billy installed himself quickly. He showed Faith off, and she let everyone know that she had the money to buy any horse Billy chose for their new venture: a stud farm. Lorraine was too delighted to have him home to worry about any criticism and Queenie was indulgently amused.

With every passing day Billy let go of the secretive, isolated boy he'd once been, finding their new interest in him irresistible. He told them stories about managing stud farms and trotted out his American jokes as he went along. Faith, not in the least shy, roared with laughter at every one.

'I think he came to help with the wedding speeches,' Queenie said.

'I think he's come to escape from business troubles,' Phil said to Lorraine.

'We thought Ireland would make a nice change for Faith,' Billy said. 'Lots of relatives for her to meet at the wedding. She couldn't wait to see my home.'

'Ah can't wait to meet the bridegroom,' Faith informed them all. 'I hear he's loaded.'

Chapter Eleven

The dawn chorus woke me. I burrowed down under the duvet and lay listening to the twitter of birds, my eyes on the spire of the church shining white in the morning light, thinking of the day ahead, scared. When I heard Mum moving around downstairs I got up. She was in the kitchen pouring boiling water into the teapot, concentrated on her task. Queenie was buttering toast.

'The flowers never arrived,' Mum said, in a tight voice. 'I sent Dad to find out what happened to them.'

'Have a good breakfast,' Queenie said fussily. 'It'll be a long time before your next meal.'

'I'm not hungry. I'll just have a cup of tea.' I could hear the panic in my voice.

Audrey had been staying with us overnight, to keep her away from Polly, who was wildly overexcited. She came bouncing in, big soft rollers falling out of her hair. 'When can I get dressed up?' she asked.

'You have to have your breakfast first,' Mum said.

'I don't want any. I want to put on my new dress.'

I sneaked back upstairs with my tea and slowly began to get ready, tucking my hair into a net. Leaning in to the dressing-table I applied my makeup carefully painting a thin, narrow line over each eyelid, slowly drawing a pale lipstick over my mouth. I was enjoying this private ritual, keeping it simple, not too much of anything. Marriage would be fun, Mum had said. She used the word 'fun' so much nowadays that she'd rendered its meaning redundant. Had marriage been fun for her? I doubted it. Dad was too quiet, too easy-going. 'Anything for a quiet life,' he had said when she organised a pilgrimage to Lourdes with Father McMahon for the amateur drama group. Dad had said, 'As long as she's happy.' He meant, 'As long as she doesn't bother me.'

I removed my dress from its padded hanger. Lifting my arms I let the fluid lacy folds drop over my head. The long, clear, fragile lines hugged my body. I was glad I was thin.

'I hear a car,' Mum called.

Then the voices of Trish and Doreen floated up the stairs.

Trish, lovely in her bridesmaid's dress, came into my room, and stopped short. 'Oh, Ollie! You look beautiful,' she exclaimed. 'Why didn't you wait for us to help you?'

Doreen, equally lovely, was behind her.

'Because I can't bear all the fuss and dressing up like a doll.' I burst into tears.

Stunned Trish asked, 'What's the matter?'

'Are you having second thoughts?' Doreen put her arms around me.

'Mind you don't crease anything,' Trish warned.

I leaned forward, my forehead touching the cold mirror of the dressing-table. 'I'll miss you all.' There was a catch in my throat.

'It's your honeymoon you're going on, for Christ's sake,' Trish exclaimed. 'Not to serve a life sentence.'

Doreen said dismally, 'You lucky bitch, I wish I was going off to enjoy meself.'

'God forbid she'd be going to enjoy herself,' Trish said, mock outrage in her voice.

Billy appeared at the bedroom door in a dressing-gown, bleary-eyed and unshaven. 'What a beautiful bride,' he said, yawning.

From the front of the house came the sound of running footsteps, loud and insistent. The door burst open and Dad stood there in his wedding suit, his white hair combed back neatly, a sheaf of lilies in his arms.

'There you go,' he said, skipping into the room, his face suffused with pleasure, his blue eyes dancing. 'Saved by the bell.'

'What happened to them?' Mum came down the corridor, stopping to take a deep breath when she saw me. 'Olivia, you look magnificent,' she said, tears springing into her eyes.

'Couldn't find them anywhere,' Dad continued. 'Maisie Byrne put them to one side yesterday evening. They got delivered to someone else by mistake. I went mad looking for replacements.' He cradled the lilies in his arms, making sure he wasn't crushing them. 'Fresh in this morning.'

'They're beautiful,' I said. 'I bet they cost a bomb.'

'Time's marching on,' he said, taking his antique fob watch from his pocket. 'We'll be late if we don't get a move on.'

Mum whipped off her dressing-gown. 'Trish, Doreen, help Olivia with her veil.'

'Such fuss!' Queenie came into my bedroom, her critical eye running over me. 'Are you all right?' she asked, adoration shining from her worn face.

'A bit nervous,' I said.

'What about a Valium to take you through the ceremony nice and calm? I'll get you one.'

The cars arrived. Mum ran back and forth, her creamy blouse fluttering over her breast, her suit jacket across one arm, her jaunty yellow hat incongruous with the worried lines on her face.

'It's good job we won't have to do this again,' Dad said, his voice choked.

'Thanks, Dad,' I said, giving him a kiss on the cheek.

Mum gave me one of her rare my-little-girl looks. 'I'll keep a hot-water bottle in your bed in case he ever annoys you,' the ever practical Queenie whispered, as I bade my room goodbye.

The aunts entered the hall as I reached the top of the stairs. Aunt Tess was first, anxious in a pink frothy hat, followed by sheepish Uncle Cecil, and Pam in a floral suit. Polly, a cherub in a long blue dress to match the bridesmaids' with a garland of rosebuds holding up her white-blonde hair, pranced in. Audrey tore downstairs in her pyjamas. 'You're ready before me,' she cried indignantly, her light voice high-pitched with excitement.

Aunt Pru, up from the country, arrived with Aunt Statia.

'Billy's here with his new wife Faith,' Mum told them.

'Fancy that,' Aunt Statia said, not in the least bit interested.

There was a collective intake of breath as I began my slow descent downwards, Trish and Doreen holding my train and veil high above my head.

'Oh!' They sighed, as I floated down the stairs in Queenie's creation as if airborne.

'Pwetty!' Polly said, through the gap in her teeth.

'Divine.' Aunt Statia was emphatic.

'I ran it up myself,' Queenie boasted. Her hands dropped to the train and she smoothed the lace, which glowed pearly in the morning light.

'You're gifted, Queenie.' Aunt Pru's dry old voice broke the spell.

Queenie pinpointed a loose thread on the lace bodice and broke it off in a lightning movement. 'Gotcha,' she cried triumphantly.

They moved across the hall, flung open the dining-room door to exclaim at the wedding gifts arranged neatly on the table: glass, china, cutlery, silver-wrapped boxes yet unopened.

Aunt Statia was hesitating over the china statue of a naked girl, her curves smooth to the touch.

'All the way from Paris,' Mum told her.

'Hmm,' said Aunt Statia, indicating that it might have been better left there.

'Oh! Such beautiful flowers.' The clear tones of Aunt Tess rang out from the kitchen.

'They liven the place up like a funeral,' Aunt Statia said, marching in.

'All set?' Dad enquired. 'The limousine's here.'

'Nearly.' Mum adjusted her hat.

Sunlight struck the church, warming the limestone. At the shallow stone steps groups of neighbours and onlookers had gathered.

'A great crowd.' Dad looked with pleasure at the mothers with prams standing at the iron railings that protected them from the busy road, and the cars that stretched its length. Lorenzo's car was parked just past the gates, Lorenzo in it.

Wolf whistles and greetings from the early-morning 'oul wans' swept down to me as I alighted, trying to smile, my face as red as the carpet that stretched inwards.

I spotted Roger Rogan from our road standing to one side with Jack Moran and another lad. 'Oy, Ollie!' he called out. 'Would ye risk it for a biscuit?'

'You're a fine thing, Olivia Healy,' Jack Moran shouted.

The sun spread shafts of light from the door, illuminating the garlanded pews, lighting the banks of flowers and candles on the altar. Inside, the immense high windows narrowed downwards, marking the distance to the altar with a crimson-magenta light. The organ burst forth with the Wedding March as we began our slow walk up the aisle, my stomach churning. Dad's hand guided me while the bridesmaids shuffled behind, giggling and tripping.

I stood stiff and hot in the restrictive lace and tulle, my groom to my right, solid, purposeful in his tails, a terrible directness about him, Trish behind me, fussing with my train, shaping it like a lily leaf. The organ blared triumphantly, note upon note, rising higher and higher, floating upwards to the realm of heavenly beings, taking me with it. From a dizzy height I looked down at the dancing, dipping candles among the vibrant roses that stretched back into the sheaves of lilies, their waxy trumpet heads vying for space amid the foliage, their overwhelming scent, combined with the odour of candle grease and incense, oppressive. The rosy glow from the sun brought a glorious gaiety to the guests. It warmed mature faces, and brightened the delicate confections of hats.

The feathers of Mum's hat floated above her face, her happiness manifest in her smile. Beside her, Queenie stood tall in her expensive lilac silk suit, her cashmere rug folded neatly beside her. Mrs Breslin was spry and splendid in pale grey, a wide-brimmed hat perched to the Kildare side. Beside her Mr Breslin was small in his morning suit. Billy and Faith merged together in a haze.

Lorenzo came into the church, hurried and quick, strange and soundless, not a draught from the door that swung behind him to stir the feathers of my mother-in-law's hat. He hesitated. The organ played again, the music rising up through the pale arches, louder and louder, dying off in a petrified shiver. Suddenly he was nowhere to be seen, only the evaporating ghost of him.

'Do you, Bartholomew Bernard Breslin, take Olivia Mary Healy for your lawful wedded wife?'

Barry's loud 'I do' brought a shudder of rapture from Mum.

'Do you, Olivia Mary Healy, take . . .'

Barry nudged me. 'Olivia!'

'I . . .' I began, my instincts protesting.

The photographer stood poised, ready to capture the precise moment. The guests pressed forward, their ears cocked.

'I don't.'

'What?' came Barry's exclaimed shock.

I turned to him. 'I'm s-sorry,' I said, to his blurred face, and hurriedly made my way down the aisle, Trish grabbing my train, whether to speed me up or halt me I was never to know.

Shivering, I stepped into the sunshine.

'Olivia, wait!' Barry had followed me out. 'What's going on?' he thundered, easing his stiff white collar from his reddening neck.

Polly was flying after him, her wreath slipping sideways, Audrey on her heels, Mum in hot pursuit, Tom Breslin, the best man, looking puzzled.

'O-l-iv-ia!' Mum ran up to me, breathless. 'What's happened?' She was edgy, trying to hide it. Behind her, Father McMahon kept his head bowed.

'Have you lost your mind?' she cried.

'No,' I said turning away.

'Olivia. What's up! Tell me!' Barry croaked, his face red and sweaty.

Audrey broke the silence with a running commentary. 'Polly, I think he's going to kill her. Look, here's Uncle Phil.'

Dad was beside me, his face angry. 'You're holding up the

whole proceedings. Not a bother on you. Get back inside,' he declared furiously.

My tiara danced dangerously as I shook my head.

Father Nobel smiled encouraging. 'Of course she will.'

'No, I won't.'

'You're totally wrong in this,' Mum protested.

Polly was jumping up and down with excitement.

'Olivia, you're not paying attention,' Mum said.

'Damn, Ollie. You can't do this,' Billy shouted, coming forward.

'Darn sure she can if she wants to,' laughed Faith, following him.

It surprised me as much as anyone else that this had happened. On waking that morning I had vividly imagined myself taking my marriage vows.

'You're right, Olivia,' Queenie said, in a low voice, coming up beside me, walking me further down the gloomy path. 'If you don't want to get married then don't.'

I started walking away.

'Come back. What do you think you're doing?' Mum was aghast, grabbing Queenie's arm, calling to Father Nobel, 'Father! She's lost the run of herself,' as if I wasn't there.

He followed me, frowning. 'Let me talk to her,' he offered. 'Come on, Olivia.' With his hand on my arm he coaxed me towards the tiny side-garden, the ring still held gingerly between his thumb and forefinger.

Slow drops of summer rain made him pause and glance up at the sky. 'Are you sick?' he asked, eyeing me up and down. When I didn't answer he shifted from one leg to the other.

Glancing over his shoulder at the church he said, 'They'll want to know what's up.' He brushed raindrops from his vestments, his eyes distant.

'I . . .'

He waited.

I turned to him. 'The game's up, Father.'

He stared at me. 'What d'you mean, "The game's up"?'

'I can't go through with it.'

'What made you decide that now, at this late hour?' he asked, his lips pursed as he waited to endure what next I was going to say.

I stared at him, dazed, as if he was asking a stupid question. 'I don't know. I didn't plan this.'

His head snapped up. 'Don't be impertinent,' he said, turning back to the waiting guests spilling out of the church, gathering on the steps. 'They'll want to know,' he repeated, lighting a cigarette as if he had all the time in the world.

I followed his gaze to the festive dresses and hats getting damp in the rain. Polly waved enthusiastically.

Mum marched over. 'Olivia, I can't take any more. Get back into the church immediately, and stop your nonsense.'

Relatives surged forward, stepping on my veil and train, in their eagerness to find out what was going on.

'Tying the knot, or not?' Uncle Tommy asked. ''Cause if you're not I'm buggered if I'm hanging around wasting me time.'

Tying the knot, tying the knot, tying the knot. I was dizzy again.

'What are you thinking of?' Mum said, looking as if she'd like to box my ears.

'What's going on?' Mrs Breslin came forward.

'It looks as if Olivia's changed her mind, Mrs Breslin,' Dad told her politely. 'She won't listen to anyone.'

So surprised at that notion was Mrs Breslin that she looked as if she'd forgotten how to speak.

Queenie said, with a wave of her kid-gloved hand, 'If Olivia doesn't want to get married don't keep her here making a spectacle of herself.' She turned to Mr Breslin, who'd sneaked up behind her. 'All this standing around's killing me poor feet,' she told him.

'Come on, we'll get you a hot toddy,' Mr Breslin said, determined not to let this mishap hinder his plan to spend the remainder of the day celebrating in the lounge bar of the hotel.

Queenie hesitated while he smiled convivially, as if waiting in the rain outside a church for a neurotic bride to decide whether to get married or not was a common occurrence. 'Right,' she said, and he took her arm. They trotted off in a great hurry.

Mum stared at me, speechless, her eyes filling up as I moved away with Trish. 'Are you off?' she asked, shakily.

'I think so,' Trish said gently.

'I wouldn't mind but we've paid out . . . Two entire families . . .'

'Come on, Lorraine.' Dad took her arm and guided her away.

'I want an explanation, Olivia Healy, and I intend to get it.' A furious Barry was lumbering after me.

'Later.'

'I'll sort you out. You bloody watch me,' he hissed, tearing off his stiff white collar and flinging the carnation from his button-hole into a bush.

'You'll pay for this,' Mrs Breslin warned.

Speechless, I stumbled into Trish's Nissan Micra, Trish cramming my veil and train in after me. 'That was a savage long wait,' she said, driving off, leaving the guests staring after us. 'I thought they'd never let you get away.'

'I feel so desperate. For a while there I didn't know where I was.'

'Where'll we head for?' Trish asked.

'As far away from here as possible.'

'Timbuktu here we come.' Trish laughed, putting her foot down. 'I'm parched.'

'Me too, and I'm dying for a pee, and I'm starving.'

'We'll stop at a pub as soon as we get to . . .'

'Right.'

Chapter Twelve

I walked into the pub with as much dignity as I could muster. With difficulty I clambered into a seat at a corner table near a plate-glass window. Another table nearby was occupied by a bulky man drinking beer, a plate of fish and chips in front of him. Outside, people walked by weighed down with shopping. Others waited by the bus shelter. Some wandered along aimlessly. A clock hanging above a chemist's said twenty to two. Trish went to the bar.

'Gin and tonic,' she called to the barman, then ordered cod and chips for us both. She put the drink in front of me. 'That should do the trick.'

I took a sip. 'Great.'

Trish swigged her gin and tonic. 'Cures everything,' she said. 'Heartaches, the lot.'

I felt a rush of love for her – her bewildered face, her jaded eyes, and for the way she sat with me without asking questions. I wanted to acknowledge my debt to her in some way, but I felt awkward.

'Penny for them.' Her voice cut into my thoughts.

'Oh! Sorry, I was miles away.' Then, leaning over, taking her hand, I said, 'Thank you, Trish.'

Her grip was strong, sure. 'Don't mention it,' she said. 'You think it's the end of the world but it isn't.' She lit a cigarette. 'Sometimes you have to do things,' she said matter-of-factly, 'and other people can't make up your mind for you. I suppose it's called growing up.' Her expression was enigmatic.

I kept my eyes on the passing traffic, and crouched into the leather seat that ran along the yellow distempered walls.

'I wanted to tell him,' I said, feeling foolish. 'But I couldn't. I thought it would be okay. That we'd be fine together. I mean I was just about to—' I hit my forehead with my palm. 'Oh, God! What have I done?' I put my head in my hands, looking like the spoilt child I knew myself to be. 'You think I'm stupid.'

'No, I don't. I think you lost faith. It'd be far worse if you'd married him and didn't love him. You did him a favour.'

There was silence. I was thinking of Barry standing there perfectly still waiting for me to take my vows.

'You can't expect Barry to accept it. Losing the one you love is the worst pain.'

'I thought I'd be able to go through with it.' I took a deep breath, thinking now of Lorenzo, the feel of his body against mine. I covered my face with my hands.

Youths gathered outside the window and looked in, pointing at me and laughing.

'Here, wait a minute.' Trish got up and hurried outside. 'What are you looking at?' she shouted at them.

'Just lookin',' they jeered.

'Well, clear off,' she yelled.

One blinked in surprise then shouted at me, 'Missed the bus, did ye?' before they ran off. The bulky man in the corner exploded into laughter, making the men at the far side of the bar laugh too. Suddenly, the fact that a bride was in a pub without a bridal party appeared to have an effect on everyone's behaviour.

'I scared them off,' Trish said gleefully. 'Little bastards.'

The sun was high in the sky over the newsagent's opposite. I gazed in the other direction, towards the park railings and the empty park.

'What can I get you?' The barman appeared beside us, his eyes popping out of his head.

'Vodka and lime, and a gin and tonic, please,' Trish said.

'Where's the rest of the wedding party?' He lingered over the table.

I was unable to find the words.

'What do you mean?' Trish asked innocently.

'Do the rest of them know where you are?' He waited expectantly. 'Only you'll be late if you don't hurry up.' He smirked at me.

'Fuck off,' Trish said, under her breath.

'Glorious day for a wedding,' he said, as he marched away.

A middle-aged couple came in and sat down. They began to argue, which took the focus off me, until we realised that they were arguing about me. The woman said, 'Of course she's not bloody getting married.'

The man said, 'All the same I wish I had a camera.'

'It's like being on stage,' I said to Trish.

'A pantomime.' She laughed.

I tried to look happy, conscious that I was acting with my eyes, forcing my lips to smile, even though my head was pounding. How often had I practised smiling in front of the mirror? I was good at it. Maybe I'd get a small part smiling in a play or a television advertisement. I wanted to leave and go into the depths of the deserted park, spend the day in there.

Trish said, 'I'm so hungry I could eat a child.'

'The smell of chips is making me starving. I haven't had a plate of chips for years.'

'You haven't had a decent meal for years. Now that you don't need to watch your waistline any more you might as well have them.'

The fish and chips arrived. Trish ordered more drinks. 'Here, have a drag of this,' she said, passing me a cigarette when our plates were cleared.

I felt better.

By now the middle-aged couple were staring and the barman was hovering, picking up the glasses and plates, waiting to see what was going to happen next, the woman insisting that there was nothing untoward about a bride seated at a table in a pub at lunchtime without the wedding party. 'Bet they're making a film,' she concluded.

'Don't be so bloody daft,' the man said. 'Where's the film crew, then? The cameras?' he said, looking around, his face like lard in the light.

'They'll be along any minute.'

'Of course they bloody won't. There's no camera or crew,' he scoffed.

'I'm telling you that girl's an actress. I recognise her face. It's what's-her-name.'

Drawn into the fantasy, I couldn't help seeing myself in a play, possibly *The Reluctant Bride* or *The Jilted Bride*. I beamed at them, star quality showing in my performance, a kind of magic oozing from me, creeping into the audience, which comprised the bulky man in the corner, the middle-aged couple, the youngsters outside the window, the shoppers, the traffic. The youths were still laughing as if I were outrageously funny.

'Don't be ridiculous,' the man said to his wife as they stood up to go, his bald head shiny in the sunlight. On their way out he said, 'She's been jilted, I can tell.' Looking back, the woman's eyes were full of sympathy.

I couldn't help feeling the bizarreness of the situation. It seemed to me that my new role could change by the hour. I was jolted back to reality by a sudden liveliness in the pub. Girls swung through the bar on platform shoes, demanding drinks, men in shirtsleeves crowding in behind them.

'What's going on here?' one girl asked.

'They're making a commercial,' a voice supplied.

It was then that I saw Barry walking along the far side of the street, his hand shading his eyes, searching. My heartbeat quickened, and I nudged Trish unable to speak, then pointed.

She couldn't believe her eyes. 'He must have followed us. Duck down.'

I scrabbled on the floor pretending to be searching for something, trying to keep calm. I'd put her through enough trauma for one day.

'He's gone. Let's go. Quick.'

We made for the door, Trish holding it open, bundling me out with the encouraging words that everything would be all right.

I didn't share her confidence, but walked out bravely into the bright sunshine, my face reddening at the surprise in the faces of passers-by. 'I'm going to faint. Oh, Trish, I can't bear this.'

'Not now.' She pulled me across the road. 'Get in,' she said, opening the car door, stuffing me and my train into the back seat. As we drove off I realised that I had nowhere to go. 'I can't bear to go home if I'm to be tortured by the Breslins.' I could hear my little-girl-lost voice. My stomach churned. 'Oh! I hope I did the right thing.'

'You did. You did.' Trish breathed sincerity into the words so that they meant everything. 'I'll never get married,' she added, 'so I'll never have to escape.'

'You don't know that for sure.'

'I'd rather be lonesome and safe.'

'Until some dark villain comes along one night and sweeps you off your feet.'

'Oh! I'll be ready for him. But not for marriage,' she concluded, glancing at me through the rear-view mirror. 'Aren't men awful?'

We giggled, her sympathy bearing me up again. She stared ahead, her eyes on the road, her thoughts on the disaster of it all.

'They're a savage lot, the Breslins.' I sighed. 'I'll never be able for them.'

'Give them time to simmer down. You'll shake them off, no trouble.'

'I will, of course.' I tossed my head to emphasise my confidence. Then, 'I'm not fit,' I said, my eyes on my scrawny arms.

'We'll join the gym, spending hours jogging. You be able to lift Barry Breslin up with one hand in a few months.'

We laughed, the thought of my future achievements bearing me up, the loneliness of my present predicament dropping me down. Up, down, up, down, down, down. That was the way this nasty experience went.

Chapter Thirteen

The reason for the cancellation of the wedding remained a mystery to the people of Abbeyville. No one had thought to give an official explanation as to why it hadn't taken place so for a long time to come it was discussed in shops and pubs, details of the events made up or exaggerated, but certainly differing from the true facts.

The marriage that didn't take place was an extraordinary tale: how Barry Breslin, a small-town businessman, had been 'dumped' by Olivia Healy, the girl from the corner shop. How she'd walked away leaving him to suffer the humiliation alone, surrounded by the wedding guests. How her brother Billy and his wife Faith left as suddenly as they'd arrived, furious at the indignity of a cancelled wedding.

After Mass the following day, the church grounds reverberated with the words 'ditched, disgrace, desperate'.

'She led him up the garden path,' Maisie Byrne, the florist

from Jaunty Blooms said to a neighbour, who promptly pronounced Olivia 'a spoilt brat'.

'Walking away, leaving him to suffer like that, and his family so respectable.'

'What could you expect?' Mona Corcoran said to Bill, the barman in the Four-leaf Clover. 'Didn't her mother do the same?'

'Well I never,' Bill said.

The story was embroidered by a vindictive Mrs Breslin, who emphasised the 'unsuitability' of the bride, a spoilt, common girl, who'd wriggled her way into the affections of her poor, innocent son.

That evening in the corner shop everyone was talking at once, no one listening. Uncle Cecil, Auntie Tess and Polly had come for tea and commiserations, bringing Aunt Statia with them.

'You won't feel it yet,' Aunt Statia confided, watching how calm and self-possessed I was as I handed round the sandwiches. 'It's afterwards when you're alone. The night-time's the worst. Believe me, I know what I'm talking about.

'Jockser was trying to escape. Only he'd done the deed, hadn't he? Me father, Lord have mercy on him, went after him and insisted that he make an honest woman of me.' Leaning forward even further she said, 'Men are bastards, you know,' giving Uncle Cecil a sidelong glance. 'But for that little warning from me father, my husband Jockser might have scarpered and things woulda been a lot different. Oh, yes, a lot different.'

Auntie Tess threw her eyes heavenwards. 'You had a narrow escape if you ask me, Olivia,' she said.

Queenie, unperturbed by the sudden change of events, said, 'I agree with you for once, Tess.'

'You'll feel strange for a while,' Statia continued, her eyes on mine. 'Keep yourself warm, take plenty of fresh air, don't neglect your health. No man is worth it.'

Mum burst into a fresh flood of tears.

'You ought to be ashamed of yourself, Lorraine,' Queenie said, 'a grown woman crying like that. Stop it at once.'

'It's the shock,' Aunt Statia said. 'Believe me, I know.'

Unable to console Mum, I sat there feeling as if I were somebody else.

'If ever you need a bit of company you must come and see me,' Statia said. 'We'll talk. Just give us a buzz beforehand to make sure that lot are out.' She nodded towards Auntie Tess and Uncle Cecil.

'Thank you.' I sat there feeling the oppressiveness of the silence that followed, before everyone started talking at once.

'The unfairness of it all,' Mum exclaimed. 'Everything was fine when we got up yesterday morning,' she said, in wonderment. 'Now it's all gone queer. I never anticipated anything like this. I just wonder what people are saying.'

'Oh, Mum, leave it!' I cried, and made for the door.

As the days went by I wished I could disappear from my own life but I had no talent for self-obliteration. More and more I became drawn into the variations of my sad story, which was echoing through the parish.

'She jilted him.'

'He'd bought a house.'

'Wealthy family.'

'Spoilt her rotten.'

'He'll never get over it.'

The only person who knew the details was Trish.

'I thought Lorenzo was a bit of fun,' she said.

'It was only a laugh to start with. Anyway, what was the point of telling you? You wouldn't have listened.'

Shrinking from Queenie's request that I return to the shop I stayed with Trish.

'What'll you do now?' she asked, suspiciously.

'Who knows?'

'Running away from your problems is not a good idea,' she said, dismissing the idea instantly.

'I suppose not,' I agreed, abandoning my hopes of a future somewhere other than my home town.

That was how I came to drift back to my old life, waking up every morning in my childhood bed. Mum's forceful nature swept me along, and the expectation of hearing from Lorenzo faded.

There were still plenty of opportunities left for me, I told myself, regardless of what Mum said. I didn't have to retreat into my shell. She continued to cosset me, with tasty lamb stews, roasts, pastries, delighted to have me back in the fold, and whenever I felt uneasy or expressed alarm at my increasing weight, my lack of a life, Mum or Queenie would plug in the kettle.

Dad went around with a face as long as a wet week in Brighton, my presence a cause of annoyance and embarrassment to him. 'To think what you gave up,' he'd say, whenever he caught me alone. 'That young Breslin will be a millionaire soon, if he isn't one already.'

I accepted their cosseting to please them – and to stop them nagging. 'I'm not staying,' I would say regularly, 'only until I feel better.'

Although I'd got into the habit of expecting out-of-the-way things to happen, life was dull. Audrey and Polly were like weasels never letting me forget that they'd been done out of their role of bridesmaid. Trish came to see me with her new boyfriend, Dave Fuller, a manager at the supermarket where she worked. There was an air of suppressed gaiety about them both, as they sat holding hands. Afterwards Trish whispered, 'How do you like him?'

'He's gorgeous,' I said, and meant it. I watched his eyes follow her across the room, secret with excitement. It was more than pride. It was a satisfaction of the flesh: Trish's celibacy vow was obviously forgotten. My stomach lurched as I witnessed it.

I walked back to the town with them, detaining them as long as I could. 'Let me go with you,' I wanted to say to Trish, but she was tucking her arm into Dave's, dismissing me. She was my best friend but she didn't belong to me, and there was no reason for me to stay any longer. I had no hold on her. I walked home alone, dreading the rest of my life, thinking of the opportunities that were slipping between my fingers.

That was when I decided to search for Lorenzo. Outside, his place was pitch dark and no one answered the door. Eventually I opened it with the key I knew he kept under the mat, stood in the hall, and thought of how he'd bounded to the front door the last time I went there, danced me across the hall to the sitting room. 'Stop it,' I told myself, standing at the balcony where we'd had dinner, the lights twinkling sadly.

I mounted the stairs and went to his bedroom. An eerie light from the street-lamp outside cast a sheen on the bedspread and the new white carpet. Everything was gone. I remained in the doorway numb with shock. He might never have been there, so thorough had he been in the removal of all his possessions. He had emptied drawers, wardrobe, bathroom cabinet, leaving nothing but the smell of his aftershave.

I thought of the time that had passed since I saw him last. All that time when I could have been with him. I thought about the way I'd felt when he'd made love to me, as if I'd been created for him, and him for me. I was back in time, a different person, living in a different world, one where only he existed. Lorenzo had led me to believe that I was the main purpose of his existence. If I hadn't been determined to take the wrong route, he might be here still.

I fell into a deep sleep, the dreams tangled together, swarms of people all talking at once. When I woke, I sat up with an effort, rubbing my eyes. My surroundings felt as oppressive as a prison as it slowly dawned on me where I was.

I returned to the shop. Time crawled by, my impatience with everyone's questions building up, work the only relief. 'Here I am', I said to myself, 'living my own life, no one to tell me what to do. I'll join the new gym, do the computer course I should have done ages ago, have a party'. Mum continued to stifle me with her caring, humiliating me in front of my friends by telling them about my sensitivity and dependence. The wedding cake sat in solitary splendour on the piano in the sitting room, a constant reminder of the event that never took place. I couldn't stand it.

'Christ, Olivia, if you don't do something about your life I'm going to brain you!' Trish said, taking the last drag of a cigarette.

'Sorry.'

'That's all you ever say.' Frustrated, she flicked back her hair, and took out another cigarette.

'What's your problem?' I watched her light up, inhale deeply. 'What's making you so edgy?'

'Nothing. I just want you to get a life.'

I shrugged. 'You got something special in yours?'

'No, but I haven't made a complete balls of it like you're doing with yours.'

'Thanks.'

'Look, if you're that mad about Lorenzo why don't you go after him?'

I couldn't explain to Trish what was going on in my mind because I couldn't explain it to myself. I was unable to think things through for fear I'd come to a definite conclusion that I'd lost Lorenzo. I looked at her helplessly.

'You're full of contradictions, do you realise that?'

'I know.'

She was shaking her head. 'What am I going to do with you? You're wasting your precious time dwelling on the past, regretting everything.' She leaned closer. 'Look,' she said, 'you're free now. For Christ's sake, go off somewhere and don't come back until you've got him back or out of your system. Get a life.'

'Easier said than done, but I think you're right.'

'I know I am.'

'Thanks.' Grateful, I stood up. 'I'll start right now.'

When I heard that Barry had left town and was travelling the country, widening his already extensive outlets for his new bread and pastry range, I decided to move into the house. I would stay there and look after it until it was sold.

'You're what?' Mum said.

'I'm moving into the house.'

'But you can't,' she said.

'Why not?' Dad asked, eager to hear of anything that might shift me out of there.

'It's not wise,' Mum said, appalled. 'In fact, it's the very worst thing you could do.'

'It's my house, too, until it's sold. Barry's away so I might as well mind it.'

Mum wasn't convinced.

'She's a grown woman,' Dad said, rattling his newspaper. 'If she wants to go there, let her. You've pampered her long enough. Anyway, I think it's a good idea. It's time she fended for herself.'

'It's not like I'm going off to Australia like Dorcen,' I said. 'I'll only be down the road.'

In my bedroom I got out my hold-all and threw things into it indiscriminately, gathering some of my belongings around me, thinking that perhaps I *should* go to Australia with Doreen, make a fresh start. Still, this was the first step to a new life. 'I'll be back for more of my stuff,' I said nonchalantly, leaving quickly.

The first thing I noticed was the for-sale sign. I opened all the windows to air the place and gazed around the room that was to have been our bedroom, at the pretty new curtains and the matching quilt Mum had bought. Beyond the window, lush green fields stretched to the sea, the village barely visible in the distance, the great church spire rising into the mist. This was a lonely house, neglected, I thought, looking down at the rusting, corrugated roof of the lean-to scullery, and the overgrown garden. It needed someone with energy to care for it, vibrant voices and footsteps on the stairs to liven it up.

But for the moment I needed it and it needed me. I would invite Trish for the weekend. That should do the trick. I would throw myself completely into looking after this house, go about finding nice furniture for it, plan the rest of the décor. Perhaps buy out Barry's share when I got a proper job.

That first night a storm came without warning. In the big empty bed I listened, terrified, to the howling wind, the sea crashing against the rocks.

Mum rang. 'I'm worried about you,' she said.

'I'm all right. I was asleep,' I lied.

The gales strengthened. The windows rattled, the doors creaked. I buried myself under the duvet and tried not to think of my chair by the range at home, hot muffins, hot drinks, my little warm bed.

Mum phoned again. 'Olivia, make sure you have a hot-water bottle. That house is very old. It's bound to be damp.'

'I'm fine, Mum. I'm in bed, nice and snug.'

But I wasn't. The storms began again, gale-force winds attacked the pier, breaking off a section. As a child I had been afraid of storms. A sudden cloudburst, the drumming of rain on our corrugated-iron roof, a clap of thunder was enough to send me into paroxyms of fear. But nothing could keep me awake that night.

When I woke up the next morning the day was calm, the sky clear, the sand washed clean, the broken pier and the seaweed on the shore the only scars from the previous night's battle. My eyes sought the gun-metal grey sea, moving calmly within the harbour. Later, walking along, the sun coming out, my heart lurched with delight at the realisation that for the first time I had survived a storm alone. Until a month ago it had been wintry, frost on the paths, ice on the bonnet of the car and rock pools, the tall grasses stiffened white blades. Now the sun was coming out, strong and warm.

I climbed the bank, and walked up to the hill, looking back across the grey pebbles towards the sandy part of the beach, silver in the morning light. Gulls arrived, swooping down slowly on the pebbles, soundless apart from the beat of their wings. In the distance cows grazed. It was a day where everything seemed possible. I was young, I told myself. Twenty-two was no age at all, really.

The path curved to the left, the sun rose high above the clouds and shimmered on the water. A friendly wind tugged at my hair, felt the collar of my jacket, dispersed my fears. All the things I had dreaded would never come about. I was alive and free and I could see for miles, past the stretch of water to the pale, ethereal sky on the horizon. The sea, the green fields to my right, the hills beyond them, farmhouses dotted here and there were all a comfort. I would walk my troubles out of my system. I kept going. I would forget the past, concentrate on the future. The memories would be discarded like old shoes, the present the only reality. I would stay well and free and, if possible, happy.

I'd buy a puppy, do the garden, tend the vegetables, take things easy until I came back slowly to a life of my own. I would allow myself the pleasure of arriving at my own conclusions. So why did my eyes fill with tears as I gazed over the hill?

That evening I went to the shop in the village to buy groceries. Elaine Evans, a waitress at Shrimps, was getting off the bus on her way home. I stopped her.

'Hi, Elaine.'

'Hello,' she said, coming to a halt, looking at me in surprise.

'How's Lorenzo?' I asked, before she could ask me any questions.

'Don't know.' She shrugged. 'He left. Went back to Italy, as far as I know.' She looked at me curiously.

'Thanks.' I was gone, walking quickly along the street, overwhelmed at the idea that he'd leave me. I was crying, realising that I wasn't gaining control over my feelings for him – where he was concerned I'd never had any control in the first place. It mattered now because he was gone, and for the first time I realised that I had been waiting for him, expecting him to appear at any minute.

I walked quickly, wanting him so badly that I could have ripped out my heart. Slowing down I listened to the sound of a car approaching, looking backwards, willing it to be his, though I knew that was impossible.

All night long I lay listening to the pitter-patter of the rain on the window-pane, my ears straining for every sound, unable to sleep. I stretched out flat and pressed my cheek to the pillow, longing for him to be at my side, knowing that he was gone. The next morning the trees were rain-soaked, the air heavy, the sky threatening. I spent the day writing letters of apology to wedding guests. Then I watched a New York cop movie on TV, blaming everyone but myself for what had happened to me. It wasn't Barry's fault that he was dull and that I'd fallen for Lorenzo. Barry was a nice guy, who'd been fucked up by his stupid, pretentious mother, his sad, drunken father, and the jealous colleagues he was always telling me about. Now I was fucked up too, having ditched the man I was supposed to marry. Immobilised by the truth, I alternated between fantasies of suicide and dreams of running off to find Lorenzo. My yearning for him filled my whole waking hours, drained me.

'Get a job for the rest of the summer,' Trish said.

'Doing what?' I was unable to think of anything big enough to fill the void Lorenzo's departure had left.

'They're looking for demonstrators in Kitchen Utensils at our place,' Trish said. 'Why don't you apply? I could put in a word for you. I'm like that with Larry, the boss,' she said, crossing her fingers. Trish was a secretary at Redmond's, a large supermarket store in George's Street.

'I suppose it's not a bad idea. But who's to say I'd get it?'

'I'll get the lowdown on it tomorrow. You'd be in the basement, mind,' she warned.

'Ideal.'

As it turned out, the job, which promised training and opportunities for advancement, was exactly what I needed. I submitted my curriculum vitae, so short that it was painless to write, and made myself available for an interview at eleven sharp the following Monday morning.

'I got it,' I shouted down the line to Trish.

'What?'

'The job,' I said, still in shock.

I stood in front of the mirror hugging myself. I was off to work. I'd be so busy while I made up my mind what it was I really wanted out of life, avoiding Mum at the same time.

Mum and Queenie were sitting in the kitchen. The folds of Mum's soft pink face shook with disgust and a cloud of smoke rose up to her shut eye. 'Stop trying to prove whatever it is you're trying to prove. Believe me, I did that. I wanted to show the world I wasn't just a pushover, that I could make it on my own.'

'It's not all that different from what you did in the circus,' Queenie chimed in. 'Olivia'll be putting on a show for the public, making an exhibition of herself, only with pots and pans instead of animals.'

Mum gave her a filthy look.

Chapter Fourteen

Having washed, dressed, and completed her early-morning breakfast ritual, Queenie felt tired as she settled into her place behind the counter to await the arrival of her first customer. She picked up a ledger, opened it and regarded the figures. All business transactions concerning the shop had been entered in neat handwriting by Jack Sweeney, her accountant. He had made his last entry the day before and had written, in the debit side, a figure that made her start. The previous day, as he was leaving, he had opened it at that page for her inspection and, seeing that she was taking no notice, had put it down in front of her. 'There's no point in keeping this hidden from you,' he'd said.

'I'll look over it tomorrow,' she had replied, yawning, then gone off for her tea.

Now, written in red biro, there were all the transactions, and those of her daughter, her son-in-law, her granddaughter, for the wedding that never took place. All the outstanding bills from Jaunty Blooms, Mrs Hope, the organist, Special Day Limousines Ltd. and the Marina Hotel had been itemised, reminding her that her family had been visited by failure and regret. She was trying to imagine Olivia beginning again, struggling with change – which Queenie herself had been obliged to do in the past but was resisting at present. Something she would have to face up to soon, before it was too late. She sighed and returned to the past, her own wedding day, the flare of excitement in Sean's eyes. Then she returned to the page and her finger moved down slowly until she got to the totals: the one they had reached and the one that they must reach before the end of the year. She knew that she would have to harness all her creditors' goodwill just to keep afloat.

Raising her eyes in supplication to the picture of Our Lady of Sorrows above her on the wall, she found herself staring at a photograph of her young husband, Sean, in his British Army uniform, his eyes soft and smiling.

The down-payment on the shop had been made from Sean's disability cheque from the Army. A couple of times after they began trading he had protested at her having appropriated his pension, but she had argued that it had been essential to purchase good stock to get herself known in the area.

Over the years she had improved the premises, widening the floor space by building on at the back, opening a back entrance for delivery vans, and concreted the yard, insuring it all. In the beginning, Sean had helped occasionally but mostly he had gone his own way, never noticing her hard work.

As she looked at the racks of coats and dresses, the hats,

the bank of drawers, she felt lonely, and tired of racking her brains for something to make the place pay. Ambling to the door, she turned the sign to 'Closed'. Peggy Noonan, Tommy Traynor's assistant, was hurrying by, her hair flying, her coat thrown open, a cigarette dangling from her lips. She waved.

Lorraine was in the kitchen making a chicken casserole from a recipe she'd cut out of *Good Housekeeping*. Gay Byrne was announcing the death of Margaret Lockwood, one of Britain's top film actresses, aged seventy-three. Lorraine had seen her in *The Wicked Lady*. She had been impressive as the highwaywoman. Lorraine reminisced as she sautéd the onions, green peppers, tomatoes and mushrooms, diced the chicken, crushed a stock cube and brought the mixture to the boil before committing it to the waiting casserole dish. Queenie walked in, sniffing the air. 'What sort of a concoction is that?' she asked dubiously, eyes on the bubbling pan.

'Poulet Provençal,' Lorraine said, in her best French accent. 'Here, have a taste.' She proffered Queenie a forkful.

Queenie made a face. 'Are you trying to poison us or what?'

'It's delicious,' Lorraine protested. 'What's wrong with you today? You're like a bag of cats.'

'Green peppers disagree with me. Anyway, my stomach's not up to anything fancy. I don't feel the best so I shut shop for ten minutes.' Queenie wanted to say that they couldn't afford Lorraine's fancy recipes, and that from now on they'd have to manage on simpler fare. Indeed, if they were to survive at all radical changes would have to be made. All she managed was, 'Business is bad.'

From the radio came the sound of Gay Byrne laughing. Queenie sat down at the table, wondering how much longer she could keep everything going. The previous week she'd fallen asleep in the shop, in her chair, her spectacles slipping down her face, leaving the till unattended.

'I've been hearing that for a while now,' Lorraine said, stirring in some crushed garlic.

'But you haven't been listening.'

'I've a lot on my plate, Mother, and I'm touchy at the moment. I keep seeing Olivia walking down the aisle in her beautiful wedding dress. If I'd known what was going to happen . . .' She paused, stirring her stew, gazing into space.

'What could you have done?'

Lorraine shrugged. 'I don't know. I just know that I'm at an awkward time in my life. I'm fifty years old and finding it all very difficult.'

The radio blared out a track from *Oklahoma*. Queenie leaned over and turned it off. 'Life has to go on,' she said practically. 'I remember your father saying, when we bought the shop, that I had a clear head for business, good ideas, and that if anyone would make a go of it it would be me.'

'You did make a go of it,' Lorraine said. 'The shop kept us all these years.'

'Not for much longer.' Queenie's heavy sigh reflected all the disappointments in her life and made Lorraine more depressed than she already was.

'I can't bear the thought of seeing it all go,' Queenie continued.

'You're dramatising, Mother. Have a drop of whiskey – that always perks you up.'

Queenie didn't argue when Lorraine got the bottle of Paddy from the cupboard and poured her a glass. She didn't believe in arguments any more. They took too much out of her. She'd been involved in enough rows and arguments, with Sean. She had got away from him into the shop, but as his health deteriorated he sat rambling to Lorraine about his childhood, the places he'd been to, the things he'd done. She was always keen to hear more. He'd told her about his longing for another child, a subject he could never broach with Queenie.

After a few sips of her whiskey Queenie began to relax. She tried to visualise herself giving up the shop, taking all her belongings and leaving, and couldn't. 'I feel better now,' she said to Lorraine. 'Right as ninepence. Ready to tackle anything.' The problems would have to be tackled, and Queenie wondered how she'd get Lorraine to take her seriously. Lorraine had a way of switching off when she was talking to her, which Queenie found irritating, but not enough to cause a scene over.

'What about Olivia's idea for a lingerie shop?' Lorraine asked tentatively.

Queenie shot her a look. 'What about it?'

'It's not a bad one.'

'I'll phone her. Have a chat with her.'

'No,' said Lorraine. 'Leave her be.' There was irritation in her voice. She was thinking that the whole place could do with renovating. She was gazing around at the cavernous kitchen: the mass of pots suspended from hooks on the walls, the barred windows, the deep Shanks sink and long wooden draining-board, the kettle that whistled all day long, the shelves packed, the dresser full of crockery, the bills and receipts on lengths of wire, the thick mugs, the refectory table and matching chairs, the old-fashioned range, the loud-ticking Guinness clock. Sitting down opposite Queenie she perused the ledger, going over it slowly, absorbing each item. Returning to her casserole, which was simmering beautifully, she said, 'You don't seem keen on this lingerie idea. What would you like to sell, Mother?'

Queenie said, 'What about fancy goods? You know, knick-knacks, cushions, artificial flowers, and the like.'

'You mean a pound shop.' Lorraine was horrified.

'Or a tobacconist's. Cigarettes, sweets, ice-creams.'

'They do all that in the shop in the supermarket complex. I think Olivia's idea is the best one.'

Queenie was thoughtful. 'We'll toss for it. Head is lingerie, tails knick-knacks. Did I ever tell you about the time your father—'

'Tossed a coin to settle your wedding date,' Lorraine interrupted, and they both laughed.

Lorraine went to get her purse. Her mother annoyed her sometimes with all her talk of the old days. You might as well be talking to the wall as try to shut her up. The coins clicked noisily. Lingerie won the day.

'Who would run it?' Queenie said.

'We'll get someone with expertise,' Lorraine offered. 'Good commission can be a wonderful inducement.'

'We'll see,' Queenie said, closing the subject, returning to the shop.

Lorraine watched her move slowly away from the gloom of the kitchen. Had she detected a hint of enthusiasm in her voice? Perhaps. It would be the price of Queenie not to let on that she liked the lingerie idea. Lorraine thought her mother an extraordinary woman. She would like to have been able to console her, tell her that everything would be all right, that she would help her. The two women had never held lengthy conversations with one another. More often than not they communicated through customers, finding it easier when a third party was present.

She wondered what her mother really thought of her – as a daughter, and as a woman. It depressed her that Queenie sat in her shop, day in and day out, letting everything fall down around her. It depressed her even more to think that she herself had spent most of her life hoping for a day to come when she would gain Queenie's approval.

Lorraine had never spoken to Queenie of when she had run off with Ginger. Neither had she told her how her livelihood had come to her, guessing that her mother might not care to know. In those days she'd had aspirations from the movies she'd seen and books she'd read full of stories about the lives of the Hollywood actresses. She'd watched them in their various roles, weeping for them, laughing with them, loving them. If she'd met them she would have known precisely what to say to them. Hadn't she shared her first moments of true happiness with them, turned to them in fierce grief at her rejection by Ginger, her first love?

A lot had happened since then. Most of it didn't matter any more.

Her mother was getting old, Lorraine reflected, capable of making mistakes, ordering too much of one item not enough of another. She was stubborn and might let the shop go altogether. Even if Queenie did get a good price for the place, would it be enough to support them for the rest of their lives? It was likely that a chain-store company would purchase it, perhaps a foreign one. Then where would they live? What kind of life could they expect? Lorraine sighed. Why couldn't they get back to normal, the way it was before the wedding débâcle, which stood in her path like a blockade. Everything and everyone associated with it had been affected in some way. Queenie, always eccentric, had a vague paleness about her that emanated from her like a shock. Phil was losing himself further in his own little world, insulating himself with trips to his beloved markets, buying and selling to keep boredom at bay. He filled Queenie's head with nonsense about a favourite horse or greyhound, paying for his keep with one hand and taking it from her with the other to pay their combined gambling debts. She herself was consumed with disappointment and sought release in cooking. Why didn't Olivia say something? Had the whole bizarre incident been deliberately staged? No, Olivia wouldn't do that. But why had it all gone wrong? Why had Olivia walked off with no explanation? She had known Barry so long, had been acquainted with his parents, and their eccentricities. The more Lorraine thought about it, the more mysterious it became.

That morning Father Nobel had passed her in the street, absorbed in his own thoughts, reminding her of Olivia in white, walking down the aisle; Olivia standing against the backdrop of the church uttering the words, 'I can't go through with it.' In particular detail she saw Olivia running to Trish's car, the swish of her train, the determination in the look she gave Lorraine. She recalled the photographer fuming that it was the 'livin' end' and the loss of a day's work for him, Phil saying harshly to Olivia, 'What can possibly be gained by you hanging around? Go now, and don't bother coming back.'

Recalling it all brought her own marriage to mind. What had happened to Phil these last few years? He couldn't be termed a bad husband, because he wasn't. Neither, on the other hand, was he a good one. But she was a good wife: she had been faithful and bossy; she had taken charge and he'd willingly let her, becoming lazier and irksome as time went on; her strength supported their marriage, and although she demanded proper behaviour from him in company, otherwise she let him go his own way.

In middle age Phil was respectable – not for him, the fleshpots of the night. Lorraine, who liked parties and dances, complained that they never went anywhere. When an invitation arrived he would make some excuse and urge her to go with a woman friend. She would describe the evening to him, detail the clothes, mention whom she'd met. He would smile pleasantly and nod. She couldn't understand why he spent so much time away from the house, but her earlier rage had given way to sympathy for a man who'd been swamped by women. He wasn't a particularly happy man, but he wasn't unhappy either. His life was simple. No bills to pay, no demands on his time. Lorraine felt she deserved more than he offered. She refused to let herself think of the happiness she'd anticipated with Ginger, knowing that Ginger would have had many women in his life. Phil, on the other hand, came home to her every night.

She picked up the phone and dialled the lingerie supplier, wondering how she'd investigate the matter further without making any commitment. However, challenged by the new idea she made an appointment for the following Wednesday to meet a Monsieur Guilbert.

In the afternoon Queenie went to take her forty winks. Returning from her nap, stepping quietly into the shop, she saw the sad expression on Lorraine's face, saw her hand at her throat, coaxing open the top button of her blouse.

'Oh! There you are.' Lorraine gave a little start. 'I was just thinking of the wedding.'

'It's all for the best,' Queenie said calmly.

'How can you say that?' Lorraine protested.

'Because it was a lot of oul cod, that's how.' Queenie thought of Olivia, the bright smile that came easily to her face, her blue eyes that danced with merriment. 'It wasn't her fault, you know,' she said. 'There was something wrong that she wasn't telling us about.'

'Very perceptive,' Lorraine said sarcastically.

'No, listen. There's some reason why Olivia did what she did in such a way.'

'Mmm,' Lorraine muttered.

As far as Queenie was concerned it was Lorraine's fault that Olivia wasn't here. Imagine giving in to Phil like that, letting him dictate who should come and go in Queenie's house. Queenie would have liked Olivia to have been there: by now she would have been in a better position to explain things herself.

The [illegible] you're taking money [illegible] advised. Stand here, at the [illegible]. Let them get a good view. Repeat the [illegible] with the [illegible] them the advantage [illegible] giving them [illegible]

Chapter Fifteen

Three weeks after the fateful wedding day I started work. Each morning at eight o'clock my alarm went off, waking me to the worst part of the day. A pitch of sorrow would overcome me, so deep in its intensity that it would knock the breath out of me. Then I would get up, shower, dry my hair, dress, put on my makeup, go down to the kitchen to drink a glass of milk and swallow the vitamin pill I'd promised Mum I'd take each morning. Finally I would slip into my white demonstration coat and leave, trying to work up some enthusiasm for the day ahead.

'The trick is not to let the customer realise you're taking money off them,' Larry, head of Kitchens, advised. 'Stand here, in the middle. Let them get a good view. Repeat the name of the product every few minutes.' He taught me how to work the various gadgets, how to keep my eyes level with the customers while gauging their mood. 'Sock it to them,' he advised. 'As if you were giving them a rare gift, and letting them in on a secret. Which, in a way, you are.' He confided his most secret tip: 'Keep talking, and listen to them as if you care. They'll love you and buy the crap.'

That first day I started at nine o'clock sharp. Feeling shy and foolish I peeled and sliced, demonstrating the new Jiffy Slicer, the latest gadget in the range, chattering away like Larry had said, eager to get the few early morning shoppers interested. By the end of the morning I was exhausted.

As the day progressed, encouraged by the nods and smiles of the customers, ignited by the notion that somebody might want to buy something from me, I kept going. I smiled at the circle of women who gathered around me, talked endlessly as Larry had advised, leading the conversation to profit, I hoped. Some customers didn't want to buy anything, just wanted to talk about recipes. Once I found myself scribbling one down for hamburgers, at the insistence of an overenthusiastic woman who'd bought a mincer from me.

I liked the work. There was excitement in demonstrating the utensils, watching faces, reading reactions. The women were usually nice to me, the men playful, often teasing.

As the days went by the rawness eased. The 'legalities', as Mum called them, were still to be faced – Barry's mother was insisting that the house be sold immediately, at a loss if need be, while Barry himself was unavailable for comment. Mum came to see me at work, her voice stilted as she assured me that everything was all right at home, but that I should keep out of Dad's way to let him cool down. 'He still hasn't got over all that wealth you turned your nose up at,' she said.

Life was getting better. I no longer dreaded waking with

the birds, and that first dropping sensation of loss that came with it. A sudden mention of the marriage, however inadvertent, didn't rouse such a deep sense of alarm in me any more. I was settling down, no longer dreading the day ahead.

On the Friday of my third week I carried on as usual, chatting with the customers, but I felt uneasy, as though something was wrong. I glanced up and saw Barry. He was staring at my neck, bare beneath my white coat. I stared back at him, saw his face whiten, his lips tremble.

I kept working, too conscious of his presence to concentrate. His gaze shifted to my hands, slicing the vegetables with the long-wired implement, and back again to my face, his own coarsened by rage. I was on the point of saying something to him when a small-faced woman leaned towards me. 'Are you all right?' she asked.

'Yes,' I stammered.

'Only you look a bit off. If you're not feeling well you should sit down. Shall I call the manager?' She caught sight of Barry, glanced at me and said, 'I hope I'm not interrupting anything.'

'Not at all,' I assured her.

Barry moved off without saying a word.

'Men are terrible,' she confided, glancing at his retreating back. 'I know. I'm married to one. I was wondering,' she continued, studying the vegetable slicer in my hand with interest, 'will it rust?'

'No.'

'Bit pricy, for what it is.'

'Carries a ten-year guarantee.'

'Oh, go on, then, I'll take one.' She spoke as if she were about to purchase the Crown Jewels. 'My son likes stews and casseroles,' she informed me, as I wrapped it up. 'He works in the city and the long journey gives him an appetite. He's only settling down, though, finding his feet.'

'That's great.'

'It's so busy in the city. My husband takes no interest in what I cook. Couldn't care less. He prefers to be left alone with his telly and his pint of stout.'

'My dad's the same.'

'Really?' She sounded surprised.

'Are you sure it was Barry?' Trish asked, at coffee break, when I told her what had happened.

'It was him, all right. He looked fit to be tied. He gave me the creeps.'

'Don't be daft.'

'No, I'm serious. He frightened me, the way he looked at me.'

'Ah, come on, Ollie. Barry wouldn't hurt a fly. The whole thing's gone to your head. Get an early night. You're worn out.'

I nodded.

'We'll prop ourselves up at some bar this weekend, or go to a disco, whichever you'd prefer.'

I wasn't consoled. 'Here I am a demonstrator in a supermarket with raw hands from peeling and slicing vegetables, and a sick ex-fiancé stalking me,' I moaned, 'when I should be with Lorenzo. Another girl will waltz into his life. What then?'

'There are plenty of fish in the sea. You'll make someone a great wife some day.'

When I'd stood before the altar that day I had felt Lorenzo's presence, felt his desire for me. I had been sure that when everything settled down we'd go on together, live in a nice house, have children, eat together, sleep together, reminisce about the day I nearly married someone else, tell our children. Now I felt that he had gone from me for ever. I shuddered.

'We'd better get back to work,' Trish said.

In the pub that weekend Doreen's brother Ken, the law student, turned up. 'I don't get it,' he said. 'Why did you clear off like that on your wedding day?'

'Because,' I said slowly, 'I didn't want to get married.'

'This could be a case of desertion,' he said.

'I don't believe you.' A most unpleasant pain began in the pit of my stomach.

'Things are never as bad as they seem,' Trish said, poking him in the ribs. 'Maybe you should go home, Ollie.'

'I'm going as soon as I finish my drink.'

'I mean home to the shop.'

'Dad's not keen to have me around at the moment and Mum's putting her energies into this French Experience she keeps talking about. She's gone amok with her plans.'

'It'll be smashing,' Trish said.

'Any excuse for her to go off on a shopping spree. She'll let her credit card go through the roof. It'll cause more trouble than Queenie's little flutters on the horses.'

Next morning I didn't want to go to work. The thought

that Barry might appear again made me feel sick. I looked awful and there were spots on my chin. The chocolate wrapper beside the bed was the culprit. I'd stop eating chocolate now, and no more alcohol ever again. It was making me fat and ruining my complexion.

I telephoned work and said I was sick.

'I'm so alone. It's unbearable,' I said to Trish, when she came round that evening with a Chinese takeaway. 'And Mum says they're saying terrible things about me in Abbeyville.'

She shrugged. 'The story is being blown out of all proportion. Swelling with the telling. Men can treat women badly and get away with it, but if a woman jilts a man! Boy, oh, boy!'

'The worst part is that wherever I go my story goes before me. It *becomes* me. "Olivia Healy, the girl who jilted Barry Breslin, the best catch in town." Already the silence when I walk into the supermarket is awful. I see them nod in my direction, feel what they're saying behind my back.'

'Good scandal is scarce around here at the moment. But you don't want to detach yourself from your own story, you want to make the most of it, capitalise on it, build it up. Give them something to really talk about.'

'Oh, but there's a bigger tragedy, far worse than anyone thinks.'

'What?' Trish asked, her eyes widening in surprise, her hands pressed together in anticipation.

'I can't say,' I said, my eyes on the ceiling, my mouth clamped shut.

'Ah, come on. We've always told each other everything,' Trish said.

'I'm in love with Lorenzo.' My eyes darted to hers, then to the ceiling, the heaviness miraculously lifting from my chest. 'Say something.'

'You can't be!'

'Go on, have a good laugh.'

She wasn't laughing. She was looking at me, shocked.

'Did you sleep with him?'

I didn't answer.

'Olivia, you didn't! I don't believe it.' Her raised eyebrows indicated that it was no wonder I'd jilted Barry. 'When? How often?'

'What does it matter? Now he's upped and gone. Just like that. And I can't face the shop in case Barry comes sneaking around again.'

'What are you going to do?'

'I want to go to Italy to find Lorenzo and tell him that I didn't get married after all.'

'Isn't that a bit drastic? Couldn't you send him a note?'

'Oh, Trish, I'll die if I don't see him soon.'

'He's gone,' she said. 'Forget him.'

'I can't,' I said, tears sliding down my face.

Next day I phoned the airport and booked a flight to Venice. As soon as I put down the phone I hunted through the chest of drawers for clean underwear, threw it into my bag with blouses, dresses, a cardigan for cool evenings, and the contents of my dressing-table. I made the bed, tidied the room. In the kitchen I washed up the cups and dishes left over from my supper the previous night, put out food lying around in the fridge. Then I sat at the kitchen table reading the newspaper, sipping tea. I was going to Italy the next day and would probably never return.

Next morning I dressed quickly. With a shaking hand I applied my lipstick, smeared it slightly, wiped it off, started again. I put on my jacket, took my bag, told myself that I must phone Mum from the post office in the village and tell her that I was going away.

'Olivia!?' Mum shouted. 'This is a very bad line. I can't hear you. You're not making sense.' Her voice faded then went altogether. I replaced the receiver and dialled again.

Queenie answered. 'What's going on?' she said, alarm in her voice.

'I'm going away for a little while.'

'Where?'

'To Italy. Don't worry about me. I'll be all right. I'll phone when I get there.'

There was a crackling sound. The line broke down.

'Olivia! Are you still there?' the faint voice said.

'Mum, listen. I'll phone in a couple of days. Don't worry about me. I'm meeting up with a friend.'

'But why on earth would you do a thing like that?'

The line crackled again. 'I'll write.'

'I can't hear you. Olivia, what's up with you? You refused to get married. Now you're off God knows where.'

'Our marriage would have been a farce.' My voice broke. 'I don't think I could ever have loved him properly.'

Chapter Sixteen

When there was no word from Olivia, Lorraine and Queenie became frantic with worry. When Trish called to see them Queenie asked bluntly, 'Do you know where she is?'

Trish said, 'Olivia has gone to Venice to search for Lorenzo O'Brien.'

'That fancy foreign fella from Shrimps,' Queenie said. 'He must have persuaded her to go.'

'Who?' Lorraine was aghast. 'Olivia never mentioned anything like that to me – but, then, there's a lot of things I didn't know about that's only coming to light now.'

'The chap that called here with a big bunch of roses one evening. Olivia said he was from Interflora, that they were flowers from Barry, but I knew he was running the new restaurant. Maisie Byrne told me about him.'

The weather turned cold and showery. Olivia's absence was arousing even more curiosity. Queenie stayed in bed, fed up with all the talk. She and Lorraine had found themselves assuring people that there was no trouble, that everything was being sorted out amicably. That Olivia had pulled back in the nick of time. Now she was fed up with it all.

'Good morning,' Mary, the help, said, coming into Queenie's bedroom one morning. 'Did you sleep well?'

'No,' Queenie snapped, hoisting herself into a sitting position. Since Olivia had left she was finding it increasingly difficult to sleep.

'I brought you your tea.' The tray rattled as Mary plonked it on the bedside table.

'I'd prefer to be up,' Queenie said grumpily.

'Take your time, everything's done. The bins are out,' Mary prattled.

'I'll get up soon,' Queenie said dismissively.

'Right you are. The French girl will be here anytime now,' Mary advised her.

Queenie settled back into her pillows, letting the sun's brilliance warm her face. The arrival of the new lingerie and the new French girl that came with it, Chantal Sage, recommended by Monsieur Guilbert, was a blessing, really, she concluded unwillingly. With Chantal's arrival the emphasis would shift away from Olivia and her wedding to this stranger.

'Meet Chantal,' Lorraine said to Queenie, when the French girl arrived, with several large suitcases, and watched anxiously to see the impression exchanged between them.

'*Enchantée*,' Chantal said, as Queenie stepped forward and shook hands with a significant lack of interest. 'So this is Ireland,' she went on, gazing around peevishly, taking in the dull walls, the bolts of material stacked in a corner, the misted surfaces of the counter, the bloom on the furniture, the fogged-up window.

Chantal was thin as a lath, foreign and smart. Her exuberance and colour brightened up the dull shop. Younger than Queenie had expected her to be, her large eyes, emphasised with kohl, stared out from her pretty, perturbed face, and her black lustrous hair, expensively cut, bounced at every move and turn of her head. Her movements had a fashion-model elegance, her clothes were foreign and smart, her exquisite legs encased in a pair of long, leather boots.

'*Il fait froid*,' she said as she entered the kitchen, with an attractive twitch of her slim shoulders. 'Your country is so chilly I forget my English.'

A pale, pampered belle, Queenie thought, and said, 'You're doomed to disappointment, what with our Irish weather and the dull lives we lead here. It's a wonder you ever came.'

Chantal widened her brown eyes. 'But I wish to improve my English,' she said, adding proudly, 'I was good at it in school, but when I was – how you say? – expelled I didn't have the chance to continue.'

'Expelled!' Queenie repeated, horror-stricken.

'I was not really a bad girl, you understand. Just full of spirit.'

'You'll be very bored here,' Queenie warned. 'Not much happens.'

'A hot bath, *peut-être*, and some champagne?' Chantal looked at Lorraine.

'Champagne! At this hour?' Queenie was aghast.

'*Mais oui*. In France we drink champagne *tout le temps*.'

'Well, you're not in France now.'

'I'll nip to the off-licence,' Lorraine broke in, 'as soon as I've shown you to your room.'

A couple of days later Tommy Traynor stepped into the shop to have a quiet word with Queenie about a favourite runner, Desert Orchid. 'Forget I'm here,' he said to Chantal. 'I won't get in your way.' His pleasure was obvious as he peered around. The word had spread and everyone was talking, not so much about the stock that was arriving from Paris but about the French piece who would sell it.

'*Allo*.' Chantal smiled at him ravishingly. 'You must excuse me. My English is not very good.'

'Mademoiselle.' He basked in her smile. 'How was your flight?'

'Bumpy,' Chantal confided, raising her chin and running a hand through her pretty hair.

'Come to have a look round?' Queenie asked, the violent defence of her shop as tangible in her tone as the uninhibited offers of assistance from the strange beauty standing beside him.

'It's the wife's birthday next week. I thought I'd surprise her with some French lingerie.'

'Hmm,' Queenie muttered, not believing a word of it.

'Something comfortable yet light. *Oui?*' Chantal spoke in a precise tone that evoked exactly what she envisioned. 'What size is your wife?' she asked, her head perched to one side, her eyebrows raised in enquiry.

'She's . . . eh . . . a size twelve, I think.' Tommy blushed.

Chantal rummaged through the delicate stock. 'Ah!'

she said, taking a Lejaby matching bra and pants from a drawer.

Blushing, Tommy looked at it. 'Sure that wouldn't fit a sparrow.'

'It stretches.' Chantal filled one of the cups with her fist, and giggled.

'I'll take it.' Wreathed in smiles, Tommy turned to Queenie who had sunk into a corner with embarrassment.

'Bring it back if it does not fit,' Chantal said, as she wrapped it daintily, then asked, 'Would you like a little drink to celebrate the new shop?'

'I don't mind if I do,' Tommy said.

'What?' shot out of Queenie's mouth.

'Just a little Cognac.' Chantal pinned down the word with a sigh as she went to her bag and took out a bottle. '*Moment*, Monsieur, *s'il vous plaît*,' she said to Tommy. 'I get ze glasses.'

The desperate Queenie took the stance of one who'd missed the boat and had been left standing on the platform. 'Would somebody mind telling me what we're running here? A pub?' she said.

Tommy stopped prowling around. 'The young lady's doing her best, Queenie. Give her a chance.'

'She's getting on my nerves.'

Tommy continued prowling and peering. 'It was all your idea in the first place,' he riposted.

'It wasn't my idea to have an over-exposed French tart behind my counter,' she hissed.

'I wouldn't complain if I had her in my shop. She'll have

the men climbing up the drainpipes to get a glimpse of her. That has to be good for business.'

'She's loud and exhausting. Olivia could have done the job just as handy.'

'Olivia's not here.'

'I just hope I took the right decision, and that Lorraine doesn't intend turning this place into a den of iniquity.'

'It's the nineties. You've got to move with the times, that's what I always say. We're part of Europe now. We've boats that sail on the right days, telephones that work, aeroplanes that fly on time.'

'And people with money who want to waste it,' Queenie supplied. 'It's all such a terrible extravagance. There are other, more necessary products.'

'Yes, yes,' Tommy agreed heartily. 'But we must keep abreast of the times.'

'A breast!' The returning Chantal burst out laughing.

'Your grasp of English is remarkable,' Queenie said sarcastically.

'*Merci*.' Then Chantal poured the drinks. '*Salut*,' she said, her eyes flitting from Tommy to Queenie, suddenly vulnerable.

'Most kind of you.' Tommy's grin stretched from ear to ear as he took the proffered glass. Watching, Queenie was remembering how she had survived the war years and poverty so honourably. She'd stuck with her shop and worked. Except for her annual holiday her business had always come first, keeping her busy, happy, important. Now she was frightened of what might happen to it in less capable hands. She hadn't needed men to flatter her, or to stand half-naked behind her counter. She must have been an attractive woman once, she mused, but she had forgotten that in her determination to do her job well. And she had succeeded. She'd looked after her child with the dedication of two parents. The price had been paid. A widow for so long, too protective of Lorraine for remarriage, loneliness had become her constant companion.

But nineteen ninety was different. Queenie had a daughter and a granddaughter who were reasonably extravagant. She knew Olivia was like her. She had been in love early, and would be again. Young men were wildly attracted to her. But at twenty-two what did she know? What had she seen? Queenie had watched the tension building up, seen the reservation in Olivia's demeanour. She had fled and she had been right to go, Queenie thought. Soon she would be madly in love again. By nature Olivia was a flirt.

The shop bell rang. Lorraine hurried in. 'Hello, everyone.' She looked keenly around. 'Is this a private party or can anyone join in?' she asked.

'You just made it,' Tommy said, raising his glass. 'A drop of this stuff would do you good.'

'I disclaim all responsibility. I'm not answerable for any of it,' Queenie said.

Chantal kept a well-bred silence.

Tommy Traynor grinned at Lorraine, his eyes crinkling at the corners. 'This new assistant of yours is marvellous.'

'Thank you.' Lorraine sighed. For all her size she seemed suddenly as light as air, as if a huge burden had been lifted from her shoulders.

'Girls come and go.' Queenie sniffed.

'I hope not,' Lorraine said.

'I don't know if I can face the winter here.' Chantal looked around. 'I miss ze sunshine.'

'Listen.' Lorraine took a bundle of rainbow-coloured leaflets from her handbag and held them up in a bright fan. 'This is the next step,' she said, handing them around. 'We're throwing a launch party. I'm sending invitations to all the men in the area.'

'Have you lost your mind?' Queenie croaked.

'No, Mother. If you remember rightly, you were the one who said that we should do something, that we were broke. You were full of schemes for retrenchment and economies. I am doing something positive, and I'm really looking forward to it.'

'That's the ticket.' Tommy scanned his leaflet, the invitation already accepted.

Queenie read hers quietly:

Paris fashion: the latest, chic lingerie from Paris. These wonderful garments will open up new vistas you've never dreamed of.

'*Très bien*,' Chantal enthused.

'Nice if you can afford it,' Queenie said drily. God knew what 'vistas' meant.

'At these prices the customers will expect a lot,' Tommy said.

'They'll get what they pay for,' Lorraine snapped.

'We'll do it,' Chantal said, confidently. 'We'll make it work.'

Tommy opened one of the brochures, relaxing into the counter to read it. Chantal poured more Cognac into his glass. Lorraine made a grab for her handbag. 'I must be off. I owe a fortune to Mr Turner at the newspaper.'

'I'm sure you have things to do, Tommy.' Queenie was dismissive.

'I'm not leaving until I've seen everything.' Tommy's eyes roamed the pages, the photographs of lithe girls scantily clad in moulded bras of refined guipure, or tulle G-strings with eye-catching embroidered flowers.

'He'll be ossified if you don't get him out,' Queenie hissed to Chantal, who shrugged helplessly.

In desperation Queenie marched to the door. 'Come on, Tommy. Time to go home.' Her command cracked the silence.

Tommy looked at her. 'Oh! By the way, Queenie, I've got tickets for the horse show. Would you like to come?'

'I'd love to,' Queenie began to relax.

'The Drysdales will be coming too.'

'I look forward to it.'

Tommy went to the door, then paused to call to Chantal, 'Be seeing you.'

'I've heard of things happening to men of a certain age, but this is ridiculous.' Queenie watched him walk down the street.

'It is the way to make money.' Chantal giggled.

Swelling with the righteousness of a community-spirited shop proprietor, Queenie felt duty-bound to consult with Father Nobel about these new developments in her shop.

Meantime, cross and hungry, she went to the kitchen wishing Lorraine was there preparing lunch as usual instead of gallivanting around Abbeyville with leaflets exposing girls in skimpy underwear.

When Lorraine returned, Chantal said to her, 'Your mudder's strange in her mind, *n'est-ce pas*?'

'Why?'

'I ask her for a list of all the men in the town. She say she can't remember any of them.'

Lorraine looked at her, puzzled. 'She's a good memory.' Under her breath she added, 'Too good.'

'I have some ideas for the men,' Chantal told her, unwrapping chiffon nightgowns and shantung négligés.

'What did I tell you?' Lorraine said to the dishevelled Maisie Byrne in her washed-out striped dress, who gasped at the magnificence unfolding before her as she entered the shop.

'Is that your one?' Maisie whispered, indicating Chantal. 'What's she like?'

Queenie appeared just then from the kitchen, wrinkled her nose and said, 'Not suitable. She has the poor men bewitched.' She shook her head regretfully. 'A silly young one. I'm afraid she'll catch her death in the clothes she brought with her. Yesterday evening I had to light the fire in the sitting room and it's the end of July. I ask you. Takes two hot-water bottles to bed with her.'

'Don't let her get you down. It's not good for your blood pressure.'

'I'll give her plenty of stick, believe you me.'

Lorraine looked from Queenie to Maisie with faint suspicion. 'Have I interrupted something?'

'No,' said Queenie. 'We were just having a bit of a chat.'

'I was telling Maisie about Tommy's invitation to the horse show.'

'Something to look forward to,' Maisie said.

'You and Tommy never miss it,' Lorraine said.

'Of course not. The biggest international horse event of the year. And with the Drysdales, this time. I can't wait.'

The Misses Drysdale were old friends of Queenie's, going back to her first days in Abbeyville. They had lived together in a Georgian terraced house since their father had died. He had also left them enough money to keep them for the rest of their lives. Yet their economical ways fascinated Queenie, as did their talent for knitting and sewing. They kept themselves busy supplying church jumble sales with beautifully crafted sweaters and embroidery, and told endless stories of hunt balls in bygone days. However, it was their accounts of trips to Newbury and Newmarket, Doncaster and Exeter that held Queenie in thrall.

Chapter Seventeen

On the bus to the airport I drifted into a reverie trying to find some flaw in my personality that was responsible for what was happening to me. At the airport I queued behind boys and girls with haversacks, thinking how strange it was to be on my way to Venice alone. I would find work, a flat, nothing luxurious, learn the language. Lorenzo would teach me, as he would teach me how to cook Italian food. I'd probably work in his mother's restaurant. We'd settle down, have a boy first then a girl. Or a girl then a boy. It didn't matter. All that mattered was that we'd be together for the rest of our lives.

The room on the top floor of the hotel, booked for me by the tour operator, was dark and old-fashioned. Its large windows overlooked a small market square. Parading past Reception that first evening on my way to the dining room was difficult, but the maid, turning down my bed greeted me brightly.

The early-morning crash and bang of the vendors, and

clatter of stalls being set out, woke me. I lay listening to the incomprehensible chatter as the smells of fruit and fish rose up and the cries of hungry seagulls floated on the morning air. In the bathroom I showered, combed my hair. To my reflection in the mirror I said, 'Hello. Welcome to your first day in Italy.'

I took the lift downstairs and secured the address of the local tourist board office. From the dining room came the sounds of breakfast. People were filing in to sit at different tables. I walked past them, out of the hotel, and went to look for the tourist office. There I was given a list of all the fish restaurants in Venice. 'Do you have the name of the proprietor?' the girl behind the desk asked politely.

'Lorenzo O'Brien,' I said hopefully, although he had told me it was his mother's restaurant.

She looked up her list. 'Sorry. No one by that name.'

Then I went to a telephone box, which was dirty and scrawled with graffiti to call each restaurant. Tiny beads of perspiration broke out on my brow as I worked my way down the list. After a while I was too hot to go on so I went to Piazza San Marco for coffee. I gazed around spellbound, took a few photographs, then walked slowly along the waterway, past gracious houses that tilted towards the tide. Boatmen sat under the water-gate as the early-morning mist, lying heaviest on the water at the far end of the piazza, drifted away through the arches.

Later, at a waterside bar I drank lemonade and gazed at the gondolas, trying to decide on my next course of action. Once I had found him and explained about the wedding cancellation, everything would be all right, I was sure.

'English?' a woman sitting at the next table asked.

'Irish,' I informed her, with a smile.

'Here long?' she asked, in an American accent.

'I've just arrived.'

'Breathtaking city,' she said, rising, folding street maps into her bag. 'I hope you enjoy your holiday. Have a nice day.'

'Thank you, I will.'

She bade me farewell and drifted off among the crowds of tourists. I kept my eyes on the gondolas endlessly disgorging passengers as the sun beat down, a pale furnace in the cloudless sky.

That evening I went out again. It was pleasant to stroll, mingle with tourists and the ghosts of history who littered the streets. The churches and buildings were grotesque in the moonlight. Here I was, alone in this strange city. There was no turning back. I had to find Lorenzo. I watched the tourists heading for the railway station as I retraced my steps to the hotel. Women in black sold flowers, trinkets, jewellery. 'You buy something for your loved one?' A toothless woman was taking coins from a German man. I wanted to cry when I thought of Lorenzo in a house somewhere in this city. He should have been with me to wander through the maze of streets and squares, over the narrow bridges, follow the canals and drink some wine at a café.

Back at the hotel I sat at a table in the small garden, watched by the ministering barman. His eyes were black and glittering, reminding me of Lorenzo.

In my bedroom I stood at my window watching the moon glitter on the dark water, its blue-black surface reflected in the two high windows opposite. Below me white muslin curtains of the windows opposite billowed in the breeze; the deep frayed fringes of blinds yellow with age hung beneath them. Listening to the strange night noises of Venice I wondered how I would manage on my own if I didn't find Lorenzo. I had never done anything much on my own.

Finally I fell asleep, my mind full of unanswered questions. I dreamed I met Lorenzo, near the water, recognition and joy coming into his face as he saw me approaching.

Next morning I wandered down to the piazza again, where stall-holders sold souvenirs, coloured umbrellas high above their stalls to protect them from the sun, which by noon had become a furnace. I turned out of the piazza, walking past advertisements for ice-creams and chocolate. Mama Mia's. I stopped. That was it! Lorenzo's mother's restaurant. How could I have forgotten it? A young man selling cigarettes at a kiosk on the corner asked, 'You lost?' He was dark and dressed in shorts and a T-shirt. I shook my head. 'You like to have a drink with me?' he asked.

'No, thanks,' I said politely.

'I show you the sights.'

I rushed back to the hotel to phone Mama Mia's. There was no reply.

I felt more desperate than ever to find Lorenzo, but it was only one o'clock, the rest of the day was mine and I wasn't going to waste a minute of it.

I returned to the kiosk. 'Do you know where Mama Mia's restaurant is?' I asked the youth.

He nodded. 'I take you there.' He locked up the kiosk and I followed as he walked past the café where I'd sat the previous evening, then on through the dim alleys. Finally we turned into a narrow street, partly demolished, washing strewn across it, and walked the length of another street until we reached a dingy little restaurant on the corner, Mama Mia's in neon over the door.

It was closed.

Disappointment made me walk up to the door, knock, then try the handle. It was locked. I peered through the dirty window, but the tables and chairs were empty. I leaned against the window-sill, deciding to wait for him to come home. The thought occurred to me that I could sunbathe on the little terrace while I was waiting. I could take off my shirt and lie there underneath the lemon tree, my eyes on the road. The boy stood leaning against the door, smoking a cigarette, his eyes on me, so I slid into a sitting position against the wall instead. A group of German tourists walked by, talking. A red car drove past, then a blue one. By now the boy had slid down too and was smoking, his knees at his chest. The sun was at its zenith and I wished the bar would open so I could buy a drink. I closed my eyes and imagined that when I opened them Lorenzo would be standing there. He would take me in his arms, and introduce me to his mother, the rest of his family.

When I opened my eyes, the youth had gone and I walked back quickly the way I'd come. Several times I nearly missed my way – all the streets looked the same.

That evening I sat in my bedroom wishing that none of it had happened; that I'd never met Lorenzo, never come to Venice.

The next day, wearing a sleeveless shirt and shorts I returned, walking fast. I had to get there quickly or Lorenzo would be gone. A man was sitting on the steps of the restaurant, his bare stomach hanging out over his trousers, a cigarette in his mouth.

I went up the first step. 'Hello,' I said.

His eyes were hostile.

'My name's Olivia,' I said and held out my hand, determined to be diplomatic. 'I'm a friend of Lorenzo.'

He took my hand. 'Lorenzo have lots of friends.' He laughed.

'Is he here?'

He shrugged, muttered something in Italian and turned away. I stood my ground for a few seconds. Then I said, 'Excuse me,' and walked past him.

Inside an elderly woman in a floral apron was bustling around, a duster in her hand. 'I'm a friend of Lorenzo's. Is he here?' I asked.

She looked at me, puzzled. 'You – Lorenzo – friends?'

'*Si.* I'm from Ireland.'

'*Unoa momento*,' she said, pushing back her hair. 'Opening time.' She indicated the bare tables still needing to be set. 'My son not here.'

'Oh!' I made to go.

Gripping my arm Lorenzo's mother led me to a table and sat me down. 'Lorenzo very busy. All the time busy,' she said, as if this meeting between us was secret. 'He in the States.'

'The States.'

'*Si*, Signorina.' Suddenly she disappeared behind a curtain of beads and returned with a letter. 'He write me this,' she said. She was watching for my reaction. 'What do you want of him?'

'Lorenzo is a good friend, that's all,' I found myself saying.

'He not coming back for a long time. I have to get my brother to help me. I have bad stomach.'

'I'm sorry,' I said. 'I shouldn't have come.'

She shook her head, smiling. 'I tell Lorenzo when I write to him. What is your name?'

I stumbled out of the door. I should have known better. I would never see Lorenzo again.

Back at the hotel I sat by the window, looking out at the changing colours of the sky as the sun set, wishing I had never come here.

I told myself I was having a nightmare, that I would wake up. I sat watching the pigeons that huddled together on the parapet opposite. I allowed myself to look the truth in the face, and acknowledge that Lorenzo would never have married me, that he had no interest in me at all. If we'd met in his mother's restaurant, he would have avoided me. I knew I couldn't face my family and friends just yet but I just had to phone Trish.

Her voice at the other end of the line was soothing. 'I'd almost forgotten what you sounded like,' she said. 'How are you getting on?'

'I'm okay.'

'I phoned your mum yesterday. She's worried about you.'

'She's always worried about me.'

'This time I don't blame her.'

'How's work?'

'Same old stuff. Life goes on, you know. We all went to the pub last night for Simon Scales's leaving party. He's off to the Canaries, repping.'

'Good fun?'

'It was a laugh.' The vibrancy in her voice was audible. She was having fun, and without me. 'It's nice to go out together after work,' she added. 'Beats watching telly.'

'Are you and Dave getting on all right?'

'We're fine.' In the silence that followed I could feel her waiting for me to say something about Lorenzo. Then she said, 'I hope you're taking good care of yourself. Eating plenty of fruit and stuff like that.'

'You're beginning to sound like Mum.'

'I mean it, Ollie.'

'The food's nice.'

'Any other news?'

'I went to his place. His mother said he's in the States.' It was finally out.

'Oh!'

'She didn't say when he'd be home. I don't think she knew.'

'Listen, Ollie, stop torturing yourself and come home.'

'I'll think about it.'

'I can't wait to see you. Don't forget the people here who love you.' There was an urgency in her voice that surprised me.

In the morning I would get the clerk at Reception to book me on the next available flight to Ireland. I got into bed and lay listening to the murmur of the voices through the partition wall for a long time before I fell asleep.

Chapter Eighteen

The days crawled by and the storms continued. There was no phone call from Olivia to either Lorraine or Queenie. Her story was told throughout Abbeyville, how she had deceived a good man, and then her flight to Venice to seek out the young Italian restaurateur who had left Ireland heartbroken, it was said, having seen her at the altar with Barry.

Gradually, Queenie and Lorraine became accustomed to the gossip. Life continued at the corner shop with meals, daily Mass for Queenie, bingo on Saturdays for her and Lorraine.

The shop was newly decorated, its inspiration drawn from the elegant boutiques of Paris, with mosaic tiles and pale green wallpaper, patherned with trees and birds. The divine underwear was shown off on a trellis rail hung on the walls: bikini panties that fitted high on the hips, slender at the waist, and dipped into a V at the front, half-cup and full-cup push-up brassières, black lace teddies, garter belts and stockings.

White wicker tables and chairs with matching glass tops

helped the customers relax. The Garden of Eden effect blossomed under Chantal's supervision and gave the shop its new name, Temptation. Queenie had to admit that it had all been done with flair and imagination. She was happy to witness the shop's instant popularity with women as well as businessmen.

Chantal had been determined to redecorate in the style of a Parisian boutique. Queenie had anxiously let her have her way, and now it was as luxurious as any shop in Paris she was sure. To Lorraine she groaned, 'Little did I know what I was letting myself in for,' because she wanted her daughter to realise that she had not found it an easy transition, but she was quick too to let Chantal know she approved of it.

Chantal was delighted with Queenie's praise. Her clothes, too, were glamorous. Usually she wore a well-cut navy or black suit with a short skirt to reveal her long legs and a white blouse with a wide collar. Her manner was teasing as she served the customers. When Matt Murtagh, the owner of the bowling alley, shuffled in, asking for a birthday present for his wife, Chantal greeted him with a big smile. He whistled under his breath when she produced an almost transparent nightdress. 'I can't see herself wearing a thing like that. She'd freeze to death.'

Chantal brushed aside his protestations. '*Mais non*. She will adore it. She will feel very loving.'

'You're incorrigible.' Matt chuckled, his hands fumbling with the garter belt and stockings Chantal had left enticingly on the counter.

Chantal reached out and squeezed his hand. 'She'll think

it's nice of you to bother.' Her huge eyes overflowed with warmth. 'And she'll dress up for you in them.'

'She will?' Matt looked as if suddenly he wasn't sure that that was what he wanted. 'You don't know my wife.'

'Trust me.' Chantal smiled.

'Bring it back if it's not suitable,' Queenie said, consumed with embarrassment, 'and we'll exchange it.'

'Thanks,' Matt said. 'It's good of you to go to so much trouble.'

Chantal wrapped the minuscule nightdress in tissue paper, placed it in a fancy green box and tied a huge pink bow around it. There was no doubt about it, she had the touch. The underwear flew out of the shop while the male customers drooled over Chantal and couldn't wait to part with their money. The women liked her too. It was only a matter of getting used to this new way of doing business, Queenie told herself.

'There's something important I'd like to discuss with you,' Chantal said, after Matt left, and they had the place to themselves.

'Don't tell me you're having problems?'

'I'm thinking that we should open another shop,' she said, startling Queenie into momentary silence. 'Eventually we could have a boutique in every city in Ireland.'

'First things first,' Queenie said, regaining her composure. 'Have you discussed this with Lorraine?'

'Yes, and she likes the idea very much.'

'I'll have to think about it,' Queenie said, with her usual caution, but her interest was obvious. With a rush of excitement she thought how perfect it would be for Olivia to have a project like that to concentrate on when she returned. Something to get her teeth into that would take her mind off marriage. She said, 'We'll have a meeting. Talk it over.'

As the days progressed Queenie became more concerned when no word come from Olivia. 'I'm worried, Father,' she said to Father Nobel when he called. 'I'm terrified of what might have happened to her.'

'Trust in God,' he said softly. 'There isn't a single moment of our lives that he doesn't know about.'

'I can't help being worried, and yet I feel so helpless. I'm afraid to say anything, Father, in case I upset Lorraine.'

'You're anything but helpless, Queenie,' Father Nobel consoled.

'I always knew there was more to this whole saga than met the eye. Now I wish I'd done something at the time.'

'What could you have done? Now, don't upset yourself. I'm sure it'll all turn out fine.'

Later that day Lorraine returned from shopping with a pile of parcels. 'Put the kettle on,' she called to Queenie from the shop door. 'I'm gasping for a cuppa. It's bedlam in the city.'

'Where are you going with that lot?' Queenie asked, casting a calculating eye on the mountain of bags, her tone disapproving.

'I had to get a few new things,' Lorraine said. 'Don't tell me you've forgotten I'm seeing the suppliers today.'

'But with Chantal sick I thought you'd postponed it,' spluttered a fretful Queenie.

'I want to see the winter stock so I'll just have to go on my own. At least I got a comfortable pair of walking shoes this morning.' She extracted a pair of moccasins from one of the bags and sat down to put them on.

'Who'll mind the shop?'

'You will. You know the ropes.' Lorraine sighed. 'You'll manage. We're not busy.'

'I haven't much choice.'

Lorraine left her to it and went upstairs to see how Chantal was and bring her the copy of *Paris-Match* she'd bought for her.

By mid-morning the following Friday Queenie hadn't sold one item, apart from a pair of the cheapest tights to Mrs Flood from Park Street. The regular customers who came to see Chantal left, disappointed, except for one man who wanted to buy a present for his daughter.

It was hard to believe, Queenie thought, that this was the same shop she had started all those years ago, now made new with fresh white paint and intoxicating underwear.

Chapter Nineteen

I slipped out and went down to the beach, walking fast on the hard wet sand close to the water. There was no hurry, I could stay as long as I liked because I didn't have to be anywhere at a particular time. I had successfully avoided the shop, and the inevitable questions, by not letting them know I was back. The air was fresh, the village curving away to the left, the long stretch of beach to the right, boats bobbing in the distance.

I was growing used to walking and I liked the solitude of early morning. The mist was lifting, the mournful wail of the fog-horn fading, the anguished cries of seagulls diminishing with the tide.

The sea merged into the clear sky, and as I walked I watched the changing patterns the wind made on the water. My hands in my jacket pockets were cold. I made my way back to the house slowly, let myself in at the back door, and went into the gloomy hall, deciding that I would scrub the place from top to bottom.

Later that evening I went shopping for groceries from the local store, and trudged home past the empty tennis courts, detouring round the village. I found myself at the quayside, and the amusement park. Its fairy-lights glimmered on the water, its piped music carried on the air and the smell of fish and chips was tantalising.

I sat on the wall to eat my chips, listening to the sea, the shooting in the rifle-range, the whine of the bumper cars. As I watched, the setting sun trailed streaks of blood in a turbulent sky. It briefly lit windows of distant houses, plunging their gardens into darkness. It was the time of day when people had returned home, and only a few stragglers were heading for the pub. I stayed there for a while, glad not to have to share the splendour of the evening with anyone.

The light was fading as I set off for home, the dusk bringing a chill to the wind that rustled through the trees heralding autumn with a whispering sigh that was almost a moan. Early dead leaves swirled to the ground. I'd been out longer than I'd intended. Still, it was good exercise. Hearing footsteps behind me I walked faster. I didn't want to meet anyone. I knew that the hurt and grief were evident in my face.

I entered the back garden through a gap in the fence. A slight movement caught my eye from behind the hedge that sectioned off the vegetable patch. When I looked again there was nothing. I went up the path letting the side gate swing after me. Once inside I locked the back door, unpacked my groceries, made myself a cup of tea, and took it into the sitting room. I pulled the curtains to shut out the bleak chill of the evening and the rain pattering against the window-pane. The glow of the lamp livened the place up and soon I had the fire lit.

After supper I went to bed, and fell asleep straight away. In the middle of the night I woke suddenly, thinking I was being suffocated. Spluttering, coughing, I struggled up, unable to make out my own hand in the inky blackness. I lay quietly under the duvet until I began to drift off into sleep again.

Suddenly I heard a light click on somewhere.

Then the door opened slowly and a dark bulk loomed large in the light from the corridor. 'Who is it?' I demanded weakly, my heart thumping wildly. 'What do you want?' My voice had risen with fright. The bulk leaned against the headboard, and I could smell whiskey. The floorboards creaked as he shifted his weight and took a step closer. A hysterical urge to scream overcame me as he touched my breast with the back of his large hand.

'What do you want?' I said, twisting away.

He grabbed my hair.

'Do it,' I said. 'Get it over with. I won't make a sound.'

He let go of my hair, pushed his face close to mine and hissed, 'Don't fight it. It won't do any good.' His stubble was rough against my cheek. He pushed me back so that I was at an angle to him, half lying, half sitting. By now my nightdress was round my waist, his mouth close to my ear.

I found the switch of the bedside lamp. 'Barry!'

He put his hand to his eyes and drew in his breath. 'Christ.' Then he barked, 'Put out that light.'

I couldn't speak. It was all going so fast. We were gazing

at each other, my heart was thumping. I was scared of him. Scared of Barry!

'You shouldn't be doing this, Barry. You're frightening me.'

He stood up swaying, his face red, reeking of whiskey and stale sweat. 'Nice greeting for someone who was nearly your husband.' His voice was ice cold.

'What do you want?'

'I've been hearing from a reliable source just how you like your men.' His laughter rose into a hysterical cry that went on and on.

'Get out of here,' I said stupidly. 'You shouldn't be breaking into your own home. It's ridiculous.' I was breathless.

Suddenly his voice was low and menacing. 'I'll show you what's ridiculous.'

I tried to jump out of bed, but before I knew it he had grabbed my shoulders. 'You can't escape me, Ollie. You're mine and you know it.' His voice was quiet, controlled, then he snarled, 'I was crazy about you, you bitch, from the first time I saw you. And look how you repaid my love.'

'Please—'

'Shut up. I wanted you by my side. I was willing to share my life with you, provide you with a good home and children. Let you have a career, if you wanted one. What I didn't want after we were married was you running around with the whores you call friends.' He was breathing rapidly, and he stood up, the bulge of his erection enormous as he unbuttoned himself. Then, suddenly, his massive body covered mine, he tugged off my nightdress and pushed at me until his penis found its target. I moaned, but he took no notice.

'Please!' I screamed as, with one brutal thrust, he entered me. A flash of pain exploded in me. 'No!' I cried out.

'You asked for it.' His voice was hoarse, his body frantic.

It was useless, I couldn't fight back. Another flash of pain ripped through me, and his determination to 'give you something to remember' brought him to a mercifully rapid climax. He slumped on top of me. 'That'll teach you,' were the only words I could make out among his unintelligible murmurings. Sated, he pulled away from me.

I drew my legs together, squinted at the clock. Five to one. Leaning back against the pillows I stayed quiet until he fell asleep. For what seemed like hours I lay still, my mind restless, my body twitching at every sound. Then I got up, padded silently across the room and let myself out, taking my clothes with me. I crept downstairs, noiseless as a cat, knowing exactly where every creaking floorboard was. In the kitchen I splashed cold water on my face and wondered what to do next.

Everything was quiet and still, my cup unwashed beside the sink. Shivering, I went to the cloakroom to get my coat.

When I got to the back door he was propped against it, a triumphant gleam in his eyes.

I pulled my coat around me.

'You're not going anywhere at this hour. I want to talk to you.' He led the way into the kitchen and ordered me to sit down while he filled the kettle.

Seated at the table I waited while he confronted me, his

hands knotted together, sweat on his brow and in the stubble of his chin.

'You treated me bad,' he said. 'You proved yourself untrustworthy.'

Eyes lowered, I didn't speak.

'You asked for it,' he said. 'You're a cruel bitch, going after other men, not caring who you hurt.'

'Please!' I stood up.

'It's obvious you've been with other men,' he said, standing up and twisting my arm back until I thought he'd break it. 'We were saving ourselves for each other, remember? You lied to me.' He slapped me hard across the face. 'What kind of life could this foreign fellow give you anyway?'

I closed my eyes to steady myself.

'I've been checking up on you. Like a bit of foreign, don't you?'

I stared out at the lightening sky.

'With all your practice you didn't do it very well,' he jeered.

I shifted my weight from one foot to the other.

'Look at me. I'm speaking to you.'

I wheeled round. We glared at each other.

'You asked for it, you know, Olivia.'

'So you've already said.'

'Thought that jilting me at the altar was some kind of joke, did you?'

'I didn't plan it,' I said.

'I'd have expected you to think more of yourself,' he said, tightening his mouth, 'and me. Leaving yourself open to public ridicule.' Looking me up and down he said, 'God, if you could only see yourself.' He gave a short burst of laughter. 'You won't be running home to your mother either.' Standing up, making his exit, he said, 'And you won't get away from me. No matter where you are I'll still come and get you. You'd better toe the line because if you think you're getting off this light you can think again.'

'Leave me alone,' I said. 'It wasn't right between us, wasn't what we'd hoped for. It never could be right between us.'

'You'd know all about that, of course.'

'I never sought out Lorenzo. Never expected to meet him or anyone.'

Barry stopped me with his raised hand. In a burst of anger he said, 'You don't care what happens to me or to anyone as long as you get what you want. You don't give a curse about love and marriage. You want fun and a playmate to run around with. You and your foreign fantasy man. What does he care about you? You'll end up on your own. Wait and see.'

'I don't love you. It's nothing to do with anybody else. I'm sorry,' I said, as calmly as I could.

His head snapped up as if I'd hit him. In that instance I knew that he didn't believe me: it was inconceivable that I shouldn't love him any more. 'I can't make it any clearer than that.' I stepped away from him.

'You've made it plain enough,' he snapped.

I gathered my things together, threw them into my bag. I came back downstairs and crossed the hall to the front door. He was standing in the kitchen doorway, laughing. 'Where do you think you're going?' he asked.

'Please unlock the door,' I said. 'I want to get out of here.'

He came to me and pulled me backwards by my collar, like a recalcitrant dog. 'You're going nowhere,' he snarled.

'Let me go!' I shouted.

'Go and unpack,' he commanded, and let go of me so suddenly that I fell forward against the banister.

Back in the bedroom I sat in front of the dressing-table, gazing at my tear-streaked face in the mirror. If Mum and Queenie knew that Barry had me jailed in here there would be ructions. When would they miss me? Surely they'd scent out that something was wrong.

I recalled Barry on the night of our engagement. He had held me close as we danced, telling me I was the best-looking girl in the place, and what a lucky fella he was to have got me, he'd never let me go. Next morning Mum had brought me breakfast in bed just to hear about the dance. I thought of the wedding that nearly was, the champagne that had never been drunk, the speeches that hadn't been given, the cake that had never been cut, and Mum's flat tone as I'd walked away.

Chapter Twenty

'Sitting here all alone in the gloom?' Lorraine said, coming into the sitting room, startling Queenie.

'I was thinking,' Queenie replied.

'What about?' Lorraine asked.

'I was thinking of all the things that have happened. Hard to believe it's only three months since the wedding day.' Queenie sighed. 'And where were you? You took your own sweet time getting home.'

Since Chantal's arrival Lorraine had been out a lot, and Queenie was torn between relief at her return, and resentment that her daughter was enjoying her new-found freedom. Lorraine placated her with treats from the city: a brack from Bewley's, or chocolates, home-made jam, a cheese.

'So where were you all day?' Queenie asked again, in an injured tone. Lorraine's forays were unnecessary, she felt, especially when she could be doing useful things in the shop and house.

'Monsieur Guilbert insisted on taking me to a fashion show.'

'Waste of time,' Queenie said, miffed at not having been invited too.

'All in the course of business,' Lorraine rejoined. 'As a matter of fact it reminded me of the fashion shows in the Hibernian Hotel years ago. You used to get free tickets for them.'

Whatever business she'd conducted hadn't taken too much out of her, Queenie noticed. She wasn't tired and irritable as she usually was after a day in the city. And there was a smell of drink off her too. Queenie suspected that Lorraine had spent a most pleasant afternoon having lunch and sipping wine into the late afternoon, and now, feeling guilty, was trying to please her with trivial details.

'Do you remember the first fashion show you took me to?' Lorraine asked. 'I must have been about fourteen. You made me a dress exactly like one that was modelled on the catwalk. It was blue with cabbage roses and a full skirt.'

'Of course I remember,' said Queenie, softening. 'Glazed cotton. An Irene Gilbert design. You ripped the bodice gyrating to that awful Elvis Presley music.'

'Jiving, Mother. I loved Elvis Presley.'

'Clothes were clothes in those days,' Queenie said, a far-off look in her eyes. 'The best material, the best cutting.'

'Monsieur Guilbert has an eye for quality,' Lorraine said.

Suddenly Queenie remembered the sheikh who used to sell Turkish carpets door to door. He was the only foreigner she'd done business with. She'd liked him. He'd made her laugh, which was unusual. She couldn't remember any other man who made her laugh. But Chantal was merrier in the company of men than women. Lorraine smiled when speaking to men, but she was more restrained. She hadn't always been restrained like that. Perhaps her age and dignity forbade vulgarity. Women made fools of themselves, Queenie thought, remembering the terrible contortions Lorraine had gone through as a teenager to attract the opposite sex. She'd been so possessive of that Ginger, following him wherever he went.

Queenie thought of those times with revulsion, but then thought, not for the first time, that it hadn't really been Lorraine's fault. She'd expected her father to be always there, reading the paper, smoking, and suddenly, when he wasn't, she'd felt abandoned. She'd married Phil because he represented a father figure. Queenie was convinced of that.

The following Tuesday evening Mrs Breslin, accompanied by her reluctant husband, arrived at the corner shop. Lorraine ushered them into the sitting-room.

What is it this time? Queenie wondered, then said, to Chantal, 'I would have sent them packing.' Eventually her curiosity got the better of her, and she went to join the guests.

Mrs Breslin, thinner and paler than the last time they'd encountered her, was saying, 'I'll have a gin and tonic.'

'Anything that's going,' Mr Breslin said.

'We want to see Olivia,' Mrs Breslin said.

'Olivia's in Italy,' Queenie snapped.

'Still!' Mrs Breslin exclaimed.

'Probably having the honeymoon she was meant to have with our son,' said Mr Breslin.

Ignoring him, Lorraine said, 'She's been gone several weeks,' wishing that Mrs Breslin would say what she had come to say quickly and get it over with.

'The sale of the house has been agreed. Olivia has to sign papers,' Mr Breslin said.

'Why didn't Barry call round instead of sending you?' Queenie asked.

'He's gone off,' Mr Breslin said, 'without a word to anyone. Not that he isn't perfectly entitled to go off. He's done it before. But this time it's different. He's upset.'

'To think that he could have had anyone,' Mrs Breslin said. 'But no, he would wear himself out chasing after your daughter.'

'I'm sure he'll fall in love again and settle down,' Lorraine said, and went to get the drinks.

'I can't bear the thought of him running round after anyone else the way he did with her.' Mrs Breslin sniffed.

'He's a grown man. He can do what he likes.' Mr Breslin sounded unconvinced.

Queenie had visions of him prowling along the city streets, desperate to get away from his mother. Lorraine came in with a tray of drinks and handed them round.

'I went to the house last night. It was all locked up, the grass overgrown, not a sinner in sight. Gave me the creeps it did,' Mr Breslin said.

Mrs Breslin began to weep quietly. 'When I think of the

way she treated my son! Who would have thought it of her? The little minx! The humiliation.'

'Come on, Mother, you're only upsetting yourself,' said Mr Breslin.

'I tried to console him, telling him that any girl would be proud to take his name. I made things nice for him at home. But it's too late. He's been damaged by the whole unfortunate business. Now I'm scared he might have taken his own life.'

'Don't!' Lorraine's voice was shrill.

'Will you stop moithering on?' Queenie was standing up. 'You've got it all out of proportion. Twisted the facts.'

'Really? So I suppose I imagined that the silly bitch wriggled into his affections, then smashed his dreams on the very day they were meant to be man and wife?' Mrs Breslin was standing up now. 'She's had her fun. Now I'm going to have mine. I'm going to see my lawyers to make sure she doesn't get one halfpenny from the sale of that house.'

'She's upset,' Mr Breslin observed.

'I haven't had a wink of sleep for nights on end,' Mrs Breslin stormed.

'I'm not surprised,' Queenie said. 'He shouldn't have gone off like that without letting you know. He's self-centred as only a man constrained by a mother like you could be. He was convinced that just because he was happy Olivia should be too. He wasn't interested in finding out what she wanted. That's why she ran away from him.'

'How dare you?' Mrs Breslin walked to the door. Her husband followed her, clenching and unclenching his fists.

'He only settled for Olivia because he couldn't marry his mother. You're the one he really wanted.'

Lorraine, shocked at Queenie's outburst, and not wanting to provoke further trouble, stayed silent.

'Your granddaughter was childish. She treated it all like a game,' Mrs Breslin said at the door.

'And your son's childish, with his big car and his toys,' Queenie retorted.

Suddenly they were speaking together, neither listening to the other, only hearing what they themselves were saying.

Queenie was seated on a bench in the park, her face tight with worry beneath the brim of her sun-hat as she thought about Olivia. There had been no phone call from her since she'd left for Italy. While Queenie understood Olivia's need to get away from home, she didn't know why she'd had to make such a clean break. In the past Olivia had always kept in touch, no matter where she was or what she was doing. This time she'd gone too quiet, Queenie mused. Worse, Lorraine wasn't concerned because she thought Olivia was having a good time. More worrying still, Barry Breslin had cleared off too. It might be a coincidence, but wasn't it strange that his parents hadn't heard from him and had no idea where he was? And the house he and Olivia bought was locked up, no sign of life there. Queenie sat on, wondering what to do, not in the least bit comfortable with the whole situation.

Queenie, resplendent in her blue suit, and Tommy, wearing his soft brown hat, followed the Misses Drysdale as they pushed through the turnstiles to the showgrounds. Eagerly they made their way through the main hall. Goldie, the elder of the Drysdales, in bright yellow jacket and boots, led the way among the stall-holders selling Irish lace and linen, past magnificent bouquets of flowers. Daisy Drysdale, subdued in grey, stopped them all briefly to admire some species they'd never seen before.

Out at the back were rows and rows of stables. Horses were everywhere, their smell pungent on the warm air. Ladies in magnificent hats stood to one side, drinks in their hands. Tommy nosed around the stables, the Misses Drysdale and Queenie following him.

People buying and selling horses jostled and pushed. Others stood around talking about horses, with no intention of buying. Finally, they went through the crowds to the jumping enclosure where the judging of the championship was taking place. Queenie sat on the edge of her seat. A current of excitement shot through her as she watched the horses.'

The show-jumping took place in the afternoon. One by one the riders cantered into the arena, a rainbow of colour, the silver and gold of uniform crests flashing in the sun as they reined in their horses to take a bow before the judges.

Queen's Glory, the dappled grey Tommy and Queenie had had in mind to purchase since the previous year, came thundering in. He pulled at his bit, and shook his head in protest, before taking off for the first fence, jumping faultlessly. Queenie's eyes followed him while she prayed. He stumbled over the last fence, kicking off a rail, and lost points on time.

Queenie was disappointed. Her hopes had been high. Edgy, she exasperated Tommy with her complaining. Goldie Drysdale had watched Queen's Glory too, as he moved at different speeds. 'I think he's a beauty,' she said.

'Wasn't he a bit clumsy on that last fence?' Queenie argued.

Chapter Twenty-one

I woke up wishing I were dead. The shutters were closed so I wasn't sure if it was night or day. The horror of what had happened bore down on me like a gigantic weight. I pressed my face into my pillow and wept. If only I'd gone straight home to Abbeyville.

Barry brought me a cup of tea and some toast. 'There you are.' He pushed open the door of the bedroom and put the tray on the floor beside my bed. He said no more, but opened the shutters, letting the sunlight in.

He poured himself a cup of tea, and drank it sitting on the chair in the corner, his eyes on me. When I refused to meet his gaze he picked up a newspaper and pretended to read it. If only he'd leave the room I could run to the window and jump out.

As my tears fell, I caught him looking at me coldly. I stared back at him, afraid. He was trying to ascertain just how mad I was becoming. Yes, I was afraid of him, and what was worse, he knew it. Finally I said, 'This place is making me ill. If you keep me locked up I'll lose my mind.'

He said nothing, just smiled at me until I thought I really was going mad. He would throw away the key, keep me here for ever, until I eventually became a lunatic.

Into the silence he said, 'I know what you've done was terrible but you've still got to eat and drink.'

I didn't speak.

Eventually he threw down the newspaper, came to my bedside and took my hand. 'You've got to eat something,' he said, and put the plate of thinly sliced buttered toast beside me. I looked at the window thinking that if I could distract him from it I could escape. I leaned towards him, put my arms around him, let him remove my clothes, my face so close to his that I shook as he held me.

'For so long I'd imagined us being together like this,' he said, 'in this house. Now you know that that foreign fellow was no good, you can forget about him. At best he was . . .' he searched for the right word '. . . a distraction.'

He was speaking as if the marriage had taken place. As if in some bizarre way the fact that we had stood before the altar, had been sufficient, my refusal irrelevant.

Never in my life had I hated anyone as much as I hated Barry Breslin at that minute. And I knew then, too, that he could never have made me happy.

His hands on the back of my neck were cold. 'Relax,' he said softly. 'I'll give you a massage to help you.'

His fingers slid to my throat. I tried to shift out of his grasp. 'Relax,' he said again, laying me face down, massaging my shoulders. 'Let yourself go. There's no need to be nervous. You used to have time for me. What went so wrong?'

'I don't know.' I was caught off-guard by the pain in his voice.

His hands were on my neck again. 'There's no benefit in it if you don't relax.' He spoke impatiently, as if I had a choice.

I closed my eyes, wishing he would take away his hands, knowing that they would be on my breasts next – if he didn't lose his temper and strangle me first. Go along with it, I told myself. Get it over with.

'If I'd only known you were unhappy . . .'

'I wasn't unhappy.'

'In the seven years we were together there wasn't a hint from you of anything being wrong.'

'I'm sorry.'

'We should have spent more time together. I was busy with the business and you were off with your pals. But I wanted it to work. I really did.' He removed his hands. I stayed still.

'There's no point in talking about it now.'

'What else is there to talk about? What else matters? It's affecting my whole life, my business. I'm eaten up with it.' Abruptly he began pacing up and down the room.

I sat up, covered myself with the sheet. He was back beside me again. 'You should have been grown-up enough to come and tell me, not run off like that.'

I was crying, hating myself for not being able to stop.

'What have you got to say to that?' he persisted.

I said nothing. What difference did any of it make now? The damage was done.

'You don't want to talk about it. Is that it?'

'There isn't much point.'

'OK. What would you like to talk about?'

I tried to think of something that wouldn't upset him too much.

'Go on, say it, whatever it is,' he taunted. 'You'd rather talk about the damage I'm doing to an innocent little creature like yourself. Keeping you here against your will and all that.'

'No!' I yelled, losing my temper.

'No need for the hysterics. Good job we've no neighbours. So what are we going to talk about then?'

'Forget it.' I slid off the bed.

He caught my arms and pushed me back. The base of the bed hit the back of my legs as I fell. He bent down to me. 'Calm yourself,' he said, holding me, lifting my face to his. He was grinning. 'Now look what you've done. That always happens to me when I get angry with you. I get excited. You shouldn't make me lose control.'

I turned away.

'I'm going out for a while. I won't be long.' Before he left he closed the shutters, and bolted them in place.

I slept for a while and when I woke I could hear him downstairs, moving around. It was cold autumn weather and the branches of the oak tree were scratching against the window-pane. Mum would be sleeping soundly and Queenie tucked up in her bed, reading.

It was raining when I woke again. I got out of bed and

tried the door. It wasn't locked. The air was chilly as I dressed quickly and went downstairs. There was no sign of Barry. I tested the front door, but it was locked and barred, as was the back door. All the windows were shuttered. I made coffee and carried it into the sitting room, to the warm embers of the fire. I was being held captive as a punishment for refusing in public to be his wife. I stayed like that for a long time. Eventually he came downstairs.

'You look so much better,' he said, coming into the room, red-eyed with fatigue, 'but I do think it was unwise of you to leave your room. I think you should go back upstairs. It's only half past twelve.'

Hostility rose in me. 'I'm staying down here.'

'That's not wise.'

Pushing myself out of the chair I made to leave. He came to me, caught hold of my wrists. Silence stretched between us. I straightened my back against the next onslaught of words, but his voice was soft. 'Don't worry. We'll see this through together.'

I shivered, my shoulders tense, determined not to break down in front of him.

'Will you sleep now?' he asked, taking my arm, leading me back upstairs.

'I think so.'

'Good.'

He locked the door behind me. Back in bed I remembered the evening of the pre-wedding dinner, bidding goodbye to the Breslins, Barry taking my arm afterwards, telling me that he would never let me out of his sight once we were married.

* * *

For the next few mornings Barry presented me with some memory of the wedding, a tendril to tempt my memory, assuring me that he would not let me forget any of the details of my defection. 'Don't interrupt,' he would snap.

'I'm sorry.' If I said that once a day I said it a hundred times. It simmered him down.

'What was I saying?' He'd start again. I could never remember. All I knew was that we were arguing. Usually there was little conversation between us. Mostly, he talked. On the rare occasions I answered it was to argue. That was only when he'd tried my patience to the limit. His words were nasty, aimed like blows to cause the maximum hurt. Occasionally, when he felt things were going well for him, he spoke soothingly, even lovingly. 'I remember a time when you hung on every word I said.'

'You weren't spending your life making me miserable.'

He laughed. 'I've cooked you a nice dinner. Come and eat it.'

Like a child I obeyed. There was no doubt about his power over me. It was building and he was thriving on it. It brought a new brightness to his eyes. I sat hunched at the kitchen table looking out at the garden while he served, moving from oven to table and back with roast duckling, roast potatoes, broccoli, mushrooms. Seating himself opposite me, the candlelight illuminating his face, he said, 'Look at you all hunched up, your face hidden in your hands. Come on, eat up. You must keep up your strength.'

If Queenie saw me now she would be horrified.

'Is it all right?' he asked.

'Yes, thank you,' I said, pushing the food around my plate, careful not to upset him, too preoccupied with my plight to notice what the food tasted like.

'You're not listening to a word I'm saying.'

'Sorry.'

'I went to a lot of trouble with this meal. You could at least make an effort to enjoy it.'

Taking a deep breath I said, 'I'd like to phone home. Let them know that I haven't had an accident or anything. They'll be anxious.' Thinking of Mum and Queenie made me almost choke with sobs.

'Let them think what they like.'

'Don't speak about my family like that!'

'I'll speak about them any way I like. You're deliberately trying to antagonise me and you shouldn't, you know, because I'm in good form this evening.'

'They'll be worried, that's all.'

'Lighten up, for Christ's sake. You're either angry or anxious about something.'

'Sorry.' I put my hand to my forehead to steady my dizziness.

'You're exhausted from the fight you're putting up. Maybe you should have a rest.'

'I'm not tired,' I snapped.

'Nevertheless.' His bright eyes gazed into mine. He was clearly enjoying himself. 'Have a nap.' He left his meal and came to me, helped me up, his head bent towards mine. 'Forget the meal, sleep is more nourishing,' he said, leading me upstairs, then helping me into bed. 'I'll leave you for a while to get some rest.'

Amazingly I slept. When I woke up he was standing over me with a cup of tea. I rubbed my eyes and looked at the clock. It was midnight. 'Here, I have a present for you. Try this on.'

I took the bag from his outstretched hand but made no attempt to open it.

'I thought we'd dress up tonight for a change. Play some music. Dance like we used to.'

Maybe if I engaged in his fantasies, let him have his mindless way, he would tire of me and let me go. I went to the bathroom, showered and put on the dress. It was of black crêpe, with a deep plunging neckline that dipped so low it exposed the full curves of my breasts. I thought of all the times I'd been told by Mum and various friends how lucky I was to have a fiancé who took an interest in what I wore, and who had such good taste. The dress was flattering, there was no doubt about that.

He came to me. 'Wow,' he said, zipping up the almost non-existent back. He was dressed in his best suit. Staring into the mirror he said, 'Let's have a party.'

'Who will you invite?' I asked, my hopes half raised.

'I only want you,' he said, holding me, gazing into the mirror with me. 'You look beautiful, my darling.'

I had never believed I was pretty. Even though I'd inherited Mum's eyes and her features, she had never once told me I was attractive, and Queenie didn't believe in looks. 'Beauty is only skin deep,' she'd say. 'It doesn't last. Use your brains. They'll serve you better in the long run.' When I had become engaged she said, 'Men aren't everything. Get yourself a career.' In spite of her good advice I'd fallen for Barry. Here I was, bowing to his every wish, not even enough brains to plan my escape.

Downstairs, he said, 'I have another present for you.' He unlocked his briefcase and took out a jewellery box but not before I'd seen the gun. My heart leaped into my throat. He was too busy removing a heavy gold chain from a deep bed of blue satin to notice. 'I intended giving it to you on our honeymoon.' I said nothing. 'Here, let me put it on for you.' He placed it round my neck and clasped it. He turned me to face him. 'There,' he said, smiling good-humouredly, pleased with the effect. 'Do you like it?'

I took a deep breath. 'Very appropriate,' I said.

He buried his face in my hair. 'Don't ever try to kill yourself,' he said conversationally. 'You're far too beautiful.'

Was he telling me he knew I'd seen the gun? Gritting my teeth I was determined to say nothing that would cause a confrontation.

'Have a drink.' He got two glasses and put them on the table. The wine was dark red. Slowly I poured it on the new cream carpet.

'Olivia!' he raged. 'What are you doing?' He grabbed my hand, took the glass from it. 'What are you thinking of?' He ran out of the room, returned with the salt, a cloth. Angrily he poured a mound of salt on the stain. 'You're not fit to live in a nice house.'

'I don't want to live here,' I protested. 'You're keeping me against my will, in case you haven't noticed.'

He put a tape in the stereo. The Chimes burst forth with 'I Still Haven't Found What I'm Looking For.' He was at my side, smiling, taking me in his arms. Trembling, I stood stiff and awkward. 'Come on,' he cajoled.

'I don't want to dance.'

'You love dancing,' he said.

For a while he was happy to sway to the music. Then suddenly he leaned down and kissed me savagely.

I squirmed out of his arms and struck his face with the palm of my hand. 'Stop it.'

He caught my hand in a vice-grip. 'Don't ever do that again,' he warned.

'Then leave me alone,' I said furiously, my eyes intent on him.

'You're sexy when you lose your temper.'

'You won't think I'm sexy when I get you jailed for this.'

'Ha!' He laughed. 'I'll tell them I never laid a finger on you. Swear on a Bible that you made it all up, that you were here of your own free will.'

'You're a lying bastard.'

'And you have no witnesses to prove your story.' He hesitated, looked across at me. In that split second I saw the uncertainty in his eyes. 'Anyway,' he smiled indulgently, 'it won't come to that.' He poured himself a whiskey. 'We'll be all right, you know, Olivia, when you accept that I'm for your good.'

'You're stark raving mad.'

'Thank you for the compliment. You have an answer for everything, don't you?'

But I didn't have an answer to this new situation. What alternative did I have now but to do his bidding? How had it come to this?

'All I need now is for you to say, "It's not fair." Go on, say it, you're dying to, aren't you?'

'It's not fair,' I mimicked, to shut him up.

'What's not fair?'

A wave of dizziness swept over me. 'I think I'm going to be sick.'

His voice was gentle. 'Calm down. Everything will be all right, once I forgive you.'

'When might that be?'

'Who knows?'

'I'm going to bed.' This time I left the room of my own volition.

He didn't try to stop me.

I felt dizzy and exhausted as I got into bed. I heard the car engine, the slosh of the tyres in the rain as he drove down the lane. Where did he go in the dead of night? I dreaded to think.

Chapter Twenty-two

Queenie got off the bus in the centre of the village and walked slowly past fields that had been harvested. Her poor, tired legs were done to death. A tractor droned in the distance. She was in the heart of the countryside, in a lane of slanting hedgerows. Further on a powerful man with enormous hands was lifting sacks of potatoes on to a lorry, thinking nothing of it, his brute strength reddening his face. She stopped to ask him directions.

As she walked she thought of childhood trips to the country. Hot summers in her uncle Tom's house, geraniums in pots on the small deep-silled windows that overlooked the purple Galtee mountains. There was an orchard out the back, large Bramley cookers and succulent eaters planted by her uncle, an authority on apples. She thought of him, dead over twenty years, buried in a peaceful graveyard at the foot of the Galtee mountains, but not forgotten. He drove his apples to the market once a week in his big old van, made a good living from them, and provided her family with wonderful holidays. She turned into the last lane before the sea, and walked past the rowan trees, and the overgrown gardens.

Her feet were sore by the time she arrived at the house. Walking up the curving path, gazing at the roof and chimneys jutting into the sky she thought what a monstrosity it was. She wondered what kind of game Barry could have been playing when he bought it. He couldn't have been thinking of Olivia's comfort and happiness. Probably fancied himself as owner of a country estate. Barry was eccentric and he had money. A lethal combination.

The shutters were closed. There was no sign of life. Queenie hummed tunelessly to keep herself company as she walked past the overgrown kitchen garden to the back door. She knocked and waited. There was no answer. As she turned to leave she heard a remote sound, like a chair scraping on a stone floor. She called, 'Is anybody there?' and waited again. She pounded the door, called out, 'Barry, are you in there?' There was no answer. Strange, she thought, and went back down the path.

'Good afternoon,' a woman at the far end of the lane said. 'Lovely day.'

'Lovely.' Queenie's quick appraisal noted her bright smile. 'I came to see if my granddaughter was here.'

In the coffee shop she ate a croissant. The young, neat-looking waitress offered more coffee, brought hot milk, a tiny pot of jam. How healthy she looks, Queenie thought, her feet aching, hoping this respite would dispel the anxiety building up behind her eyes.

A picture of Olivia came into her mind, rushing to meet Barry, returning to tell them all about him. 'A brief fling,' Queenie said at the time. But when Olivia brought him home for the first time that Christmas and Lorraine pronounced him 'perfect', Queenie knew he was there to stay. By perfect Lorraine must have meant the big house on the hill, the bakery, his social status in the town. She had filled his plate with turkey while Queenie observed the dumb shine on his face.

He was a little on the fat side, his hair was a bit wild and his face was too serious, as if he had all the cares of the world on his shoulders. He was a boy in man's shoes. It was understandable that Olivia had run off. The thought of being lumbered with Barry would have sent Queenie running too. Sitting there in the little café she sensed that Olivia had escaped something Queenie dreaded. It had been far from the cowardly, selfish act people had said it was. Only the timing had been wrong. She should have done it sooner.

Lorraine's buying trip to Monsieur Guilbert's warehouse the following week took up the whole day.

The warehouse was full of all kinds of frilly underwear: bras and briefs, suspenders in rich lace, stockings, catering for all tastes and requirements. Men were buying easily, the women serving them not discouraged by their comments.

Monsieur Guilbert said, 'Our new brands are a force to be reckoned with. High quality, wide-ranging cup fitting, good value for money. Models in fashion shows all over the world have worn them.'

'They're an extravagance,' Lorraine said. 'Far too expensive.'

'Money well spent,' Monsieur Guilbert assured her, knowing his reassurance was paramount because she was a new customer and he would have to look after her. 'You shouldn't count the cost when you're buying quality. Years from now your shop will be remembered for the quality. Look at the lace trim, the colours.'

Lorraine recognised the truth of that as she fingered the garments, revelling in their neat perfection.

Monsieur Guilbert waited, a benevolent smile on his face, as Lorraine made her choices. Then she stood at the counter, bargaining for more discount, counting out twenty-pound notes. A look of pure pleasure crossed Monsieur Guilbert's face as he put away the money.

'I must be off,' she said, looking at her watch, picking up her handbag.

'Let me take you to lunch,' he said.

Over their meal they discussed the garments she had seen, Lorraine nervous at first. However, as Monsieur Guilbert rambled on, speculating about the future of her shop, she was flattered by the shine in his eyes, the excitement in his voice. 'You will adapt to this novelty in a surprisingly short time,' he said, his foreign tongue sliding beautifully over his words.

'I thought I was too old for change,' she said.

He laughed heartily. 'You're young!' he exclaimed. 'Your eyes are like a teenager's eyes when you talk about this new venture.' There was a measure of passion in his own as he asked, 'Out of all the stuff you saw this morning, which did you like best?'

Unnerved by his lopsided grin, and surprised at the question, she tried to think of a suitable answer. 'All of them,' she said. She rose and buttoned up her jacket, not giving away that she had seen a glimpse of his feelings for her. Driving out of the city she thought of all the things she would have to get used to. Dealing with men like Monsieur Guilbert was one of them.

Queenie and she argued when she got home. 'I hope you didn't overspend just because that Monsieur Guilbert fancies you,' Queenie said.

'Of course not. You have to trust people sometimes, Mother,' Lorraine protested, but was upset by Queenie's remark.

'What's the matter?' Phil asked, his kind face perturbed. Lorraine told him she was upset because she had quarrelled with Queenie. 'I'm sick of being undermined all the time. And in front of Chantal too.' She sniffed.

Phil said, 'It'll all have blown over by the morning.'

But things didn't blow over. Queenie went around in a superior state as if she was dealing with strangers who couldn't be trusted. Lorraine wished that Phil wasn't so accepting of Queenie, that he would interrupt her sometimes, bang his fist on the table, correct her. His patience and acceptance infuriated her.

That night when she lay beside him the events of her meeting with Monsieur Guilbert slipped into place. A teenager, he'd called her. Suddenly her body felt light, and her breasts ached for new excitement.

The next morning they stayed in bed late and took Queenie to the last Mass. Lorraine thought of Olivia, imagining her dashing around Venice enjoying herself. She thought of Barry, respectable and solid. They should have been married a month now, living in the house they had bought, Olivia caring for him, cooking his favourite meals. How time flies. Not a bad thing for time to pass quickly, especially for Barry. Where had he gone to? Why wasn't he in the bakery?

It was amazing to Lorraine how quickly routine had been re-established. Even the new way of doing things in the shop had evolved smoothly, and the household chores were now split between Queenie, Mary and herself, when she was there. Chantal ruled over the shop and Queenie did the paper work in the evenings. She liked correspondence, sitting at her roll-top desk, going over the order books, the stock, keeping the accounts, paying all the bills.

Yet no matter how busy she was, Lorraine was lonely, which Phil never suspected. He got on with his visits to the market, always hopeful that some day he'd find an ornament, painting, piece of china that would make him rich. 'You took a real chance when you married me,' he remarked to Lorraine from time to time.

'You think so,' Lorraine would say, agreeing, smiling, thinking how open and trusting he was, how lost in his own little world, happy to let her get on with her life. How absurd their lives were, how innocent.

She had to get on with it, be satisfied, gracefully accepting.

It would be stupid to let Queenie get on her nerves, and she must not become discouraged by her mother's lack of faith in her.

Tommy Traynor returned from Doncaster a richer man. Snurge had roared home in the St Leger, and Tommy had had a tip from the tout.

'I won quite a bit on him too,' Queenie said.

'What do you say we buy a share in a racehorse with our winnings?' Tommy asked. 'Could be very lucrative.'

'That's a wonderful idea.'

'I'll find out about it and let you know.'

[illegible]

[illegible]

[illegible] hands and knees. I searched for my shoe but couldn't find it. I crawled up the grassy bank and waited for the pain to subside. Then I hobbled off down the path.

[illegible] the end of [illegible] had grown [illegible] dark. I found [illegible] [illegible] crept down the [illegible] the wall [illegible] When [illegible] the house

Chapter Twenty-three

The bathroom window was open. Hoisting myself up on to the ledge, I swung my legs out and jumped on to the slanting roof of the shed below, slithered towards the edge and prepared to drop to the grass. The wind whipped against me, blowing rain into my face.

My left ankle twisted beneath me as I hit the ground and my shoe flew off. Gasping with pain, I stumbled in the darkness, my chance of a quick escape snatched away. Slowly I got up and tested my foot beneath me. The ankle gave way and I almost screamed. Scrabbling around on my hands and knees, I searched for my shoe but couldn't find it. I crawled up the grassy bank and waited for the pain to subside. Then I hobbled off down the path.

By the time I reached the end of the garden my eyes had grown accustomed to the dark. I found the gap in the hedge, scrambled through it, crept down the road, staying close to the wall, my hand on it for support. When I got to the house on the corner I dragged myself up to the door, and rang the bell. No sound came from within. I rang again and hammered with all my strength. Eventually the light snapped on.

'Who is it?' a woman's voice asked.

'Can you help me, please?' I called back. 'I've twisted my ankle.'

The door opened. A woman in a dressing-gown peeped out. Holding the door between us, the chain still on it, she said, in a Scottish accent, 'Who are you? What are you doing out at this hour of the night?'

'I'm from the house up the road,' I said, clinging to the door frame to prevent myself falling. 'I've had an accident.'

She reached out a hand to help me in. 'What happened?'

'I'm in trouble,' I said, suddenly choked up with tears.

'Jim!' she called out, shutting the door firmly against the wind. 'Jim!' she called again. 'Get down here quick.'

'What is it?' A young man came reluctantly downstairs in his pyjamas, his voice hoarse with sleep.

'The wee girl here's in trouble,' she said. 'She's from the end of the laneway. Help her on to the sofa, will ye?'

'I twisted my ankle,' I explained, limping forward.

'Take your time,' he said. 'Here, let me help you out of that jacket. It's soaking. I'm Jim Goodall.'

The woman's eyes widened as they travelled from the dirt on my hands to the bruises on my arms. 'You've had a bad fall. That knee's nasty too.'

I looked down at the cut in my knee.

'Shall I call a doctor?' Jim asked.

'I don't need a doctor,' I said, flinching at the pressure of his hand on my swollen ankle.

'Just making sure there's nothing broken,' he said. 'I think you'll live but it's a bad sprain. You have to rest up for a wee while.'

'I'm sure that won't be necessary.' I put my weight on it to prove the point, and fell back into the sofa with the pain.

'Let me bathe it for you – get the swelling down,' Jim said, and left the room.

'How did it happen?' the woman asked.

'I fell into a pothole.' I was unable to think of any other excuse.

She laughed. 'You should write and tell Gay Byrne. I'll make you a pot of tea,' she said.

'That's very kind of you.'

Jim returned with a basin of water and a bottle of Dettol. Carefully he submerged my ballooning ankle in the water. 'That should do the trick. Can you bear it for a little while?'

'Yes, thank you. It's very good of you.'

'Let me see to that knee,' he said, dabbing it with Dettol. It stung.

'You haven't been living here very long.'

'Only a couple of weeks.'

'We've been on at the council about those potholes,' Jim said.

'Where were you heading for?' the woman asked, handing me a mug of tea.

'I was on my way to the bus terminus.'

'There are no buses at this hour,' the woman said, concern in her voice, 'and it's lonely along this laneway at night.'

Jim smiled amiably. 'You can take your ease. No need to rush off. Let me get you a proper drink, then I'll drop you back.'

'Oh, no! Thank you. If I might use your phone?'

'Certainly,' Jim said, winding the bandage around my ankle and bringing it up my leg. 'There you are. Right as rain. Keep it off the ground as much as possible.'

The shrill ringing of the doorbell made me jump. The woman's head jerked up. Jim's eyes caught mine, saw the fright in them.

'I'll get it,' he said, making for the door.

'What a night it's turning out to be,' the woman said.

The pounding on the door interrupted her.

'Is there somewhere I can hide?' I asked pleadingly.

'Take her into the bedroom, Ma.' He gave me a brief smile.

The front door shook violently with the next pounding. 'I know you're in there,' Barry's voice cried out.

'All right, all right. I'm coming,' Jim shouted. Grim-faced, he went slowly to the door.

'Where is she?' Barry demanded, bursting through the door, pushing past Jim.

From the bedroom I could hear his footsteps marching down the hall into the sitting room.

'There's no one here,' the woman said.

'I don't believe that,' he said. 'Olivia!' he shouted

Somewhere a dog barked, and Barry roared, 'For the last time, where is she?'

Jim said, 'Calm down. Have a drink.'

'I don't want a fucking drink. I want her.' I heard him leaping up the stairs and he had reached the bedroom door. He flung it open.

'Don't go in there,' Jim shouted.

'Ah!' Barry was smiling, brandishing my broken shoe. His eyes were glassy, and sweat glistened on his forehead. 'I knew you wouldn't get far.'

'What do you want?' I asked.

'I want you to come back home with me.'

'No.'

He wagged his finger. 'Naughty, naughty,' he said, stepping towards me.

I moved back.

Cold with fury, his right hand in the inner pocket of his jacket, he said, 'Are we ready now?'

I knew he could pull out his gun in a flash so I made no attempt to pull free as he put his arm around me.

'We're off,' he said to Jim, leading me towards the door.

'I hope you'll be all right.' Jim looked anxiously at me.

'She'll be fine. I'll take care of her,' Barry said.

'Fine,' Jim said, turning to go. Then, with one swift leap he was on top of Barry, driving his fist into his face. Barry scrambled to his feet, blood spurting from his lip, the knuckles of his clenched fist white. Jim swung at him again and Barry's knees buckled under him. As he slid to the ground his head struck the sharp edge of the doorknob. He fell in a heap on the floor.

Jim dropped to one knee, felt Barry's pulse, ran his hands over his body. 'He'll live,' he said, removing the gun from Barry's inside pocket, and holding it to his throat. 'All right. I've got you now.'

Barry mumbled incoherently and groaned. His eyelids fluttered open.

'Try any more stunts like that and you're a dead man,' Jim said. He sat Barry up, then pulled him to his feet. 'On your way,' he said, half dragging, half carrying him out of the door. 'Now clear off or I'll call the police.' Coming back into the room he said, 'That'll cool his ardour.'

'I'm so sorry to have caused you all this trouble,' I said.

'I don't blame you for running off on him. He's crazy.'

'I know.'

'We'd better go before he comes to. Would you like to phone your family to let them know that you're safe and on your way home?'

'Yes, please.'

'We'll be off, then.'

In the car Jim said, 'He must have done something terrible to you.'

'He kept me imprisoned in that house,' I said, and then I told him everything, about the wedding and how I had dumped Barry at the altar.

'I admire your courage,' he said, 'getting away from him like that. You're a brave girl. But you must have suspected that he was a rat when you ditched him like that.'

'Not in my wildest dreams did I ever imagine he was that bad.'

Jim glanced into the rear-view mirror. 'There's a car behind us.' His face was expressionless. Just as I turned to look back the car overtook us and shot ahead, travelling so fast that it swayed from side to side before it disappeared around the next bend.

'That's him,' I said.

Jim turned left down a lane. 'We'll wait here for a while,' he said.

Chapter Twenty-four

It was strange to stop in front of the corner shop and see it so changed, but Queenie was waiting inside the door. When she saw Jim's car she came forward to embrace me. Mum was behind her and, Mary was hovering in the background.

'Olivia.' Queenie's arms were around me. 'We were frantic.'

Mum and I looked at each other. 'I'm sorry,' I said to her, and waited for her to say, 'I told you so,' but she only took me in her arms.

'Come on in. You'll have something to eat with us?' Queenie said to Jim.'

'No thanks. I'd better head off. I'll call in to see you, Olivia, when you've settled down.'

'I can't thank you enough for all you've done,' Mum said, shaking his hand.

Jim blushed. 'Anyone would have done the same.' He left

quickly. 'Take care,' he called to me, before getting into his car. 'I'll phone you.'

'I'm thrilled you're back home,' Mary said, then removed her apron. 'I only waited to say hello.'

Nothing had changed in the living-quarters. My bedroom was the same, the bed made up. I paused at the window, looking at the church spire. Here I was, back in my own bedroom.

'You're safe and sound now,' Queenie said, bringing me a mug of tea. 'All's well that ends well.'

When I'd stumbled into Jim's cottage, rain-soaked and terrified, I wasn't sure if I'd ever make it. Now, as I touched the silver hairbrush Queenie had given me on my twenty-first birthday, I couldn't believe I was home. Nora, a birthday doll from Queenie, was where I'd left her. I had loved the annual ritual of the birthday trip to the city to choose a doll, and Queenie loved buying them. I had chosen this sweet-faced rag doll on my ninth birthday, because I couldn't resist the soft tendrils of red hair falling from beneath the poke bonnet that matched her smocked dress. I remembered the journey home, my arms weighed down with her. That Christmas Queenie had made a whole wardrobe of clothes for Nora from old scraps of material in her work-basket. She even made her a midnight blue coat trimmed with white fur from an old rabbit collar. Now I sank my face into her. She gave me the same comfort she had provided when I was a child.

'Tea's ready,' Mum called up.

The clock ticked loudly in the kitchen.

'How's the shop doing?' I asked.

'Wonderful,' Mum said. 'Chantal's marvellous. She has a way with the customers. And wonderful ideas.'

'Good.'

'She gets on well with everyone, doesn't she, Mother?'

Queenie nodded. I couldn't think of anything else to say.

Chantal came in for her tea. In black leather skirt and high heels, her nails painted cherry red to match her lipstick, she looked like a film star. '*Bonsoir*,' she said. '*Je m'appelle Chantal.* You are Olivia, *n'est-ce pas?*'

'Yes.' We shook hands.

'I've heard all about you,' she said, smiling.

I was mortified.

Father McMahon called to check that I was 'safely home' as he put it.

'Well,' he said eventually, lifting his glass, 'here's to your homecoming.' He waited for me to say something but, still lost in the shock of it all, I sat silent. He listened while Mum spoke of some of the dangerous things that had happened to her in her youth, and Queenie made an effort to join in, the priest's presence making her feel obliged to fill the gaps.

'You'll stay for supper, Father?' Mum asked. It was a mere formalilty. She assumed he would.

'If you insist,' he said.

Later, I went for a drive with Trish. We skirted the city and took the road to Abbeyville. The weather was cold for the time of year and dusk was settling over the town, shadows lengthening. 'I'm always in trouble of one kind or another.'

'Stop fretting. You're home now.'

I assured Trish that I was all right, but I wasn't and she

knew it. Finally I told her everything that had happened from when I had set out for Italy.

She was appalled. 'You must be feeling terrible.'

I recalled my imprisonment. 'No one to talk to, that was the worst part,' I said. 'I can't believe how stupid I've been.'

'No, Ollie. You've been unfortunate.'

The summer was over. It turned cold. Life went on. I slipped further into introspection. 'I'm perfectly all right,' I reassured Mum.

Mum and Queenie were like watchdogs: they sat looking at me as if they were sure I was about to explode. I spent days on end either in bed or soaking in the bath, keeping out of their way. Queenie kept coming upstairs to see if I needed anything. For the few short hours I was up she would follow me around the house.

'You'll wizen up like a prune if you stay in that bath too long,' she'd admonish me. But I couldn't help it. I tried to act as if I wasn't shaking all the time, as if I could find the armholes of my sweaters.

Eventually Queenie's concern for me got the better of her. 'I have to talk to you, Olivia,' she said. 'Something terrible has happened to you. It's all to do with Barry Breslin, isn't it?'

I wanted to tell her everything. In the end all I said was, 'He kept me imprisoned in the house.'

'I knew it!' Queenie blazed. 'I'll report this to the police.'

'Don't,' I pleaded. 'We can't afford to get involved with the Breslins. Besides, what would the neighbours say?'

'To hell with the neighbours.'

'What about Mum? She'd have a fit if she knew. Please don't tell her, Queenie.'

Like a wounded animal I crawled into my bed and lay there for days on end, refusing food, drink, company, not getting up except to trek to the bathroom and back.

'She's very sick,' was all Queenie said to Mum, and she was right.

Apart from crying most of the time I withdrew into myself, and stayed in that dreamlike state. It rained continuously. I lay watching raindrops chase each other down the window-pane. I'd made a mess of my life, and Queenie's sad old face was tight with worry as she paced up and down outside my bedroom door,

The minute darkness descended, my bedroom became a place of pure terror. I lay paralysed in bed, my eyes on the street-lamp outside. If I shut them Barry became the maniac who would enter and kill me the moment all the lights in the house went out. It was the same every night.

I should have told Queenie I was afraid. She would have sat with me and talked to me comfortingly like she did when I was a child, but to confess my fear would have been to admit what had happened to me. And that would have drawn down fury against the Breslin clan, the thought of which I couldn't stand.

'You look very nice,' Queenie said to Chantal one evening when I came downstairs to find her all dolled up. 'That colour suits you.'

'Thank you,' Chantal said delightedly. 'Are you getting

dressed up, Olivia?' she asked, humming as she arranged cocktail sausages, and titbits on plates. 'We're having a little party to launch the winter stock.'

Her enthusiasm had the effect of an open window on a stuffy room. 'In fact, I think you'd better get ready,' she said, looking me up and down. 'In a quarter of an hour the shop will be open and you have no makeup on.'

'I'm sure no one will notice,' I said.

'Of course they will,' she said briskly, glancing at her watch. 'Go and put on a sexy dress. I'll lend you some false eyelashes, and let you use my Christian Dior perfume.'

'I don't want to look sexy.'

'Of course you do. It'll cheer you up.'

In less than an hour the shop was full. Chantal passed among the customers with a jug of punch, Mum poured wine. Queenie remained in her seat behind the counter. Voices chattered, faces smiled, as more people squeezed into the shop. Chantal poured punch for the men, vying with Mum in simpering, steering them towards the new stock.

Women chatted with Mum. 'Excellent,' was the verdict on the new brands as money was handed over and items were wrapped with speed. A long-haired woman whom nobody knew objected to the prices.

I watched Chantal in action: she was a free spirit, uncluttered by family, the responsibility of conventional behaviour and 'standards'. Her flirting was gloriously refreshing. 'I don't know how you do it,' I said, marvelling at her skill.

'Simple.' She lowered her voice. 'The men who come in here are in search of erotic adventure. I am helping them to discover their dreams by listening to them and recognising their needs without considering them foolish.'

'I can't imagine any of the middle-aged married men I know seeking erotic adventure,' I said, glancing around.

'In most cases the wife would rather hang up her suspender belts and be done with it. But he can't imagine why she doesn't want him in the same way, so he buys her sexy underwear to encourage her. Sometimes it works, sometimes it doesn't.'

'And when it doesn't?'

'He buys it for someone else.'

I gazed at her long-lashed eyes, her lustrous hair.

'No woman knows exactly what goes on in her man's mind,' Chantal continued, 'but mostly she doesn't bother to find out.'

Queenie, who had been listening, threw her eyes heavenwards. 'You do talk rubbish sometimes, Chantal,' she said, and went to talk to Mr Murphy, the school principal, about vandalism and thieving.

Chantal didn't argue. I found her casual approach to men and morals refreshingly wholesome in this town of hidden marital strife. I wished I could talk to her alone, tell her the terrible things that festered within me. 'I wish I was like you,' I said, under my breath. It sounded childish but it was meant as a compliment.

'You are,' said Chantal, and suddenly I wasn't surprised that she thought that. There was something remote about her – and something in me, too, was unassailable since my return and my silence.

'It's business,' Chantal explained further. 'I make sure the customer is happy. *Voilà!*' she said, wrapping a pair of silk stockings. 'People spend lots of money in the pursuit of happiness. I do myself.'

Then Trish appeared at my side. 'Come and meet the girls from work on Thursday night,' she said. 'A few drinks and a bite of food afterwards. It'll get you out of yourself.'

I imagined having to get all dressed up. 'No, thanks,' I said. 'I'm not up to it.'

'Oh, come on! It's Sandra's birthday. You remember Sandra, in Shoes? She's a laugh! They'll all be there, and they'd love to see you. I know they would.'

But I didn't want to go, didn't want to do anything.

After everyone had left we put away all the underwear, Chantal teaching me the art of folding and packing with precision. Her pleasure in attacking a pile of garments, arranging them in neat, uniform groups to return to their boxes or shelves was obvious. The radio was on softly in the background and when Kylie Minogue came on with 'Tears On My Pillow' both of us sang along together.

The cold weather made Chantal irritable. She stayed in, was silent in the evenings, often sulky. She couldn't be persuaded to take a walk. I was getting by, though, learning something from all that I'd been through. One thing I knew for sure was that I hadn't got over Lorenzo. I could still remember everything about him, how he could strike shocks off my body by his touch, his long, curving limbs, how tender his skin felt. I shivered, recalling my willingness to be overwhelmed by his passion.

I was in a trance, unwilling to share my feelings with anyone. I tried to convince myself that it was a period of recovery, but I knew it was really a period of illness.

'You fuss about everything,' Chantal said. 'I think, So what?, and do as I wish.'

'I don't know anyone who can do as they like,' I said.

Chantal shrugged. 'I can. Now stop fussing and go out with your friend,' she ordered.

I had a shower and sprayed myself all over with Cool Water. I put on my new jeans and the pale grey top I'd bought as part of my trousseau. Brushing my hair back I let it fall loose around my shoulders, and appraised my reflection as I applied a little makeup, not wanting to draw attention to myself.

We drove to Redmond's where Sandra, Cindy from Cosmetics, Betty and Irene from Groceries and Willie from Trish's office were waiting.

'Happy birthday.' I handed Sandra the parcel Chantal had wrapped beautifully.

'I hardly dare open this in front of these men,' she exclaimed, peeping at the pale lilac French slip in its bed of white tissue paper. 'It's gorgeous,' she said, holding it up for inspection.

'If that doesn't do the trick, nothing will.' Larry Moore, the Kitchens manager, laughed. 'She's been after the boss for years,' he said to me.

'I have,' Sandra agreed.

'If you slip into that and slip into his office some evening when he's working late, you might get lucky,' Larry advised.

Irene, touching the lace, said, 'One of these should be compulsory in every girl's wardrobe.'

'I heard about your new shop,' Sandra was saying. 'I'll definitely have to pay it a visit now.'

'Who hasn't heard?' Larry joked.

'It's amazing.' Trish sighed. 'I wish I were rich enough to buy one of every item in it.'

'For your trousseau?' Irene asked.

Trish shook her head. 'I'm not ready for commitment yet.'

'You mean, Dave isn't.'

They all guffawed.

Trish laughed. 'You know how attached he is to his mother's cooking.'

'Are you working in the shop, Olivia?' Larry asked.

'Not at the moment.'

'Who wants another drink?' Trish called, diverting Larry's attention.

When the pub was so full and the smoke so thick that I thought I was going to choke, I said, 'I think I should be getting home.'

'No, you don't,' Sandra said. 'You're not getting away that light. Have another drink. It's my birthday.'

'How about coming back to work with us?' Larry asked, determined to put me at my ease. 'We're looking for a demonstrator who'll go from store to store. A week here, a week there. You wouldn't be stuck in one place all the time, and the money would be better. There'd be a petrol allowance too.'

'I'll think about it,' I promised him.

'Who knows? You could get to the top in Kitchens one day,' Sandra said, and everyone laughed.

'She's right,' Larry said. 'It's a good company with a sound product.'

'It's worth thinking about,' I said, and watched him go to the bar. That's when I saw Barry, also at the bar. He took his drink and moved away with exaggerated care, looking neither to right nor left, choosing a table in the other corner. He took a newspaper out of his pocket and propped it up in front to him. I held my breath, knowing that he'd seen me. Larry returned with the drinks. I said to Trish, 'Don't look now, but Barry's here.'

'Where?'

'In the corner.'

I stood up, excused myself. Trish followed me across the room.

Chapter Twenty-five

The morning mail lay open on the desk. Nothing urgent to be dealt with – it was Friday and I was looking forward to a quiet weekend. There was a memorandum from Chantal, which detailed certain changes to the shop to accommodate the increasing stock. In the lead-up to Christmas we women had banded together, working all hours to get everything ready. Over the past year terrible things had happened to me, which had devastated me and left me vulnerable. Now I was working hard, hiding the trauma I'd endured under a cool exterior, and a pleasant manner. Queenie was surprised at how diligent and shrewd I was becoming, and told me so repeatedly. Later in the morning, folding away a batch of tights newly arrived from Paris, I heard, 'Olivia!'

I looked up and blinked in surprise. 'Jim.'

We stared at one another. 'How are you?' he asked.

'Fine, thanks. How are you?'

'Great.'

In the grey business suit he looked well. Stockily built, muscular, he was about my height. I hadn't noticed that he was good-looking and sexy – yes, definitely sexy.

His presence was unsettling, though, bringing the memory of Barry flooding back. 'I wasn't expecting to see you again so soon,' I said.

He leaned towards me. 'Are you feeling better?'

I blushed. 'Not too bad. I'm getting back to normal. What are you doing with yourself?' I asked, to take the focus off me.

'I'm working for a computer company in Sandyford. Would you like to come to lunch with me?'

'That's very kind of you.' I looked at my watch. 'I could go now, I suppose.'

'Smashing.' He grinned boyishly.

'The Nook do a good lunch, if you don't mind queuing.'

'Great.'

I locked up, and followed him out the door. We took our places in the queue. 'What would you like?' Jim asked, reading the menu from a blackboard on the wall.

'Greek salad, I think.'

Jim was surprised. 'You won't get fat on that.'

I made a face. 'I don't want to get fat.'

'I don't blame you. You're perfect as you are,' Jim looked me up and down admiringly.

'Thank you.'

When we were seated I began to relax. 'What have you been doing with yourself?' I asked.

'Bit of sprinting, weight-lifting. There's a gym near the office.'

'You like to keep fit?'

'Comes in handy if I have to rescue a damsel in distress.' His eyes glinted with amusement. 'Have you heard any more from Barry?'

'No.' I cut him dead.

'Sorry. I didn't mean to pry. You're trying to forget all about him and I come barging in bringing it all back.'

'I should be able to talk about it, but I can't. I told Queenie what happened, but I've kept Mum in the dark. God knows what she thinks.'

Jim said, 'Might be for the best. She'd go mad if she found out.'

'The strange thing was that no matter how much I told him I wasn't in love with him any more it didn't sink in.' I was opening a tiny door, letting in a chink of light. 'He was my first boyfriend, and that made things even more difficult.' Tears stung my eyes.

'You'll find a new one.' Jim's eyes glittered.

'It's not as simple as that.'

'I couldn't agree more. You always imagine you'll never fall in love again, and it's silly, really, I suppose.' He sounded as if he knew what he was talking about.

'It was silly to have ever thought I could make it work with Barry. Sillier still to have thought that I could get away from him.'

'Don't be harsh on yourself. He's sick.'

'He wasn't always like that.'

'It took courage for you to decide not to marry him. But how's life treating you now?'

'I like being back home. It seems essential to my sense

of identity. For the moment anyway. Of course, I won't stay there for ever.' Without warning I dissolved into tears. 'Sorry,' I said, ashamed and embarrassed.

Jim took my hand. 'You poor girl,' he said.

I kept my head down. He leaned closer to me. 'You've been so unlucky,' he said. He clenched his fist. 'I should have finished that Barry off when I had the opportunity.'

'Don't be daft.' I laughed through the tears. 'But maybe I'm not doing as well as I thought.'

'Perhaps you should see someone,' Jim said gently.

'Who?'

'A counsellor or a psychotherapist. Someone qualified to help you deal with all of this. Bottling it up may not be the answer.'

My tears stopped abruptly. 'You think I'm going mad, don't you?'

'Of course I don't.' There was nothing but kindness in his face.

Relieved I said, 'Why did you suggest I see a counsellor, then?'

'To help you sort yourself out.'

'Maybe I should. Mum and Queenie are exasperated by the fact that I refuse to go out with my friends.'

'I don't blame them for worrying about you. It must be awful for them to see you so unhappy.'

We looked at one another unaware of the clatter in the background.

'I know of a therapist who has a great reputation. Would you like her name and address?'

I sat up straight, watching the door in case someone I knew came in. Spying Mona Corcoran out of the corner of my eye, I said, 'Yes.' Then, desperate to change the subject, 'Tell me about your new job.'

'There isn't much to tell – I'm only there a couple of weeks – but so far so good. Long hours, up to eighteen at a stretch sometimes. Lots of holidays as well, though.'

'The money to afford them?'

'Of course.'

We finished our coffee.

'I'll walk you back to the shop.' Jim led the way out.

'Thanks for the lunch. I enjoyed it.'

'We must do it again.'

'Are you coming in to say hello?' I asked, when we got to the shop.

Jim glanced at his watch. 'I've got to be back. Next time. Tell them I was asking for them.' He leaned towards me and kissed my cheek. 'Take care of yourself.'

I watched him walk to his car.

'You should ask him to dinner sometime,' said Mum, when I told her he'd called.

'We've no time for entertaining at the moment,' Queenie snapped and began talking about the shop, the subject closest to her heart.

'What do you think, Phil?' Mum asked.

He raised his head. 'About what?'

'The renovations.'

'What renovations?'

'Forget it.'

* * *

Dr Fenlon, the psychotherapist, was a neat little woman, with tight-permed hair and a warm smile. She began by saying, 'This form is for our medical records. I'd also like you to answer a few questions about your life.'

My stomach turned to jelly.

She smiled. 'Don't be nervous.' Her pen aloft and a sheet of paper in front of her she added, 'This is strictly private and confidential. If you meet me on the street or anywhere at any time, don't feel you have to say hello to me.'

'OK.'

'Let's write a little history of your childhood.'

I recited the names of my parents. She wrote them down.

'Was it a happy childhood?'

'Yes.' I fidgeted, knowing that if I were to start at my earliest memory I'd be worn out by the time I got to the nub of the problem.

'Go on,' she encouraged. 'Begin at the beginning.'

I had dim memories of dark rooms, and blinding sunlight when the shutters were opened. Memories of food and clothes and children's parties came next. I could remember customers in the shop whispering dark secrets, me standing behind the counter, next to Queenie, in my little beige coat with the brown velvet collar. Other memories of Mum catching me playing in the street with Trish and Doreen, in our good pumps, when we should have been at dancing class, or hanging from my window calling out to the boys. My first period was frightening: the white linen sheets bloodstained, my nightdress ruined, Queenie coming into the room, alarmed, Mum changing the sheets and the subject at the same time, Dad alarmed at the fuss.

'Were you happy?' Dr Fenlon asked.

'Yes. My father was absent a lot, but that didn't seem to make much difference. Everything went on as normal.' I warned myself not to give away too much.

'Are your parents happy?'

'Yes, I think so. The fact that they scarcely see one another and that there's a twenty-year age difference seems immaterial. There's a bond between them.'

'You get on well with your mother?'

'Reasonably so. She expected so much for me from this marriage. Now she sees me as a distorted version of herself, someone who made a lot of mistakes.'

'Do you think she's disappointed in you?'

'Definitely.'

'What was it about Barry that put you off?' Dr Fenlon looked at me squarely.

'Another man.' I gave a light embarrassed laugh.

'All the same it must have been a terrible shock when he turned on you so viciously.' Dr Fenlon said.

I pondered this. 'When I think back there *was* something inhuman about him, something remote, elusive.'

'But he'd never been violent.'

'No.'

'Were you very frightened of him?'

I shook my head. 'I was too furious with him at first. We were furious with each other, then, for a while, we lived in that intimacy of hatred. At what point he frightened me, I can't remember, but all my energy evaporated and so did my resistance. The hatred was replaced by numbness. All I wanted was to die, to get beyond pain, beyond harm. I thought about death a lot when I was locked up. I thought that if some night it stole a march on me, removed me from the living hell he'd put me in, I wouldn't put up a struggle.'

Dr Fenlon looked at me intensely. 'You don't really mean that.'

'I would have welcomed it with open arms. Not that it was always like that. Sometimes I longed to see Queenie and Mum again.'

She listened.

'Barry was clever. He made sure I survived. Watched me like a hawk. Everything was so wrong between us, yet he seemed to grow more attached to me, and didn't mind the awful long evenings we spent together. Occasionally he cried and that made him seem more human. Other times he paid no attention to me. Certainly he never listened to a word I said so, in the end, I stopped speaking altogether.'

'How did you escape?'

'Sometimes, at night, when everywhere was locked up he would drive off, God knows where, and not return for a couple of hours. One night he forgot to shut the bathroom window.'

'And now? What do you want now?'

'I'm not sure. I like working in the shop.'

'Do you like dressing up, going out?'

'No.'

'Boyfriends?' She arched her eyebrows.

'I'm not really interested,' I said. 'I'm particularly averse to the idea of marriage.' The idea of being alone for the rest of my life was even more frightening and unpleasant, but I didn't say that. 'I know I'm lucky to have a home, a job, enough to eat. Yet I feel like a fish out of water.'

'There are lots of things we do in the pursuit of happiness, but its attainment has nothing to do with any of them. What we don't realise is that happiness is an elusive condition, not easily analysed. Things are not always the way they seem.' Suddenly she said, 'Have you told your family about this?'

'I haven't had the courage to tell my mother or say much about it to my grandmother,' I said, anguished.

'What did you tell her?'

'I tried to describe it to her without horrifying her, and I found it impossible.'

'It's your experience. Really, it has nothing to do with anyone else. What do you want of life, Olivia?'

'To be happy.' I felt tears behind my eyes. Suddenly I laughed. I couldn't help it. The laughter wouldn't stop. Dr Fenlon was unperturbed. 'Sorry,' I said, and laughed again, inexplicably.

She waited patiently. 'I'd like to see you again, soon.' She was businesslike. 'This is not going to be unravelled in one session. How about coming back in a fortnight?'

Chapter Twenty-six

It was spring and the days were brighter. I visited Dr Fenlon every fortnight, walked a great deal in the fresh air, worked all day in the shop and sometimes drove to the city to look at other shops and compare notes. There were nights when I couldn't sleep. In my dreams I would relive the nightmare of incarceration. Sometimes Queenie would shake me into wakefulness. I would cling to the edge of the bed whimpering and she would sit with me until I felt drowsy again. Only once did I dream of Lorenzo, a long, sexual dream that I woke from covered in perspiration.

I bought new clothes. A black trouser suit for work, a dress for evenings. It was April, a new month, a new year. Hopefully, a better year.

'How's everything?' Queenie asked, poking her head around the door one Monday morning.

'Fine,' I said.

'You got a minute?' Her voice was urgent.

'Yes, of course.'

She shut the door carefully behind her and marched across the room. 'I want a word with you before that bloody Chantal comes down.'

'What's the problem?'

'She's moving out.'

'Oh! She didn't say anything to me.'

'She told me she's got a place of her own.'

'I suppose that was inevitable. She's not leaving the shop, though, is she?'

'No.'

'Well, what's the problem, then?'

Queenie sighed. 'God knows what she'll get up to when I'm not around to keep control. Now, if she were a good girl like you are, that would be a different matter. But she's not. I have to keep an eye on her all the time.'

'You can't control her life outside working hours, Queenie. That's not fair.'

'Really?' Queenie drew her mouth down. 'What if she gets involved with unsuitable company and gets a reputation? It wouldn't do us any good.'

'So far Chantal has behaved perfectly well.'

'That's because I sat on her. But I'm telling you the minute she gets a place it'll be the talk of the town.'

'The topic of the week,' I suggested.

'You know what men are like where she's concerned.' Queenie grinned ruefully as Chantal came into the shop at the same time as Una Gun, manager of the Nook.

'Can I help you?' Chantal asked, all smiles.

'Just looking.' She picked up a hand-embroidered slip.

'That's not your size,' Queenie snapped.

Una stared at Queenie, then moved awkwardly to another display. 'Very expensive,' she remarked to Chantal.

'Oxfam's at the far end,' Queenie retorted.

Una scurried out.

'What eez your problem?' Chantal turned on Queenie, furious.

'She never buys, messes up the place. Can I help you?' Queenie said to a man, who praised the shop and said, through moist lips, that he was looking for the large sizes.

'I'll deal with this.' Chantal pushed Queenie to one side, and laughing an elegant, high laugh, pointed to the extra-large rail at the far end, behind the silver Gossard bust.

There was something suspicious about his behaviour and Queenie, her eyes never leaving his face, wasn't having any of it. 'Have you found what you fancy?' she queried, in her high commanding voice.

Quietly, he slunk out. Through clenched teeth Chantal said to Queenie, 'You frightened him off.'

'Disgusting type,' Queenie observed. 'Coming in here, poking around, sniffing and squeezing. I've never seen the like.'

I looked at Chantal. We roared.

Uneasy, fidgety, Queenie was about to say something. Instead she donned her hat and coat. 'I'm off to collect me pension,' she said.

'Don't rush back,' Chantal called after her. 'Have a coffee.'

'Cheeky strap,' Queenie said, and left.

'What is ze matter with her?' Chantal asked innocently.

'She's a bee in her bonnet.' I shrugged.

'I don't understand.'

'She's fretting about something.'

I knew what Queenie's problem was. The shop had lost its challenge since Lorraine and Chantal had taken over. She had always thrived on challenge, and playing guard dog to them left her frustrated. She missed the wheeling and dealing that kept the juices flowing. No one consulted her about anything to do with the day-to-day running of the business any more. The struggle that she had always thrived on was over.

Chantal eyed me shrewdly. 'I'm moving out. She told you, *n'est-ce pas*?'

'Yes.'

Chantal sighed. 'I can't stand her bossing me around. Oh, we are polite to each other and civilised, but she's too sharp for me.'

'She's marvellous for her age,' I said, looking on the bright side, thinking Queenie should have been beyond criticism, knowing, of course, that she wasn't.

'*Merveilleuse*,' Chantal mocked, throwing her hands up in despair.

'She looks after you well. The food's good. You're kept warm.'

'I hate the food. It makes me big.' Pettishly she blew out her jaws. 'All I want when I'm finished work is a Cognac and soda. I'm bored with living here.'

'Mum's very fond of you.'

She looked at me and for a moment I thought she would deny this. Instead she said, 'I want to go dancing, have dates, come and go as I please.'

'Where's the flat?'

'Blackrock. You must come and visit me.'

We sipped our coffee watching early-morning shoppers, mainly women, march busily along, their shopping-bags held aloft.

'Why are you really moving out, Chantal?'

'I met someone when I was in London. I'm hoping he will come and stay with me for a leetle holiday.'

'Oh!'

'Queenie wouldn't approve.'

'No, she certainly wouldn't.'

The sun struck the street, a blade of light searing off the new office block. Chantal, sleek as a cat, sat by the window soaking it up, her eyes narrow against its brilliance.

She was about to speak.

I waited. 'What is it?' I asked finally. 'What were you going to say?'

She searched for the right words. 'You don't miss it?' she asked eventually, in a whispery voice.

'Miss what?'

Chantal glanced towards the door to make sure nobody was coming in. 'Sex,' she hissed.

Taken aback I said, 'No.'

'Not even *un tout petit peu*?' She measured a tiny space between thumb and index finger.

I shook my head, recalling Barry's rough hands yanking

my hair back, and the smell of boozy breath. Seeing the revulsion in my face she moved closer. 'My new boyfriend has the magic, the fireworks. It's like nothing on earth. You must know what I'm talking about.'

A shiver ran down my spine. I wanted to cry.

'I don't blame you for not fancying ze Irish blokes. Zey is hopeless. It's all over in a couple of seconds, then they roll over and snore.' She spoke with regret.

'Here's a customer,' I warned.

A man wanted to buy the red satin ensemble he'd seen in the window. Humbly he sought Chantal's advice on size.

Queenie, coming into the shop, said, 'What's keeping you?' to him.

'Take your time,' Chantal said, in the low, pulsing voice she used with male customers.

'You can't go biting off the heads of the customers like that,' I said to Queenie over supper.

'That Chantal gives me the pip. Anyway, the shop's overcrowded with us all,' Queenie complained.

'I know. We need to expand.'

'What?'

'That's the easy solution. Get another shop. A big shop with a wider range of goods.'

Queenie's eyebrows shot up.

'The lingerie market's not big enough to sustain the customer. We'll have to produce something else.'

'Such as?'

'Perfume! Our own label blended by a perfumery in France

to go with our line of lingerie, beauty products, that kind of thing. What we need to do is capture more customers yet maintain our name for quality with a more popularly priced market.' Leaning forward I took Queenie through my ideas step by step. 'Why don't we try and get a foothold in the city where there's a larger, younger population?'

Queenie was silent, thinking.

'We could pull it off. We did in the past.'

'I see you've been thinking.'

'More than that, I've thought of every aspect of it.'

'Except where the money'll come from.'

By the expression on her face I could see that Queenie was interested in the idea. 'The last thing I want to do is put you off, Olivia,' she said. 'You're making such an effort to forget the past and get on with your life. But it's a big undertaking.'

'There's another thing,' I said. 'If we tighten our belts here, cut down on expensive stock Mum's been ordering from Monsieur Guilbert, we'll be able to afford a wider, more versatile range.'

'But the number of men that come through that door looking for that stuff . . .' Queenie protested.

'I hate to tell you this but they're not all buying. They're coming to see Chantal. If we were to supply the same quality but from a cheaper source, they wouldn't know or care about the difference.'

There was a slight pause.

'Where, in the name of God, will we get that quality cheaper?'

'Buy in bulk from Parisian warehouses. We need to expand our range too. Go for more variety in underwire bras, bikini briefs, thongs and deep suspender belts. More colours, too.'

Queenie was silent for a minute. 'You have certainly thought it all out.'

I smiled. 'You'll think of a way of financing it.' Queenie was the one person I could trust.

Queenie's face tightened. 'Oh!' she said. 'I haven't been paying as much attention to the books. Left it to Lorraine when she accused me of penny-pinching.' She lifted herself out of her chair and walked slowly to the window.

'You could become more active in the shop. Make more than an occasional visit, if only to stir things up. See for yourself what's going on.'

'I hate the atmosphere. Chantal's so morose these days. I can't even guess what goes on in her mind.'

'Boyfriend trouble?'

'Boyfriend trouble indeed,' Queenie scoffed. 'She should keep her troubles to herself.'

'Don't worry about her. She's well able to make the men behave themselves.'

'All the same,' Queenie said. 'I wonder is it more than men that Chantal has on her mind?'

'What do you mean?'

Queenie shook her head, her eyes narrowed under her wrinkled lids. 'I couldn't say at present.' She would have to go over the books again, study them carefully.

Chantal's place was dark when I got there.

'I'd never guess why you chose this place,' I said.

'What a day.' She groaned, flicking off her high heels, massaging her toes. 'I am peessed off. And I'm broke.'

'How come?'

'First of all I spend a whole day in the shop. This maniac come in and wasted my time telling me he want to go to bed with me. He said he could tell from looking at me that I needed it. I got him out before Queenie came in. I had to pay the rent and now I'm broke. The guy I met in London hasn't contacted me. The bank won't lend me any more money. This is a crazy place. They only lend you money if you have it already. If they don't give me more money I won't be able to stay and I will have lost the rent.'

I felt sorry for her. 'Take a lodger,' I said

She shook her head. 'I need my own space.' She took a bottle of wine from the fridge, Camembert and rolls.

Suddenly it occurred to me that it would be nice to have a place of my own too, away from Queenie and Mum, and a good mate to share it with.

'What about if I come and stay with you for a while? Until you get straight.'

Her eyes narrowed. 'Queenie wouldn't approve.'

'On the contrary, she'd be delighted to have me as chaperone.'

'*Merveilleux*.' Chantal laughed. 'Have some cheese. It's the perfect ripeness. *Bon appetit*.' She poured wine and bit into a roll.

We drank too much. Chantal rolled a joint, wrapping it in thin paper, damping the edges with the tip of her tongue as she talked about abandonment, isolation, men in general. 'Stupid,' she said, over and over again. She spoke to herself in French, all meaningless to me. I wished I could help.

'Write to him,' I suggested. 'Invite him over again. He may need a bit of coaxing.'

She didn't see it that way. As far as she was concerned she was a failure, with the misfortune to attach herself to a succession of unsuitable men. If she'd been insignificant in appearance or ugly I would have understood. But she was beautiful and it didn't make any sense.

I didn't know how to help her. I hated men and the idea that I could be fulfilled only with a man made me feel sick. But it was my hatred of Barry that disturbed me most. No matter how hard I tried I couldn't shake it off. I wished with all my heart that I could.

'Trish is having a bit of a party tonight. It's her birthday. Want to come?'

Chantal brightened. 'I'll change.'

She returned in a short black dress, her face freshly made up, the scent of Giorgio all pervasive.

'You look gorgeous,' I said, admiring.

'*Érotique*. Tonight I will go out on the town and drive men wild.' She lifted the phone. 'Starting with the taxi driver,' she said, with a wink.

I didn't doubt her. No man could fail to notice her cat's eyes and deep plunging neckline.

At the party she said, 'I am going to enjoy myself, not like the rest of you,' distancing herself from us, something she'd never done before.

All night she danced frantically, centre-stage, laughing, rocking back and forth, her eyes glinting in the light.

When I told her I was going home, she said that she was having a good time and wouldn't be leaving until the small hours. Watching her, I wished she could meet someone nice, settle down.

Suddenly Barry barred my way. He stood there, a bottle in one hand, a cigarette in the other. 'Peace-offering,' he said. 'Let bygones be bygones.'

I stared past him at the opposite wall. I couldn't breathe. I couldn't hear what he was saying. I didn't need to. I'd heard it all before. He looked angry when I didn't respond. I turned and pushed through a group of people towards the door.

Chapter Twenty-seven

Queenie returned to the shop full-time, much to Chantal's disgust, and sat erect, alert, missing nothing. Each morning she arrived as soon as Chantal had pulled up the blinds. While Chantal arranged the racks, Queenie checked the stock. She loved the early mornings in the shop. She would sit near the window, watching it all, and count her blessings.

The past no longer troubled her. Olivia was safe and sound. And to her that was more important than anything else. She felt better, and her renewed energy was centred on the business. Olivia was right. The shrewdest move would be to open another shop.

That April morning she settled back into her chair, unlocked the drawer of her desk and took out a folder. Her mouth set in a line of concentration as her eyes travelled down the columns of figures. It would mean starting all over again, pitting her wits against the business adversaries of the city. Everything she owned would be on the line. Lorraine would object. But the business she had built up single-handed was hers and hers alone. She could do as she wished.

Lorraine, with her dogged loyalty, could not be bypassed and her instability had to be taken into consideration. Lorraine was self-indulgent as her father had been: deep down she was as untamed as the day she ran off with Ginger, and as unhappy as the day she returned with baby Billy. For all her appearance of respectability and *savoir-faire* Lorraine was to be pitied, married to that useless husband of hers. Her life was tragic, really.

They didn't talk much these days, Lorraine and she. In fact, they were barely on speaking terms over the handling of Chantal. The French girl's indifference to Queenie's feelings, her skittish behaviour with the men, and her tantrums angered Queenie. But her angry outbursts had no effect: Chantal remained aloof in her presence. Queenie froze as she thought of Chantal gallivanting around in the most scandalous manner and dating the customers – mostly the married ones. But what could she do about it? Sack her? That wasn't an option. Chantal did the job she was paid for and did it admirably.

Olivia was her main concern. Queenie felt a rush of love when she thought of her granddaughter, solid, hardworking, dependable. She was turning out fine, had Queenie's own vision in business, and was willing to weigh up situations, make compromises. Where the shop was concerned Olivia kept things in perspective and didn't let her personal life intrude. Given the supervision of her own shop, Olivia would continue to grow and gain a good understanding of every aspect of the business. For years now Queenie had been training her, preparing her for the day when she would take over.

Her initial shock at the sight of Olivia when she returned had been replaced by a ferocious anger against Barry Breslin that she kept hidden while she continued to monitor her granddaughter's progress. Evaluating her worth in business was one thing, watching her like a hawk during her recovery from her ordeal, praying that there would be no repercussions, was another. Queenie knew that whatever had happened to Olivia might have been much worse. As she turned Barry Breslin's name over and over in her mind, she was unable to subdue the nagging suspicion that he was still a potential adversary. She had nothing to go on but instinct, which had never let her down. Queenie knew that somehow Olivia had outwitted Barry Breslin and had left him in some desert of his own making. He was now an enemy, and a powerful one at that.

The idea of acquiring a new shop filled her with fresh energy. Faced with the dilemma of what location to choose, she waited and watched, and scoured the property pages, until she found the ideal premises in the *Irish Times*. It was beside the fire station in Donnybrook, a desirable area, close to the city centre. Queenie realised that immediate action was imperative.

Rather than use up her cash for this venture she would lease the equipment for the new shop. She would love to get her hands on that property in Donnybrook, but she had to be careful. If they kept to the plan she'd mapped out, things wouldn't go wrong.

She returned her folder to the drawer, locked it and put the key in her pocket. Chantal was at the dentist's; Lorraine was shopping, due back at eleven. She would be on time. Queenie lifted the phone, a smile hovering on her lips. As she spoke to Mr Hill her confidence grew.

Later on she said, 'I've decided to go and look at these premises,' showing Olivia the advertisement.

'That would be perfect.' Olivia kissed the top of her head.

'Hold on a minute. We haven't seen it yet.'

'I know by the advertisement. Oh, Queenie! You're the best woman in the world.'

'Go on with you,' Queenie's voice was gruff. Head bent, eyes moist, she sifted through some papers. 'There is a lot of considerations, mind. I won't decide anything until I'm sure it's the right place for us, and that the leasehold's in order.'

Chapter Twenty-eight

May, with its green freshness, brought something to look forward to. I reassured myself as I unpacked the stock in our new shop, Paradise, that I would forget the past and everything that went with it. I would make a new start.

The shop had been redesigned by Chantal under Queenie's close supervision. Glass panels divided the two fitting rooms, wall mirrors created an illusion of space, and glass cabinets displayed eye-catching new perfumes and beauty products, introduced to lure customers into spending more of their hard-earned cash.

Pristine white and floral designs, in cotton and stretch lace, featured heavily in the collection for the young and sporty. Classically designed co-ordinated ranges, in gold and black, were also on show. Glamorous underwired and padded bras, matching briefs and suspenders, patterned and plain, lined the walls.

People queued up to get into the opening party, their

faces pressed to the window. A man tried the door, then a second man. 'We're not ready yet,' Chantal, back from a week's holiday at home in Paris, called. 'We open at eight o'clock,' pointing to her watch.

'You don't speak English?'

'What do you zink I'm speaking?' Chantal looked at them as if they were mad.

'Hey, lads, look at her! She's lovely.'

Queenie was first in the receiving line to greet the customers, I was beside her as manager, then Mum and lastly Chantal.

The shop was full and Queenie, moving among friends and acquaintances, looked happier than she had for a long time. She was proud of the shop, her new 'baby', and I felt fearful that I wouldn't live up to her expectations. I took a glass of wine and got caught up in a group of people inspecting the perfumes.

It was the culmination of weeks of preparation. Queenie had called a meeting and had detailed, in a harsh voice she hadn't used for years, everything she wanted done. But it was evident that no matter how she couched her requests Chantal would do things as she always had.

Wine and savouries were served. Chantal had dressed the window. She had a penchant for matching colours and ensembles with style. Jim crossed the floor to the perfumery, glancing at the eye-catching, inviting displays. People were coming and going, looking and buying, lured by the soft lights and seductive music. An excitement hung in the air that had been absent in the corner shop. I loved the activity.

The aunts arrived. Aunt Statia was so thin she was almost transparent.

'Who's that lovely young wan?' Uncle Cecil said.

Queenie gave him a warning glance.

'Over there.' He was pointing to Chantal, who smiled triumphantly at him as if to say, 'I know you can't resist me,' and said, 'Ooh la la,' as he reached out and touched her arm. His unsolicited adoration surprised everyone, except Chantal, and annoyed Queenie, whose eyes were far too bright from her couple of glasses of wine. She led him away, saying to the air, 'Being the object of so many men's desires doesn't make her public property.'

Chantal glared at her.

Mum said, 'It isn't Chantal's fault that men chase after her.'

'No?' Queenie rapped out clearly. 'Of course it's her fault if she acts like a whore.'

'Mother, you don't mean that,' Lorraine gasped, hoping Queenie would retract her statement.

'I do.' Queenie flounced off.

People were all talking at once, but glancing over their shoulders. I kept my eyes on Queenie's retreating back as she moved through the crowd in a blur of blue, heading for the door, Uncle Cecil firmly in her grip, Auntie Tess following.

'Beetch,' Chantal said, through clenched teeth, her eyes blurred with tears.

'It's—'

'Hello,' Jim said. He was holding a bottle of wine in one hand, a bunch of lilies in the other.

'Jim!' I said. 'How lovely to see you.'

'What beautiful flowers,' Chantal exclaimed. 'I'll put them in water. Some wine?'

'I like your shop.' Jim stood before the watercolour painting of a Greek goddess, the name Paradise picked out in a golden halo around her head. 'I think you should do very well,' he said.

'You zink so?' Chantal smiled as she handed him the wine, Queenie forgotten, her charm and efficiency enticing him towards the clothes. 'Would you like to buy a present for that somebody special in your life?' she asked, shooting a glance towards me.

There, before my eyes, Jim was transformed into a discerning customer, purchasing presents for his mother, his sister, and all his family if Chantal had had her way.

'Perhaps.' He laughed.

He drove me home.

'Will you be all right?' he asked.

'Fine, thank you.' I gave him a goodnight kiss on the cheek. Then slightly dizzy, I turned away.

'Ollie, I'd like to take you out sometime,' Jim said, catching me by the elbow. 'Will you come? On a proper date?'

'I'm not ready to get involved with anyone.'

'You don't have to. An occasional meal together or a show isn't getting involved, is it?'

'I suppose not.' But I felt nervous even though it was Jim, the kind man who'd rescued me.

'I'll phone you,' he said, and was gone.

*   *   *

Chantal got to know the new clientele, and kept them coming back with her bargain sets and special outsize offers. Queenie saw to the accounts, and with Mum's careful management the stock was holding. We had discovered several new sources of supply whose prices were keener than Monsieur Guilbert's.

Things were going well, I reflected, contemplating the future of the business as I looked through the photographs of our new spring range that were to be used as advertisements. I placed them against the background of sharp white wall. They stood out beautifully. The delivery van arrived just as Jim called into the shop. 'How are sales?'

'Very good. We've been pretty lucky so far. Lots of interest.'

'Well done. You never cease to amaze me.'

'Don't sound so surprised.' I laughed.

'Oh, I knew you'd go far, but this is all so sudden.' Catching my fingers across the counter, he squeezed them. 'You're working too hard, though.'

'I'm feeling much better now. Truly I am. My visits to Dr Fenlon have done me the world of good. I'm sleeping much better too.'

'Isn't it time you had some fun, though?'

'I am having fun.'

'Not the kind of fun I've got in mind. Going places, meeting people. Dating!'

'I don't want to date.'

'Surely you haven't written off men just because of Barry Breslin.' Jim watched for my reaction keenly. 'We're not all like him. And you don't realise how attractive you are, how sexy.'

'I haven't the time, to be honest. I don't want a man around at the moment. I'm too busy.'

'See? It's back to business – and what a lonely life you're letting yourself in for.'

'I'll worry about that when the time comes. For the moment I want to look after myself. I get a kick out of it. I don't want anyone dishing out advice.'

'Sorry. I shouldn't have interfered.'

'No, I'm sorry. I didn't mean to be rude.'

Chapter Twenty-nine

'Queenie,' I asked, 'have you ever thought of us making our own brand of lingerie?'

She looked at me askance. 'Are you out of your mind, girl? Haven't we enough to be going on with?'

'Wouldn't it be exciting, though? Manufacturing our own exclusive ready-to-wear Paradise ranges? We could do made-to-measure too, if we liked.'

'We wouldn't have that volume of sales, Olivia.'

'We could sell to other retail outlets all over the country. Do exclusive parties.'

'That would mean employing designers, machinists, not to mention acquiring premises. Think of the advertising and promotion we'd need. Sure that alone would cost a fortune. It's so much easier to buy well-established brands.'

'We could get Monsieur Guilbert to organise the making and labelling of our brands.'

'I suppose so.' She regarded me thoughtfully. 'If we were to consider it we'd have to get bigger premises.'

'We could keep an eye out.'

Queenie smiled. 'You're persistent if nothing else.'

A few weeks later, Queenie said, excitement in her face, 'I think I've found what we're looking for.'

'And what are we looking for now?' Mum's voice was tolerant.

Queenie pointed to the newspaper. 'Breslin's bakery is closing down. There's an article in the newspaper about it.'

'What?' I was stunned.

'If this report is anything to go by they've run it into the ground.' Queenie smiled, a hint of mischief in her eyes.

'Is it actually on the market?' Mum persisted.

'No, but we could approach the owners. It isn't as if they're strangers.' Queenie looked puzzled. 'I can't understand why Barry Breslin let his business slip through his fingers.'

The report in the business section of the *Irish Times* was there for all to see. It seemed that everything we needed for the expansion of the business was there, and Queenie read out the details: 3,000 square feet of floor space, offices, staff canteen, a shop-front, sheds at the back. 'It's ideal, right here in the town,' Queenie went on. 'With flair and expertise we could easily turn it into a large shop.' Her lips were set resolutely as she turned the pages.

'It's far too big!' I exclaimed

'We could lease some of the space to Tommy Traynor

for a betting shop. He's looking for somewhere in the town centre.'

'What a good idea.' I shot her an admiring glance.

'I don't think we should consider it,' Mum said. 'Who in the world would have thought up such a thing only yourself?' She continued indignantly, 'Of all the notions you ever got in your life, Mother, this has got to be the worst. And the Breslins of all people.' Mum was horrified.

'Business is business,' Queenie snapped. 'I know from past experience that you can't allow feelings to dominate decisions.'

So this was Queenie's way of striking back at Barry. Over the next week she laid her plans. First she called a meeting. 'Barry Breslin had become excessively careless about his business, and left it to his father to deal with,' she told us.

'God help us.' Mum sighed, leaning forward to look at the newspaper, putting it down quickly. 'The whole idea stinks. You should know better.'

'Calm down, Lorraine,' Queenie said, her lips compressed. It was obvious that Queenie was dying to get her hands on the bakery and turn it into her own little enterprise. Convinced that the premises were suitable, she wasn't going to be put off.

'Barry Breslin wouldn't sell to us. He hates us,' Mum said.

'We've got the cash. He needs it. That might persuade him,' Queenie pointed out. 'And that place is perfect for us.'

'It's a good idea to get Monsieur Guilbert to organise the manufacturing end of things,' Mum said. 'He's reliable, his garments are top quality, and he's never let us down.'

'It's a necessary move if we're to compete with the big stores,' Queenie insisted. 'By producing good-quality cheaper goods we can capture the more popular-priced markets, and eventually sell to the retail trade.' She sat back, satisfied with her little speech.

'It's risky,' Mum said.

'Think of the savings on import duty, transport, packaging,' Queenie offered. 'Monsieur Guilbert can absorb all those costs in his overall charge to us for his services. I'm sure he'll be reasonable.'

'It's either that or shut up shop when the British moguls move in,' I told her.

'How much will it cost to do all the refitting of the shop?' Mum asked anxiously.

'I've discussed it with Mr Hill at the bank. He's analysed every aspect of the plan. Here are the figures he gave me.' Queenie passed them across the table. 'We can build on what's there. One way or the other we should do it reasonably with local builders.'

Mum took the proffered pages.

Queenie had already studied the figures. 'Builder's fees, building materials. He's done his homework all right,' she said. 'Yes, I think it's a good idea to have our own brands. Well done, Olivia, for thinking of it. You're on the ball.'

'Thank you.' I was delighted. Her approval was of paramount importance to the scheme.

Mum said, 'Who'll design them?'

'Chantal's aunt,' I said. 'She's worked for all the leading lingerie houses in Paris.'

'Another bloody Frenchwoman! I was afraid of that,' Queenie said.

'Who else knows the business like the French?' Mum was enthusiastic for the first time.

'Who indeed?' Queenie conceded, a smile in her candid eyes. 'We'd have to start small, keep down the running costs.' She was getting down to basics.

'What about staff?' Mum asked.

'There are plenty of out-of-work staff from the bakery. We'll advertise.'

'Good idea,' I said.

'What would they know about lingerie?' Mum asked.

Queenie gave her one of her penetrating looks. 'With their jobs at stake they'll soon learn.'

'We'll get a designer who knows about shop management to design our brands,' I suggested. 'Have the place effective immediately it's ready. No penny-pinching on the equipment either.' I had their undivided attention.

'Where will the money come from to fund all this?' Mum asked.

'We'll sell this place,' said Queenie, 'move lock, stock and barrel into the bakery.'

'Do you expect us to live there too?' Mum was horrified.

'No, of course not. We'll buy the Breslins' house.'

'What?'

'Make a clean sweep of it.'

'Is it for sale?' I asked, horrified.

'If it isn't now it will be,' Queenie said. 'They're bankrupt.'

Mum's jaw dropped. 'How are you going to deal with Mrs Breslin?'

'Leave it to me.' A smile hovered on Queenie's lips as she closed the subject.

Queenie, a tough negotiator, had every confidence that she was equipped to deal with this, and that I, too, had developed into a shrewd enough businesswoman to handle it. With the success of the new shop my confidence had grown.

Mum wasn't convinced. 'Surely you should be a lady of leisure by now, Mother, enjoying little luxuries like holidays, staying in nice hotels playing bridge instead of buying that awful bakery, and that cheerless house. It'll put us in hock for generations to come.'

'It's a bargain,' Queenie snapped, 'which I find I can't resist.'

'The bakery is one thing, but what will Barry have to say about you buying his home?' Mum glanced at me.

'He finds money irresistible, like the rest of the Breslins,' Queenie said.

'Don't be surprised if he turns nasty, and don't say I didn't warn you.' Mum left the room.

'Why is she acting like this?' Queenie asked, puzzled.

'I suppose because we didn't consult her.'

'What have we been doing for the last hour except consulting her?'

'Ah, but your mind was made up.'

Queenie laughed. 'You've got the measure of me, Olivia.'

'If I don't have it by now I never will.'

'Right. I'll prepare a list of builders' names.'

Lorraine was tossed about in the sea of Queenie's ideas. Queenie never felt the need to explain anything, and if her ideas were misunderstood or carried out wrongly, she lost her temper, and never allowed for the inadequacies of others.

Mollified and strengthened by the attentions of Monsieur Guilbert Lorraine phoned him to ask him if he'd consider supplying the Paradise label. He sent her flowers and took her out to lunch on a beautiful day when the air was crisp.

While they ate Monsieur Guilbert talked about the success of the project, and told Lorraine how beautiful she looked. The wine made her head swim. He promised his support. He was her knight in shining armour, her saviour from Queenie. It wasn't just the business that interested him: he was interested in her too. It struck her that she was in love with him.

Queenie phoned Tommy Traynor. 'I'm going to buy Breslin's bakery,' she told him.

'I can't imagine you going into the bread business, Queenie,' he said, surprised.

'I'm going to turn it into a couple of shops. Would you like to lease space in it?'

There was a pause before Tommy said, 'I'd prefer to buy some.'

'Done.' Queenie smiled to herself, knowing that she could do with the extra capital.

In Queenie's dining room we were grouped uncomfortably around the table, Queenie at its head, then Mr Hennessy, Mr Hill, Mum, Madame Renard and myself, briefcases and computers at the ready. We exchanged pleasantries as we waited. Tommy Traynor came into the room, followed by a tall man with a beard.

'Let me introduce Bernard Bellows. Mr Bellows is the architect who designed and built some of the largest shopping centres in the country.'

'Good morning.' Mr Bellows nodded at the group, opened a large portfolio, and placed a sketch on an easel. 'This drawing is the altered version of the bakery.'

At that moment Mary entered with a tray. 'Sorry to disturb you,' she said, banging it down on the table.

'Thank you.' Mum's eyes rushed her out of the room.

Mary closed the door quietly behind her. Mum dispensed the coffee.

'What I propose,' Mr Bellows went on, 'is to keep the façade the same, but incorporate within this area a restaurant, a couple of shops, a children's play area. A car park to the rear.'

'This isn't a shopping centre, is it?' Queenie asked suspiciously.

Bernard Bellows answered patiently. 'I thought of having more than one shop in the bakery, a combination, clothes shop, or gift shop, or a coffee shop and restaurant. I've loads of ideas.' He leaned back into his chair, a wide grin splitting his face.

'In time we'll need the other outlets,' Bernard Bellows explained patiently. 'In order to maximise the facilities we will have to buy the site behind it. It's a commercial site, owned by Sam's Shoe Repairs, which can be acquired on good terms. This gate at the front, with its tall archway, will be a feature. We can use it as a logo for all our advertising.'

Queenie should have employed an architect of her own. It had been a mistake to let Tommy Traynor engage this know-all on her behalf with his gates and archways. Tommy's enthusiasm to take a shop in the bakery had bowled him over with high-falutin' ideas.

'There's just one thing,' Queenie interrupted.

'Yes?' Bernard Bellows waited.

'Won't these be very expensive?'

'We're at the exploratory stage, Mrs Boyle. Everything here is open to suggestion.'

'You obviously know what you're doing, and it's certainly a fine structure. What'll we pay for it with?'

Heads turned to Mr Hill.

'This proposal will appeal to certain people with business interests already in the town.'

'I have a team of builders standing by to start,' Bernard Bellows said.

'So we have,' Tommy backed him up.

'I'd think we should keep the commercial investment to a minimum,' I said.

Mum nodded distractedly.

'That shouldn't be a problem,' Mr Hill said. 'I have a lot of interest. I'll pick and choose.'

Mr Hennessy nodded his approval.

Mary stuck her head round the door. 'There's a telephone call for Olivia.'

'If you'll excuse me . . .' I said, standing up.

Bernard Bellows folded his sketch and placed it in his portfolio.

Chapter Thirty

'I have a proposal to make, and I hope you'll hear me out,' Queenie said, easing herself into a chair in Breslins' drawing room, her sharp eyes on Mr Breslin.

'Fire away,' Mr Breslin said.

'We've been discussing your problems and we think we have a solution that would suit everyone concerned.'

'I see.' Mr Breslin stroked his chin.

'We find we have a use for your bakery. We would pay a good price for it, taking it over in its entirety.'

Mrs Breslin sat upright on her chair, po-faced and unyielding. 'Impossible,' she declared.

'Let's hear what they have to say, Bernie.' Mr Breslin threw his wife a cautionary look.

There was silence.

Queenie noted the interest in Mr Breslin's eyes. 'I've done some investigating, talked to certain people. It seems your company is shaky financially. I'm prepared to purchase the bakery immediately.'

'Sounds good to me.' Mr Breslin rubbed his hands.

'There's one condition,' Queenie said.

'What's that?' He cast a glance at his wife's direction.

'That you sell us the house as part of the deal.'

'The house is not for sale.' Mrs Breslin rose from her chair.

Queenie sat up, straight as a reed, and faced her. 'That's not the information I was given. Mr Smith, the auctioneer, assured me that it is indeed for sale by private treaty.'

Mrs Breslin shook her head. 'Not to you.'

'We'll leave it so,' Queenie said, rising stiffly. 'Come on, Lorraine. Let's go.'

'Hold on a minute.' Mr Breslin turned to his wife.

They looked at each other with the desperation of two people caught in a terrible dilemma.

'You and I go back a long time in business, Queenie,' Mr Breslin said. 'I used to deliver the fresh loaves to you meself when you had the lodgers, remember?'

'That's not today or yesterday,' Queenie conceded.

'All we're asking is a fair deal. We don't want to part with the house, and with cash for the bakery we could hold on to it. Wouldn't you say that was fair?'

Queenie said, 'In order to buy the bakery I have to sell the corner shop, living quarters and all. We'll need somewhere to live. So, you have no choice, if you want cash and a quick sale.'

'The bakery will sell independently of you, and the money

from the sale will enable us to keep the house,' Mrs Breslin's voice was slow and insistent.

'You could be a long time waiting. There's a recession and, if my memory serves me right, you haven't got the time,' Queenie reminded them. 'Anyway, who's going to make you an offer as quick and as fair as mine?'

The look Mrs Breslin gave Queenie was one of pure hatred. 'You'd like to see us on the scrapheap.'

'There's no need to be abusive,' Queenie said. 'We've made you a good offer. Taking everything into consideration it's the best you're likely to get. As I said, we've got ready cash, and a purchaser for the corner shop.'

'We're not interested.' Mrs Breslin moved towards the door.

'That's it, then.' Queenie rose slowly. 'Come on, Lorraine. We'd better go.'

'Wait!' Mr Breslin's tone was conciliatory.

Queenie said, 'There isn't much point in continuing this discussion unless we're talking about the whole lot.'

Mrs Breslin's face was gaunt, and anxious.

Mr Breslin sat down. 'I have a great deal of respect for you, Queenie,' he said. 'I've always admired your honesty and fairness. You can imagine my shock when I discovered that Barry was running up debts, borrowing against the business, bleeding us dry. Now we find ourselves destitute.'

'I can't believe Barry was so foolish.' Queenie sat herself down again. 'Tell you what, we'll pay the full asking price, which is more than generous. But you must accept an offer for the house too. That's the deal. Otherwise, we'll buy somewhere else and you'll go into liquidation.' Queenie looked directly at him. He turned to his wife.

Mrs Breslin wailed, 'I'm still the majority shareholder and I don't want to sell it to them.'

Queenie shifted in her chair. 'You can fight it out between you when we've left.'

Mrs Breslin stormed out of the room, her back stiff with anger, slamming the door behind her. The sheaf of paper on the table fluttered to the floor like leaves scattering in the wind.

'I don't know why we bothered coming here,' Queenie said, drawing on her gloves. 'We had hoped for a little civility.'

'Sorry, Queenie.' Mr Breslin was mortified. 'Leave her to me. I'll talk her round.'

'You'd better hurry up.'

Mr Breslin had tears in his eyes. 'Poor Barry was full of crack-brained schemes and ideas but that's typical when everything's going wrong. I don't like to say it in front of Bernie but we will have to sell everything, one way or the other. You might as well have it.'

Queenie gazed at the china cabinets bulging with Sèvres. There was no answer to this frank confession of necessity except, 'I'll be glad to.'

'Good,' Mr Breslin said.

'Now that you've got me here, I'm not leaving until I've seen everything in this house. There could be some very good bargains.' Queenie got to her feet and went to the door. Without an invitation she advanced down the hall, resolute and precise. Mr Breslin, in hot pursuit, babbled about the history of the house, his voice swelling as Queenie gazed around.

Mrs Breslin appeared again from nowhere. Queenie said, 'You have some nice bits and pieces.'

Mrs Breslin said, 'This is not a junk shop,' but knew it would be impossible to stop Queenie having a good look round.

Nothing daunted, Queenie was off, opening doors, peering at everything. Lorraine was mortified. From the landing Queenie said, 'It's damp here. Don't you ever light a fire?'

'Your visit was a little unexpected,' Mr Breslin said.

'The cold makes everything so uncomfortable. If we could discuss the matter further another day I'll have a clear understanding of what fixtures and fittings are in with the property,' Queenie said.

'Let's get a clear understanding of the situation right now,' said Mrs Breslin, seeing Queenie's eyes on the antiques. 'They're not for sale.' She stepped forward, between her husband and Queenie. Her chin jutting out, she said to Mr Breslin, voice trembling, 'Kindly get this rude woman out of our house this minute.'

Mr Breslin nudged her. 'Get a grip of yourself, Bernie. They have the money to sort us out.'

'Don't let her bully us,' she said, in tears.

The Breslins had owned the house for over thirty years. Mrs Breslin had given birth to Barry upstairs. 'What next?' she asked her husband now, a great uncertainty taking hold of her as she saw herself being rushed out into an alien world.

'Mrs Breslin seems to have taken a queer turn,' said Queenie, then moved off down the steps. 'I want to arrange a meeting to discuss your workforce, things like that, Mr Breslin.'

Mr Breslin followed her, and whispered, 'Don't mind Bernie. Her nerves are in bits with everything that's going on.'

Queenie said, 'I'll make an offer through our solicitors today.'

It was all too much for Lorraine. Shuddering, she followed Queenie down the chilly path to the car, saying, 'Thank God that ordeal's over.'

'All that fuss,' Queenie rejoined, 'when they should be grateful.'

'Those poor people are being forced out of their home,' Lorraine said, 'and you showed them no mercy. A bit more persecution and that poor Mrs Breslin will go over the edge.'

'Don't exaggerate,' Queenie said. 'We're the solution to their plight, not the cause of it. I won't take any of their nonsense.'

Mr Breslin ran down the steps after them. 'Drop in again if you feel like it.'

'Thank you, Mr Breslin.' Queenie smiled ravishingly at him. 'But no, we've seen enough. Anyway, being blessed with a good memory I'll remember everything.'

'Don't worry about Bernie. She'll be grand. I'll see to that.'

As they swept off down the drive, Queenie said, 'Quite

a decent sort, Mr Breslin.' She gave a last look at the place as they turned left at the gate. 'Nice solid house.' She sounded pleased with herself. 'Who would ever have thought that we'd be the owners?'

'Fine house,' Lorraine agreed, glad to be away. 'All the same, it seems like a bad joke to me.'

Queenie lay back on her pillows, the sale agreement in her hand.

'When are we moving?' Lorraine asked.

'Who wants to know?'

'Mrs Cleary from the post office was asking me yesterday.'

'I'll let you know when it's decided, tell her.'

Lorraine sat down on the bed. 'I know Olivia's your main concern in all of this upheaval, but what about Phil and me?'

'What about you?'

'I'd like to know where we stand in all of this. We're not getting any younger and we need security.'

Queenie sat up. 'I don't know if you realise it but I've invested a lot of money in you, especially since you married that feckless fellow. He's been a real drain on me over the years.'

'I've worked hard all my life in the shop and the house.' Choked with anger Lorraine swept out of the room and out into the garden.

The concept of buying Breslin's bakery and the house filled

Lorraine with terror. From the beginning, her life had been bound up with the business in so many different ways. Her father had invested his disability pension in it and had worked for Queenie while he could. She had served in the shop as a child and since she'd returned from England she'd slaved in it from dawn to dusk.

Queenie had taken the best years of her life. Granted, she'd got her living out of her, and a comfortable one at that. But in having a mother who was negligent of her daughter, she'd missed out. Now, she observed, Queenie was doing it again. Her selfish preoccupation with herself and Olivia had her walking into a situation that would cause nothing but misfortune. Queenie would take off on a mad skite with Olivia, and leave everything to Lorraine and Chantal, with no acknowledgement of their investment of hard work and expertise. When the shop had been in real financial danger Queenie had depended on them. They'd tackled the problems together, made this new venture possible. Where had Olivia been then?

Watching Queenie and Olivia together, seeing their special closeness develop, Lorraine seethed with jealousy. It was strange that Queenie could give so much love and affection to Olivia having always withheld it from her.

Still shaking with resentment Lorraine drove to the supermarket. The glorious red-gold autumn leaves of the trees that lined the route did nothing to lift her mood.

In the car park she met Father McMahon. 'Are you not well?' he asked anxiously, his keen eyes missing nothing.

'I'm all right,' Lorraine said impatiently, wishing she could hurry by, knowing she wasn't looking her best. 'What are you doing here?'

'I'm just getting a few bits and pieces. Mrs M's taken a week's holiday.' He indicated the shopping in the back of the car. 'Is it true that Queenie has bought Breslin's?'

'I'm afraid so. The bakery and the house.'

'My word!'

'I think it's a mistake but Queenie won't listen. She says it's a good move.'

'She's a good businesswoman. Don't worry about her and don't overdo things, will you?'

'No, I won't.'

She put her shopping in the boot of her car, packing the parcels neatly together.

Father McMahon was beside her again. 'I've bought some nice ham and fresh bread. Would you like to join me for a sandwich and a drop of wine?'

'I'd love to,' she said, guilty and elated as a naughty child.

As she drove to his house she wondered how much she could depend on Queenie to sort things out, and how much they could hope for from the outcome, now and in the future. I'm only a nuisance to Queenie, she thought, a worry she can do without right now. Wishing desperately that she had some power over her mother, she drove on.

Chapter Thirty-one

Mum came into Queenie's bedroom and sat beside her, a sheaf of papers in her hand. 'We'll have to do something about a Christmas celebration,' she said, looking down her list of social contacts, business contacts, and people crucial to the business who should be invited.

Queenie's eyes snapped open. 'What?'

'Christmas,' Mum said. 'What about a celebration?'

'I heard you.' Queenie hoisted herself up into a sitting position, switched on the telly for the race at Doncaster. All Mum got was Queenie pointing out her favourite horse stepping neatly along the track, sighing exasperatedly, 'He'd be quicker if he walked,' groaning at the idiocies of horses and jockeys alike. Christmas parties weren't her cup of tea. She'd much rather conserve her energy for the Leopardstown races on St Stephen's day.

'Get Tommy Traynor to help you organise it,' she said dismissively.

The idea of crowds in her home appalled her.

Tommy convinced Mum to invite our guests to the Chamber of Commerce ball in Killiney Castle Hotel, on Christmas Eve, and offered to arrange it all.

'I've nothing to wear,' I moaned to Queenie, when everything was all arranged.

'I'll make you a dress,' she said, warming to the idea.

Leafing through a copy of *Vogue* I found a Dolce and Gabbana black chiffon evening dress with draped bodice and sash. Queenie sketched it on tissue paper and I bought the fabric.

In the dining room she cut it out carefully. Then she pinned it on me, pinching in the waist so that the skirt billowed outwards. Scissors clutched in her hand, she swooped around me, snipping off edges, muttering to herself as she worked, standing back to survey her handiwork. 'Good,' she said, satisfied with the shape her creation was taking. She removed the lid from her Singer sewing-machine, threaded the needle and began to sew, her foot working furiously on the old treadle. Eventually, she said, 'Try this on.'

I slipped into it, and the folds of chiffon fell gracefully to the floor. 'You'll look like a princess by the time I'm finished with you.' She smiled.

Mum laughed as she came in with the tea-tray. 'You're too feckin' thin, even for a princess,' she said, jokingly spoiling our pleasure with her practical eye. Putting down her tray she gazed into the mirror at her own strong, well-cushioned body. She said, 'Come and have a cup of tea and a slice of sponge cake. You could do with it.'

I struggled to get my dress over my head. Queenie swept it up determinedly. 'I'll have it,' she said to me.

'You're spoiling her,' Mum said.

'A bit of spoiling never did any harm. It's Christmas.'

'Don't remind me.' Mum looked at her impatiently. 'I dread it.'

I stayed quiet, determined not to make matters worse, wondering, as I tidied up the pins, threads and bits of material, why Mum had to spoil the fun.

Queenie watched with disgust as Mum cut a huge slice of cake and put it down in front of me, saying, 'Eat up, I'd hate to see it go to waste.'

'No thanks.' I got up, hovered near Queenie for a moment, thanking her, leaving her to get on with her sewing.

How much more pleasant things would be if Queenie and Mum got on well together. Their continuous slighting of one another had a corrosive effect on everything. Alone, Queenie and I were comfortable with one another.

On the night of the dance we swept through the tall gates, up an avenue to park in front of the Killiney Castle Hotel, its towers and turrets rising up to the darkening sky. Light shone from the long windows and we walked up wide steps to an enormous door. The commissionaire, in a navy uniform and top hat, ushered us into the lobby, where Christmas flowers and decorations fused with the red carpet in sumptuous splendour. A log fire blazed in the open hearth. Chantal tore past me to the bathroom to 'fix her makeup'.

The commissionaire appeared again, then led us upstairs

through a series of corridors to a closed door behind which voices were raised in conversation and laughter. Inside, people sat in groups on sofas, the men in tuxedos, and the women in extravagant evening dresses. Queenie stood to one side, in a long midnight blue velvet and lace dress, a feather boa thrown casually round her neck. 'Over here.' She waved.

As I moved to her side, she said, 'Lovely,' eyeing me.

Chantal, dangerously coquettish in a leopard print lamé dress, made Queenie shiver

Tommy Traynor took one look at her, gave a low whistle, and said, 'I'll see to the drinks.' He rushed headlong to the bar.

'Such beautiful men.' Chantal sighed, looking longingly around.

'Married, most of them,' Trish complained as she joined us.

'*C'est la vie*.' Chantal shrugged.

Tommy returned with Jim, whom he had bumped into at the bar, and a tray of drinks: sherry for Queenie and Mum, wine for the rest of us.

Mum sipped her sherry. 'I was dying for that,' she said. 'Oh! There are the Misses Drysdale.' She moved off, her long silver earrings dangling, her black skirts swirling.

Chantal finished her drink, handed her glass to Jim with a nod towards the bar, and looked around the room. As the band started up she made a beeline for Tommy Traynor and grabbed his hand. They moved to the floor, Tommy dithering in the company of such an appealing partner, Chantal coaxing, her upturned face sensitive to his response.

For a few blissful minutes they swayed together in harmony, Tommy transported back to his youth, transformed, in his own eyes, from bookie to young lover.

A man they both knew slightly broke the spell by touching Chantal's arm. She uncoiled herself and disappeared with him among the dancers. Tommy, taut and disappointed, waited patiently. She returned, not to him but to the bar where champagne corks were popping. Jim handed her her glass. She drained it, then proceeded to dance with one man after another, irresistible to those who partnered her graceful steps. It was in their eyes, and in their laughter.

Dave Fuller arrived. He caught my eye, raised his glass and called 'Cheers.' Tommy Traynor sidled up to Queenie, his recent investment transforming him in his own eyes into some kind of royalty.

Queenie said, 'Well, you're having fun.'

'So I am, and I'd a good day at Navan too. Here's mud in your eye.'

'Won all before you, did you?'

'Lost me shirt on the last race. Devil of a horse, too temperamental. It was off and away, first for ages, fell back, riderless.'

'Unfortunate. What do you recommend for Leopardstown?'

They were off with their familiar banter. Strains of the 'Blue Danube' floated towards them.

'Come on, Queenie. Let's show 'em.' Tommy put down his glass.

They moved gracefully together, a stiff Fred Astaire and a hesitant Ginger Rogers, the past in their eyes. Tommy hummed along with the tune as Queenie's large feet tapped out a painful rhythm. As soon as it was over she made for the nearest chair.

Jim brought me a drink and we joined the group who were watching Chantal dancing on a table, cheering her on. Her graceful body swayed and bent, this way and that, like a reed on the tide of the men's pleasure. As they cheered and whistled, her eyes grew wild and her laughter rose in that helpless quality of the inebriated. Effortlessly, she held them in thrall, a Cleopatra to her reckless slaves.

'She's drunk,' Queenie squawked to Tommy. 'Do something before she falls.'

'Can't stop her now.' Tommy laughed. 'Might do her an injury.'

'She's nothing but trouble,' Queenie declared, exasperated.

As the music stopped Tommy caught hold of Chantal's waist, lifted her into his arms, his skill forestalling disaster.

Dancing with Jim was not the fun it should have been. We moved together to the music, he awkward and close, too anxious to please. Queenie looked on approvingly. She was admonishing Polly, 'Don't lick your fingers in public,' for picking a cherry out of her tropical fruit cocktail, as I returned.

'Who says so?' Polly asked.

'Don't be cheeky. Go and wash your hands.'

'Come on,' Tommy said to me, as a Ladies' Choice was announced. 'Let's dance.'

The space between us closed. Tommy, smiling at me,

hummed the tune and couples swirled around us. It was then that I saw him.

'Is that—' I stopped, looked at his familiar face, saw the worship in Chantal's face. 'That isn't . . .' I felt that he saw me too, but either he didn't recognise me or I was less important than Chantal.

I refused to let myself look again because it was so ridiculous. We resumed dancing, me rocking against any acknowledgement of what I'd just seen, wild with the rhythm, Tommy desperate to keep up, gasping for breath. When the music stopped, I looked round, but there was no sign of them. Surely I was wrong. My heart raced. I crossed the floor to the far door, and looked down the gloomy corridors. There was no one in sight.

'I don't know about you, but I'm having a wonderful time,' Jim said, sweeping me back to the dance floor, our feet moving in different directions as he said, 'Shall we? I like this tune. Jason Donovan, isn't it?'

'"Too Many Broken Hearts",' I informed him, as we circled the floor.

'Thirsty work,' he said, when the music stopped, and he led me towards the bar.

'May I have this dance?'

I looked round, the magic words ringing in my ears. Dave Fuller stood there. 'No! Thanks. You must excuse me.'

I scurried across the ballroom again, back to the far door, where Mum, talking to Auntie Tess, cornered me. 'Looking for someone?' She asked.

'Chantal. Where is she?'

'I haven't seen her.'

'Have a brandy,' Auntie Tess said. 'It'll settle your stomach.'

'There's nothing wrong with my stomach,' I said offensively, though at that minute I felt it swell conspicuously and wished I hadn't eaten such a large dinner.

Mr Hill, stately in tails, advanced purposefully. 'I'm not as nimble as I used to be, but would you like to . . .' We were off, waltzing around the ballroom.

Suddenly I was saying, 'Sorry, I have to go,' escaping from his fumbling footsteps. I ran back down the maze of corridors to the hall, pain gripping me as I blundered down the stairs. Doreen was coming towards me, a man I didn't recognise on her arm. 'Terrific night,' she said, stopping to introduce us.

'Have you seen Chantal?'

'No.' Doreen looked at me, puzzled.

'Excuse me.' I continued my journey. Once out of sight I hurried to the ladies', thinking she must be in there but she wasn't. Where to try next? How could she have disappeared so quickly? The french windows to the garden were open.

I ran outside. It was cold, rooks shifted and stirred, birds rose up stiff from sleep as I flew past. The chill seeped through my dress. I stood with my arms hugging my body. I could smell cigarettes. Chantal was out here somewhere, smoking. It was colder in the conservatory, where I sat down to take a breath. It, too, had been decorated with streamers and balloons, the windows framed with fairy-lights, poinsettias and evergreens among the red-berried holly.

At that moment I saw them through the window. They were sitting on a garden seat together, his dark head bent towards hers. I waited, willing the scene to become bearable. But no, she turned her face up to him, kissed him. There was a playfulness between them, her flattery sharpening his interest. I turned my attention to Lorenzo and took in his beloved face, the perfect clothes worn with casual distinction. Why had no one warned me that he was here? But, of course, they didn't know. And all I knew now was that Lorenzo didn't love me, that he never had and never would.

Now, they were rising, walking deeper into the darkness, holding hands. I couldn't watch them any more.

I couldn't bear the terrible truth. Everything I'd searched for was lost to Chantal, whose desire for Lorenzo was expressed in every line and curve of her sleek body as she walked off with him.

Alone, leaning against the cold wrought-iron seat, I longed for him but knew that to follow them would cause an emotional outburst I would not be able for.

Wordless, half-blind with tears and shaking, I retreated down the path behind the clipped hedge, taking refuge in the trees, stepping on the slugs that slid unobserved, leaving only their silver trails as proof of their presence. I breathed in the air like a lost animal, grief draining me of all sense of the world.

Eventually, the turmoil ceased. Numb, I sat alone, heavy with despair that sapped my strength, thinking of Chantal with hatred. I didn't feel the first warning drops of rain until my dress was soaked. I felt empty. A knifelike surge of regret seared through me, overwhelming me, How could I have let him slip away from me like that?

Jim found me at the bottom of the garden by the pond.

'Ollie.' He came forward slowly. 'Whatever's the matter?'

'Oh, Jim.' I stood up, wiped my face hastily, trying not to let him see the state I was in.

'You OK?'

'I'm fine.'

'Would you like something to drink?'

'No, thanks. I have a glass of wine somewhere.'

'All you sure you're all right?'

I looked at him, hardly believing how everything had changed so suddenly. 'Oh, Jim!' I cried.

He stepped forward and took me in his arms. I clung to him like someone drowning. 'There, there.' He held on tight for a long time, mopping my face with his handkerchief, like Queenie did when I was a child.

'I saw him,' was all I managed to say. I felt lost and so ashamed of my unbearable grief.

'It's all right,' he whispered, his arms tight around me, rocking me back and forth.

'I don't usually do this.' I took his hanky and blew my nose. 'Queenie always says that a well-behaved woman shouldn't cry in public, or draw attention to herself.'

'Cry all you want.'

'It's awful to appear to mind so much about anything. I can't believe I let him go while I still had a chance with him. He loves her.' I bit my lip to stop myself from crying again, then pulled myself together. 'I have to go to the loo,' I said.

Jim followed me. The party still blazed in the lighted windows above us. We ploughed through the people chattering at the entrance, and hurried past the group at the bottom of the staircase. 'I'll wait for you,' he said. 'Take as long as you like.'

'Jim said I'd find you here,' Trish said, coming into the ladies', looking at the drowned rat before her. 'What's up? You look as if you've seen a ghost.'

'Don't let's talk here.' My eyes flew anxiously to the door.

'All right. Come to the lounge. There's a fire going.'

'No, I have to go. I saw Lorenzo.'

'Lorenzo!'

'He was . . . with . . . Chantal.'

'Oh, my God.' She put her arms around me.

'I'm all right.' I sniffed. 'I'll get over it.'

'You won't. You'll get hard. That's a different thing. Come on. Jim'll take you home. I'll stay to the end, make sure everything goes all right.'

Jim held out my coat for me to slip into it. Tommy Traynor was at the door. I thanked him, my voice small as I tried to keep it steady.

'Glad you enjoyed yourselves.' Tommy clapped Jim on the back, called, 'Go carefully,' and returned inside. He was swallowed up in a pool of light.

In the car Jim wrapped a rug around my knees. I

felt his sympathy as I slumped down, the darkness a relief.

'Cigarette?' he asked, proffering the packet.

'No, thanks.'

'Believe it or not, you'll feel better sooner than you think.' His voice was soothing as he drove.

'I'm not going back to Chantal's flat.'

'Queenie's?'

'Yes.'

'Why don't you get away for a while?'

'I might.'

'I'm here to help you,' he said, before stepping out to open the car door for me.

'Thanks Jim, you're so kind.' Fearful of bursting into fresh tears I got out, and ran towards the arc of light over the door.

The hall was dim, the back stairs dark as I went down to the kitchen.

Queenie was in her dressing-gown putting a small saucepan on the top ring of the cooker. 'What an unexpected surprise,' she said. 'Grand party, wasn't it?'

'Brilliant.' I held my breath so as not to cry.

'I'm not long back myself. Perished I am. Would you like a mug of hot milk?'

'Why not?'

I sat at the table while she boiled it up, shook cinnamon over it, and poured it into two mugs; her unfailing love holding me as sure as my hands held my mug of hot milk, her cure-all in a time of crisis.

'Lorenzo O'Brien was at the party.'

'Oh!' There was silence.

'He's the fellow I followed to Italy.'

'Yes, I remember him. He brought the flowers that day to the shop, and you said they were from Interflora.'

'He was with . . . Chantal.'

'Chantal!' Queenie threw her eyes to the ceiling. Thoughtfully she said, 'Had you known him long?'

'Not very. Oh! I'm a fool.' I burst into fresh tears.

'Here, drink your milk and don't talk about it now. You're only upsetting yourself.'

'But I love him.'

'I know.'

'He was the reason why I could never marry Barry, or anybody. I thought I was over him. But there's no one else for me. I don't want to live a single day of my life without him. If I could get him again, I'd hold on to him. Oh, Queenie, how long will it be before I stop loving him?' I was plunged into renewed crying, a wild creature hiding nothing, because Lorenzo was gone. Gone, gone, gone for good. I said, 'He's gone,' in a half-whisper as I slipped down into my chair.

Queenie looked thoughtful as she came to me, smiling and silent, reaching out to hold me firmly. Time ticked away as she waited for the crying to ease, healing her broken child in the only way she knew how.

'Maybe it's not what it seems,' she said, eventually.

'I think it is.'

'Remember, he loved you once. Who's to say he won't love you again?'

It was true, but I shook my head. 'He loves Chantal now. I'll never see him again.'

'How do you know? It's a long road that has no turn. Come on, I'll make you a hot-water bottle. You can sleep in my bed.'

She didn't say another word as she boiled the kettle, filled our bottles, hopping around sure-footed and nimble, like the Queenie of my childhood.

I went to bed light years removed from the young girl who had walked out on Barry Breslin, and had gone to search for Lorenzo. As I lay awake, I realised that Lorenzo was gone from me because of outside forces. If only I could retrieve him from Chantal I would hold him until he was himself again.

Chapter Thirty-two

Chantal's flat seemed cold, unwelcoming. Everything was the same, tables and chairs, sofas in their usual place, yet the perspective had changed. Chantal was in bed, leaning back against her pillows, reading. '*Bonjour*,' she said, never taking her eyes off her book.

'What's the matter with you?' she said, when she looked up. In my despair I blurted out, 'I saw you with him. I saw you with Lorenzo.'

'Oh!' Chantal looked brazenly at me, like a bold child caught stealing sweets.

'You knew about him. I told you.'

She pouted. 'You never told me his name. And, anyway, it was only a bit of fun,' she protested.

'It didn't look like a bit of fun to me.'

'Don't be such a misery,' she coaxed. 'What does it matter?'

'I saw you together. I saw the way you looked at each other.'

'What way was that?'

'If I'd found you in bed together it couldn't have been more obvious.'

'Don't be stupid.' Chantal spoke as if she were giving a warning, the truth of my accusation unacceptable. 'And stop that silly crying.'

'I'm not crying.' I straightened my back, my chest heaving, tears running down my face at the thought that Chantal had betrayed me so ruthlessly.

As she gazed at me I felt awkward, ugly. 'I've lost him,' I cried, the tears falling like rain, 'and it's all your fault.'

'He was never yours in the first place.' There was no pity in her.

'That's not true.'

'Anyway,' she ignored what I'd said, 'what's the big deal? It was nothing. I fancy him, but so what?'

'But you're my friend and he's my—'

'Your what?' Chantal's arms were flung out. Her head was dark against the pillows, her cat's eyes were trained on me, her nightdress barely covered her breasts. She looked ravishing as she waited for my reply.

She laughed suddenly. 'Have him, you silly thing. If you can. See if I care.' She looked at her watch. 'You do what you like, but stop crying. I'm going to sleep – I've got to be up early in the morning.'

She burrowed deep under the duvet, pulling it over her head. I was dismissed, an inconvenience. Trembling, I packed my belongings, bundling everything into a bag, floundering around in the semi-darkness, the bedroom we'd shared a foreign place to me now.

Next day I was in the Nutmeg with Trish when I saw him through the window. I said, 'Lorenzo!' pointing at him.

Trish looked up. 'So it is.'

'I have to go.'

'He's gone.'

'I know.' I jumped out of my chair and hurried through the coffee-shop, calling over my shoulder, 'Pay the bill. I'll phone you later.'

I raced up the road. He was turning the corner. 'Lorenzo!'

He stopped as I caught up with him. But it wasn't Lorenzo. It was a stranger who turned and asked, 'Who are you looking for?'

'I'm so sorry. I could have sworn you were someone else.' I pretended to laugh, too, at my mistake. I stood back, gazing disbelievingly after him.

Trish was beside me. Taking my arm she said, 'Come on. Let's go.'

'I did see Lorenzo, didn't I? I wasn't dreaming?'

'No. It was definitely Lorenzo. But he's gone.'

Chantal was in Paris for the Christmas festivities and would not be returning until 6 January. I buried myself in my work to stifle my despair. Lorenzo had been within touching distance yet I had missed him.

I moved into a flat of my own, and continued in the mundane routine: getting up, having a shower, brushing my teeth. My head was full of images of Lorenzo with Chantal, his exquisite beauty matched only by hers. She had won. I had lost. But what had I lost? Apart from that brief interlude he had never been mine to lose. Alone, I would burst out crying. To continue to live knowing that Lorenzo would never be mine seemed too much to bear. But live I must. I couldn't let Queenie down.

I shrank from Chantal when she returned to work.

'What is ze matter?' she asked me, puzzled. In her opinion her only crime was that men found her attractive. 'Lorenzo is gone back to Paris. I won't be seeing him any more,' she said.

I didn't believe her. I yearned for him.

Obsessed, I made plans, insisting Queenie give me the job of buyer. It would keep me out of the shop.

With buying trips to London and Paris I was escaping, severing links with the past quickly, cleanly. It was time for business. In hotels, in airports, I exchanged pleasantries with anyone I met. All my contacts, no matter how obscure, were important to me now, as I kept abreast of things in my work. I laughed outwardly with customers and colleagues, no joy inside. Would there ever be again? In my own eyes I'd grown into a mature woman, alluring, amusing, teasing, adorable, always with an air of isolation. Often I thought of Lorenzo. No matter how far I travelled, no matter how successful I became, I would never catch up with him.

Jim phoned me at my hotel in London. 'I'll be over there on Thursday. Why don't we go out to dinner?' he suggested.

He arrived at the hotel, dapper in a dinner jacket and black bow-tie. 'I want you to try this new restaurant. Gorgeous dishes from all over the world.'

We walked to our destination. The wet streets were bright under street-lights, the lanes, fitfully lit, hid their secrets. The restaurant was in a basement, in a small square, and was half empty.

'Come on,' Jim said, seeing my reluctance. 'They do wonderful fish.' Once inside he said, 'It has charm and character, hasn't it?' his eyes seeking my approval.

Looking around the shadowy tables, I said, 'Yes, it has something.'

He was right. The meal was delicious. Seated with my back to the door, my mind on the lobster, I felt a draught and looked up to see Jim staring past me, gaping.

'Who is it?' I turned towards the door surprised to see that no one was there.

'I thought for a second . . . I could have sworn . . .'

'What?'

'Doesn't matter.'

'Kylie Minogue?' I prompted, laughing.

'Don't be daft.'

'She saw you recognised her and was scared to come in.' I grinned and returned to gouging my lobster out of its shell.

After a while Jim said, 'Olivia, why don't you come home?'

'What's the point? I'd rather be miserable here than with Queenie and Mum breathing down my neck.'

'Has it occurred to you that they might need looking after

for a change? I called in to see them yesterday. They're not doing very well. The new house is a shambles. Queenie looks awful. I think they got more than they bargained for.'

'Dad's there.'

'He's not interested. As he said himself, he knows nothing about builders. Your mum's unhappy. You've no idea what it's like for the two of them in that mausoleum, avoiding each other like the plague.'

'I don't know anything about builders either.'

'It'll take time and money to restore the house completely. With the purchase of the bakery, they have neither, and Barry Breslin yanked out everything, only left the four walls. I think you should go back and help them. They need someone to keep an eye on them. They need you to get involved. They're not getting on at all.'

I thought of Queenie and the sterile house that would sap her energy and yield her no return on her investment. I felt sad.

'There's nothing to keep me away except . . . Chantal.'

'She hasn't a clue about what's going on. And she's not with Lorenzo because she was moaning to me about having no steady boyfriend.'

A flicker of interest flared inside me. 'I suppose you're right. Maybe I should go back.'

'Come on, let's get out of here. I'll take you back to my hotel for a Gaelic coffee.'

'I don't think I've room for anything else.'

He laughed. 'Come on.' He was holding my coat, shrugging into his own.

A wave of tenderness swept over me for kind, generous Jim. How stupid he must think me. He was always looking out for me, for ever giving. I must stop pitying myself and do as he said.

In his hotel room we sipped our coffee, he in trousers and shirt, relaxed. 'What's the matter,' he said eventually, touching my arm. 'You've gone very quiet.'

I swallowed nervously.

'What is it?' he prompted.

'I'm tired. I haven't slept much since I left home.'

'Poor you. I'll take you back to your hotel.' As I stood up he moved towards me. Uneasy, he hesitated, studying my face. 'You're beautiful, and I've wanted you ever since I laid eyes on you that night I rescued you.'

'I don't know what to say.'

'You don't have to say anything.'

'I know you want to sleep with me.'

'And you don't mind?'

'I don't want to make another mistake.'

'I don't blame you for reacting like this. I won't treat you badly. I promise.' He held out his arms. 'Come 'ere.'

Obediently I went into them.

He stroked my hair gently. I was shaking. 'Relax. I won't do anything you don't want me to do.'

We stayed like that for a little while.

Jim took my hand, led me to the bed. We lay down. He stroked my hair again, his hands gently massaging the back of my neck, the side of my face, until I was relaxed.

'Sleepy?' he asked, pulling me closer.

I lay my head on his shoulder. We were as close and familiar as a long-married couple. It wasn't as if I was in bed with a stranger, after all. We were friends, comfortable together. We both slept. When we woke up he reached for me, pulled me close again, ran his fingers down my back, slid off my top. Without a word he kissed me gently, his body taut against mine.

'Are you all right?' he asked.

I nodded my head, hardly daring to breathe, hardly believing how much I wanted him to continue.

His fingers touched my breasts. Trembling, at the end of my resistance, I summoned up an erotic pose, casting myself as a naked nymph, frail and ethereal, lying on my fern bed, obedient to my master's lust. Slowly, like an actress playing a part, I pulled him down to me. He caressed me, from my neck to my thighs. I reached out for him. He was real, not a dream I was chasing, and I was warming to his touch.

I wanted to be loved, and Jim loved me. He was there, I needed him. That was all there was to it, I told myself, as I abandoned myself to the pleasure he gave me.

As soon as it was over I felt guilty. I went to get out of bed.

Jim attempted to hold me. I pushed him away.

'Ollie, what's the matter?'

'I shouldn't have done it.'

'Why not? You enjoyed yourself, didn't you?'

'Yes,' I said shyly. 'But I'm not in love with you Jim.'

'I can live with that for the moment.'

I took my clothes, went into the bathroom, and showered. 'I'd better get going,' I said, returning to put on my clothes.

'Ollie, listen . . .' Jim was beside me, reaching out to me. 'Don't go. Stay. We'll have breakfast together.'

I shook my head. 'No, thanks.'

While he showered, I put on my makeup. When he returned to the bedroom, I was waiting, my bag under my arm.

'Are you sure you won't stay?' He looked at me like someone who had lost his way.

'I've got an eight o'clock appointment. I really should get going.'

Traffic moved silently in the night. Outside my hotel Jim said, 'Don't feel bad, Ollie. There's no harm done. We're still friends.' It was an affirmation.

'The best of friends,' I reassured him.

I held myself in check until I was safely inside my hotel bedroom.

Once inside I thought of Lorenzo, and wept uncontrollably.

It was late evening when I arrived outside the Breslins' house. I was shocked at its deterioration since I had been here last. It was evident in the overgrown lawns, the rotten timber piled in the drive, the open front door, the black sacks filled with rubbish outside it. Mary greeted me at the hall door. 'Come on in.'

'What's going on?' I asked, looking towards the planks

of new timber shoved through the gap that had been the dining-room window. The shriek of a Black and Decker came clearly from the dark recesses.

'We're replacing the floorboards.' She spoke as if she were doing the work herself. 'Dry rot,' she confided.

The hall, vast and empty, was freezing, and as gloomy and unfriendly as it had been on the first day I'd entered it. The carpet on the staircase looked shabby in the evening light, and the stair-rods lacklustre. Dining-room chairs were stacked neatly in one corner; the dismantled dining-table and sideboard were shrouded in dust-sheets, and the place was tomb-like.

This was not our house. It belonged to the days of Mrs Breslin's strict attention. In our possession it had gone downhill. The tick of the grandfather clock, reminding me that we didn't have much time to get everything done, caused me to drop further down into a black anxiety.

In the sitting room the curtains were drawn against the chill and the low lights gave a cosy feeling to the only warm room in the house. Queenie and Mum were sitting on opposite chairs, huddled over the fire, the tea-table between them, sandwiches and fruit cake waiting. Queenie, in her pink dressing-gown, her shawl wrapped round her shoulders, smiled a warm welcome as I hugged her. Mum, spooning jam on to a scone, stopped and stood up. 'Hello, my dear,' she said, hugging me. 'Good to see you.'

'Good to see you both.' I sat between them, going along with their welcoming ceremony, their reassuring love evident in Queenie's eyes and in the way Mum buttered a scone for me, and poured me a cup of tea.

Queenie eyed me. 'You look pale. How was your journey?'

'I'm tired, that's all.'

Mum said, 'It's great to have you home. Have more tea. Cake?'

'No, thanks.'

There was no mention of the bakery, only polite conversation about the shops, and the increasing orders for our own brands.

'We'll have to get the show on the road if we're to fulfil those orders,' Mum said to Queenie.

'We will.' She yawned. 'I'm off to bed.'

'Me too.'

I unpacked, staring at the huge bed, with its white quilt, as cold as a marble slab. Queenie's silver head bowed over it, as she put a hot-water bottle between the sepulchral sheets, did nothing to allay my feeling of isolation. This was not my home. This was not my room. Nothing in it was mine.

I woke up late. It was cold. In the hall, on the table, the day's post lay unopened. I checked through the manila envelopes, wondering why Queenie hadn't bothered with them.

I went upstairs to see her. I found her leaning back on her pillows, her eyelids drooping, her expression peaceful. Her new bedroom was well proportioned. The long windows, lavish drapes pulled back to let in the light, and the marble fireplace were luxuries beyond anything she'd ever known. Lying back comfortably she said, 'I thought about opening the letters and bills, then decided against it. I've had a nasty dose of flu, Olivia, and I don't want to have to think about the money on this glorious day.'

'You haven't seen the bakery yet?'

'Time enough in a week or two when I feel better.'

Later, when she came in from Mass, I drew her attention to the mail again. She stood for a long time looking at it, her hat askew. 'I can't be bothered with all that legal stuff. Have them readdressed to Mr Hennessy. I pay a fortune to that man to look after it all.'

'Some of them are just bills,' I pointed out.

'Send them to Mr Hill.' She picked up the envelopes and handed them to me.

I didn't argue but doubts crowded in. What had she let herself in for with this preposterous house?

Chapter Thirty-three

Her heart like stone, Lorraine sat in an armchair near the fire. Finally she leaned back against its cushions and let herself relax. In letting Queenie have her way, and agreeing graciously to move into the Breslin house with her, she'd averted a nasty row.

When Queenie bought the leasehold on the shop in Donnybrook Lorraine's first reaction had been admiration. The conversion of the bakery into two large shops had been a good idea, in principle. But Queenie's purchase of the Breslins' house had been a different matter. All her money from various savings accounts had been used up in this unnecessary extravagance. As she planned to refurbish the property, get fitted carpets, install central heating, Mr Hill, the bank manager, was advancing cheques for immediate expenses only. For a while they would have to be careful, Queenie had agreed, when Lorraine had spoken to her about it. But Lorraine was worried. Unhappily, she saw Queenie's vanity as the motive that had compelled her to eradicate the Breslins as quickly as possible.

Queenie had been itching to get her hands on the place so that she would be the undisputed queen where the Breslins had imposed their superiority for so long. All her plans for her elevation were in the estimates for decorating, central heating and new bathrooms. She'd insisted that everything be done quickly, until they ran into financial difficulties. Then she'd become insufferable; scolding everyone who came within her sight.

With Chantal in Donnybrook, Olivia travelling all over in her purchasing capacity, Lorraine had been pushed to one side, her opinion no longer sought or wanted. She missed the corner shop. It had been a haven where she'd lived and worked for so long. She'd done a good job, devoting herself to her family. Now, idle, waiting for the new shop in the bakery to open, she was miserable. Perhaps she ought to do something for herself with her new freedom. Break away from her mother, get a job and a small house for her and Phil. Anything was possible. The future was hers and Phil's now, and she had chances she'd never had before. She'd talk to Queenie about selling that horrible house and taking her share.

She went shopping. The house was quiet when she returned, nobody at home. 'I'm home,' she called out, but there was no answer. She went into the sitting room and drew the curtains. Then in the kitchen she made herself a pot of tea and a ham sandwich, calm and ready to discuss her options with Queenie when she returned. Everywhere was cold, the silence oppressive. The evening news was no comfort. Hands clasped together, she walked up and down, thinking it only natural to want her freedom.

Phil came in, washed his hands, sat at the table, his shirtsleeves rolled up. She noticed that his hair was thinning and he walked more slowly, but his body was still lean and muscular, his arms sinewy. His day at the market, lifting and hauling, kept him healthy and fit. His answers to her few questions left huge gaps about his day, and she was unsatisfied with his answers. Yet she was glad to have him in the kitchen, especially when he listened to her fears about Queenie's finances. 'What happens if she runs herself into debt?'

'I wouldn't know.' He coughed, embarrassed. 'Don't think about that.'

'Someone has to think about it. Mother doesn't seem to care.'

'Queenie knows what she's doing.'

'I wonder.'

'It's her life. She's following her instincts. She's mistress here. Free to do as she pleases.'

'I've worked for her all my life. Aren't I entitled to some say in it?'

'Keep an open mind. There's nothing you can do unless she asks you for her help. Obviously she feels it's worth the risk. She's taken a few of those in her time.'

Lorraine folded her hands and sighed. 'I'd like to get away from it all. Travel the world. See Egypt, India, places like that. Wouldn't you?'

'I suppose so. But you can't desert Queenie – not yet anyway. We're one big happy family here and for that we should count our blessings.'

The conversation had never flowed between them. Phil lived with her, sat down to the table, ate his breakfast, put on his jacket, his baseball cap, and left each morning as if going off to work but he never seemed at home. There was something unreal about the situation, as if they were living on a stage or in a film.

Still, his words took away the edge of the emptiness she felt. She smiled with relief. She wasn't alone. 'There's so much I haven't done,' she said, more to herself than to him.

'Don't do anything without consulting me.' Phil took his paper, sat back with just enough politeness to make his withdrawal acceptable.

His words had a certain finality about them, instantly curtailing her plans for selling up, moving away or going abroad.

She sat alone for a long time afterwards, depressed. If she cleared off with Monsieur Guilbert what would the neighbours say? Who would look after Phil? She knew she couldn't desert Queenie, leave her on her own to be looked after by Phil or, worse, strangers, would no doubt stir disapproval.

Lorraine thought about Monsieur Guilbert. He'd told her about his life in Paris, his wife and children. He wanted her, she knew that, but on his terms. She was afraid of her new-found love, and fearful that her want of Monsieur Guilbert would make her forget everything: Queenie, the business, everything important at that moment. Also, she was fearful of the despair this love would bring. Her best plan was to keep her distance.

In the sitting room she lit the fire, and wrote out her grocery list. Ashamed that she wanted to be rid of her mother, the woman to whom she'd been bound to for over fifty years, the woman who'd stood by her through thick and thin.

Chapter Thirty-four

In the bakery I opened the post, staring at the staggering bank statements.

In the stark morning light the whole enterprise seemed like a terrible mistake. Queenie's fortress was turning into a joke.

'Cash is what's needed,' Mum said.

'And fast, to pay wages, and keep things afloat,' Jack Sweeney said.

'But where are we going to get it?' I thought of all the people who depended on Queenie, and felt sick. She'd always said that being an employer had responsibilities, and that we must look after our workforce. Now what was she going to do?

The bakery roof was leaking, the ceilings blistered and flaking. Rain dripped down from blocked drains, forming puddles everywhere. It would all take far longer than expected. We'd never get it done in time. I stood with the bills in my hands, exhausted and appalled at the undertaking. Where was Queenie to get the cash? Suddenly I longed for something undemanding and small, like the corner shop had been.

I crossed the empty space to the office. My thoughts were on the people Queenie would take down with her if she could not save the situation. People would say it served us right, we'd been too hasty in our acquisition of the bakery. I was exhausted with trying to think of a way round it all, wondering what direction to take next. I picked up my briefcase and left, walking to work to calm the anxiety that seethed through me.

That afternoon, the familiar back roads were sunny. The house, grey and sullen in the shade, looked down over the town. I hurried up the drive, not because I was anxious to arrive, but because I had to tell Queenie how bad things were. Though she wouldn't be pleased, she had to know the truth.

I crossed the threshold, my heart pounding, wishing there was something I could do – anything but shatter Queenie's dream.

'What's up?' Queenie asked.

'Things are bad at the bakery. Worse than we thought.'

Queenie's eyebrows shot up. 'Oh?'

'The place is falling down, bills from all over, and the roof repairs will take ages and cost a fortune,' Mum blurted out.

Queenie drew in her breath. 'That's why the Breslins wanted a quick sale.'

I nodded.

'The roof's falling down, rain's pouring in. The bills

are pouring in too. I'm sorry it's bad news but it had to be said.'

Mum and Queenie exchanged looks.

'I knew something would go wrong,' Mum said, choking back the accusation in her voice. 'Almost everything we had is made over to the bank. And there's this house – nothing but a liability. No return, no promise. All that money spent for nothing.'

'I'll get us a drink,' I said, rising.

'What are we going to do?' Mum's hysteria was evident in her voice.

'The Surveyor passed it, let's not forget whose money has been spent,' Queenie said, struggling to her full height. 'What I did was necessary, not extravagant. I didn't know the place was in shreds. Trust the bloody Breslins.'

Mum said, 'I suppose the installation of the central heating will have to be cancelled, no new wallpaper or curtains for the bedrooms.'

'Only for the present,' Queenie said.

When Mum left the room, we went over the bills. Queenie's poise was shaken at her miscalculation and she looked exhausted. She, more than anyone, understood the terror that loss of money brought. Her money had meant we could live comfortably in the past and her money sustained and indulged us now. Failure was alien to her, but it was that failure, manifest in the bills before her, that had me sitting watching over her shoulder.

She waited in dread of reproach. When none came she threw the bills to one side and, with an effort, looked around the room, as if searching for reassurance. All the possessions that were gathered about us only served to remind us of the years of struggle the Breslins had put in to get them, and their failure in the end to keep them.

'Leave this to me. I'll think of something,' Queenie said, eventually.

I was cast aside while she plotted and planned. Each day I monitored the post and waited. One morning I found Queenie in the hall, a bunch of unopened bills in her hands, looking defeated. Mum, her hat and coat on, said, 'I'm on my way to the shop. Anything you want?'

'Here's a bill from the butcher.' Queenie handed it to her. 'Have it checked. There must be some mistake. And another thing. Do you think you could restrain yourself at the supermarket? Just get what we need.'

'That's what I usually do,' Mum reminded her.

'We don't have cash-flow,' Queenie explained. 'It's gone on wages and stock before we get a look at it. I don't know where you expect me to get money from.'

'But . . .'

Queenie raised her hand. 'I don't want to hear it. You've done nothing since we moved in here except bypass my authority and go your own way. If you were only willing to economise, eat less, cut down! Look at the size of you, and the size of the food bills! You will insist on having your own comforts.'

I looked at Queenie after Mum had left. 'That's not fair. She has cut down, and she's been to see Mr Hill at the bank.'

'He's a dead loss at finding money. The last thing he seems to have available to him is money. And he works in a bank! I ask you.' She wasn't asking, she was telling, her hands stretched out to the non-existent fire. 'Wouldn't you think he'd help out, seeing as he got us into this jam in the first place?'

'You'll have to go and see him yourself. Cutting down on electricity and fuel and the butcher won't solve the problem. The place is freezing. You'll catch your death.'

'Sacrifice,' Queenie muttered. 'That's a word this generation doesn't understand. In my day we knew nothing but sacrifice. Mary will have to go. Lorraine will have to get back to the cooking and like it.' Her hands holding the bills were turning blue with cold, her sharp tongue belying the defeat in her eyes.

'I could see Mr Hill for you if you like.' I wanted to help her. I wanted her to depend on me. I wanted life to be warm and cosy the way it had been in the corner shop.

Queenie was insisting that she could do it all by herself. She sacked the Breslins' gardener, cut Mary down to one day a week, and sat in the evenings over a meagre fire, her head bowed to the books. Eventually one evening she said, 'I've thought of a rescue plan, Olivia.'

'Is it going to be difficult? Can I help?'

'Not at all,' she answered, almost jovially, her eyes looking far away at something I couldn't see. 'What you can do is take me into town tomorrow to see Mr Hill. I hate the man but I mustn't be selfish. Oh, and I'll call to Dr Ross, too, for more tablets.' These orders were given in an imperious tone but I didn't mind because it was a sure sign that she was back to her old self again.

'Wrap up warm. Take a blanket in the car,' Mum fussed.

'Don't fret yourself,' Queenie said, not unkindly.

We drove to the bank, the rain trickling down the icy windscreen, Queenie silent for once. Mr Hill, tall, thin, greeted us with a smile and led Queenie off down a corridor to his inner sanctum. Twenty minutes later he returned her to me. 'Everything sorted for the present.' He gave me a reassuring smile. 'Bills taken care of. Our new arrangement should keep the wolf from the door for now.'

Queenie gritted her teeth. 'Thank you, Mr Hill.'

'Glad to be of service, Mrs Boyle.'

Queenie leaned towards him and gave him her gloved hand. 'It's what you're overpaid for,' she said, and marched to the swing doors, calling, 'Come along, Olivia,' over her shoulder.

Back in the car she sank into her seat. 'What an awful man,' she complained. 'You've no idea the humiliation I've been through. Dreadful business having your debts trotted out before you, like a list of sins. I felt like a pauper. Lord, how I hate bank managers.'

'I'm sure,' I agreed, 'but at least you got some cash out of him to keep afloat.'

'Hardly enough to last the month, and I'm one of his oldest customers.'

'At least we can pay the wages.'

'And sure isn't God good for tomorrow! Now what about

a little visit with the Misses Drysdale to take my mind off that meeting. They're just back from Newmarket. I'm sure they have some tales to tell.'

Goldie greeted us with delight. 'Oh, how lovely to see you, come in,' she cried.

Though no explanation for our visit was necessary, Queenie said, 'We were just passing. I brought you a little something,' and handed over a bottle of homemade wine.

'How kind.' Goldie placed it on the sideboard in the sitting room, like a trophy. Daisy was sewing before a blazing log fire. She apologised for not getting to her feet. 'It's my leg,' she said. 'Little accident at the races,' she explained.

'Some of the courses were closed because of the bad weather,' Goldie said, 'so we drowned our sorrows, didn't we, Daisy?'

Her sister giggled. 'We did.'

We sat down to scalding cups of tea and fresh-baked soda bread. Goldie thrilled us with snippets of scandalous gossip about their escapades, and the glamorous people they'd met.

'Isn't your garden looking perfect?' Queenie said, her eyes on the blaze of dahlias.

'And how are you since you moved?' Goldie asked.

'You've no idea what I've been through.' Queenie threw off her scarf and launched into her tale of woe.

'Monstrous.' Daisy clucked with sympathy. 'Oh, that lovely house. What a shame.'

'Whatever happened to all Mrs Breslin's beautiful pieces of Regency and Chippendale?' Goldie asked enviously.

Queenie's voice lifted slightly. 'The place is coming down with it.' Her eyes were sharp and purposeful. 'What with our own furniture we're stuffed to the gills. I know you love good furniture so, if you'd care to buy a few bits and pieces, I could let you have them at the right price. That's really why I'm here.'

A change came over the sisters as they deliberated conspiratorially. Queenie sat sipping her tea, her desperation cloaked with a smile.

'Would you sell us that beautiful drum table in the hall?' Goldie asked.

Queenie hesitated for a split second. 'I'd consider it.'

Goldie was up off her chair, heading for the door, speed and certainty in her movements. 'I'll write you a cheque this instant to secure it.'

'Thank you,' Queenie said.

Daisy picked up her embroidery and stitched on. 'I fancy the card table,' she said dreamily.

'It's yours, my dear.' Queenie's eyes admired the beautiful flowers blossoming beneath Daisy's industrious hands as she snapped her handbag shut on Goldie's cheque. 'Wonderful colours. Is there no end to your talent?'

Daisy bowed her head graciously.

As the afternoon passed I realised, from the gleam in Queenie's eye, that not only was she intent on flogging the favoured furniture she'd bought for a song, but good paintings as well – in fact, anything she could unload to the sisters, or anyone else who was willing to pay for them. Helped on with a drop of brandy in her tea, she told them about the bakery. 'Needs rebuilding, rewiring, everything. For that I need investment. But as soon as it's up and running we'll be out of the woods. You know me. I won't take long to get it going.'

'We might be interested in investing a little. We've every confidence in you, Queenie,' Goldie said.

'You're a great businesswoman,' Daisy agreed.

Their nods to each other emphasised their conviction.

'Is that the time?' Queenie lifted herself out of her chair. 'Lorraine will be wondering what happened to us,' she said. 'Now, do come soon and see the other bits of furniture for yourselves.' She was putting her coat on, calling to me to get a move on. 'And don't forget, Daisy, to call into the shop as soon as your leg's healed. Your order's in.'

'We'll be over,' they chorused.

'We'll make plans,' Goldie promised, smiling delightedly as if a kindly benefactor had visited her.

Sidestepping the potted plants and huddled together under Queenie's big black umbrella we made our way to the car. Reality struck me as we waved the sisters goodbye. 'However are you going to get money out of them when they see the state of the bakery?' I asked, helping her into the car.

'Simple,' she answered, wrapping her coat around her. 'They won't see it.'

A wave of anxiety swept over me. 'But they're coming over. Surely they'll want to see their investment.'

'Leave it to me,' Queenie said. 'It'll be sorted by the time they see it.' She sat back in her seat, chuckling. 'With the help of Tommy Traynor's money too. Do you know, I feel better already and I saved meself twenty quid on the doctor?'

That evening she phoned Tommy Traynor. In the old days he'd extended her credit, small loans, even, charging very little interest; their shared hobby added the edge to their odd friendship. He'd always given help in times of trouble, and was ready to confide his own difficulties to her. She'd ask him to invest heavily in her business too. He'd had a lot of money on Desert Orchid when it romped home at Sandown as he'd predicted. Too cautious to risk him, Queenie had missed out.

The race meeting was exactly the place to bring up the subject. If she were to accompany him, she was bound to find the opportunity to bring up the subject before the last race or on the way home.

'Would you like to come?' he asked, knowing her love of the races. 'I'll take you,' he said, determination in his voice as though Queenie had refused.

'I wouldn't want to inconvenience you.'

'No inconvenience at all.'

'By the way, Queenie,' Tommy said, 'did you hear that the Breslins have bought a small pub somewhere in Cork?'

'It's a wonder she let him,' Queenie said. 'He'll drink it in no time.'

Chapter Thirty-five

Two men guided the cars to the grass verges of a sweeping field where rows of cars were already neatly parked. Tommy Traynor, small and distinguished in his best suit, stepped out. Next, Queenie and Statia disembarked, Tommy giving them a helping hand. Lorraine got out last, full of apprehension, the circus-like quality of the enclosure, and the billowing entertainment tent with its colourful streamers bringing back memories of the circus.

The smell of grass and cigarettes reminded her of the delight when she first encountered the circus, in 1955 when it came to Glasthule. That's when her love affair with Ginger and his string of ponies had begun. Since then her life had been a performance, an act to be kept up at all times. She closed her eyes and saw the rippling bodies of acrobats on ropes and ladders, the white-painted face and scarlet mouth of the clown, the lions growling and restless, Nellie, the great docile elephant, bedecked in bright jewelled cloak and matching cap.

She had escaped one year, went lumbering down Eden Road, and turned into Mona Corcoran's granny's back lane. Mona Corcoran's granny was sitting in her deck-chair in her garden, sunning herself, when Nellie's trunk appeared over the fence. Never having seen an elephant and thinking it was a snake she ran screaming for the shovel and her bottle of holy water . . .

It began to rain. Shivering, Lorraine turned towards Tommy Traynor.

'Come on,' Tommy said, grabbing Queenie's arm, then Statia's.

Off they trotted to the enclosure, as graceful as horses, in unison and harmony in their shared sport. There they discussed form and weight with racegoers in brown felt hats, who smelt of old money, their hands clasped around their shooting-sticks as they watched the horses go. Preoccupied with the anticipation of the long day's pleasure that stretched out before them, they laughed, talked and contradicted each other.

In a world of her own Queenie ran her expert eyes over the racehorses' quarters, checking for quality and muscle tone. They greeted old friends warmly, and questioned the horses' chances before going under the canopy where a hawk-eyed man was taking bets.

'I'll give you Carvill's Hill for the first winner today,' Tommy bragged.

Queenie looked surprised. 'What makes you say that? He's had a succession of injuries.'

'He has to start somewhere and he has the form, the handicap.'

'Do it each way,' Queenie said, ignoring all other advice, giving herself up to the vision of his glorious win, hearing in her head the drumming hoofs of Carvill's Hill. She placed her bet while Lorraine held her bag, remembering the old days when Queenie never missed a big race meeting.

Once the racing started the talking stopped. Queenie was hardly aware of what happened that moment, her horse's start was so fast. She lifted her binoculars to watch, oblivious of everything except the galloping hoofs, the flash of colours, the crowd roaring, 'Come on, come on.'

Their selection finished first to everybody's amazement. Disappointed friends offered congratulations, and after that Queenie relied on Tommy as her sole tipster. Recklessly he gave a second winner. After they collected their winnings they walked back to the tent where they sat with their sandwiches and flasks.

'You must be gasping for a cup of tea,' Statia said.

'I'm sick of tea,' Queenie said, looking towards the bar.

A gust of wind shook the tent and glasses clattered in protest. 'All this dressing up,' Statia moaned, from under the veil of her black velvet hat, 'waste of time if you ask me.'

'No one asked you,' Queenie responded. 'I love it all. Such gorgeous style.' Her eyes were on the hats and colourful suits. 'Gives it a sense of occasion.' She removed her white gloves, laid them on her lap and sat in violet splendour, her coat wrapped gracefully around her, and the matching feathers in her hat fluttering in the breeze.

Tommy appeared with a bottle of champagne.

'That's more like it.' Queenie's eyes twinkled.

'We're on a winning streak,' Tommy said, pouring it out, handing glasses around.

Queenie sat back, her glass at her lips, the world her playground.

'Lovely,' Statia said, drinking quickly, licking her lips. 'It's all the excitement, churns me up.'

'Have a drop more.' Tommy refilled her glass.

'Go easy on it,' Queenie warned her. 'It's dynamite.'

'Never did me a bit of harm.' Tommy laughed, raising his glass, pledging their good luck.

'You've a galvanised stomach,' Queenie said.

Statia said, 'That's what took poor Jockser in the end. His stomach.' Her eyes clouded over.

'Come along, my dears, come along.' Tommy put down his glass. 'The next race is starting. You don't want to miss the fun.'

'It's raining,' Statia wailed, as they plodded through puddles, Tommy's umbrella over them, his arm protectively around Queenie.

Lorraine linked Statia, giving herself up to her predicament with good grace. Aloof and separate she kept a watchful eye on them, wishing she were part of their magic circle, but she could never share Queenie's pleasure at race meetings because horses reminded her so much of Ginger. Queenie was deep in conversation with racing friends when Father Nobel and Father McMahon appeared.

'Lorraine, I won.' Father McMahon was thrilled to share his brief moment of delight with her, the touch of his hand on her arm dispersing her unease.

'Come on,' he said, his enthusiasm compelling her forward, 'I'll give you a tip for the next one.'

They joined the drift of crowds passing the determined tic-tac man. The next race began. Father McMahon cheered the horses on, jumped up and down as they finished with childish conquest in his eyes. Tommy and Queenie placed their bets, Tommy tempering his advice with caution this time, whispering the odds in Queenie's ear. They returned to the tent defeated, and went to get a hot whiskey each.

'Irish?' Tommy asked, stooping towards Queenie.

'Irish. We won't see much more of the races if we keep this up.' Finding the opportunity she told him of her problem.

He listened, their friendship valuable to him. 'Bad news,' he said, shaking his head. 'Criminal, really, because you could have been on to such a good thing.'

'I didn't realise the extent of the repairs.'

'So,' he said, eventually, drawing on his pipe, 'what do you intend to do about it?'

'Getting rid of the house would be a bad idea, but if we don't we'll end up with not enough to eat.'

'You always were dramatic, Queenie. How much do you need?'

'A lot, if I'm to rebuild the bakery, but it's impossible to find.' She swirled her glass, her eyes transfixed by the amber liquid as if it were gold. 'What I need is an investor, someone with a bit of capital behind him or her. Otherwise I see no improvement in prospect.' Her voice was lifeless. 'Someone I'm well acquainted with. Someone like yourself, Tommy.'

Tommy sucked on his pipe silently. 'I'll think about it.'

'Done. We'll work out the details tomorrow.' Queenie said

'Where's Statia?' Queenie asked, remembering her suddenly.

'Over here,' Statia called, extending a full glass of champagne. 'That nice Mr Breslin insisted I share his champagne with him.'

'Sit down and have a drop,' said Mr Breslin, raising his head sparrow-like, his smile loaded with mischief.

'No, thanks,' Queenie snapped.

'Have you anything in the way of a tip for me for the next race?' he asked Tommy.

'No,' Tommy barked.

'Coming, Statia?' Lorraine asked.

'We're grand here, aren't we, Statia?' Mr Breslin said, ordering another bottle of champagne, with a wicked gleam in his eye.

Queenie turned away and gazed at the passing crowd.

'Couldn't you stop now,' Father McMahon said to Mr Breslin, 'while you're sober?'

'Me only pleasure these days.' Mr Breslin sighed. 'I'm too old for the fillies.'

Queenie, her eyes shuttered, said, 'We must go.'

'Go ahead,' Statia replied. 'Mr Breslin can drive me home.' She took his arm.

'You're coming home with us,' Queenie said stiffly.

'I'd prefer to go with Mr Breslin,' Statia said to Lorraine. 'That old fool Tommy Traynor is a terrible driver.'

Lorraine knew that only her patience would head off

disaster and said, 'It's been a long day, Statia. I think you should come home now with us. Queenie's dropping.'

'I am not,' Queenie denied, marching towards the car park, Tommy mincing after her. 'I'm delighted with my day.'

Statia took Lorraine's arm. 'I'm too tired and tipsy for an argument.'

As they crossed the hall, went past the bills on the hall table, Lorraine felt the constriction of living in the Breslins' house returning, squeezing the daylights out of her.

'Me poor feet,' Queenie said, crouching over the fire, putting a log on it, angry that it had gone out. 'Where's Mary? What about our bite of supper? Phil!' she called, sneezing suddenly.

Phil came up the back stairs. 'How did you get on? You look miserable, the lot of you,' he said.

'It rained,' Queenie said.

'And you've had a drop too.' He tut-tutted.

'Champagne,' Statia hiccuped, reeling into the nearest armchair.

'You'll catch your death after the soaking you got,' Phil warned.

'Can we not have a bit of fun without worrying about our health?' Statia moaned.

'We won,' Queenie said.

'Lucky you,' Phil said sarcastically. 'I'll bring the tea.'

Chapter Thirty-six

'Are you not feeling well?' Mary asked, delivering Queenie's breakfast tray to the bedside table.

'I've got a touch of a headache,' Queenie said, gazing up at her. 'I don't seem to be able to get warm. Me feet are perished after the drowning I got at the races, and I've got indigestion.'

'I'm not surprised you've got indigestion. I'll get you a hot-water bottle. How did you sleep?' she said, straightening the quilt with clinical competence.

'Like a log.'

'There's nothing else to do but stay in bed.'

'I'll get up later, see to this correspondence.'

'I don't recommend it,' said Mary, handing her a pair of pink bedsocks. 'It's freezin' downstairs.'

'Light the fire in the sitting room.'

Queenie dozed, and was woken by a pain that seemed to engulf her ribcage. She called but not loudly enough for

Lorraine, who was getting into her car to drive to the shops, or Mary, in the kitchen with the radio blaring, to hear her. Returning with the promised hot-water bottle, Mary was shocked to find Queenie doubled in agony, perspiration pouring off her.

'In the name of God, Mrs Boyle, what ails you?' Mary cried, catching up the sinking Queenie in her strong arms and pushing her back into the pillows. 'What is it? Talk to me?'

'Get the doctor,' Queenie rasped.

Panic-stricken, Mary ran from the room, down the stairs to the telephone. The doctor said he'd come at once, then Mary rang Lorraine before she rushed back upstairs to Queenie's bedside.

Dr Ross took the stairs two at a time, Lorraine following him.

By the time I arrived Mum was sitting at the bedside while Dr Ross gave Queenie an injection. 'You're all right now, Mrs Boyle,' he said. 'That should do the trick.'

Washing his hands then drying them, his eyes steady on his patient, he said reassuringly to Queenie, 'No need to panic.' Then he cast a conspiratorial glance at Mum and me. Once we were outside, he said, 'Keep her warm and no fuss. She won't feel like eating but give her plenty of fluids. I'll call in later.'

Mum said, 'Yes, Doctor.'

'I'll take up her tray,' I insisted at supper-time.

'Don't forget the evening paper. She'll want to study the form for Newmarket or Doncaster or whatever's on,' Mum reminded me.

I found Queenie sitting up, her pillows behind her head, looking comfortably refreshed. She was feeling much better. 'It's all my own doing,' she said. 'This weather is frightful and I shouldn't have gone out in it for a whole day. But I enjoyed meself.'

'I've brought you some chicken broth.' I laid the tray carefully on the bedside table.

'I'm not hungry. Take it away and pull up the blind, I'll read the paper instead.'

Mum came into the room and marched over to the bed. 'It's a harmless bowl of soup, eat it.'

'How dare you speak to me like that?' Queenie lashed out.

Mum stormed off. I opened the window slightly and left Queenie to read her newspaper in peace.

A few hours later a knock on her bedroom door woke Queenie. Thinking it was Mary, she called, 'Come in.' To her astonishment Tommy Traynor's head appeared around the door.

'Oh! It's you.' Queenie sat bolt upright and pulled the sheet up to her chin.

'Hello, Queenie. I'm sorry to barge in, only Lorraine said it was all right.'

'Did she, indeed?'

'I wanted to say that if there's anything I can do for you, don't hesitate to let me know.'

'I've caught a chill. You can't do anything about that.'

Tommy came into the room, squeezed himself between

the screen and her bed, then sat down beside her. 'I can do better than that. I've got the answer to your problems.'

'What?'

'I've decided to invest in your business in return for a stake in it.'

'I see.'

Relieved as she was, Queenie wished that she didn't have to entertain him and his talk of business while she was in bed.

'All legitimate and above board. It's in a letter to Mr Hill.'

She touched the envelopes on her tray. 'I haven't opened them yet.'

Pointing to the bedroom plasterwork Tommy remarked, 'That's in a terrible mess. I'll get my builders to fix it when they move into the bakery.'

'Mmm.'

'I think I should have a good look around the bakery again. See what's involved.'

'If you must,' Queenie said. 'As soon as I'm well enough I'll take you.'

A few days later, Queenie put on her best coat and hat and took Tommy to the bakery. Together they stared at the four walls stripped bare of every last piece of machinery and furnishing. Tommy whistled through his teeth and Queenie shuddered, taken aback at the skeleton she saw before her eyes.

Gone were the shelves that had held sacks of flour, the huge ovens, the trays for the bread, the slicing machines, and the rolls of waxed wrapping paper. All that was left was a sweeping brush and the ghostly breath of baking bread.

'At least now we can see the problem areas,' Tommy said, Armed with the plans and measurements, Tommy moved around with the quick assurance of possession. He poked at the flaking walls with a stick, trying to locate the source of the damp. 'You've got dry rot too,' he said, pointing to a corner, before turning his attention to the fungus in the skirting board. 'It's everywhere,' he continued crossly. 'The place reeks of decay. It'd be easier to knock it down and rebuild it.' His rebuke made Queenie feel inadequate.

'Do you still want to invest?' she asked. 'Because if you don't I know other people who will.' She was thinking of the Misses Drysdale.

'There's nothing that we can't handle,' he said, recovering himself quickly.

'Come on, let's go, then.'

'We haven't finished yet. What about the offices out here?' He went outside, leaving the door wide open.

Queenie followed him.

'Plenty of space here for the staff. The builders will start as soon as we get the paperwork in order,' he said.

Queenie felt uncomfortable. 'Fine,' she said.

With the unfolding of Tommy's plans and his investment in the business, Queenie's position was undermined. As head of the family she had been both owner and managing director. Now Tommy would pop over to Queenie's house, making himself indispensable with his protectiveness over her, her shops, her bakery and her home.

'You're like God, you're everywhere,' a weary Queenie would sigh, discovering him in the sitting room or in the kitchen having tea with Mary. Sometimes he'd appear for no other reason but to remind her of his existence. He couldn't wait to inform her of the builders' progress, the strict economies he'd insisted upon.

A workman arrived at the house. 'Hello, love,' he said. 'I'm here to do some repairs for Mrs Boyle.'

'I'm sorry, she's not here today,' Queenie said, keeping her eyes downcast.

'That's funny. Mr Traynor arranged for me to call.' His eyes searched her face. 'You look surprised. He phoned me in answer to an advertisement in the paper.'

'I don't know what wants doing,' Queenie said, looking around, puzzled.

Nothing gave Tommy more pleasure than to break into her home with reminders of details previously given as if her memory was faulty. Her views held no sway. Once he had listened to her he carried on with his own plans, making it obvious that no help from her was needed. Queenie kept her eyes on him, and paid another visit to the bakery.

Great piles of timber lay in the yard, beside a cement mixer and a load of sand and gravel. The sounds of demolition deafened her. Hammer blows resounded off the roof, and saws seared the air. Workmen whistled, dogs barked, and the piles of rubble grew higher. Tommy was running from one man to another, his hand punching the air for emphasis.

As time went on Queenie berated him for the slow or

shoddy workmanship of his men, if only to reinstate her position as boss. As she pored over her accounts, checking every penny that was spent, her desire to strangle him was restrained by his competence. Much as she hated to admit it, the place was taking shape. Progress was being made. Just as she began to relax Chantal gave notice. The persistent cold weather was her reason for returning to Paris, but Queenie suspected she was chasing after some man she'd set her heart on.

The phone rang in Donnybrook. It was Trish. 'I got your message. Would you like to meet for lunch?'

'What a good idea.'

At one o'clock I walked into Searson's in Baggot Street. Trish was waiting, elegant in a red suit and frilly white blouse. 'Are you here long?' I asked, slipping into the chair opposite. 'We were up to our eyes. I couldn't get away.'

'Poor you. The trials and tribulations of being your own boss.'

'It's no joke,' I agreed.

'I'd swap with you if I could. Do you know that no matter what goes wrong at that damn store I have to carry the can for it?'

'The price of promotion.'

'They're pleased with me and even praised me for my dedication to duty.' She laughed.

'Don't complain, then,' I said, reaching for the menu.

'Trouble is they don't pay me enough for the hours and the aggro. I hate being pushed around,' she said fiercely.

She ordered two vodkas and tonic, which the barman poured.

'I have an idea,' I said.

'What's that?'

'How about you coming to work for me?'

Trish took a sip of her drink. 'This is unexpected.'

'I know.' I hurried on, not giving her a chance to refuse, 'I could do with an expert book-keeper and you could do with a pay rise.'

Trish sat back, thinking. 'Have you talked to Queenie?'

'No, but she'll think it's a great idea. If you were willing to take over the accounts I could concentrate on the rest.'

Straightening up Trish said, 'You'll have to give me some details of what's involved,' a note of caution in her voice.

I outlined what I had in mind, Trish listening intently.

'Are you serious?'

'Business is something I never joke about. We could have a great little enterprise with the right staff and the backing of the bank.'

'I thought you said you were broke?' Trish said, baffled.

'We are, but we need you, Trish. What's wrong?'

'I'm flattered, overwhelmed really.' Trish sat forward. 'I've been doing accounts for years.' She stopped, at a loss for words. Finally she said, 'Are you sure?'

'You're ideal for the job.'

'Give me a day or two to think about it. It's a big responsibility having to make it all pay for itself. Mind you, I enjoy a challenge. But I wouldn't want to let you down.'

'Take as long as you like,' I agreed, watching the enthusiasm surface. 'And isn't it time we ordered something to eat?'

Chapter Thirty-seven

The flight of Madame Renard, the new shop manager, was overdue.

'She's late.' Queenie sighed, her eyes on the clock, the airport business proceeding around her.

'There she is.' Tommy rushed towards her, anxious to relieve her of her bags.

A tiny dark woman, barely visible behind a trolleyful of luggage and a large bunch of exotic bird-of paradise flowers, came through the barrier.

Tommy took her hand. 'You must be Madame Renard.'

'Mais oui.' Wearing a burgundy velvet hat cocked to one side and a matching coat, she smiled up at him.

'Mrs Boyle's over there. She's going to be thrilled to see you.'

Madame Renard's eyes found Queenie's. Ceremoniously she handed her the flowers. 'A present for you, Madame. I am so sorry. They are crushed.'

They moved towards the exit. Tommy was battling through the throng with the trolley. Madame Renard hastened to keep up with him. Queenie, upright and dignified, lagged behind.

'You brought the sunshine.' Tommy glanced up at the sky over the car park.

Madame Renard looked skywards doubtfully and drew her coat around her.

On the way home Tommy insisted they stop at the Skylon Hotel for a drink. Madame Renard relaxed a little over her large brandy.

'This is nice,' she declared, gazing around.

Queenie brought the conversation round to business. 'We've found ourselves in a fix with the bakery. But we've got things going.'

Tommy smiled at her. 'Plenty of time for all that. Another small one?' he asked.

Madame Renard hoisted herself up on the bar stool. 'I'll have a large one.'

'Good. Hungry?' His fascination with her showed in his admiring glances.

She nodded, dimpling up at him.

'A plate of assorted sandwiches will sort us out,' he said to Queenie, before skipping off to order them.

When he put down the plate Madame Renard took a bite out of one and said, 'I'm a greedy girl.'

'And a good-looking one,' said Tommy.

'Married,' Queenie reminded him.

The time slipped by, unnoticed by either of them.

Queenie said, 'We'd better get a move on. The day

won't wait.' Madame Renard looked doubtfully into her glass.

'Sure I can't tempt you to another?' asked Tommy.

'But why not?'

Delighted he ordered another round.

Finally Queenie stood up. 'Come along then,' she said.

Madame Renard, her hat crooked, got to her feet. 'I'm so happy to be here.' Her eyes floated up to Tommy's.

Tommy gripped her arm, and led her along. A disgruntled Queenie followed.

They drove to Abbeyville and Tommy swept to a halt outside Queenie's house. He got out and hurried round to open the passenger door. He waited, hand outstretched to help the scrabbling Madame Renard. Queenie was forgotten.

'Take it easy,' he advised. 'Lean on me.'

Madame Renard floated towards him, giggling.

Queenie made her way up the steps ahead of them, glancing back disapprovingly. On the last step Madame faltered. Tommy lifted her in his arms and carried her in.

Queenie remained composed until they reached the sitting room. Then she said, 'Put her down.'

Madame Renard dropped into an armchair, her hat leaped from her head, and she fell instantly asleep.

'We've had it,' Queenie thundered to Lorraine in the kitchen. 'She's paralytic. Bring the coffee and lots of it. I should have known better than to trust another Frenchwoman.' But Lorraine shook her head. 'She's a stylish woman,' she said. 'She might just do the trick for us.'

And Lorraine was proved right. Until the shop was ready

one of the bedrooms was turned over for Madame Renard's exclusive use and she got to work. Wrapped in a pink housecoat, her hair caught up in a matching chiffon scarf, she threw herself into perfecting her designs.

Patterns were laid out, materials scattered everywhere. Scissors, pins and threads were ready at her elbow. Surrounded by fashion magazines, she sketched a pattern on to tissue paper, then cut it out. 'Just wait,' she ordered the impatient Queenie.

Taking black satin from a suitcase full of materials, she pinned her pattern on it. She cut carefully. Then her sewing-machine ran up precise seams. Now and then she stopped to survey her work, pounced on a problem, plucked pins from her pincushion to rectify it.

'*Voilà*.' She lifted the garment up for Queenie's inspection. 'We can do the same in pink, and cream, coffee, burgundy, any colour you like,' she advised, settling into her seat.

'Quite.' Queenie was begrudging in her approval.

As she continued, a sense of ease overcame Madame Renard, as subtle as the collection she was making for the discerning woman, or the glamorous one. Queenie's irksome ways were forgotten as her prototypes took shape.

The shop became an extension of Madame Renard's personality. She had designed it, from the large plate-glass counter to the central fountain. Each morning, in trousers and pale silk shirt, she would inspect it. Her yearning to express the warmth within her came out in her choice of colours. Purple and white, coffee and cream, chocolate, vermilion and violet were all matched together. Happy, she flew about, a lively bird, giving orders. Her staff of two assistants, the Jackson twins, had been selected for their tasks because they had trained in sales in Breslin's bakery shop. Their minds and hearts warmed to her as she worked on her exquisite creations. Swathes of slippery black satin, lavender cobweb lace and champagne chiffon cascaded from her case, and fell in clouds to the floor. Swiftly her range was extended to produce the sexiest lingerie imaginable – lace bras, matching briefs, suspender belts, G-strings, chiffon négligés, and baby-doll pyjamas. Next came satin nightdresses, soft as a sigh, and glazed cotton ones too, chosen to appeal to young tastes.

Lorraine's 'Wow!' broke the silence as she searched for the right word to describe the magnificent display. Panic overtook Queenie, who declared the whole ensemble too naughty. But everyone else went wild with delight at M. Guilbert's garments. Drifts of mascara slid down Madame Renard's cheeks as, overcome by their praise and support, she took a bow and a huge bouquet of flowers from Tommy Traynor. His assurance, spoken with true conviction, that the bras and briefs would sell in 'massive' quantities, comforted Queenie.

Out of the blue Queenie had a big win on a horse. Happy for the first time since Madame Renard arrived, she invested the money in her business, her mind on mass production.

The designing was left to Madame Renard. Relieved to have Queenie on her side at last, she got to work. Soon the place was buzzing. Queenie, gruff and taciturn alternately, kept her distance, embroiling herself in the accounts.

The next few months sped by. Each day Queenie came

to the shop and although she was caught up in the swing of it, she left the day-to-day running to her staff. But her shrewd eyes missed nothing and she gave sound advice when it was needed – advice Madame Renard didn't always welcome.

'I wish you would take yourself back to the accounts,' Madame Renard said exasperatedly when Queenie made suggestions for the spring collection. 'I am a bundle of nerves,' she continued. 'Your interference shatters me for days.'

'I'm only trying to help,' Queenie protested.

'I've got a lifetime in the trade, and, the last thing I need is your advice.' Madame Renard swaggered off to devote herself to the planning of the next collection.

Chapter Thirty-eight

Queenie had changed the décor throughout the house, repainting the walls in delicate, airy colours, matching them with pale carpets and chintz curtains. The few antiques she'd kept and the delicate china cabinets stayed as they were, huge bowls of lilies adding brightness and the scent of autumn. 'If Sean could see us now he wouldn't believe it,' she said to herself.

'Mother.' Lorraine stood in the doorway. 'Are you all right?'

'Of course. Why?'

'I thought I heard you talking to someone.'

'I was wondering aloud if your father would have approved.'

'He'd probably have found it a bit grand,' Lorraine said.

'He had social aspirations of his own, you know, and he liked to be surrounded by nice things.'

'I know,' Lorraine said. 'And he'd have been proud of our achievement. By the way, I suppose we should have a party to celebrate your seventy-first birthday.'

'Yes, something small.'

'If we're going to do it, we'll do it properly,' Lorraine insisted, and began to make elaborate arrangements, glad to be back in action. Thankfully she had energy to spare, and Queenie had the money. Lorraine drew up the guest list, contacted the band, organised a marquee, dealt with Maisie Byrne, the florist, and phoned the caterers. By the time she'd finished there wasn't a detail left to chance.

On the day of the party the weather was glorious. The sky was blue the sun shone brilliantly. All day long Lorraine worked, while Mary scrubbed and polished. Gifts were wrapped, tied with ribbons, and laid out at the top table next to the birthday cake.

Thanks mostly to Lorraine's efforts the garden looked magnificent. All shades of lupins marched alongside hydrangeas. Deep red roses and stephanotis stretched to the wrought-iron gate, their scent heavy on the air. Inside the marquee rows of tables were extravagantly laid for dinner. Vases of flowers were placed strategically here and there. Pale candles waited patiently on the enormous birthday cake for the flame of celebration. Helium balloons rose in glorious shades of blue, Queenie's favourite colour. Everything had been planned with precision, and was perfect.

Wrapped in her dressing-gown, Lorraine sat brushing her hair resolutely, her mind jumping distractedly as nervousness overtook her. It was the same unease she had felt in the circus, before the show started, when she would parade up and down outside the back of the tent, fidgeting with the buttons and bows on her costume, making sure that everything was in place. This evening, Queenie's party was going to be a magnificent affair, a night to remember. Tying a chiffon scarf around her head, she applied her makeup expertly, then stepped into her long black velvet dress. Her love of parties, her pride in all she had done, her good intentions made her strong. This house was homely now, cosy with their own unsophisticated stamp on it. She loved it: Queenie had been right to buy it. In fact, her mother had been right about most things. Caustic as Queenie was, Lorraine understood that she was kindly and well-meaning. One last check in the mirror: she saw that her face was glowing, her dark eyes great with anticipation.

Queenie stood in a long, floating dress of mist blue, and her scent of lavender mingled with the smell of roast turkey. The guests came to meet her, congratulations and good wishes tumbling from their lips.

Later, at the top table she was seated next to Lorraine, with Olivia on her left. She and her granddaughter were engrossed in conversation. 'You're doing well, Queenie,' Olivia said encouragingly.

Queenie shook her head. 'I'm not able for all the fuss. The last thing I want is to be swept off my feet. Listen, my pet, tonight I'm depending on you to keep the balance. Distract them. It's been such a rush and fuss.'

Olivia looked at her, consideringly. 'How do I begin? I don't know if I'm magnetic enough for what you're asking. You're the one they want to celebrate tonight.'

'You know what to do. With your charm and your wit you'll distract them, believe me. I'm just an old lump of wood in the corner.'

Queenie's desperation was not lost on Olivia. She said, 'You'll be all right.'

'All I want is to put my feet up with a nice hot cup of tea.'

Tommy, at the table opposite, sat between his wife and Madame Renard, and held Madame Renard's attention with his wisecracking and his constant pouring of wine.

Leaving Queenie alone for a moment Olivia, immersed in conversation with Aunt Pru, glanced around the tables, her eagle eyes missing nothing.

'Delicious,' Tommy called to her, his mouth full. 'Any more of this?'

His helpless wife looked at Trish, who hissed, 'Daddy!' under her breath.

Quickly he turned his attention back to Madame Renard. 'As I was saying . . .' His voice faded into the hubbub.

'Lorraine knows how to do things in style,' Aunt Pru said.

'That Olivia's damned attractive,' Uncle Cecil declared.

'Really,' said Queenie, whose strength was ebbing. She continued to look thoughtfully at the people who were eating her food. What did they know of the struggles she had endured? The pain, frustration, defeats and losses, all part of her life before the achievements and success?

Dinner over, Tommy stood up. 'Here's to your good health, Queenie,' he said, raising his glass. 'Happy birthday.'

'Happy birthday!' Cheers went up as Queenie stood to cut the cake, her eyes on the garden. She wished she could be released like the balloons floating above her head.

'Thank you all for celebrating with me,' she said simply, and sat down again.

Long speeches were made, champagne flowed. Everyone was talking gaily and at once. It struck Queenie with brutal force how meaningless it all was. The breath was gone out of her. She missed her evening exercise among her flowers and shrubs.

Smiling, she got up quietly and went into the garden. She felt tired yet relieved that she'd questioned Tommy Traynor's loyalty with Mr Hill – not that he'd believed her for a minute. His respect for her money made him mouth polite responses. She knew his vanity wouldn't let him accept what she had had to say about a man like Tommy Traynor, Tommy had been a customer of his for as long as Queenie had. His admiration for Tommy overrode all reality.

The spring wasn't in Queenie's step now, and her shoulders were stooped. There was a lessening of the force within her too, and she did not seize opportunities and plan any more. She was sad that she wasn't as brave as she used to be. She didn't want to look too far ahead. The fact that Tommy was part of her business, and it wasn't all her own, dismayed her. If only he'd stayed out of it, a sleeping partner, as she'd intended him to be. But he insisted on full participation. His entire personal endeavour seemed to be to grab as much of the limelight as he could get, push Madame Renard to the fore, and obliterating Queenie's achievements in the process.

Sitting on the garden seat by the pond she thought back to when she'd climbed out of the rut she'd been in and widened her world. She thought of all the customers she'd served over the years, the friends for whom she'd made outfits in her spare time. She thought of Olivia, in those featureless hotels, always impatient to get home, then itching to be off again, Jim sullen when she'd gone. If only she could smooth things between them, make the magic happen for Olivia. Jim was good with Olivia, and Queenie would have done anything to feed the flame that Olivia was starving. Perhaps the time was right to put into practice the idea that had been in her mind for a long time. Out of her handbag she took her bulging notebook.

Then she thought of Lorraine, who had been a healthy child, a luscious teenager. She'd loved glamour and dancing, and Ginger, whose desertion had destroyed her. When she'd brought Billy home from England, with his pink cheeks and his bottle permanently stuck to his lips, Queenie had taken him over. On fine days she'd taken him to the seaside, leaving Lorraine to mind the shop. He adored their picnics on the rug, sandwiches, crisps, and his plastic mug of orange juice.

Billy phoned to say he'd be home for her birthday.

A longing to see him again overtook her. She recalled his face, lively and young, as surely as if she'd seen it yesterday. Her desire to hug and kiss him was so strong it almost bowled her over. She stood up and walked down the path. The graded heights of the fairy-lights illuminated her way, adding strange texture and colour to the garden. Her odd sense of being with Billy, was overpowering. Now, on this perfect evening, all she had achieved in her life was as nothing compared to her desire to see him.

Next day, when she was gardening, she heard his voice calling, 'Queenie', so plainly that she was rooted to the spot.

She turned, and saw him coming towards her.

'Queenie.' His voice was hoarse yet gentle.

'Billy!'

He rushed towards her, and took her clumsily in his arms. She clasped him to her. She longed to hold him, stroke his hair as she had when he was little, but Faith stepped forward and Queenie greeted her. 'Happy birthday, Queenie' Faith said, and kissed her. They all linked arms. 'It's like old times,' Queenie said.

'The old times were never like this.' Billy made a sweeping gesture with his hand, taking in the gardens and the house. 'You got all this since I was here last and never told me.'

'That was our surprise for you,' Queenie explained.

'Ain't it terrific?' Faith broke away, looking up at the large squares of light in the upstairs windows, the curtains not yet drawn. 'Ah'm sure glad to be here. We might even stay for good.' Shivering, she said, 'Isn't this climate chilly?'

'Go and get your wrap,' Billy said.

'If ya'll excuse me?' Faith smiled at Queenie, and strode ahead, her hips swinging.

Faith loved the new shop. Quickly and unemotionally she examined everything. 'What a surprise! How thrilling!' she said to Queenie, her face aflame with delight. 'So very exciting. Billy never said.' Without a pause she continued her exploration, of the pretty garments, the coloured silks.

'Billy didn't know,' Queenie informed her. 'And you didn't know, Billy, that I'm giving you a ten per cent stake in the business'.

Beside her, Billy, his eyes hard as cash registers.

That evening, he said, 'Wow!' 'I've so much to ask you about, Queenie. I've been thinking about the factory, making plans.'

Billy made his second trip to the factory without Faith, his face set, his mind on work. 'I'm not just here for a holiday. Not when there's so much to be done,' he told Lorraine. He was going to bring the twentieth century to Abbeyville, and end the old-fashioned ways. It was obvious that Queenie, poor soul, was practically caving in with it all and needed him.

'I'll have to stay to rescue Mum,' Billy told Phil.

'From what?' Phil asked, puzzled.

'Can't you see she's being swamped by Queenie and Olivia?'

'It's a bit late to change that.'

'Has Queenie treated her badly?'

'Of course not. A bit rough on her at times, but that's all. She's very useful, your mother. Queenie wouldn't go too far.'

'It'll take me a while to catch up on things, but I can smell a rat already.'

Perplexed, Phil looked at him. 'Watch him or he'll take over,' he warned Lorraine.

'Nonsense. Billy's not materialist, never was,' Lorraine insisted.

'It's that southern belle he's hooked himself up with. She's a gold-digger if ever I saw one.'

Queenie was enterprising. She liked change, and would

be on Billy's side, providing he didn't force his wishes on her. Tact, he explained to Lorraine, was the key to get Queenie to go along with his views. Once he'd gained her confidence she'd let him speak to the employees. Once he'd got their co-operation he'd put a stop to their slack ways. First, he'd reschedule their working hours to make sure of achieving the maximum benefit, and that Queenie wasn't being exploited.

Next, discipline would be introduced into the easy-going atmosphere. Long tea-breaks and leisurely lunches would be cut out. No more sick days for long-suffering shop assistants, and no more floating about, chatting and gossiping. Once the staff saw the error of their ways, and the bulge in their bonuses, they would all welcome this new efficiency. Things would be done the way they were done in the States because, as far as Billy was concerned, America was the best country in the world to be in.

He began by saying to Queenie, a reproachful look in his eyes, 'There are no men on the staff.'

'What do we need them for when we've got perfectly able-bodied women?' Queenie shot back.

'Not even a handyman?'

'We do it all ourselves.'

Olivia wasn't impressed with her half-brother's tactics. She saw in his loving interest in Queenie a trap to ensnare her. He was unaware of the self-sacrificing efforts Queenie had put into the making of the business, not to mention the exhaustion, the discomfort and the sheer physical pain at the end of each day. He had left, a raw youth, to learn about bloodstock. Now he'd come home to see for himself what the slow, relenting hours of work had yielded and he wasn't satisfied with their success. He wanted to control it.

When Faith decided to look for a small house, Billy was thrilled, seeing her settling down in Ireland for good. They tore off in Billy's new sports car one warm afternoon. Queenie was worried. Tommy Traynor's involvement in her business had been one thing: she had known she could handle him because she was still the boss. But Billy, with his views on changing everything, was a different matter.

Chapter Thirty-nine

As the months went by, inflamed by his intention to take charge, Billy went around the shop with the air of a soldier off to war, a feel for battle in his blood, battle he pretended to be waging on Queenie's behalf. On the first morning when he stood at the entrance his blond hair illuminated by the sunshine, his hands in the pockets of his jeans, the staff nodded a cool good morning, wondering why he was there listening attentively to their chatter as they clocked in. As time went on they knew by the serious tone he adopted when he and Queenie talked together confidentially that he meant to make changes.

Queenie watched him carefully. He had spent long days in the shops interfering in every area, with Madame Renard and her designs, and upsetting the staff with petty rules and what they suspected were his plans to take over. Resentful and dispirited, they would try to escape him.

In the evenings he stayed late in his room, while the rest

of the family watched TV. She knew that then, he would open the account books and study the figures. At first Queenie had underestimated his interference in the business, but slowly the significance of his actions dawned on her. And then there was Faith, with her expensive shopping trips to the city.

Queenie watched and waited, knowing that she would strike when Billy's actions threatened to destroy. She realised that he was only happy when he was turning the wheels of mischief in his own grasping favour.

Queenie played along with him, flattering him, and observing him mutely. She remembered the stunts she'd pulled in the past to save her skin. Yes, she'd pulled many a rabbit out of a hat, and she was about to do it again. She'd no choice. A feeling of power rose in her as she made her decision. She took up her diary, leafed through the pages and checked the date of the next board meeting. Be careful, she warned herself, then got up to telephone Mr Hennessy.

Then she decided to take some exercise in the garden. Instead, however, she sat in the garden seat to think over the last few months and the course things had taken since Billy's return.

'There you are,' Billy called, coming down the garden path.

'Hello, Billy.' Be patient, she told herself. 'Where's Olivia?'

'At the hairdresser's, I think.'

Queenie looked at her watch. 'I wanted a word with her.'

Billy frowned. 'She won't be back for hours.'

'I can't wait for her. I'm in a bit of a rush.'

'Anything I can handle?'

'No, thanks.'

'You stay here and rest yourself. Let me handle it.'

Queenie shook her head.

'You're not thinking of making any sudden moves?' he asked, suspicious.

'Such as?'

'Selling off any of the family jewels,' he joked.

'Don't be daft.' Queenie stayed cool. If she told him where she was going, what she was about to do, the game would be up. Head bent, hands in her pockets, she wandered along the path.

Faith was coming to meet them, pretty as a picture in a pale pink suit. 'There you are,' she said, grasping Billy's arm possessively, her head a shade too close to Queenie's.

Queenie moved back. 'You look very pretty,' she said.

'I'm just about to take Billy off to view this darling little house I found in Ballsbridge.'

'Isn't that a very expensive area?' Queenie asked.

'We should manage it.'

'I suppose you know what you're doing.' A woman with a mission, everything under control, Queenie allowed herself a smile of indulgence as she glanced at her watch. Is that the time? she thought, suddenly anxious. 'I must get on too,' she said aloud. 'There's so much to be done.'

'Want a lift anywhere?' Billy asked.

'No, thanks, I need the walk,' Queenie said.

'Come on, Billy,' Faith said, and there were secrets in their exchanged glances as she led him away.

Queenie watched them walk off across the garden. Billy turned and came back to her. 'It's getting cold, Queenie. You should take your coat.'

'I'm all right,' she assured him.

With Billy and Faith gone, Queenie went indoors. Her call to Mr Hennessy had given her strength.

Billy and Faith took Lorraine to Killarney for a weekend break. They left early on Friday morning leaving Queenie alone. She was glad to have time to herself and to think. Hearing a car advance up the drive she wondered if they'd returned having forgotten something. The vehicle pulled up at the house. Who was the man crossing the gravel, and what did he want? As he walked up the steps, it occurred to Queenie that there was something familiar about him.

'Good morning. Did you want to see someone?' Her voice was nervous.

The man leaned against the door, curiosity in his posture. Queenie was silent, waiting what seemed ages for him to speak.

'What a splendid place you have here.'

There was a whine in the voice that sent her heart galloping through some sealed-off part of the past. She said, 'Who are you?'

'You mean to say you don't recognise me?' The familiarity persisted in the insolent smile of the man who continued to stand in the doorway, his face pinched, his red hair receding.

They stared at one another. Queenie gathered her wits and

peered closer at the stranger's face, then straightened her back and demanded, 'Who are you?' with a force she didn't feel.

'You *don't* recognise me!' He walked into the hall and shut the door behind him. 'I recognised you instantly – even though you've smartened up since I saw you last.'

'Just tell me who you are.' Her instinct to protect herself and her home gave way to faintness. She looked up at the stranger again. With his arm around her shoulder, he said, 'Hello, Queenie.'

Her resolve to keep calm evaporated. 'I didn't say you could come in.' What if he was carrying a gun? Olivia was at the hairdresser's.

'You look wonderful, Queenie.' The flattery made her more edgy. 'Strange you should have forgotten me.' He looked at her. 'All the times you tried to get rid of me. You thought you'd succeeded but you hadn't.' His eyes were up and down the hall. 'It's great to be back. I was going to phone, but then I thought, why not surprise them? What will Lorraine think after all these years?'

'Ginger.' The name shot out of the shocked Queenie, the memories it conjured up like poison. How could this man possibly be the laughing fellow who'd wooed her daughter with his animal-training tricks? The snotty-nosed country kid, who knew how to tame a horse, snare a rabbit, catch fish with a string. The fellow who'd lived by his wits, who'd loved then cruelly discarded her daughter; the same man who had made Billy agonise throughout his boyhood about his father's long years of absence. Ginger had been a shadow in their lives they'd all learned to live with. Now his presence made him a reality. Seized with weakness she sat on the nearest chair.

'Correct. Only I'm not Ginger any more. There's nothing of that time left in me.'

'And what should I call you?' Queenie gazed at him.

'George. It's my real name.'

'George!'

'George and the Dragon,' said Ginger, squaring his shoulders.

Queenie croaked. 'There's a lot of the boy still in you.'

'Insult me all you like.' Ginger smiled genially. 'And you needn't play the petrified old woman either. I know you too well for that.'

'I thought you were in America or somewhere.'

'I was, only things got tough.' Stepping further into the hall, he said, 'Aren't you going to invite me in properly, for old times' sake? What I need is a whiskey.' The request had an edge to it.

'Whiskey,' repeated Queenie.

'Correct.'

She'd better get him a drink. Calming herself, she went into the sitting room.

Ginger followed, going to the cabinet, getting out the whiskey bottle.

'What do you think you're doing?' Queenie's feeble effort to regain authority failed.

'Saving you the trouble.' His voice was quiet. 'It's really Billy I came to see.' Nonchalantly he poured his whiskey. 'He contacted me before he left the States. Where is he?'

'He's away.' Queenie's mind raced to the upstairs room and the antiques in the trunk, the jewellery in the drawer, the money in the strong box in the wardrobe.

'Where's Lorraine?'

Clearing her throat, she said, 'If you give me a lift into town I'll take you to Lorraine. She's in the shop.' The lie that hopped easily out of her mouth calmed her.

The delight in Ginger's face put her in a position of authority once more. Suddenly his face crumpled. 'I never wanted to leave her, you know. The night before I left I said to her. "Tell me if you don't want me to go."'

'That's not my recollection of events. But you can discuss that with her when you see her. Come on.' Queenie walked out into the hall and looked steadfastly towards the front door, determined to get him out.

Following her, Ginger said, 'You know, I would've given anything to get her and Billy back, all those years ago. But you had me stopped, you ugly old cow. Funny, though, I never stopped caring about her.' He looked bitter as he spoke.

'Tell that to her,' Queenie said, unsympathetically, walking ahead, wondering how she'd endure his company on the short journey into town.

Ginger drove fast. Queenie leaned sideways against the passenger door. Not a word was spoken. Queenie was thinking of his sudden reappearance, and the eagerness to see Lorraine that seemed to be eating him up.

'I'll get out here, if you don't mind. You'll find Lorraine at the shop. It's at the far end of the town.' Queenie got out.

'I know where it is.' Ginger's car shot off.

Queenie watched him drive away. Had he been in touch with Lorraine in the past and, if so, why had she kept it secret? She wondered what trouble he was about to make now as she made her way to Mr Hennessy's office. Ginger would go mad when he discovered that Lorraine wasn't in town.

The sun shone as Queenie walked along. When winter comes where shall I be? she mused, ringing Mr Hennessy's bell.

'Congratulations, Queenie.' Mr Hennessy took her hand. 'Wonderful party.'

They talked about the new shops. 'You're on a winning streak, Queenie,' Mr Hennessy said.

'Thank you,' was all Queenie managed. She always found it difficult to express deep emotion in words. I'm a silly, sentimental old fool, she thought, filled with nostalgia, and trembling a little.

'You're a great woman.'

'You had faith in me even when I was worried to death.'

'You showed us all. You, with your brilliant ideas, your theories and your willingness to take a gamble, taught me a lot.'

'Are you on for some startling news?' She looked at him coyly.

'Of course.' He looked at her, uncertain of what she was about to say. For all his business ability, his stature, in her lights he was still the junior she'd started out with all those years ago when his father had been her solicitor.

'We've got to move fast. Billy's father's just shown up.'

'What?'

'Lorraine tipped him off that Billy was back, I'd say. They're all in some kind of conspiracy, I wouldn't wonder.'

'*What?*'

'The shock I got when he turned up on the doorstep. Walked in as if he owned the place.'

'Lorraine wouldn't do anything behind your back.'

'Where that Ginger's concerned I wouldn't trust her. She could never see his faults and failings.' She leaned forward. 'They're in cahoots, I'll bet.'

Mr Hennessy shook his head. 'Lorraine's a sensible woman. She's been in the business most of her life. She's hardly going to do anything stupid . . .'

There was a pause. Queenie pulled a face. 'Like I say, where Ginger's concerned, she's stupid, and she's soft about Billy too.'

Mr Hennessy listened with the greatest respect and attention, as he always did.

'As for that Tommy Traynor, he's genuine enough, but he's greedy too. I see it in his eyes. It's that Madame Renard. That's when his mischief started. Since she walked in all coy and girlish he's pathetic.'

Fumbling for words at what he was hearing, thinking that the shock of seeing Ginger had brought on one of Queenie's little turns, Mr Hennessy said, 'How can you be sure?'

Queenie leaned further towards him as she said, 'Mark my words, given time he'll play us up, probably side with Lorraine and Billy. Then there'll be real trouble.'

Mr Hennessy looked at her with sly eyes. 'Be careful with this kind of talk, Queenie. It's dangerous without proof.'

At that moment his secretary popped her head round the door. 'Mr Hill's here.' She looked from one to the other.

'I phoned him and asked him to pop over.' Queenie was defying Mr Hennessy to say a word.

'Right you are,' Mr Hennessy said. 'Tell him to come in,' he added to the girl.

Mr Hill, affable as usual, shook hands with Queenie and Mr Hennessy, and sat down beside Queenie.

For the office-boy at the bank he'd gone far, she thought, taking in his elegant suit, his silk tie.

'Now, this is what I plan to do.' Queenie spoke clearly and precisely.

Before she left, Mr Hennessy read out the minutes of their meeting to make sure that everything Queenie had said was written down. He linked her arm, just as he had in the old days when he would escort her from his office after she'd succeeded in procuring a hefty loan.

'I'll drop you home,' Mr Hill offered, as they said their goodbyes.

'No, thanks, I'll get a lift from Olivia. She's at Tony's having her hair done. She should be finished soon.'

Chapter Forty

'There's something I have to discuss with you, Olivia.' There was a self-important air about Billy as he spoke. I saved the computer file I was working on and followed him into Queenie's office.

'I heard you were looking for me. What's up?'

'It's a family matter.' He glanced briefly towards the door, then gave me a confident smile. 'I want you to do me a favour.'

'If I can.'

His blue eyes settled on me. 'I want you to ask Queenie to step down.'

'What?'

'It's not such a big deal. She hasn't been involved in the day-to-day running of the business for a while.'

'As you said yourself, it's family matter and it needs to be discussed with Queenie.'

Unnerved by my outburst, he dropped the pretence. 'Look, Olivia, she has to go.' His voice was cold.

'Says who?' I lifted my head, and waited, unable to believe that this clean-cut man with the candid blue eyes and the innocent smile was willing to betray his own grandmother.

'I was hoping this wouldn't take long.' The smile was replaced by a look of puzzlement. 'Under Queenie's management Paradise Properties has serious problems.'

'Such as?'

'Financial restrictions for one, bad management for another.'

My stomach muscles tightened. Struggling for composure I said, 'Shouldn't we wait for Queenie to be present before saying any more?'

'No. She shouldn't be bothered with all this at the moment, but if Paradise doesn't get an injection of capital to meet our expansion programme, we'll go to the wall.' He sat back and watched me digest this information.

I was stunned. 'That's ridiculous. I know everything there is to know about the company. It belongs to Queenie. Everything she has worked for has been channelled into it. We just succeeded in closing some good deals with outlets around the country.'

Billy laughed dismissively. 'And unless we have the money to pay wages and suppliers we won't be able to fulfil the orders. Already she's lost an enormous amount of the business by not expanding quickly enough.'

'Queenie would never consider stepping down. You're wasting your time.'

Billy smiled, his expression optimistic. 'She's getting on. It's all too much for her.'

'I'm not convinced. I know Queenie. She loves business. It's been her lifeline since she was a girl.'

'All the same, maybe you should have a word with her.'

'I'd be wasting my time. She wouldn't be interested.'

Billy shrugged. 'Only the other day she was talking about taking a trip to the States in August to visit us. Think of the freedom she'd have. No business worries. Talk to her, Ollie.'

'It won't work.'

Billy levelled his shrewd eyes at me. 'It's like this. Myself and this party I'm involved with are anxious to buy out her share.'

'Really. And what "party" might that be?'

'Confidential.' Billy sat back smugly. 'She's getting on and, to be honest, they don't think her health's the best,' he explained.

'She's in fighting form.'

'I might as well be honest, Olivia. As far as my party's concerned the business could do better without her input. She's too old.'

'She's no such thing.' I met his gaze head on. 'I refuse to continue this conversation.'

'Face it, Olivia, she's an old woman whose influence could be done without.'

Appalled, I said, 'How dare you speak about her like that? She's dealing with the business in her own way, the only way she knows how. It makes her feel useful and wanted. She needs a reason to keep going.'

Billy was shaking his head. 'I don't mean to be disparaging but she nearly lost the lot recently through recklessness.' His eyes were on the figures in front of him.

'But she didn't lose it.'

'Thanks to Tommy. He knew what to do with this place, getting in the right builders at the right price . . .' His voice trailed off as he threw in his last triumph. 'He had the cash, and got it ready on time. She'd never have managed without him.'

I gaped at him. 'So you've roped Tommy into your little scheme.'

'Of course.'

'Queenie likes to keep an eye on everything herself.'

'That's what I'm saying.' Billy was forceful. 'She should go now and let you run it your way. Otherwise it'll only be harder on you later on when she does pop her clogs and you've been trained all wrong. The damage will be done.' Seeing my face he raised both hands defensively. 'Sorry, Ollie. I'm only telling you for your own sake. Queenie's a strain on everyone.'

He wasn't sorry. His cold ruthlessness was in his eyes.

Furious, I said, 'You're being disloyal to Queenie, betraying her trust like this. And you're wrong. If it weren't for her we wouldn't have a business. She's the largest shareholder, the founder of the company, the boss. She can make people sit up and take notice. Perhaps it's her power you resent, and that she's quick-witted, always one step ahead.'

'It's none of that. She's old, that's all.'

'Just because she's not a man.' I stopped to take a breath.

'With all due respect to you, Billy, we don't want an unknown quantity in the business.'

'Now, now. Men don't make all the decisions, only the big ones.' Billy grinned. 'Don't think for a minute that we won't move against Queenie, my party and me.' He gave me a direct look. 'That's part of the reason why I'm being honest with you.'

'You have no authority to shift Queenie. Just who do you have in mind for the job, if it's not too rude a question?'

Billy shrugged nonchalantly. 'Someone who's better equipped to handle the growing business.'

'Someone like you?'

He smiled. 'My party's investment in Queenie's stock, my ten per cent, they give me a big say in the matter. Anyway, don't worry your pretty little head about it. You've plenty to do looking after the shop in Donnybrook, now that Chantal's gone. I'll take on the new shop and all the additional pressure if you can persuade Queenie that her stepping down would be a good move. There'd be money involved. She could make a huge profit.'

'I can tell you here and now that the money won't sway her. She's doing fine financially. And when she's ousted, you and your party will turn on me.'

Billy threw down the Biro he was fiddling with. 'Give us a break, Ollie! I'll make sure that doesn't happen. You're a smart young woman. I'll be right there with you every step of the way. Especially if you encourage Queenie to hang up her boots.'

'I won't do that, but what I will do is tell her every detail of this meeting. She'll be curious to know who it is who wants to buy her out.'

'You can't do that. It's confidential.' Billy sat back, in full control, a glint in his eye. 'And you couldn't even begin to guess.'

'But it was "this party" who thought that you should raise the matter with me immediately.'

'That's why we need Queenie's stock. It will give us a say in the running of the company.'

'Control is what they call it, and Queenie won't be interested. I know.'

Our eyes met. 'As a matter of fact it just fits in with my ideas for the future. I haven't told you about them yet.' He drew a long breath, patting the folder on his desk.

'I don't want to hear them. We're doing fine with the way things are now. We've paid off the overdraft.'

He nodded. 'Very commendable but we can do better than that. And I'm going to do it.' His arrogance made all Queenie's efforts seem puny and unimportant.

'It was a big overdraft,' I reminded him.

'That was all part of the business before I came on the scene.'

Shaken by his determination I feared for Queenie. The years raced through my mind as I sat opposite my brother, whose words threatened everything that had been important to Queenie for so long. Her reason for living had been the struggle for and the maintenance of her business.

Looking at him squarely, I said, 'We all love Queenie. We all depend on her and confide in her. Even Madame Renard.'

'Leave Madame Renard out of this,' Billy snapped.

I thought of her dedication to her job and retaliated, '*You* leave *her* out of it. You've been brain-washing her against Queenie since you arrived.'

Billy shook his head in denial. 'I've done no such thing.'

'She's our most useful asset. We need her designs. Not you and your destructive influence.'

'Queenie bullies her.'

'She reacts.'

'What do you expect her to do?'

'She's an expert. Designers like her are rare.'

'And earning a fortune.'

'We're lucky to have her.'

He got to his feet, head erect, poised; his eyes on me travelled downwards, suggesting something unpleasant. 'Queenie's money will have gone down the drain if she's not careful. That's all I'm saying.'

I didn't want to hear any more so I stood up and said, 'I really must go. I've an appointment. We're planning a promotion week.'

'You'll do your best to talk Queenie round?' Billy's eyes were anxious.

'It's up to her.'

I didn't talk to Queenie that evening. Instead I went for a walk along the seafront. The setting sun, the sea below it a mass of changing colours, enriched the soft, muted skyline. Boats bobbed on the ebbing tide and everywhere was calm. My desperation to defeat Billy welled inside me. I couldn't accept his interference. He was erecting terrifying scaffolding in which Mum and I, Tommy and perhaps Madame Renard were being used to topple Queenie. Still young and strong, he was relentless in his willingness to make her the sacrificial lamb to further his own ends.

I paced up and down like a fish caught in a net. Billy was a bastard. He'd always been out for himself, ever since he was a child. His attempt to betray Queenie in his own interest was typical of him. But he wasn't going to get away with it.

I loved the business. I had developed a passion that I couldn't have anticipated. I had kept a check on Queenie. Each night I'd gone to bed looking forward to the next day with impatient anticipation. I'd worked hard and found contentment. The business was where I could forget hurt. Work sustained me, and occupied my thoughts. It had no connection to Lorenzo. There was no living in the hope that he would return, just gratitude and optimism for the future of the business. As long as there was work to be done I would survive – or so I had thought.

Now my thoughts drifted on a wave of despair. I was numb, but every fibre of my being was filled with resentment at my powerless status as only daughter, and granddaughter, the child of the house. The spoilt brat who had lived in the shadow of Mum and Queenie.

Chapter Forty-one

'Olivia! Olivia!' Tony was running out of the salon down the street after me. He caught up and grabbed my shoulders. 'It's your grandmother. She's been knocked down. We've got to get help.' I stood rooted to the spot. 'Come on.' He shot up the road, calling, 'Phone the ambulance,' into the salon as he flew past. I raced after him.

A bicycle was lying in the middle of the road. Tucked into the kerb sat Queenie, her handbag and umbrella lying beside her, her hat tilted at an absurd angle, blood oozing from a cut on her cheek. She looked dazed.

'Queenie!' A huge surge of relief came over me and I threw myself down beside her.

'Bloody fool of a cyclist,' she said. 'Didn't look where he was going.'

I put my arms around her and cradled her against me. 'The ambulance is coming,' I told her.

'I don't need a bloody ambulance. Help me to me feet, Olivia, and we'll be gone before it arrives.'

'Wait, Queenie,' I held her down.

Tony covered her in a blanket. 'You'll be all right,' he shouted at her, as if she were deaf.

'I know that.' She tilted her head back, a drowsy look in her eyes, a slight droop to her mouth.

The ambulance tore up the road, its siren scattering the crowd.

Queenie was lifted like a doll on to the stretcher, and propped up with pillows. Though she pretended she was all right, I knew she was in pain.

'You'll stay with me?' she whispered, shifting in discomfort.

In Casualty a young doctor came quickly to examine her. 'What happened to you?' she asked, in a bossy, efficient tone that made Queenie cross.

'Silly fool cycled out in front of me,' Queenie answered bluntly.

Before she was taken for X-rays she said to me, 'Don't worry about me. It's hard to kill a bad thing,' and gave my hand a squeeze.

I felt her fear in the pressure, and worried about how much damage had been done.

She was allowed home the next day. The phone rang constantly with well-wishers asking for her. Friends and neighbours called to enquire about her progress. Routine went out of the window. Queenie resisted all orders to stay in bed and sat by her window, bored and sullen.

Mr Hennessy visited. 'You had a lucky escape by all accounts,' he said.

'I suppose so,' said Queenie.

Mr Hennessy said, 'You had a lot on your mind that day.'

Queenie silenced him with a look. 'No permanent damage,' she said. 'I'll be right as rain in no time.'

I wondered what Queenie had been up to. How much did she remember? It was hard to tell.

That evening a strange man called at suppertime. I could hear him in the hall, explaining, in a peculiar lilting accent, that he was a friend of Queenie. Mary called me up from the kitchen. 'It's someone to see Mrs Boyle.' The shrug of her shoulders, and her derisive glance towards the hall, put me on my guard.

The man was in an armchair, incurious about his surroundings, leafing through one of our new brochures. The evening sun glinted on his receding red hair.

'Hello,' I said, politely. 'I'm afraid Queenie's asleep.'

'How is she?' he asked.

'Not great.'

'That's not giving much away.'

'We don't really know yet. Only time will tell. The shock to her system and all that.'

He threw down the magazine and stood up. 'I'll call back when she's up and about again.'

'Who shall I say?'

'George. Hasn't she mentioned me?'

'No.'

'And who are you?'

'Olivia, Lorraine's daughter.'

The indifferent veneer slipped away. He said, less politely this time, 'I've heard of you. Where's Lorraine?'

'She's gone away for the weekend.'

'Don't tell her I called.' His voice coarsened. 'I'll surprise her. I wonder what she'll say.' He chuckled to himself. 'At least one thing's certain,' he said, 'she'll be glad to see me, not like that mother of hers.'

I felt sorry for Mum. She'd be enjoying her dinner by now, her attention riveted on Billy and his wife, no knowledge of Queenie's accident or her ebbing strength to spoil her little holiday.

When Mum got back, though, she was furious that I hadn't phoned her. She bent over Queenie, pecked her cheek. 'Why didn't you send for me?' Her voice was aggrieved.

Queenie looked from one of us to the other. 'We didn't want to spoil your peace.'

'I'd rather have known what I was coming back to,' Mum said. 'What's more, Mary's complaining that she hasn't been paid. Why haven't you settled up with her, Olivia?'

'You usually do it,' I reminded her.

'What does she do, anyway? Only moan and groan that I don't eat what she dishes up,' Queenie put in. 'By the way, we had a visitor while you were away.'

Mum's eyes widened. 'Oh?'

'Let's talk about it later,' I said. 'You're tired, Queenie.' I tucked her sheet in around her.

Mum took over the care of Queenie. She went about

her duties briskly, treating Queenie like a baby. Billy, with his wisecracking jokes, was banned from her bedroom, and Queenie's efforts to keep her concentration from slipping became a real struggle.

Faith, still househunting, was out all the time.

'By the way, Ginger called to see us,' Queenie said to Lorraine one day, out of the blue.

'She's losing her grip on reality,' Mum said. 'Of course, she's not eating properly. That accounts for most of her problems.'

'I make her as comfortable as I can. Change her sheets every day,' said Mary.

'She's not making much progress. The doctor's due a visit tomorrow. I'll see what he has to say.'

'It'll be a long haul,' Dr Ross said, no comfort in his tone. 'Sure what can we expect at her age? I'll give you a prescription for painkillers, and keep her as comfortable as possible.'

'She's not happy having to stay in bed.'

'Rest is the only cure. You're doing a great job, Lorraine.' He put the prescription in Mum's hand and hurried off on another important call.

Though doubts persisted, and all the warning signs were there, I refused to believe that Queenie wouldn't make a complete recovery. In the evenings after work I sat with her and told her about the day's events, tasty morsels of gossip to keep her interest alive.

'Don't keep her awake,' Mum would urge, coming to say goodnight to Queenie and pounding her pillows into shape. 'Is there anything you want?' she'd ask, before she left.

'No,' Queenie would say, impatiently, wishing Mum would leave so I could start reading to her.

Each night I read her a chapter of her book, *The Sport of Queens*, Dick Francis's autobiography about his racing life. It was the glorious hour before sleep, the house quiet, and the shadows round the walls huge in the dim light from her bedside lamp. Queenie would lean towards me, her eyes alert at the magic words, her mind drifting easily into the gripping tale. Sometimes she would fall asleep before I got to the end.

As I pulled the curtains, I would look out at the stars from her window and think of God. Queenie had always said that God was good. 'Dear God, make tomorrow a better day for Queenie,' I would pray. 'Show us some improvement.'

'She's getting better,' Mum said to me. 'She said she was looking out for Ginger,' she said, laughing.

'Great,' I said, thrilled.

'We'll see how good she is after she's tired herself out,' Mary said, with her usual pessimism.

'I'll take her up this letter.' Recognising Mr Hennessy's handwriting I knew it was important.

'You'll do no such thing,' Billy said, appearing from the shadows at the end of the hall. 'You don't want her to overdo things. I'll take it.'

I held the letter against my chest. 'You won't,' I said, and walked past him.

It was cold in the sitting room, with the damp air of early autumn about the place. The leaves on the maple tree were trembling, ready to fall. I lit the fire. Mum came in with her knitting. I was going over the books for Queenie when the doorbell rang. I heard Mary's footsteps pass the door on her way to answer it, then a man's voice asking for Mum.

'If you would like to wait here, I'll see if she's in,' Mary said, with put-on politeness.

The sitting-room door burst open, and George flounced into the room. I jumped up. Mum's hand was over her mouth.

'I suppose you didn't hear the bell,' he said, and stopped, his eyes on Mum. 'Lorraine!'

'Ginger!' Mum's knitting fell to the floor.

'I told him to stay in the hall, but he wouldn't,' Mary complained.

'Shut up, you,' Ginger said. 'It's freezing cold out there. I called last week. Didn't they tell you?' His words tumbled out in a torrent.

'You told me not to tell her,' I said to him.

Mum shook her head.

'I told Queenie off, Lorraine,' he said, his voice defensive. 'That old bat came between us. I told her what I thought of her for stopping us being together.' Mum stood rooted to the spot. I knew she wasn't taking it all in. 'And what's more,' he continued, 'it gave me the greatest pleasure to do so. Now that I'm here I want to make up to you for her twisted narrow-mindedness. To think that I was kept away from you and my son by that conniving old . . .' He went to her. 'I want to see my son.'

She pushed him away. 'I've told you before. Stay away from me.'

'Billy'll be glad to see me,' he whined.

For an instant I felt sorry for this mean man, the way Mum was looking down on him.

'I've been patient long enough. I need to see Billy urgently.'

'Just a minute,' Mum said, coolly. 'It's a pity you didn't say all this a long time ago. You deserted me.'

'Lorraine, they wouldn't let me,' Ginger protested.

'It's too late now. I'm happily married with a fine daughter, as you can see.'

'I'm here to help you run your business. I realise what you're up against with that oul wan Queenie running the show.'

Mum went to Queenie's desk, took a key from the key-ring she carried around her waist, opened it. Rifling through bills stuffed into a drawer, she took out a chequebook, wrote a cheque and handed it to him. 'That should cover your fare to wherever it is you're heading.'

Ginger seemed appalled. 'I don't want your money. How could you think that that's what I came for?'

'Just go back to where you came from, and leave me alone.'

'That's not a nice thing to say, Lorraine. A lousy bit of cash for all those years we've known each other, and our son Billy? You're not a very generous person.'

'Get out,' Mum said.

'I want us to be friends. There's Billy and his wife to consider.'

Mum bit her lip. 'That's something we never were. And, anyway, over the years I've given you more than you deserve.'

His hand tightened on her arm. Mum shook it off.

We stood together. Ginger backed away. Then, his face brightened. 'I'll wait here for Billy. I'm in no hurry.'

Somewhere upstairs a door banged. Ginger's eyes shot up to the ceiling and came back to rest on me. 'Go and see who that is. It might be Billy.'

I didn't dare leave Mum's side.

The door opened. Queenie came slowly into the room, leaning on her walking stick. I went to her. She pushed me aside. 'What do you want?' she asked Ginger.

'I'm waiting here for Billy.'

'You'll find your resourceful son in the pub, I'm sure.' Marshalling all her strength she stood tall and straight, as angry as I'd ever seen her. 'If you don't get out I'll call the police.' She pointed her stick to the open door, its gold tip threatening. Ginger, filled with indecision, looked from one of us to the other. Mum, behind him now, pushed him. He edged backwards into the hall and said, 'I'll get you for this, you old shrew.'

'I resent your familiarity,' Queenie snapped.

'As for you, Lorraine, I thought you had feelings for me.'

'I do.' Mum heaved him towards the door with a strength I never knew she possessed. 'I can't stand the sight of you.'

We watched him go down the wet steps towards his car, brushing down his jacket as he went. 'You'll regret this,' he called out. 'Wait till Billy hears about it.'

Mum slammed the front door, and leaned against it,

the strength gone out of her. Her voice exhausted. 'He needed telling.'

Queenie, turning back from the door, said, 'You should have told him long ago. But no! You couldn't let go.'

Mum lifted her shoulders helplessly. 'He's Billy's father. I don't like throwing anyone out on the streets.'

'He's a nasty piece of work. Now that's all I'll say on the subject. What we all need is a stiff drink.' Queenie was as practical as ever.

I looked at my mother. Queenie's unpleasant implication seemed to have no place in her world. Yet she hadn't denied it. There and then I realised that I didn't know my own mother very well at all. As I dispensed the drinks curiosity crept into me. When Queenie was tucked up in bed, warm and snug, I said. 'What did you mean by saying that . . .'

'A clinging vine, that Ginger,' she said. 'He always left a taint in the air, like a pig after a roll in muck.'

'Has Mum kept in touch with him all this time?'

Her warning look was enough to satisfy my curiosity.

And now there was a more important matter for us to consider. Faith's sudden flight. Mum's news that Faith was threatening to return to an old flame in Florida put all thoughts of Ginger out of my head.

'What brought this on?' I asked in amazement.

'Don't know.' Mum shrugged. 'Came out of the blue, according to Billy.'

'Don't you believe it,' Queenie said. 'I smell a rat.'

'Who is this other fellow?' I asked.

'Some sugar-daddy she's known for years, far richer than Billy could ever hope to be.'

'And far older too, I bet,' Queenie said.

'Oh! How could she?' I cried.

'I don't know how Billy'll face it if it's true,' Mum said. 'He'll be heartbroken.'

Ginger's appearance in Billy's life had been one thing Faith either couldn't or wouldn't cope with. And the lovely little house she'd set her heart on had been sold elsewhere.

Mum, too, was subdued: Ginger's unexpected appearance had taken its toll.

'I should never have kept in touch with that man,' she confided in me, one evening when we were sitting by the fire together.

'But weren't you still in love with him?'

She laughed. 'I couldn't stand him. I only did it for Billy's sake. On the few occasions we did meet I couldn't wait to get away from him.'

'I don't blame you,' I said. 'He's a creep.'

'I can't stand the winter,' Queenie said, looking miserably at the rain. 'I've planted hyacinth bulbs. They're under the bed, keeping warm.'

'I'll take you for a walk in the garden soon,' I promised.

Queenie said, 'We'll take sandwiches with us. Picnics like the old days.'

'Not in the garden!'

'No, no!' Queenie hated to be caught out in her confusion. 'To the beach. Billy can fish for tiddlers.'

Mum looked sideways at her. 'And what's-his-name can come too. Billy's friend.'

'Maggots Corcoran?' Queenie said and nodded. 'I'll have a little snooze now.'

'Poor thing. She's exhausted all the time these days.'

Chapter Forty-two

The good thing that came out of the row between Lorraine and Ginger was that Queenie's spirits were up. She sat by the fire in the afternoons, bright as ninepence. Mum would apologise for the distress Ginger had caused but Queenie would laugh about it. With this new charge of happiness between them, Mum became more amenable. She would phone Tommy the bets and bring Queenie's winnings home to her in an envelope.

Mr Hennessy phoned occasionally; so did Mr Hill. Queenie talked to them, happier now to let matters in their hands take their course. A lot of her time was spent waiting for Mum or me to come in from work. Sometimes, when I got home, Queenie would be in the sitting room. I would know she was there because her lavender scent would be strong in the hall as I opened the door. Mum was often with her, knitting or reading the newspaper. Whatever she was doing she would stop immediately Queenie made a request.

Queenie was making a great effort towards a full recovery and Mum eased her struggle. She combed Queenie's hair, creamed her face, put her own strength and will to continue into her.

Sometimes Queenie stayed in bed, Mum sitting in a chair beside her, watching the leaves fall, waiting for her to wake so that she could feed her thin bread and butter with her afternoon tea.

'You don't have to stay here all the time. You must have other things to do.' Queenie would say. She slept lightly, always listening for the phone, or a ring on the doorbell, always watching for Ginger's return.

'That tinker thought he'd get the better of us,' she said to Mr Hennessy one day.

'Sad,' Mr Hennessy said, bent over his business, putting papers into a file when I came in with the tea. 'All those years he held Lorraine to ransom.'

'Your mother's much better,' he said, on his way out. 'You're doing a great job, Lorraine.'

Delighted, Mum said, 'Thank you,' and shook hands with him.

But the doctor reminded us, 'We can't take any chances. At her age and with the winter coming in you must keep her in an even temperature at all times.'

I sat with Queenie one evening, and noticed her efforts to speak to me becoming increasingly difficult. She leaned towards me. 'Another thing I want you to do is give all those business letters in that box there to Mr Hennessy.' She looked towards the drawer where she kept her bills, her breath loud, her eyes hazy. But her speech was clear. After that we spoke sporadically until she said, 'I'll have a little rest now.' I held her hand while she slept. Once or twice she opened her eyes and looked at me. 'She's much better since he left.'

I knew she meant Mum and Ginger.

'I know.'

Suddenly she became alert. 'What will you do? The nights are so lonely on your own.'

'Don't worry.' I laughed. 'I'll find someone to share them with.'

'Poor Jim,' Queenie said. 'Don't you fancy him at all?'

'Between you and me, Queenie, I don't know.'

'You'll kill him if you keep turning him down. What will we do at all?' She sighed, her attempts to rein in her thoughts frustrating her. 'I blame that Lorenzo. I remember the summer you met him as if it were yesterday. I made you that white linen suit with the black trim. Don't you remember? Black and white was all the rage.'

I went for a walk in the clear evening September light. Talk of that suit Queenie had made for me had unleashed a whole cache of locked-away memories. Lorenzo arriving with the flowers, playing with Polly and Audrey in the park, his hand under my chin, the feel of his cool cheek against mine when we danced, that first kiss, the texture of his lips.

I could still think of him as if it were yesterday. I would dream of holding his hand, drifting along the sand, dressed in white muslin.

That night I read to Queenie. Under my hand hers went limp as I got to the end of the chapter. I held it while she slept, her face composed, all the stress and strain gone out of it. I stayed with her for a long time, afraid to take my hand away for fear of disturbing her. Her breathing stopped. I didn't move, or call out. Here, tonight, with her, I could survive. I recalled her caring: hot milk at bedtime, my toes tucked safely under the blankets while she told me stories; Queenie at the beach dispensing tomato sandwiches and lemonade, her eyes loving under the confection of roses that was her summer hat. All the things she'd given me, all the things she'd promised, were my security now. Tonight was real, her cold hand chilling me. With her promise that she would never leave me I was already looking forward to the prospect of her return before she'd fully gone.

'I think it's time to let her sleep,' Mum said, coming quietly into the room.

'Open the window a little,' I said.

'Don't be daft. She'll freeze. Whatever will you think of next?'

'She won't,' I murmured.

'You can't imagine the warning I've had from the doctor. Nothing's worth letting her get cold.'

I couldn't speak. Mum looked at me, then down at the bed. 'Nothing's worth letting you get cold, is it, Mother?' she said, taking Queenie's hand. 'She's dead,' she said, in disbelief.

I nodded.

Kneeling, a far-away look in her eyes, Mum made the sign of the cross and said, 'Hail, Holy Queen,' Queenie's favourite prayer, my presence forgotten.

Mum took charge of everything, making sure that fires

were always lit and that food was in plentiful supply. She stopped at nothing to keep us all comfortable in the days following Queenie's death, even prowling around after me, asking if I was all right.

I wanted more than anything in the whole world the one thing I couldn't have: I wanted Queenie back. I wanted her to be here with us, tucked up in bed, cosy and warm. In those hours after her death I wondered if I'd made light of her suffering, if I could have made her better by taking more notice of her aches and pains. Mum had taken her over, and I'd let her, rejoiced with her in a job well done.

I went for walks, determined to avoid Mum and Mary's fussing. One night I sat in Queenie's room, reading the racing pages, as if she were there. I longed for her groans about stupid trainers and jockeys. When I heard Mum approaching, her step on the stairs, her voice calling me, I didn't answer because I couldn't allow her to distract me from the matter in hand. The business of keeping Queenie alive was all-absorbing: I couldn't bear to think of her in a wooden box, waiting to go down into the ground. Sitting in her bedroom made me feel some semblance of normality; in stifling my grief in her pillow I could pretend her death had never happened.

Telegrams arrived, wreaths, tributes of all kinds. In the dark, gloomy church I sat next to Mum, her face hidden under the wide brim of her new black hat. Dad, close beside her, was watchful of her. Next to him sat Aunt Statia, in her usual black, then Aunt Tess and Uncle Cecil. Further along sat Polly and Audrey, silent for once. Billy's absence was obvious. Not wanting to tell anyone who asked that he was chasing after Faith, we said that they were away on holiday together.

As Father Nobel, assisted by Father McMahon, began the Mass, my grief for Queenie went through me as a cold, shivering weakness. Father Nobel told us all how blessed we'd been to have had Queenie's love, and reminded us that no one could take that from us now. I didn't want to listen. Instead, I wanted to hunker down beside Queenie's skirt while she sat working at her sewing-machine. The notion of her leaving me was impossible to grasp. I thought of the corner shop, the kettle on the range, the thin bread and butter she would coax me with when I couldn't eat my dinner.

'Sad.' Tommy Traynor stood outside the church, dignified in a smart black coat. Madame Renard, flounced and feathered in black, looked sleek as a well-fed cat. Queenie's kindness had stretched to all her employees. They looked prosperous, from the twins, identical in black coats, to Mary swamped in a hat several sizes too large for her.

They all spoke as if Queenie's death had been a blessing. 'She had a good life.'

'God was good to take her.'

'She'd have hated to have been a burden.'

Mum, beside me, said little, accepted their condolences with dignity.

'I only heard the sad news yesterday.' Jim's tone contained real regret. He'd been in Santa Monica on a training course. 'I had to come. I hope you don't mind.'

'Thank you so much.'

He took my hand, helped me into one of the waiting

cars. 'I'll see you at the graveyard,' he said, loath to let go of me.

During the burial I was determined to keep my dignity among all Queenie's crowd, and not let her down, no matter how much willpower it took. She was happier now, I reminded myself, in her rightful place in heaven with the saints, her watchful eyes on us all.

I recalled a summer's day of our holidays in the Galtee Mountains, when I was only six years old and had stolen money from her purse to buy sweets. She'd slapped me hard and I'd run away from her, across a field. She had come tearing after me, grabbing me from the path of Brady's bull.

The wreaths were removed from her coffin, and laid to one side. Slowly and awkwardly it was lowered. I moved forward wanting to say, 'Wait!' My red rose was light as air as it fell in after her. Crumpling to my knees, my longing for her almost choked me. Father McMahon lifted me up and led me back along the path.

'She's where she wants to be,' he said, assuring me that Queenie hadn't really left me. 'She's only a breath away. She'll live in you as you continue her work. You'll make her proud.' As he spoke of Queenie's new happiness in heaven the sun came through the surrounding trees, bringing with it the reality that I would survive.

Mum was in the back of the car, Dad beside her, waiting for me, and for the crowds to disperse so that we could go home.

I dreaded going home: the sweeping drive, eerie in the evening light, the crunch of the wheels as we drew to a halt. On the way Mum and Dad discussed ordinary things, made everything that was happening seem incredible. Up the steps we went slowly. Dad said, 'Lean on me. One step at a time,' his arm a band of steel around my waist. It reminded me of that day we'd walked down the aisle together, in slow procession, to a wedding that never took place.

'You still have us,' he reminded me.

'I know,' I said.

Composed now, I followed him into the hall, his back straight, his step light, his burden lifted. In the hall, Mum looked over his shoulder to see if the mourners she had invited back were arriving. She preceded us to the kitchen. Mary was already there, the table laid with sandwiches, sausage rolls and cakes.

'I gave the graveyard a miss,' she said. 'You should have plenty there.'

'Thanks, Mary. I couldn't have faced it without you.'

'Go and take off your coat,' Dad said. 'I'll make us all a cup of tea.'

Tommy Traynor's voice boomed in the silent hall. 'Poor Queenie. Gone for good. End of an era.'

'And no word of Ginger either,' said Dad, his voice light. Mum was his and his alone now, no Queenie or Ginger to share her with.

'What'll you have, Tommy? Whiskey?'

'I don't mind if I do.'

Madame Renard sat in the sitting room fumbling with a tiny handkerchief. 'I shall miss her so much.' Astounded, I examined her face closely. She meant it.

'It was cold at the cemetery,' Dad said to Father Nobel, handing him a glass of whiskey.

Father Nobel looked into the distance. 'Cold as the grave,' he said.

Mum burst into tears.

'It comes to us all, my dear.' The priest spoke kindly to her.

'Queenie's turn came too soon,' she protested. 'We weren't ready for it. She wasn't even sick.'

'Who are we to question God's decisions? After all, her work on this earth was done, wasn't it?'

'I blame the rascal on the bike,' Tommy said. 'It's a wonder you didn't sue him.'

'We considered it,' Dad said, 'but there were too many witnesses to say that she wasn't looking where she was going.'

'We'll have to soldier on,' Aunt Statia said.

'That'll be no joke,' said Aunt Tess. 'You could always rely on Queenie's good advice.'

'You could always rely on a lash of her tongue,' said Aunt Statia.

Jim arrived and stood to one side looking uncomfortable, silent. Mary came in then with a tray and said, 'Will someone put a bit of coal on the fire, or is that asking too much?' She gave Jim a sharp look.

'Of course.' He rushed to oblige.

Trish tried to haul her father home. He looked at his watch. 'It's early yet,' he protested.

'Everyone's tired. You have a good night's sleep, Ollie,' she advised me. 'I'll phone you tomorrow.'

'God, I dread tomorrow. There's so much to be sorted out,' I said to Jim.

'They'll be gone soon,' he consoled, and began clearing the glasses on to trays.

In the kitchen, he said, 'What'll you do tomorrow?'

'I don't know. I haven't thought about it.'

'You needn't be alone. I'll come round if you like.'

'Thanks, Jim, but I want to work.' It came out sharper than I'd meant it.

He looked at me. 'You won't be able to concentrate for a while.'

'Doesn't matter. I'll try anything to keep myself from thinking.'

'You should have a good cry,' he suggested.

I was starting already and he was looking at me with the same sympathy he'd shown when I'd caught Chantal with Lorenzo. He came to me, put his arms around me, held me.

'I'm all right.'

Gently, he wiped away my tears. 'You have my mobile number. You can get me any time you want me.'

'Thanks. I'll be all right.' I spoke with forced brightness.

He caught me. 'Let it out, Ollie. Don't fight it.' He kissed the top of my head. 'I'd do anything for you. You know that.' Then he drew breath and looked at me. 'I'm not asking for anything, Ollie, just trying to help. You've got to get through it as best you can.'

There was a pause while I wiped my eyes. 'Thank you,' I said, moved by his kindness.

I bent over the sink washing glasses, thinking of his kiss. He stayed watching me as if I was a small, helpless creature in need of protection.

Mum came in with another tray of dirty dishes. 'They're leaving,' she said, with relief.

Jim took the tray from her and began to wash up.

'That's very kind of you,' Mum said, putting things away, her face pale.

'We'll finish up, Mum,' I said. 'You're tired.'

'I'll have plenty of time to rest after this.' She looked lonely as she spoke.

'I'm sure you'll find plenty to do,' Jim said.

'There are so many things I've never done in my life,' she said reflectively. 'But I'm not going to make any plans yet, apart from going to the hairdresser and buying a few new clothes. Oh! Don't I sound awful? Queenie just in her grave.'

'As I was saying to Ollie, you've got to do the best you can.' Jim was his matter-of-fact self.

'You're right,' Mum agreed.

'I wonder why Billy hasn't shown up yet?' I said.

'He phoned to say he's on his way,' Mum assured us.

The thought of him returning made my skin crawl.

Chapter Forty-three

Billy returned, annoyed at Queenie's nerve in dying as soon as his back was turned. He had Faith in tow – recaptured by the prospect of Billy inheriting his grandmother's estate.

Mum, tight-lipped, kept her dislike of the woman who threatened Billy's happiness barely concealed. 'Have I got this right?' she probed, when she found Faith on her own. 'You were on the point of leaving him?'

'No,' Faith denied strongly. 'Ah just wanted to teach him not to take me for granted. As it turned out we found we couldn't live without each other,' she insisted, fluffing up her hair.

Faith, certain of Billy's love, said to me in the privacy of my bedroom, 'Ah thought Ah'd escape for a little break from him, without hurting him, but he got into a rage over my friend Marvin. That's the guy I was staying with. We've been friends for years.'

'I see,' I said, not understanding any of it.

Faith sniggered conspiratorially. 'He was fit to kill ol' Marvin.' Her eyes were wild with the telling. Trembling she said, 'Ah was weak with fright. Marvin's not as strong as Billy.' Thoughtfully she said, 'Ol' Marvin sure brings out the beast in him.'

'You can do that too, Faith, without any help from Marvin. You probably like that about him.'

'Yeah, Ah do.'

'I wonder how long Billy will put up with you taking a hike every time there's a spot of bother between you?'

'For ever, if A'm the one dishing it out.' Her laughter was full of a crazy sense of fun. When she saw the expression on my face she said, 'Ah didn't mean any harm. Ah just wanted to bruise Billy's pride a little. Let him know that he couldn't take me for granted.' She spoke like a child who'd suddenly remembered which was her favourite doll.

Billy came looking for her. 'I thought you'd done another bunk,' he joked.

Faith said defensively. 'As if Ah would, Billy darlin'. Ah'm here for the duration. Especially now that you've lost your beloved grandmother.'

'Listen, dearest,' Billy took her hand, 'I know you're going to feel hurt and left out, but I'm afraid I can't bring you to the reading of the will tomorrow. Family only.'

'You're playing with me, Billy. Ah'm family. Of course Ah'll have to be there. Ah want to hear exactly what she's left you. Not that Ah don't trust you, darlin'.' She winked at me.

'Sorry.'

'This is your mama's doin'. She don't like me. She's mountin' her own crusade against me.'

'Don't be such an airhead. Of course she isn't.'

'Don't you dare call me that.' Faith flounced off, Billy following.

Later I said to Billy when we were discussing the business, 'I don't know what we're going to do.'

'There'll be plenty for you to do,' Billy said. 'You'll always have a job with us.'

'Us!'

Ignoring me, he continued, 'We'll ensure that everything's kept going the way Queenie would have wanted it.'

'We!'

'Sure. Mum and me.'

'Oh, Billy, work is what Ah need too.' The appeal in Faith's tone was sickening.

As far as Faith was concerned, now that Billy had stepped into Queenie's shoes anything she needed to keep herself afloat could be relied upon.

'So you're taking over?' I asked him.

Billy looked from Faith to me, a hand to his forehead. 'One thing at a time,' he pleaded. 'You don't have to concern yourself with the business, Olivia. All that's taken care of.' His voice was cold with authority. 'Mum and I will see to everything.'

Mum came into the sitting room.

Billy said, 'I was just saying to Olivia that she doesn't have to worry about anything any more with me back in the business.'

'It's a blessing to think that you two are getting on so well together. It's wonderful to see it.' Mum looked from Billy to me, with evident pleasure.

Weakness overcame me as I thought of the business without Queenie, Billy in charge, aided and abetted by Mum, and Tommy most likely, while I had to carry out his commands.

Next morning, Mum said, 'We have to be in Mr Hennessy's office about the will at three o'clock. You're very pale, Olivia. If you don't feel up to it, I'll make your excuses.' She meant it kindly.

'I really ought to go.' My voice sounded feeble; the thought of Queenie's estate being discussed upset me already.

Billy put his arm round me. 'Always one for duty. Queenie's death took more out of you than you thought. You should take things easy for a while. We'll manage everything, won't we, Mum?'

'We will.' Mum beat a cushion briskly.

'Poor Queenie,' Mum said to Billy. 'Little did we think all this would happen so soon.' She stood still, her eyes on the maple tree outside the window. 'She loved that tree.' Her eyes misted. 'In fact, I think it was that tree that made her buy this house.'

'I thought it was the fact that the Breslins owned it.'

She ignored me. 'I thought she was mad at the time. Of course she knew exactly what she was doing.'

'Didn't she just,' Billy agreed, consolidating their new alliance, shutting me out.

Gulping back her sorrow, Mum went to change. She returned wearing a black suit, with her diamond brooch in the lapel. 'Come on,' she chivvied us.

Faith came bouncing down the steps after us. 'Ah'll ride into town with y'all. Look at the stores while I'm waiting. Ah'm not stayin' here on my own.' Ignoring Mum's protest that we might be delayed she hopped into the back seat of the car beside me.

Billy, blazing with the power and authority he'd bestowed upon himself, drove us to Mr Hennessy's office

Mr Hennessy was waiting, drinks ready on a side-table.

'Hello, Mr Hennessy.' Billy looked him up and down as if he were of no consequence.

'Hello, Billy.'

Mr Hennessy took Mum's hand and gripped it tightly, before he shook mine.

Seating himself, Queenie's last will and testament on the desk in front of him, he didn't speak immediately. 'Now I have here . . .' he began slowly.

Billy looked at his watch. 'We mustn't keep you,' he said rudely. 'You're a very busy man.'

Mr Hennessy peered at Billy from behind his bifocals. 'Take all the time you need. I'm not rushing off anywhere. Are you?' he asked grandly.

Billy squirmed visibly and Mum shot him a look.

'It's just that Mum and Ollie are still a bit rattled with everything that's happened. They won't be up to much of that legal jargon.' Billy pointed to the papers.

'We'll be as expedient as we can.' The dismissal in Mr Hennessy's voice silenced Billy, and he sat quietly now, his arms folded across his chest.

Mum leaned back in her chair, her hands folded in her lap, her eyes on Mr Hennessy.

First he read out the gifts: small amounts of money for Queenie's favourite charity and for Mary.

Mum looked as if she wished it was over so that she could have a good cry. I kept my arms folded across my chest to keep the tears from bursting out.

Billy sent me a look that warned me to keep my anguish to myself so as not to delay the reading.

Mr Hennessy enquired, 'All right so far?'

Billy's glance at Mum encircled them both, and left me out in the cold.

Mr Hennessy loosened the buttons of his jacket and read on. I was so concentrated on keeping in my grief that I didn't take in what he was saying. It was Mum's intake of breath that made me look up sharply.

'What?' Billy exploded, shooting out of his chair.

Mr Hennessy glared at him. 'It's exactly what it says here.' His finger was poised on the page. 'Queenie's forty-five per cent of the shares and everything she possessed in the business are left entirely to Olivia. Please sit down, Billy.'

'Me?' It was my turn to jump up.

'You're Olivia Mary Healy.' Mr Hennessy spoke slowly, his eyes on me, confirming my existence.

'I am.'

'Queenie was the largest single shareholder in the company. That means that, with your own ten per cent, you have the largest stake in the company.'

'Mum, did you hear that? What are you going to do about it?' Billy was flabbergasted. He looked ready to burst.

Mr Hennessy smiled convivially.

'But—' Billy shouted.

'No buts,' Mr Hennessy interupted. 'That's the way it is.'

'It's ridiculous.' Mum got to her feet. 'You've got it wrong. Let me see it.'

'It's all here.' Mr Hennessy looked up at us all standing there before him. 'I haven't finished.'

Mum and Billy sat down.

Dazed, I stayed standing as I tried to breathe normally. I was in the same room, surrounded by the same people, but everything was different. By a stroke of her pen, Queenie had turned my world upside down. I was Olivia Mary Healy, and I was in charge. Queenie had recognised in me the same talent for business that she herself had possessed. Hadn't she always said so? How could I have doubted her love or her faith in me? 'I'll never leave you in the lurch,' was what she'd always said. She hadn't. I could feel her presence in the four walls that surrounded me, and in the delight in Mr Hennessy's eyes.

It was sinking in with Billy that his 'inheritance' was fleeing from him, like a thief in the night. 'I'm afraid I didn't hear you read it out the first time, Mr Hennessy,' he said. 'Would you mind reading it again?'

' "To my beloved granddaughter, Olivia, I bequeath everything I possess in the company. I also leave her my home, and its contents, which was bought for her in the first place, in the hope she marries the man she truly loves, and settles down happily. To my daughter, Lorraine Healy, and her husband, Phil, the contents of my personal bank account. To my grandson Billy I bequeath my share in Bright Star, in the hope that he wins lots of races and makes himself a fortune." '

'Useless bloody horse.' Hate and distrust were pouring out of Billy.

'Queenie didn't forget you.' Mum was sobbing helplessly.

Billy turned away.

'I'm so sorry that this is causing such pain,' Mr Hennessy said, 'but I can only tell you what's here before me.'

Billy moved closer to me, his hands deep in his pockets as if he were afraid he might throttle me. Mum hopped between us, saying, 'As long as it's all kept in the family. Isn't that right, Billy?' She looked at him, willing him to behave.

'Let's have a drink.' Mr Hennessy got to his feet.

Billy looked at his watch, 'No, thanks. I'd best be off,' and raced out of the door, leaving a surprised Mr Hennessy looking after him.

'You'll have a glass of sherry, won't you, ladies?'

'Thank you,' we chimed.

'Here's to your good health. Now, what I want you to do, Olivia, is to drop in and see me as soon as possible. There are quite a number of things Queenie wanted me to go over with you. She was meticulous in her instructions about certain matters as she was determined that you should run the business.'

'I should have guessed.' Mum sniffed. 'You were the only one for her.' There was no bitterness as she took my hand in hers. 'Come on, let's not keep poor Billy waiting.'

At that precise moment his car roared off at full throttle, the wheels squealing in protest.

'He's gone.' Mum shrank back into her chair, hardly believing her ears.

'I'll drop you home,' offered Mr Hennessy.

'That's very kind of you, but we can't impose. We'll get a taxi.'

'If you'd like to take a taxi, Mum, I'll stay on with Mr Hennessy and go over the papers with him.'

I sat back, waiting.

'What a good idea.' It was Mr Hennessy's turn to check his watch. In my employment now, he smiled politely.

The taxi arrived. Pulling down the brim of her hat as if to ward off a blow, Mum faced outdoors alone.

Chapter Forty-four

I went for a walk along Sandymount strand to absorb everything that had happened to me. I reached the end of the beach, thinking that I'd have to buy new outfits, clothes fitting my new position. Mr Hennessy had explained things perfectly to me, including the delays that would occur before everything was settled.

'There's no doubt who's boss now, though.' He'd laughed. 'You've got to hand it to Queenie. Taking everything into consideration, she was a prudent woman.' There was admiration in his voice.

'And a cunning one,' I added, thinking of her various U-turns in life and in business.

Mr Hennessy had said that her business bank account was to be used at my own discretion, but with the interest of the business foremost. I was giddy with plans for the future.

Looking out at the cold sea I shivered, thinking of my freedom to make decisions. I could please myself about the day-to-day affairs. It was a concept I would have to get used to. The house was mine too. Perhaps I should sell it.

Mum and Dad were moving out, leaving me all alone. The house was bulging with useless objects Queenie had acquired over the years. Then I knew I couldn't sell it and buy an apartment. There was more to it than just a house. Queenie had bought it because she believed that owning it would be my salvation and sanity. It had been retaliation for the way Barry Breslin had treated me.

I walked back down the beach, the tide out, the sand smooth and shiny, late gulls crying. I must honour Queenie's wishes, do nothing to embarrass her. I must never shut her out by selling her home and possessions. I must honour her memory by continuing with her business, as she'd have wished.

Glad of my decision I went home. The life I'd lived with Queenie would continue, my employees and friends sustaining me. I might even expand, take a risk here and there. Queenie would approve of risks. She'd taken plenty in her time, always certain that she was doing the right thing, refusing to let arguments interfere with her decision. She was mistress of her own home, and in business always followed her own instincts.

Mr Hennessy phoned and asked me to call in to see him.

'I don't want to alarm you, but now that you're in control, I think you should get rid of Billy.'

'That's a bit drastic, isn't it?'

Mr Hennessy eyed me reflectively. 'If you don't do as he

wants you might have more trouble on your hands than you bargained for. Billy's ruthless and he's unstable.'

I frowned. 'What makes you say that?'

'I've checked up on this "interested party" he spoke about to you. It's his father,' Mr Hennessy said.

'Ginger? Are you sure you're not mistaken?'

'Certain. Apparently Ginger persuaded Billy to try to get rid of Queenie. Ginger wanted to buy her shares so that Billy could become chairman of the board and Ginger could nail Queenie for cheating him, as he saw it, out of his family all those years ago.'

'I can't believe Billy would be stupid enough to permit Ginger any leeway in the company.'

Mr Hennessy nodded. 'Seems he owns a lucrative circus and now wants to retire and get involved with Billy. It was Ginger who alerted Billy to Queenie's business in the first place.'

'I'd no idea that he had anything to do with Ginger.'

'I think it might be advisable to talk to your mother about it.'

'I can't do that. It would worry her too much.'

'I probably seem over-cautious, but it's better to be careful. The point is, Olivia, you can't trust Billy, especially when you're away. God knows what he might get up to next.'

'What can he do? He can't take the company away from me, can he?'

'Of course not.' Mr Hennessy laughed. 'Don't even think such a thing. But you're not off the hook with him. He won't give you an easy time over the will.' Mr Hennessy's eyes were grave. 'In fact, he can make life very unpleasant for you in an effort to get things his way. He's contesting the will on the grounds that Queenie was not in her right mind when she made it, and he's prepared to go to any lengths to prevent you taking over.'

'Why can't he settle for a good job with Paradise and leave it at that?'

'Because he sees you as an accomplished young woman, with great potential, and he resents your power. He's using your career as an excuse to punish you for your place in Queenie's affections. He sees himself as the neglected, long-suffering, rightful heir, who was cast aside in favour of you.'

'I feel sorry for him. He was out of touch with the family for so long, and now he seems intent on making enemies of us all.'

'He's his own worst enemy. I know I paint a gloomy picture but it's my duty to warn you.' Mr Hennessy sat back reflectively, hands clasped together.

'It doesn't have to be like that. I'll talk to him, try to make him see sense.'

'That won't work. I think you should make a plan of action. Offer to buy him out, and be fair about it. Give him over the odds for his shares on condition that he resigns. That should do the trick. Money is his main interest.'

'Suggest a figure and a date and we'll put things into operation.'

Mr Hennessy smiled sardonically. 'Leave it with me and I'll come up with a reasonable settlement. It won't be easy.'

He escorted me to the door. 'It'll work out fine in the end.'

I left, dreading having to rid the company of Billy. When I got home Jim was waiting for me in the sitting room.

'What are you doing here?'

'I was worried about you, with Billy's carry-on and everything.'

'I'm sorry you had to wait.'

'I'm off to Scotland for the weekend. Thought you might like to come?' He raised quizzical eyebrows.

'Oh, Jim,' I hesitated, 'that's sweet of you, but I can't.'

Jim's face fell. 'Have a drink with me when I get back.'

'I'd love that.'

The next morning I sent for Billy. 'I want a word with you. There's something important we have to discuss.'

Since the reading of the will Billy had been openly hostile to me. It was unnerving to face him. How could my brother be such a nasty schemer?

'So you want me to take over. It's all too much for you,' he said. 'You know I can do the job with my eyes closed, and one hand tied behind my back. I'm smarter than anyone else. I hope this won't take long.'

I looked at him. 'I want you to resign.'

He gaped at me. 'You're kidding! This company had serious problems when I took over, big financial problems, and I'm a shareholder.'

'I'm appalled at your disloyalty to Queenie. She was kind and generous to you, giving you ten per cent to bring you back into the fold.'

'A measly ten per cent after shutting me out for all those years. What would you know about it?'

I ignored him. 'You tried to bring poor Tommy into your plot – anything to discredit Queenie.'

'You're a liar. Of course, you've always hated me.'

'You had it in for me because I was Queenie's favourite. Now I want you to clear out your desk.'

Billy laughed. 'What right have you to talk to me like this, you silly little bitch?'

'Every right. I'm the managing director. What I say goes. I'll give you a good price for your shares.'

'Poor little rich girl,' Billy mocked. 'Look at you sitting there imitating Queenie. Well, you won't get far. My shares are not for sale and I'll prove that Queenie wasn't in her right mind when she made her last will and testament, which I happen to know was only recently.' His eyes were blazing. 'She was ga-ga.'

'Cut the crap, Billy. I know everything there is to know about your shady secret deals with your "interested third party". You could have lost us our busines by bringing your father into it without anyone's permission.'

Billy retaliated, 'I wouldn't do anything to harm it.'

'You should have thought of that when you let Ginger dictate to you. I'm afraid I'm not as forgiving as Queenie. She tolerated you, even though she suspected you of being a liar and a cheat. You let her down in the worst possible way.'

Billy's mouth opened and shut like a fish. 'I'll get you for this, you little cow.'

He was storming out as Trish dashed in. 'What's up?'

'Out of my way.' Billy pushed her aside.

'Nasty situation?' Trish said.

'Let's get out of here.' I grabbed my bag.

Over lunch in the pub, Trish said, 'I've no sympathy for Billy. He deserved everything he got. He's rotten.'

'I don't think I can dismiss him just like that. He'll try to make more trouble for me.'

'Idle threats. He won't succeed. Forget him and Ginger. They're powerless to do anything to you.'

'I suppose.'

'I was thinking that maybe you should put Jenny in charge of the shop. Make Madame Renard general manager. She has a good head for business, and with a bit of promotion I think she could do wonders.'

'That's a terrific idea. Why didn't I think of that?'

Jim phoned unexpectedly one evening when I was working late.

'Hello, Jim.'

'You sound a bit down,' he said.

'Tired, that's all.'

'I was wondering if you'd like to have dinner with me on Saturday night?'

'If you like.'

'You don't seem too enthusiastic.'

'Sorry, I'd love to.'

'Good. I thought I'd book a table at the Grey Door, make it a bit of an occasion. I got promoted today, and I wanted to share it with you.'

'Jim, that's wonderful.'

Since our night of passion our friendship had been strained. In a moment of weakness I had supplanted Lorenzo with Jim, and now I felt guilty. Though we tried to behave normally we were both awkward and embarrassed.

'Thank you for coming,' Jim said, when we met in the restaurant.

It took a bottle of wine and a few glasses of Bailey's before the atmosphere thawed sufficiently for us to relax with each other. By the end of the night the comfort I'd always felt with Jim was back and we drove home in companionable silence. 'It must be strange living here all on your own,' Jim said, outside the house.

'I'm getting to grips with it. Besides, Mary's here most days, and Mum pops in regularly with casseroles and all the fattening food I don't want.'

'It's no life for a beautiful woman.'

'Don't start,' I warned him.

He hugged me tight. 'Sorry, I didn't mean any harm. I wouldn't hurt a hair of your head, you know that.' He kissed my cheek and let me go.

'Thank you for a lovely night,' I said, went up the steps and let myself into the dark, empty house.

Chapter Forty-five

The winter was over. With the spring came new growth. I was alone now, every waking minute of my time taken up with business. The grief that had shattered me was under control, except for the times when Queenie's death would return to me briefly, like a slap across the face.

It didn't take long for me to become accustomed to being the boss. It helped that Queenie had put me in charge during her absence. I took pride in my efficiency, never leaving things until the last minute, everything in my briefcase shipshape and ready to hand. I continued what I'd being doing, leaving the house early, neat and tidy, fresh to face the day. I had made changes in my personal life, enrolling at the Leisure Centre, and joining the library. I owed it to Queenie to keep my life brimming with occupations, not dwelling on the past.

I set up an office in the dining room so that I could leave work early and concentrate on the accounts at home. Under Mr Hennessy and Mr Hill's tutelage I learned everything there was to learn about the business, my mind soaking it up quickly.

Each Monday morning we held a meeting. Mum, Madame Renard, Tommy, Trish and I would get together in what had been Queenie's office but which was now mine, and go over the future collection, discuss the progress of the current one. Our new collection, designed to appeal to the younger customer, was the main topic of conversation. The younger brand had achieved rapid success but still had a long way to go. I saw it as our major growth area. 'We have the essential ingredients, fashion, quality, value for money and innovative fabrics and designs. We want Paradise to be the top brand in this country.'

'That's a bit ambitious with so many French brands already well established here,' Mum said.

Madame Renard agreed with me. 'It's a realistic aim for the next five years.' Her willingness to listen and take action gave me the confidence to make sure that our aims were achievable.

'I was thinking of a collection that embodies the essential qualities for a young woman. Contemporary, clean lines, excellent fit, value for money. Basic but sophisticated. Maybe we could extend to sportswear, swimsuits.'

'Not beyond the bounds of possibility,' Madame Renard said, sketching madly.

Promotions were discussed. 'Buy two bras, get the matching briefs free', was going well. We talked about the new computers.

Trish and I often had a drink after work, always to discuss

business. Her relationship with Dave had fizzled out and we joked about becoming old maids. Deep down I knew it would be nice to have a man in my life, someone who would raise excitement in me when he phoned, the sight of whom would make me flush with pleasure. Someone who would brighten my life, make me feel more alive.

There was a message on my answerphone from Jim. 'Ring me, it's important.'

'I got your message,' I told him.

'Can you meet me tonight? We need to talk.'

'About what?'

'Lots of things to be sorted out.'

'I'm working late.'

Jim sighed. 'Shall I pick you up?'

'No. I'd like to get home and have a shower first.'

'Tell you what, I'll book a table at Tosca's. You'll probably be hungry. Say, half past eight.'

As I came into the restaurant Jim stood up. His smile was anxious.

'Sorry I'm late,' I said. 'I got here as soon as I could.'

'Thanks for coming. I know you're busy.'

'Oh, Jim! I'm glad to see you.'

'Hungry?'

'As you would say, I could eat a scabby horse.'

He handed me the menu. I chose spaghetti carbonara. Jim settled for the same.

'So, what's the news?' I asked.

Jim smiled. 'I'm going to Santa Monica for a couple of weeks.'

'I'll miss you.'

His eyes were moist as he said, 'We've something special. I don't want to let it go. I wanted everything to be perfect. Instead, it all went pear-shaped.'

'Jim, it wasn't your fault. If anything it was mine. I wasn't ready for romance.'

Jim looked at me. 'Take time off. Come to Santa Monica to visit me. The break will do you good.'

I gazed at him, thunderstruck.

'Put Trish in charge. She's reliable and experienced enough by now.'

'I couldn't consider it at the moment. I'm up to my eyes in new designs and there's the trip to Paris next week to see this new designer.'

'At least say you'll think about it.'

'This is all so unexpected. I'm very flattered, Jim. I don't know what to say.'

Jim took my hand across the table. 'Say you'll come to visit me there.'

'I'll think about it.'

The circus came to town. Polly and Audrey were dying to go but none of us wanted to take them: the circus had been tainted for us by the obnoxious Ginger. In the end I agreed to go because they pestered me, and I felt sorry for them.

'The circus, the circus,' they cried, desperate to get inside the tent. A pony came prancing into a circle, a girl in a sequined tutu riding it bareback, her golden hair caught up in a diamanté crown. The pony trotted round the ring the girl dancing, leaping in the air, turning somersaults backwards, a golden cartwheel. 'That's what I'd like to be,' Audrey said.

Everyone clapped as a young man entered, cracking his long whip, a string of ponies forming a circle around him.

The clown in wide white trousers and huge red boots staggered in, squirting water from the flower in his hat. His face was painted white, his red mouth an enormous O. The crowd clapped. He danced around in a circle, his feet tapping out the tune of the organ-grinder, the bowler hat in his hand tipped towards the audience.

'I hate clowns,' Audrey muttered.

Polly gave her a dig in the ribs. 'Shut up. I love them.'

'Why should I?'

'Stop it,' I screeched beneath my breath.

Next came the crimson-clad lion-tamer followed by his snarling lions. He cracked his long whip, and opened the cage. Silently they followed him, dancing on their toes, hopping on to a stool to take a bow. The crowd roared, the lions waited, sleek cats, eyes glinting.

With a great effort I concentrated on the shape of the lion-tamer's head, the receding hairline, the tufts of red hair sticking out at the sides, the tooth that glinted gold, as he smiled and took a bow, the familiar voice returning the lions to their cage.

'I want to be a lion-tamer,' Polly said.

'I want to ride a pony in a circus,' Audrey said.

I sat watching Ginger swing away, his mincing steps almost dancing with delight. I thought of Mum and wondered what she would have said if she had seen him. How foolish she'd been made to look when he returned after all those years demanding money. The shame she'd endured at the hands of that man was inconceivable. He hadn't told us what he did for a living, only that he travelled the world, and trained animals.

That night in the kitchen Dad made a pot of tea. 'Don't tell your mother you saw him.'

'Would it upset her?'

'Everything about him upsets her. He's a nasty piece of work, just like his son. You know me, I hate drama of any sort, but that Billy was a heap of trouble.'

'He thought he could walk in and take over,' I said.

'He lacked the resolution to see anything through, never mind run the business. You're the one my money's on, Olivia.'

Chapter Forty-six

In Paris I decided to explore the shops, keeping to those near the hotel. The streets were full, tourists strolling along, others exercising their dogs, all well dressed and respectable. I walked slowly along the promenade, gazing at the Arc de Triomphe. It was a beautiful city, a pleasant evening. I should come here more often, leave Trish in charge. I paused, wondering which way to go. Not wishing to return to the hotel so soon, I sat on one of the park benches, near a bandstand where music was playing.

Later I looked out over the balcony of my hotel room at the towers of Notre-Dame, the boat sliding along the Seine towards it. Stepping back inside I combed my hair, freshened my lipstick and went downstairs to sit at one of the sidewalk cafés and soak up the atmosphere. I chose a table facing the busy Boulevard Saint-Germain and watched waiters serving the constant stream of people who came in.

I thought of Chantal. She had lived in Paris most of

her life, had travelled to big cities like London and Milan, and was probably in Bangkok now or somewhere exotic like that. I envied her free and easy existence. Travelling opened the mind, kept a person lively and interesting. Standing behind a counter in a corner shop, listening to Queenie, had stunted my own growth. Now a whole new world had opened up for me and I hoped I'd meet the challenge.

A man had come into the café and was signalling to me, calling my name. I stared at him, hardly believing my eyes when he stood before me, excited, smiling shyly.

'Lorenzo!'

'Olivia!' he said. 'It's really you.'

I took the hand he held out and a chasm seemed to open between the Lorenzo who had gone away and the man who stood before me. He was as strange as any other man in a crowd. A thousand emotions coursed through me as he kept my hand in his. I moved back from him a fraction, and waited.

'May I?' he asked, indicating the chair opposite me.

'Of course.'

Tossing back his dark hair, blushing like a schoolboy, he sat down. 'What are you doing here?' he asked.

'I'm in Paris on business.' I looked at him expectantly. 'I'm so glad to see you.'

'You look wonderful.'

'Would you like coffee, a drink?'

'Coffee would be great.' He smiled, lit a cigarette, his exaggerated gestures suddenly familiar.

We sipped coffee, and I told him about the last couple of days spent trying to get my bearings.

'I can't wait to show you everything,' he said.

It was too early for dinner, so we went for a walk. He took my arm and led the way, as though he were hurrying somewhere exciting. It felt strange to be with him again. He'd been in my thoughts and dreams for so long. At the traffic lights at the end of Boulevard Saint-Germain he caught my elbow.

'Where are we going?' I asked.

'What does it matter?' He laughed.

'We're lost,' I said, when we found ourselves in a maze of crowded streets.

He looked at me, his blue shirt making his eyes sparkle. The time fell away as we laughed together. Once again I was the girl he'd fallen in love with.

'I'll buy a street map.'

We sat at another café, to study it. The waiter brought wine and two glasses. I told Lorenzo about the business, the suppliers I'd already met. He listened intently, with the look that made me feel shy.

His eyes possessed me with the appreciation of a stranger, nothing hidden, his delight obvious. Our mutual attraction was still there as we sat and talked. Here I was, in the city of romance, hundreds of miles from home, gazing into Lorenzo's eyes like a lovesick teenager.

He was shaking his head in disbelief. 'If only I'd known that you'd been searching for me. If only I'd known that you were free. All I ever wanted was to love you. When

I went into the church and saw the two of you standing there, the priest's hands raised in blessing, the organ music, Barry's face so happy, I could hardly believe that you'd gone through with it. For months I imagined you and me together like that, sipping champagne, everyone enjoying themselves. I will never forget a single detail of the few minutes I stood in that church, the priest's voice asking you to accept him as your husband.'

With an air of unconcern I said, 'There's no need to go into that now.' I enjoyed trivialising what once had mattered so much and was too proud to tell him it still hurt. 'Anyway, you met Chantal.'

He laughed. 'Chantal was a big mistake. It was you I loved.'

'I loved you too, or I thought I did.' I tried to step back into the place I'd only ever known once, with Lorenzo. By reflecting on it, I thought I could recapture that magic state.

'That's why I decided to go to America.'

'What did you do there?'

'I worked hard, had a good time, went sightseeing, and went to lots of nightclubs. I told myself I was being stupid, that you were a happily married woman. So I went out with lots of girls to get you out of my system. But I missed you.'

'You did?'

There was silence for a moment.

Finally Lorenzo said, 'And what about you? A girl like you must be in great demand.'

I laughed. 'I'm too busy.'

'And you so beautiful! Such a waste.'

'It's not that bad. I enjoy my life.'

Lorenzo smiled. 'So, we're both happy. Just goes to show. People do recover.' He sounded convinced.

As he spoke I realised that I had told him the truth. I was enjoying my life, or had been until I came face to face with him again. After all this time of searching for him, thinking of him, I was finally sitting here with him, feeling as wretched inside as the day we had parted. I wasn't over him at all.

We talked of other things as we wound our way back to the hotel. When we got there Lorenzo said, 'May I take you to dinner tonight?'

'I'd love that.'

'I'll come back at seven.'

I felt ill-mannered for not inviting him to dinner at my hotel or even asking him where he was staying. Restless, I ran a bath and soaked in it for a long time.

At seven o'clock sharp, in a black velvet dress I'd purchased the previous day in Le Printemps, I met him on the hotel steps.

'You look gorgeous,' he said, looking at me admiringly.

'Thank you.'

'I passed a nice little restaurant on my way here. Would you like to try it?'

'Sounds great.'

We strolled through the gravel paths of the Luxembourg Gardens until we reached the restaurant. We sat at a table overlooking the peaceful green lawns and statues. He leaned towards me, his hand on my arm, and said, 'I'm so glad you're here.'

'So am I.'

The restaurant was filling up. As soon as the waiter arrived with aperitifs we gave our order, Lorenzo selected *foie gras* and laughed at me for not wanting to try the frogs' legs.

A street violinist appeared on the little terrace, close to our table, and played for us, bowing when Lorenzo put coins in his copper cup. We ate, and sipped our wine slowly.

'What time will you be free tomorrow?' he asked, as we left the restaurant.

'Midday.'

'We can go sightseeing, shopping, anything you want.' He was watching me with eager, excited eyes. 'What's the matter?' he asked solicitously.

'We're like two children in a conspiracy.'

He took my hand. 'Let's go,' he said, taking charge.

Back in the hotel we had a nightcap, sitting in the bar nursing Cognac until the place was empty.

'Where shall we meet tomorrow?' He rose to leave.

'The Galéries Lafayette.'

'I'll be there.'

'I may be a few minutes late. Wait for me.'

He left, walking quickly away, then turning at the entrance to wave to me.

As soon as I reached my bedroom I felt the emptiness of being alone again. Going to the balcony I stepped out in time to catch sight of him below, turning the corner.

'Lorenzo,' I called, but he was gone.

Chains of fairy-lights stretched across the city. Pleasure

boats twinkled on the Seine. The Eiffel Tower rose majestically to the sky, the moon behind it.

The sun, shining through the curtains, woke me. Lorenzo was my first thought. Excited, I jumped out of bed and went to the window. Sunlight filtered through the tall buildings opposite and the city, in the gap between them, glowed. I showered, put on my makeup with a slow, steady hand, anxious to look my best and as natural as possible. I put on my black suit and white blouse, then gazed into the mirror, turning sideways, examining myself from all angles, wishing I were slimmer, amazed that I cared so much again.

The hotel lobby was busy. I caught a glimpse of myself in the full-length mirror as I got out of the lift, then walked out into the sunshine and hailed a taxi.

The meeting took longer than I had expected. When I finally arrived at the Galéries Lafayette Lorenzo was waiting for me. I felt an overwhelming urge to rush to him, and had to make myself take my time. As soon as he spotted me he came towards me.

'I'm sorry. It took longer than I expected.'

'It's all right. You're here now. Sit down.' He pulled out a chair. 'How did it go?'

'Very well,' I said, nervous again.

'All finished now?'

'Yes.' We sat for half an hour, drinking coffee and relaxing, talking of this and that. Then he paid the bill and took my hand with a flourish. 'Let's make the most of every minute of our day together.'

We went shopping. Lorenzo bought a Givenchy silk scarf

for me and a pair of 501s for himself. I bought a present for Mum. We went back to the hotel slowly, Lorenzo carrying the bags. 'I'll bring these up for you,' he said.

'Thank you,' I said.

I unlocked the door to my room and stepped in, not looking in Lorenzo's direction. He stayed in the corridor, the bags clutched in his hands.

'Leave them anywhere,' I said.

He came into the room, put the bags on the chair, and turned to leave. 'I thought perhaps we'd make tonight a bit special,' he said. 'I want to make love to you.'

I said, 'I've an early flight to catch in the morning,' scared of the depth of my feelings, and the hurt that came with them.

He held me, whispered into my hair, 'Let me show you that I still love you.'

Lorenzo O'Brien wanted me still. After all this time. I never thought I'd hear those words again. Delight surged through me.

'Couldn't we try again?' he asked.

I drew back, looked at him. 'No, Lorenzo. I'm very tired.'

'We'll meet again? Soon?'

'Yes.'

He pulled me to him, and kissed me. 'You're so beautiful,' he whispered.

My legs felt weak as if they were going to give way. I could feel my cheeks burn. I had to get away from him.

'Maybe there's a chance for us to be together?'

My heart somersaulted in my chest. Time stood still. 'It's all so sudden. I don't know how I feel.'

'We'll keep in touch. Meet soon again?'

'Yes, we will.'

Chapter Forty-seven

'I've got a surprise for you,' I said to Trish.

'Oh!'

'I bumped into Lorenzo.'

'What? Where?'

'In Paris. We had dinner together.'

'But, Ollie, how could you? He broke your heart.'

'Nothing happened,' I protested. 'We caught up with things.'

'Chantal didn't last long then?'

'No.'

'If I were you . . .'

'I'm not looking for advice,' I said.

'All right.' Trish's eyes were weighing me up. 'Don't talk about it if you don't want to.'

'There's been too much talk already.'

'Not from you there hasn't.' She was watching me intently.

Putting my head in my hands I said, eventually, 'I feel so silly. I'm not fit to be let out.'

'Do you still love him?'

'I don't know.'

'For God's sake, Ollie, he's a liar, a cheat, and at this very moment is probably with somebody else. When are you going to get sense and forget about him? He'll only hurt you again.' She spoke to me as if I was a ten-year-old child in need of a good slap.

'I'm in control of my feelings.'

'Where Lorenzo O'Brien is concerned, Ollie, you were never in control. And what's more,' she went on, 'you've kept poor Jim waiting in the wings for just a kind word from you.'

'I didn't give him any encouragement.'

'Don't I bloody know it.'

I turned from her chilling words, heedless. What did she know? Lorenzo was back in my life. No more wondering, no more listening for the telephone, no more being stuck in the empty gilded cage that Queenie, my fairy grandmother, had provided for me. No more loneliness.

Jim returned from Santa Monica.

I arranged to go for a walk with him on Dun Laoghaire pier.

'Didn't you get my messages on your answering-machine?' he asked.

'Why do you think I'm here?'

'I was beginning to wonder if I'd ever see you again. You seem to spend most of our time avoiding me.'

'Well, here I am.' I sounded sharper than I'd intended.

Jim was leaning on the sea-wall, watching the boats, the sunset. 'I've hardly seen you since I got back.'

'I know. I'm sorry.'

'It doesn't have to be like this, you know. Things could be so different.'

I shook my head. 'I don't think we should talk like this.'

Jim looked up sharply. 'Why? What's happened?'

'I met Lorenzo in Paris.'

'What?'

'I bumped into him.'

'Are you going to see him again?'

'I suppose so.'

'You're making a big mistake.'

'I don't think so.'

'Think carefully, Ollie. You'll get hurt again. He's a figment of your imagination. You don't even know him, for God's sake.'

'Of course I know him.'

He swung round, caught me by the shoulders. 'He played with you like a cat with a mouse, picking you up, letting you down.'

'Don't be so theatrical.' I turned away.

Jim was furious. 'He crooks his little finger and you go running.'

'My mind's made up.'

Appalled, he looked at me. 'You can't go off just like that!'

I turned on him. 'Why not? Don't you think I've worked hard enough to deserve a break?'

'Olivia, think carefully. You've been hurt already.' The plea in Jim's eyes mirrored the sadness he felt.

'Don't think anything you say will stop me. I'm going and that's that. Anyway,' I protested, 'it's the right time for a change.' I walked away.

He came after me, and stood in front of me, barring my way. 'It's madness. Remember how he hurt you before?'

I put my hand on his arm. 'I must go, Jim. I have to.'

'Olivia! I love you a lot more than he does. I'll never stop loving you. Never.'

I was afraid. 'Don't let's talk about it.'

'He'll walk off like he did before.'

'He thought I was getting married to Barry.'

'He's a messer. He'll destroy you.'

'And you want to be my saviour,' I said sarcastically.

He seized my hand. 'I want to be your lover.' He leaned towards me. 'Queenie was hoping you'd choose me.'

'I've fulfilled all Queenie's wishes in every other area. I'll marry whom I please.'

He dropped my hand. 'Have it your own way. There's no point in forcing myself on you if you don't want me.' He sounded reasonable but his eyes were desolate. 'I'll be off then.' He was pushing me away with his tears.

'I'm sorry, Jim. Truly I am.'

He was gone without a backward glance.

That night I packed my bags to go back to Paris. My cream linen jacket was a must, and my straw hat for sitting in the sunshine.

* * *

He came bursting through the swing doors at the airport, his eagerness displacing the air around him.

'Lorenzo.' A shudder of pleasure ran through me at the sight of him. 'I didn't expect to see you so soon.' I was shy suddenly. 'I wasn't even sure if I should come.'

'I couldn't wait to see you.'

'Oh, Lorenzo,' I said, into his shoulder.

'Now that I've found you again you're not going to get rid of me that easily.'

Laughing together, we left the terminal. We had breakfast in the hotel where I was staying. We sat at a corner table eating hot croissants and drinking coffee.

'How are things?' he asked.

'Busy. We're expanding. Too rapidly, I think, but my accountant insists that it's necessary.'

'You've changed, Olivia. You're more confident, even more desirable. I want to take you in my arms right now, this moment.'

'We're going to the Musée d'Orsay, remember?'

His face fell. 'I'd rather look at you than any painting.'

'Charmer!'

We looked at paintings, seeking out favourites. After a couple of hours we sat in the shade of a street-café umbrella, watching groups of tourists wandering around. I leaned back, the heat draining me.

'This reminds me of Venice.'

'Come to Venice with me. See it properly.'

I shivered, thinking of the fiasco it had been. 'I think I'll rest for a while.' I stood up.

Lorenzo got to his feet. 'I'll take you back to your hotel.'

When we reached the room Lorenzo said, 'Would you like some coffee or a drink?'

'No, thanks. I'll have a siesta. Meet you later.'

He took me in his arms. 'It's me you want,' he said, all restraint gone. He was fumbling with the buttons of my blouse.

'We shouldn't be doing this,' I said, breaking away from him.

'What's wrong?'

'I'm nervous.'

'Ssh.' He silenced me with a kiss, open-mouthed and urgent. In a frenzy of excitement he unbuttoned his shirt, pulled it off, and threw it to one side. His perfect body, made for love, filled me with longing. We kissed again, and moved to the bed where we lay down. My heart beat wildly, everything forgotten except the tingling in my body as he stroked me.

Shamelessly he teased me with kisses as he pulled me towards him, desperate in his urgency. I quivered with excitement as he pressed me closer, the moment of surrender imminent.

I knew it was wrong, that I shouldn't be doing this, that it could only lead to trouble and heartbreak.

'Do you remember the first time we made love, in my apartment?'

'How could I forget?' He was holding me, his presence comforting, familiar. I moved closer to him.

He kissed me and held me, whispering my name, his smell

familiar, everything just as I'd remembered it. Thrusting into me he cried out, 'Olivia,' in a strangled voice, then fell forward sobbing.

I lay in his arms for a long time, feeling the love I'd almost forgotten. I slept, and woke to find him fast asleep, his arm thrown wide, making him look young and vulnerable. What would he say when he woke up? Would we make love again? Or would he leave, embarrassed?

'We're perfect together,' was what he said, wonderment in his voice.

Silently we showered, dressed and went to a brasserie at the corner of Boulevard Saint-Michel where we had *filet de boeuf sur sa galette aux pommes*. Afterwards we wandered aimlessly along with the drifting crowds, acutely conscious of time passing, both anxious to get back to the hotel room.

Later, he held me, kissed me, helped me undress, stroked me, and made love to me again. This time it was different. I made him wait until he could wait no longer.

Afterwards I lay still, listening to the faint hum of traffic below, the music from the bar next door. When I woke up he was gone. How could I have been so foolish? Didn't I know it would happen again? Trish and Jim had tried to warn me. Easing myself out of bed I went to stand at the window, thinking how stupid I'd been. The telephone brought me out of my reverie. 'Olivia, are you all right?'

'Yes,' I said. 'I'm fine. Oh, Lorenzo, I thought you'd gone.'

'I had to go to work. I didn't want to disturb you.'

'I'll phone you when I get back to Ireland,' I said.

'I love you,' Lorenzo replied, and put down the phone.

Sunlight slanted in through the dining-room window, highlighting the daffodils in Queenie's big vase. The scent of spring was in the air, and I was in love. Happy, I swept up the papers I'd been working on into a folder, and put it into my briefcase. There was music in my blood as I whizzed around, tidying the table, the sunshine glancing off the silver on the sideboard and the coffee-pot in my hand. My heart raced in the thrill of the secret I must not share with Trish, or anyone. I was flying to Paris today ostensibly on another buying trip but really to see Lorenzo. He'd said on the phone that he couldn't wait to see me again, so I was going to surprise him at his restaurant. I checked the card he'd given me and my thoughts flitted to the future, the promise of happiness.

Le Petit Oiseau was not difficult to find. Just inside the eighth *arrondissement*, it was a stylish restaurant with a wide bay window. The door was ajar. Lorenzo was sitting at a table in the window, a girl opposite him. She was gazing at him, her dark hair falling forward, adoration in her familiar painted face, her hand holding his. I stood rooted to the spot.

'Olivia!' Immediately he got to his feet, astonished at the sight of me. 'What a surprise!' Ushering me out of the door and up the stairs to his apartment, he became his suave, sophisticated self. 'I love surprises,' he said, as he opened the door and welcomed me in.

I will never forget the pain. I shall always remember it with those words, 'I love surprises.' He was describing the food he would cook, *loup de poissons et royales roties aux petits legumes croquants*, followed by *la cristalline de fruits rouges en blanc-manger et sorbet.*

'Olivia!' He was beside me.

I was dreaming. In a few minutes everything would be all right. His arms were around me. I broke away, making no excuse for my tears.

'Olivia, it was only Chantal. She's in trouble again with her boyfriend. She came to me for advice. See? Nothing to worry you.'

'Oh! Well, that's all right then.' I sighed, but the tears were unstoppable.

He relaxed. The fact that he'd ruined everything between us was lost on him.

'Now dry your eyes and let's have a glass of wine.'

Gathering myself together, I let him face me.

'Perfect,' he said.

'Yes, perfect,' I agreed.

He took my handbag, placed it in a corner, helped me to remove my jacket. While he hung it up I had time to absorb the wide mouth, the dark hair falling in a long sweep into his eyes, the rippling muscles beneath the snow-white shirt, the neat waist, the muscular legs, the surprisingly small feet.

'I love surprises,' he said again and laughed joyously.

'You have surprised me for the last time, Lorenzo. I saw what was between you and Chantal with my own eyes.'

'You're wrong. You're wrong,' he said dramatically, his eyes blazing.

'Lorenzo, I don't know why you need me, why you're

dependent on my approval. You obviously have plenty from Chantal and others.'

I took my jacket off the hook.

Lorenzo's poise deserted him. 'Olivia! Listen to me. Please don't go.'

I turned away from him and ran down the stairs, past the restaurant, along a flagged path, where flowers in dark pots flowed from tiny balconies, and old men sat in the shade dreaming of better days. I leaned against the wall, trying to hold on to what strength I'd left, the horror of it all beating against my brain, refusing to let me think.

Chapter Forty-eight

'Back to normal?' Jim asked me when he phoned me at home that night.

'Yes. And how are you?'

'I want to see you. Come to Santa Monica for a holiday. You've been working like a slave. You need the break.'

'Oh, Jim, listen,' I whispered. 'It's no good. Don't you see that?' I closed my eyes, wishing that he'd understand. 'We're going over the plans for the new extension. It's a big step. This Shopping Centre. I'm not sure if it isn't too big.'

'Then take a break to think about it.'

Mum came into the hall followed by Tommy, who pushed past her. 'Can I borrow your car, Olivia? It's an emergency.'

'Of course. What's up?'

'Madame Renard's not feeling well. She needs to see a doctor.'

'Jim, I'll phone you back. I have to go.' I put down the receiver and phoned the doctor.

Madame Renard was shifting from one leg to the other, like a hen on hot coals, her face pinched in agony. 'Pain,' she said, pointing to her side.

'Appendix,' Mum diagnosed.

'Too much booze,' Mary said under her breath.

Bernard Bellows, the architect, hovered. 'Well,' he said, 'what do you think?'

'We'll go ahead,' I said, 'perhaps on a slightly lesser scale, provided that Mr Hill can organise suitable investment.'

'Of course,' Mr Bellows said, pleased.

Realising how empty my life would be, with no one special to praise my achievements, I decided to take a holiday with Jim in Santa Monica. I crossed the landing to Queenie's bedroom, and stood looking at the stripped bed.

Perhaps Queenie's command of the place would prevail if her bed were made up. I got out sheets and pillowcases and made her bed. Her lavender scent hung in the air. My sense of order restored, I returned to my bedroom and packed.

I would take many holidays, and business trips abroad, but I'd always come back to Queenie's home. Her spirit would be here waiting to keep me company, her love continuing.

Who knows what the future holds for me? I might open a factory to manufacture our brands instead of having Monsieur Guilbert manufacture them. I might even marry Jim. On our wedding day Queenie's house will never look more beautiful. Her presence will be there, then and in the aftermath, her spirit in the trees, and in the nights and days, the lapping water, the cry of the birds, the wind and rain, storms and sun. Her laughter will be in the clinking champagne glasses, her joy in it all, regretting nothing.

For now my happiness is bound up with Paradise, the business she built up for me. Through the stars she looks into our future with me, perhaps at the beautiful babies Jim and I might have together. Perhaps she looks at a little girl called Queenie.